DALY CITY PUBLIC LIBRARY
DALY CITY, CALIFORNIA

P9-DMZ-388

GOOD-BYE
DISCARDED
MARIANNE

THE GRAPHIC NOVEL

IRENE N. WATTS

ILLUSTRATED BY KATHRYN E. SHOEMAKER

TUNDRA BOOKS

For Adam, and in loving memory of Joseph Selo — I.N.W.
To Irene N. Watts, dear friend and dear writing partner — K.E.S.
Thanks to Lauren Bailey for her input and enthusiasm throughout the process, Irene Watts

Adaptation copyright © 2008 by Irene N. Watts
Illustrations copyright © 2008 by Kathryn E. Shoemaker

Based on Good-bye Marianne by Irene N. Watts, published by Tundra Books, 1998

Published in Canada by Tundra Books,
75 Sherbourne Street, Toronto, Ontario M5A 2P9

Published in the United States by Tundra Books of Northern New York,
P.O. Box 1030, Plattsburgh, New York 12901

Library of Congress Control Number: 2007938845

All rights reserved. The use of any part of this publication reproduced, transmitted
in any form or by any means, electronic, mechanical, photocopying, recording, or
otherwise, or stored in a retrieval system, without the prior written consent of the
publisher — or, in case of photocopying or other reprographic copying, a licence from
the Canadian Copyright Licensing Agency — is an infringement of the copyright law.

LIBRARY AND ARCHIVES CANADA CATALOGUING IN PUBLICATION

Watts, Irene N., 1931-
    Good-bye Marianne / Irene N. Watts ; illustrations by Kathryn E.
Shoemaker.

Ages 8 to 11.
ISBN 978-0-88776-830-9

    I. Shoemaker, Kathryn E II. Title.

PS8595.A873G6 2008   jC813'.54   C2007-906214-8

We acknowledge the financial support of the Government of Canada through the
Book Publishing Industry Development Program (BPIDP) and that of the
Government of Ontario through the Ontario Media Development Corporation's
Ontario Book Initiative. We further acknowledge the support of the Canada
Council for the Arts and the Ontario Arts Council for our publishing program.

ONTARIO ARTS COUNCIL
CONSEIL DES ARTS DE L'ONTARIO

Cover illustration: Kathryn E. Shoemaker

Printed and bound in Canada

1 2 3 4 5 6   13 12 11 10 09 08

CHAPTER ONE

EXPELLED

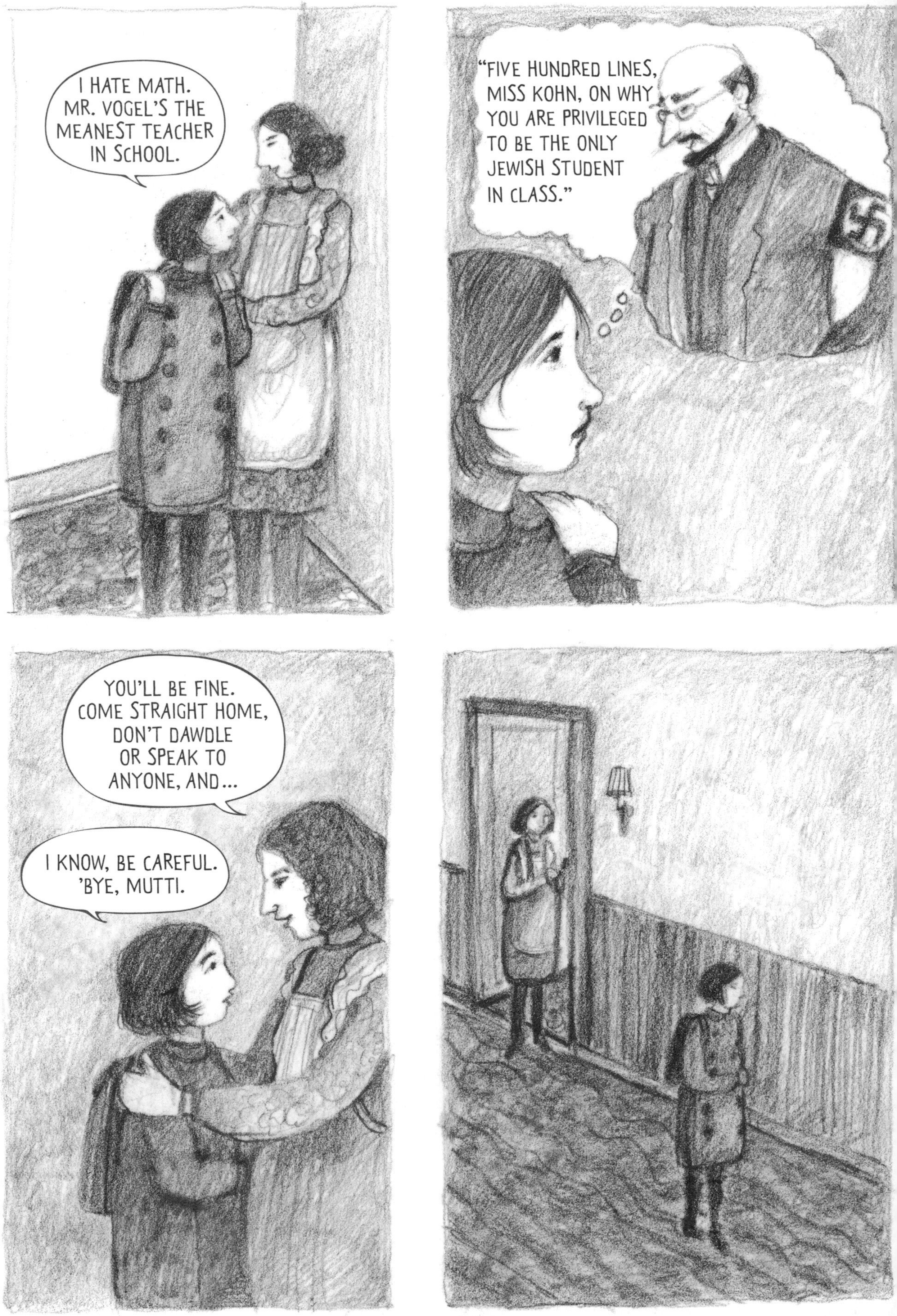
I HATE MATH. MR. VOGEL'S THE MEANEST TEACHER IN SCHOOL.
"FIVE HUNDRED LINES, MISS KOHN, ON WHY YOU ARE PRIVILEGED TO BE THE ONLY JEWISH STUDENT IN CLASS."
YOU'LL BE FINE. COME STRAIGHT HOME, DON'T DAWDLE OR SPEAK TO ANYONE, AND...
I KNOW, BE CAREFUL. 'BYE, MUTTI.

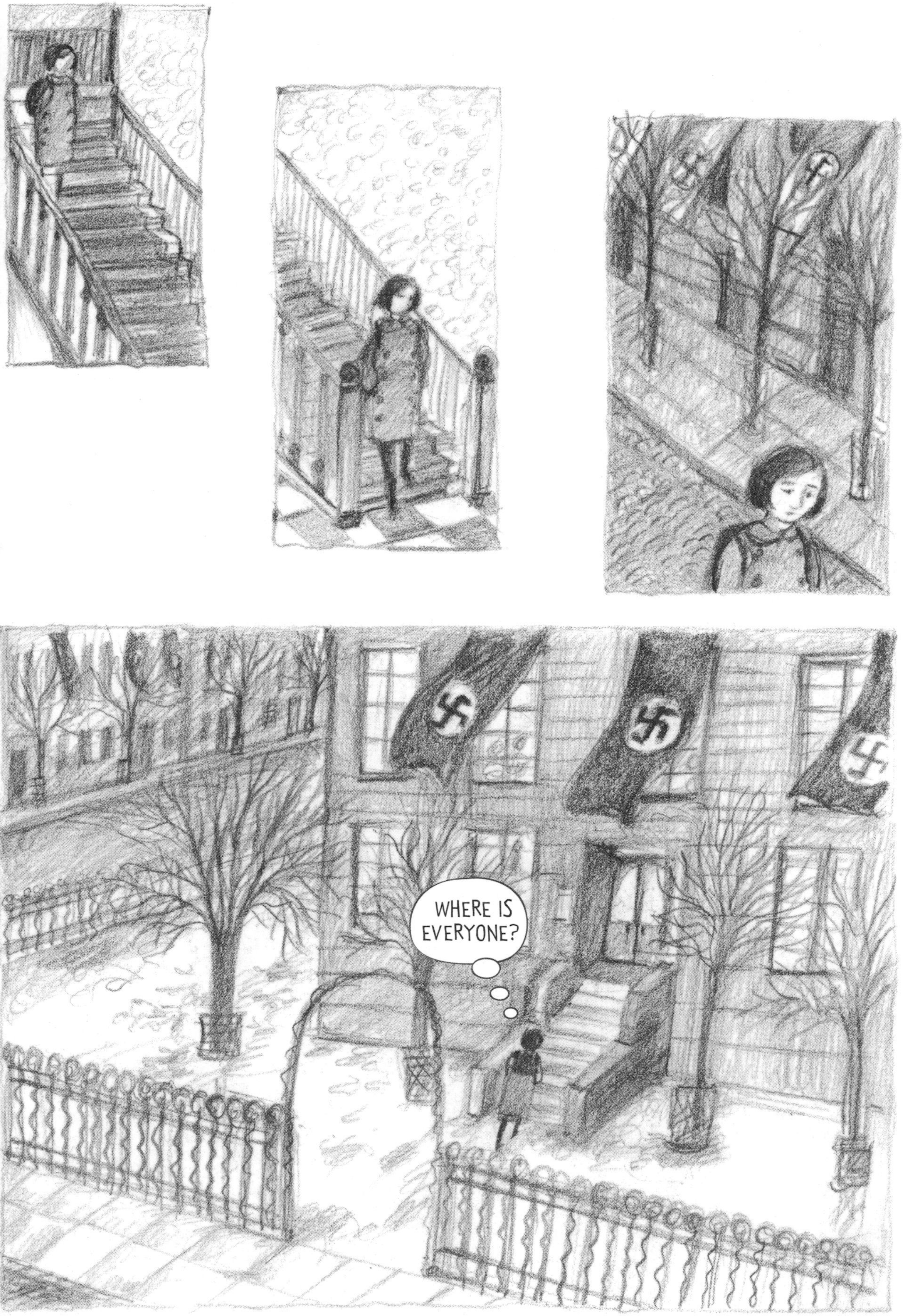
WHERE IS
EVERYONE?

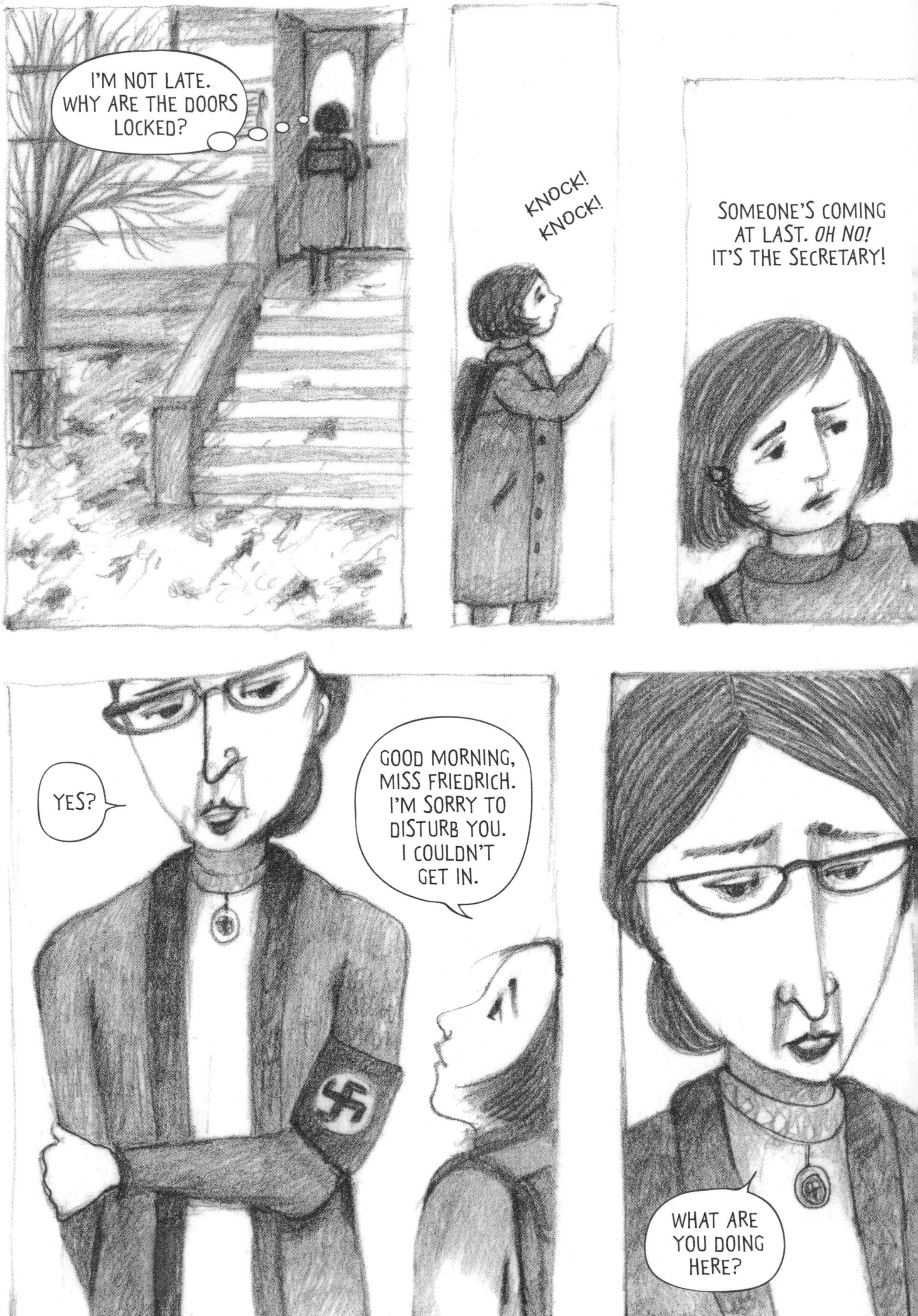
I'M NOT LATE. WHY ARE THE DOORS LOCKED?
KNOCK! KNOCK!
SOMEONE'S COMING AT LAST. *OH NO!* IT'S THE SECRETARY!
YES?
GOOD MORNING, MISS FRIEDRICH. I'M SORRY TO DISTURB YOU. I COULDN'T GET IN.
WHAT ARE YOU DOING HERE?

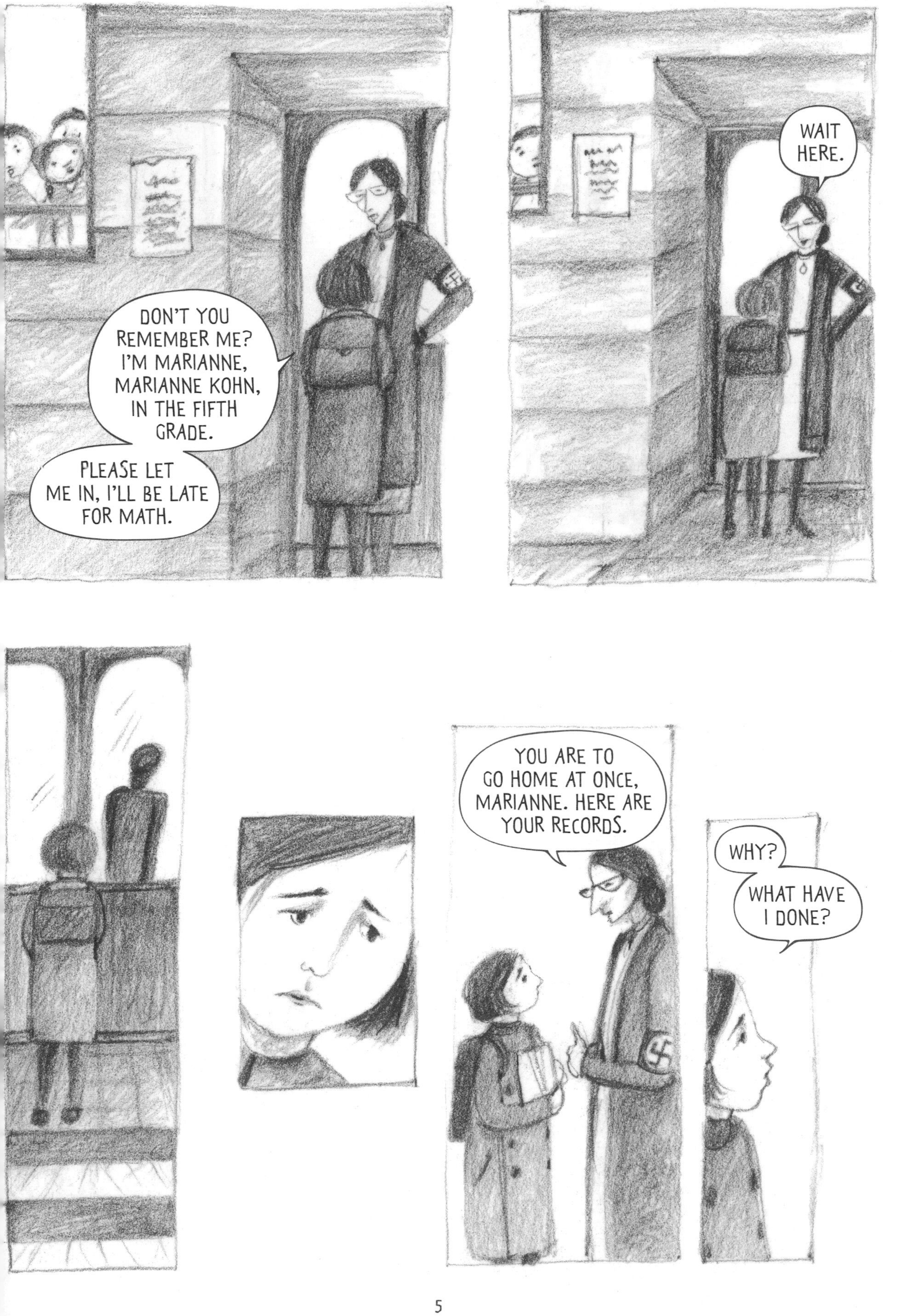
DON'T YOU REMEMBER ME? I'M MARIANNE, MARIANNE KOHN, IN THE FIFTH GRADE.
PLEASE LET ME IN, I'LL BE LATE FOR MATH.
WAIT HERE.
YOU ARE TO GO HOME AT ONCE, MARIANNE. HERE ARE YOUR RECORDS.
WHY?
WHAT HAVE I DONE?

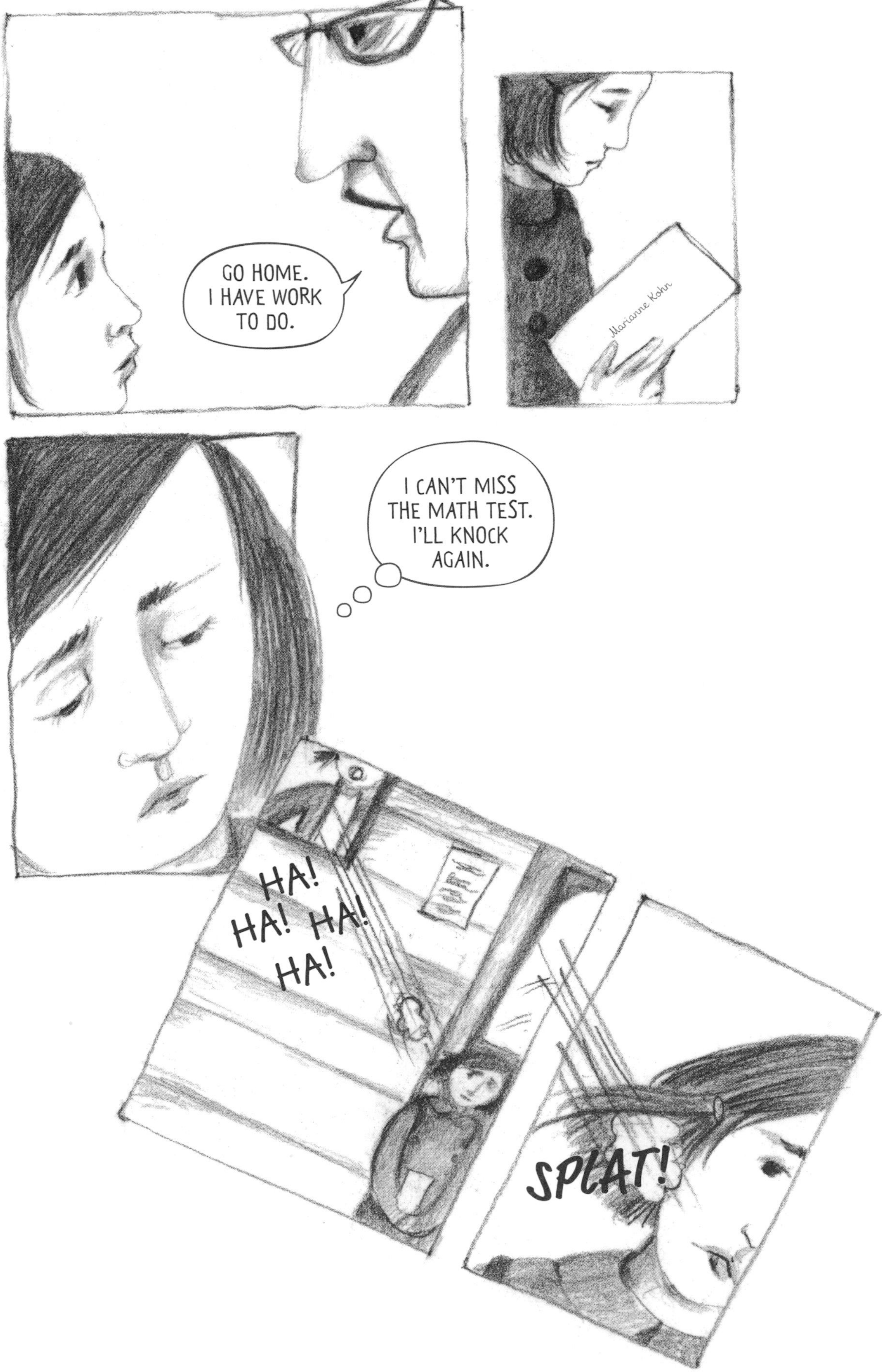
GO HOME. I HAVE WORK TO DO.
Marianne Kohn
I CAN'T MISS THE MATH TEST. I'LL KNOCK AGAIN.
HA! HA! HA! HA!
SPLAT!

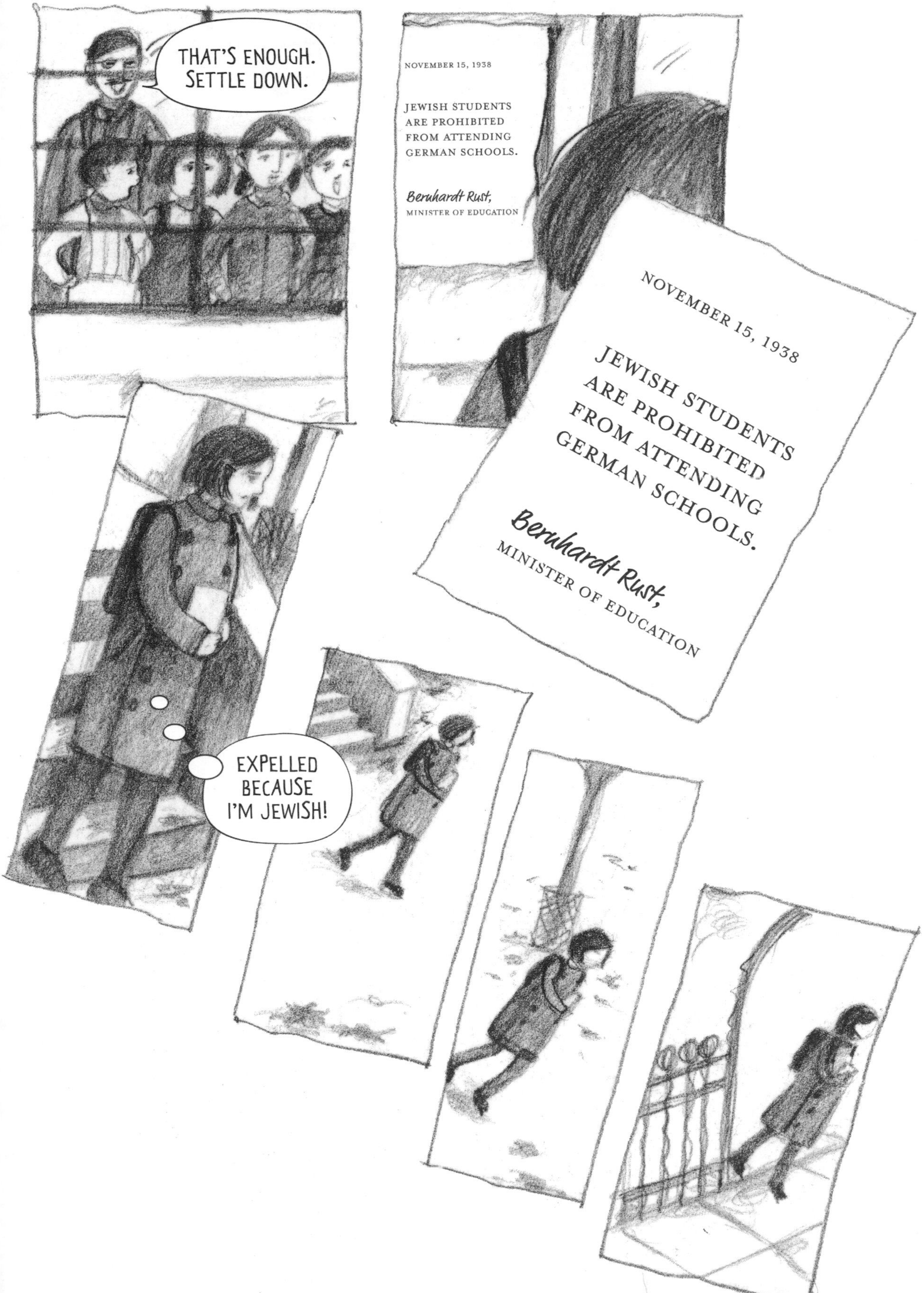
THAT'S ENOUGH. SETTLE DOWN.
NOVEMBER 15, 1938
JEWISH STUDENTS ARE PROHIBITED FROM ATTENDING GERMAN SCHOOLS.
Beruhardt Rust,
MINISTER OF EDUCATION
NOVEMBER 15, 1938
JEWISH STUDENTS ARE PROHIBITED FROM ATTENDING GERMAN SCHOOLS.
Beruhardt Rust,
MINISTER OF EDUCATION
EXPELLED BECAUSE I'M JEWISH!

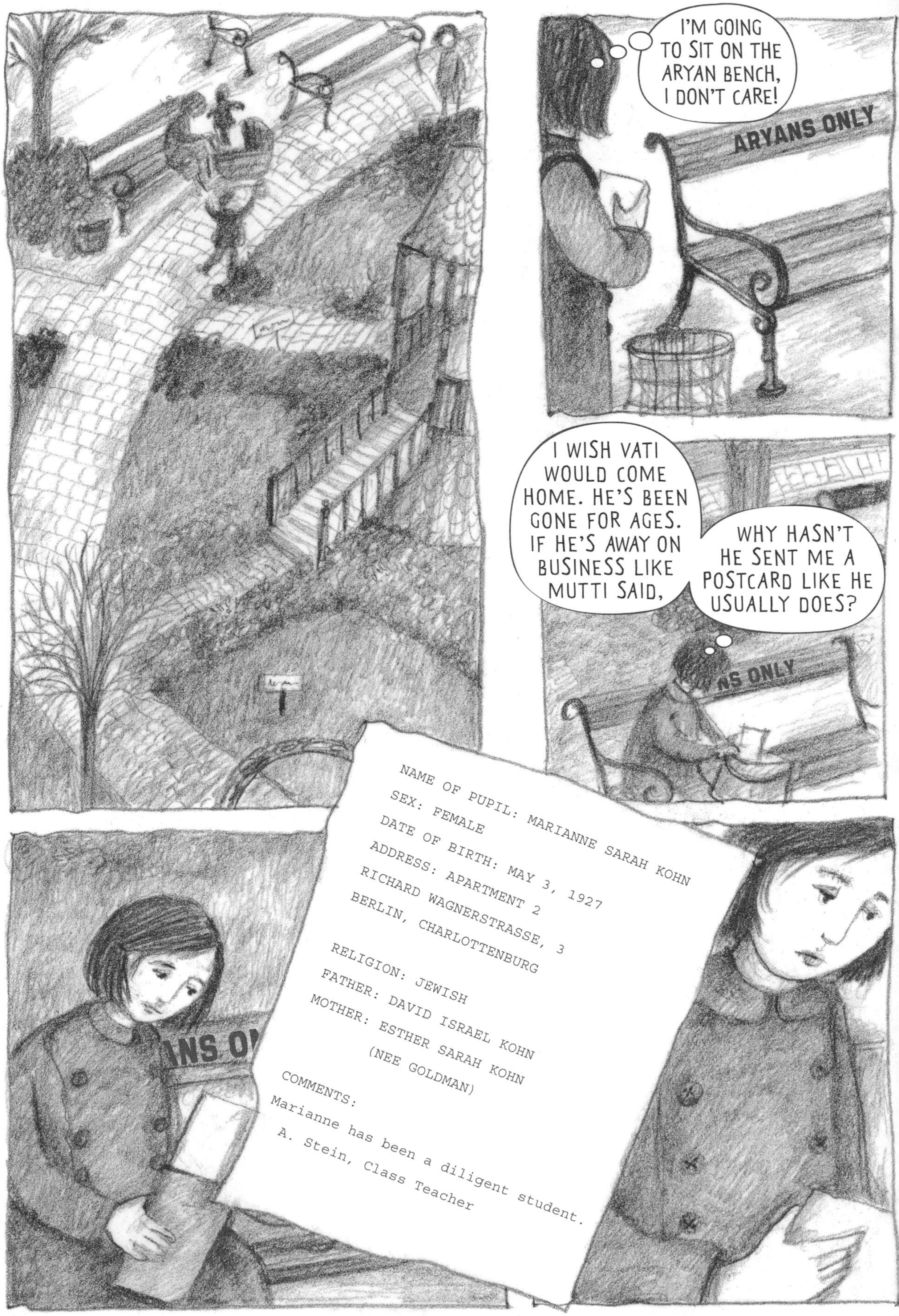
I'M GOING TO SIT ON THE ARYAN BENCH, I DON'T CARE!
ARYANS ONLY
I WISH VATI WOULD COME HOME. HE'S BEEN GONE FOR AGES. IF HE'S AWAY ON BUSINESS LIKE MUTTI SAID,
WHY HASN'T HE SENT ME A POSTCARD LIKE HE USUALLY DOES?
NS ONLY
NAME OF PUPIL: MARIANNE SARAH KOHN
SEX: FEMALE
DATE OF BIRTH: MAY 3, 1927
ADDRESS: APARTMENT 2
RICHARD WAGNERSTRASSE, 3
BERLIN, CHARLOTTENBURG
RELIGION: JEWISH
FATHER: DAVID ISRAEL KOHN
MOTHER: ESTHER SARAH KOHN
(NEE GOLDMAN)
COMMENTS:
Marianne has been a diligent student.
A. Stein, Class Teacher
ANS O

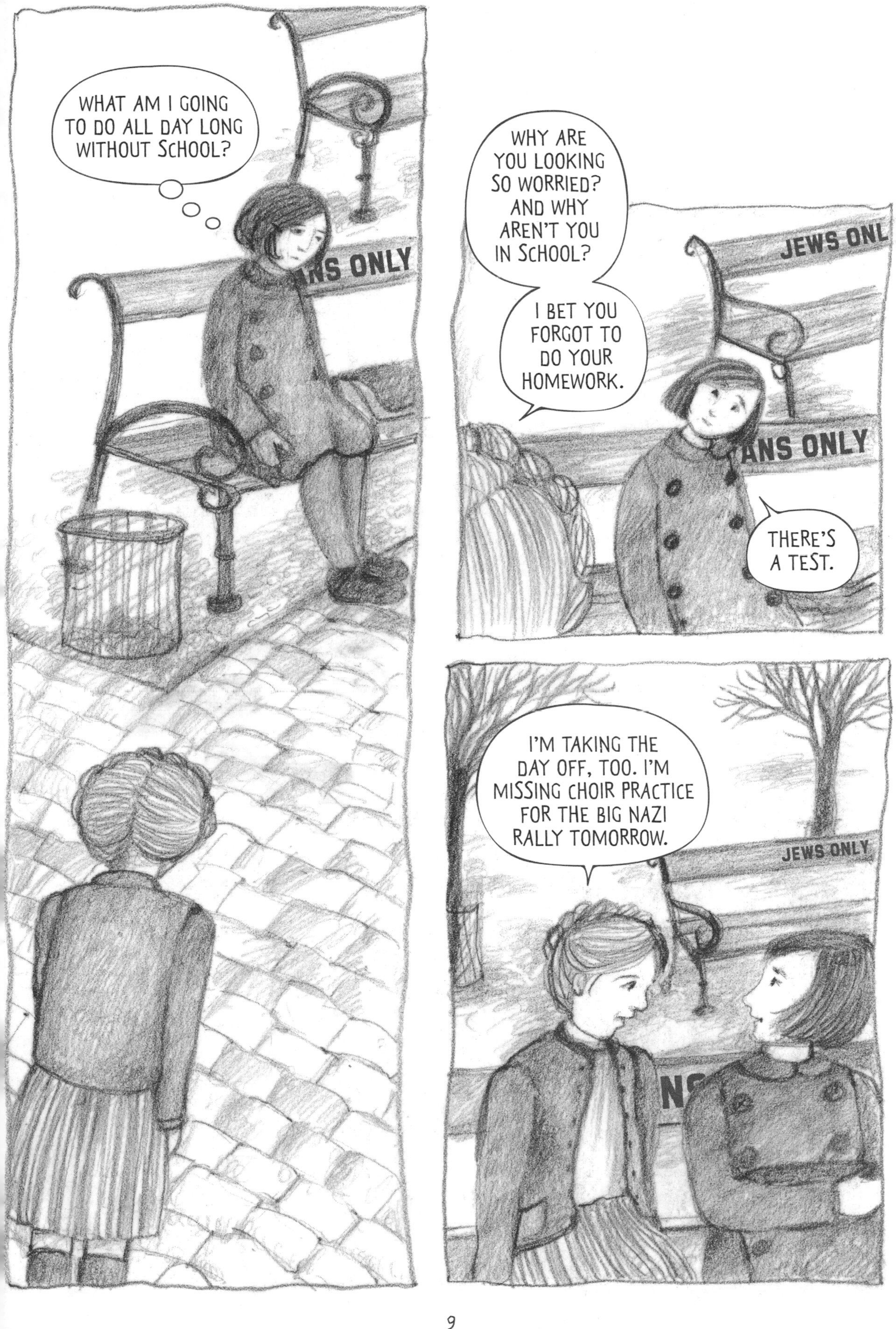
WHAT AM I GOING TO DO ALL DAY LONG WITHOUT SCHOOL?
ANS ONLY
WHY ARE YOU LOOKING SO WORRIED? AND WHY AREN'T YOU IN SCHOOL?
I BET YOU FORGOT TO DO YOUR HOMEWORK.
JEWS ONL
ANS ONLY
THERE'S A TEST.
I'M TAKING THE DAY OFF, TOO. I'M MISSING CHOIR PRACTICE FOR THE BIG NAZI RALLY TOMORROW.
JEWS ONLY

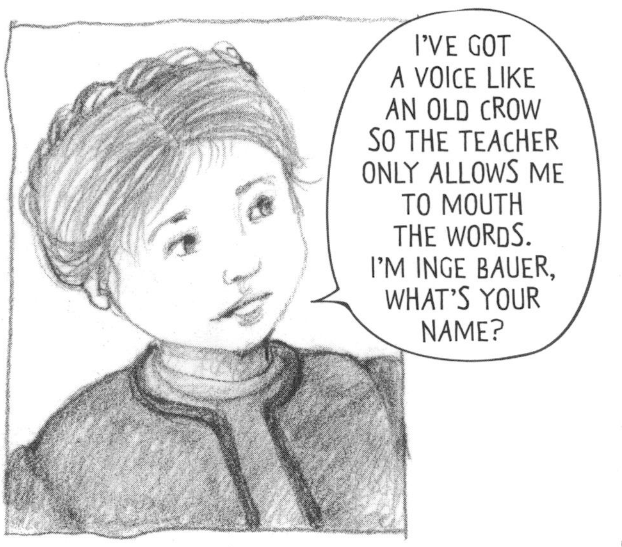
I'VE GOT A VOICE LIKE AN OLD CROW SO THE TEACHER ONLY ALLOWS ME TO MOUTH THE WORDS. I'M INGE BAUER, WHAT'S YOUR NAME?

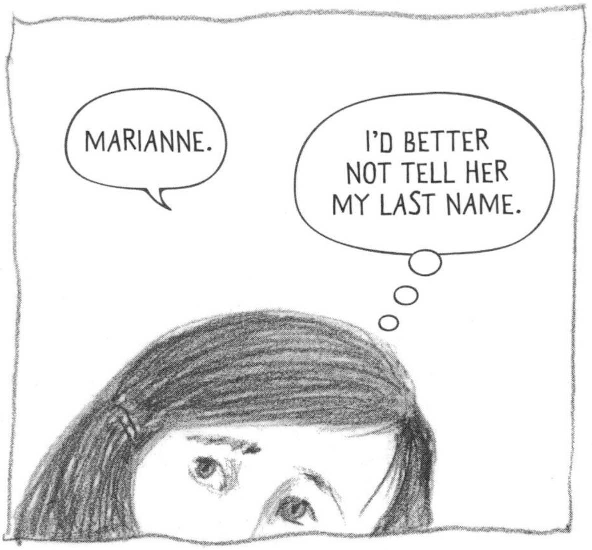
MARIANNE.
I'D BETTER NOT TELL HER MY LAST NAME.

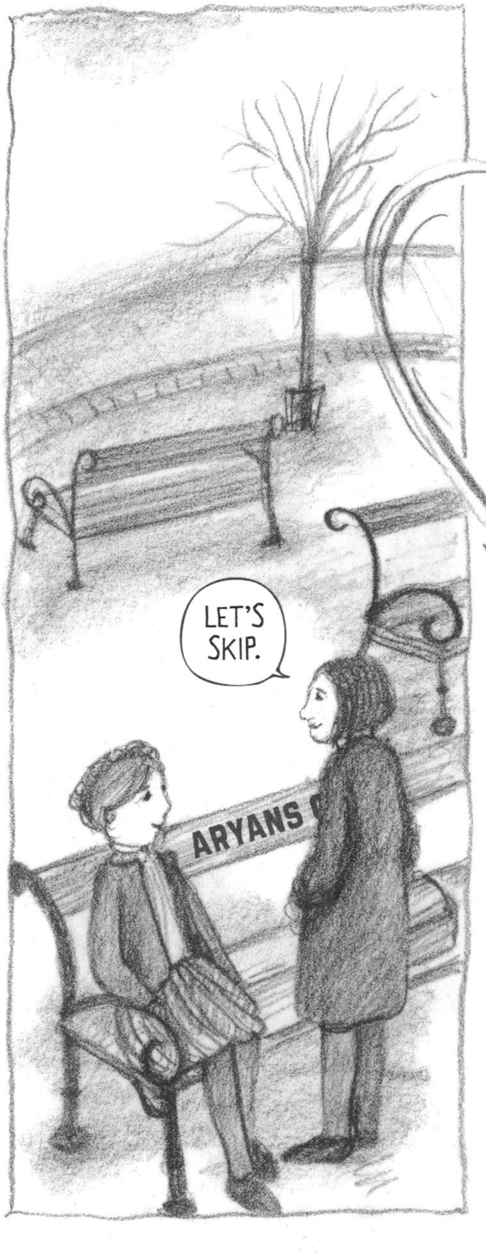
LET'S SKIP.
ARYANS

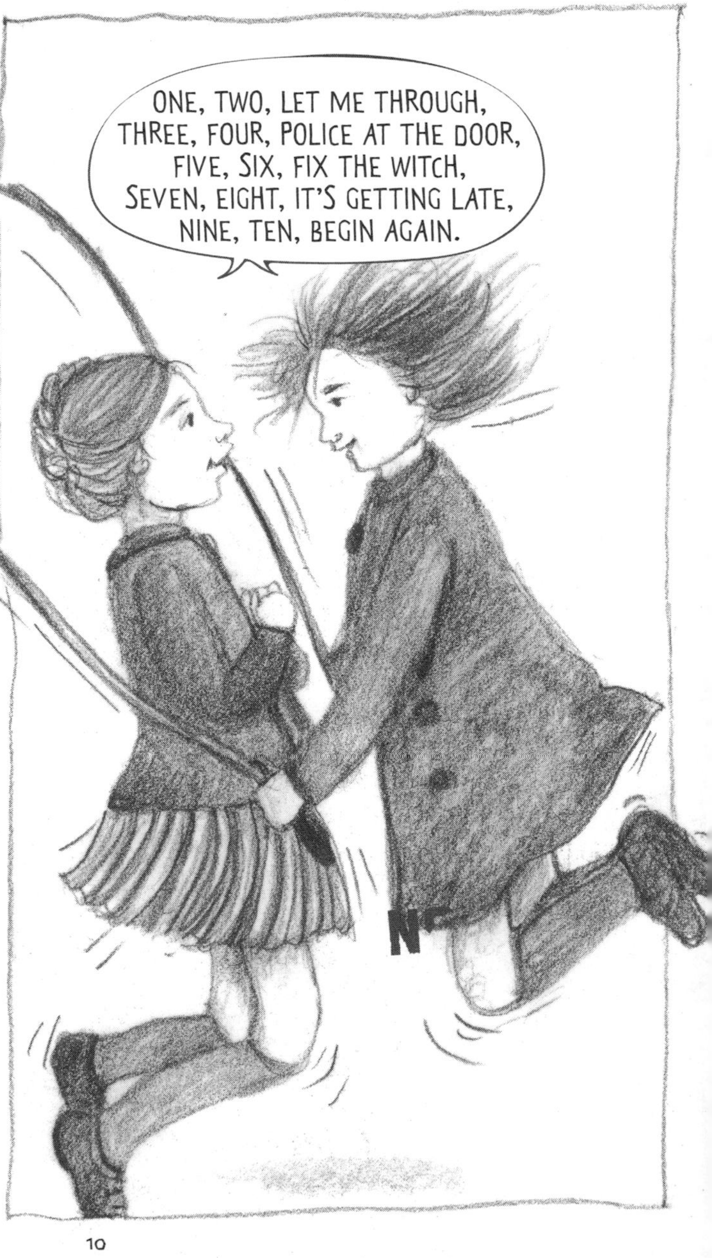
ONE, TWO, LET ME THROUGH, THREE, FOUR, POLICE AT THE DOOR, FIVE, SIX, FIX THE WITCH, SEVEN, EIGHT, IT'S GETTING LATE, NINE, TEN, BEGIN AGAIN.

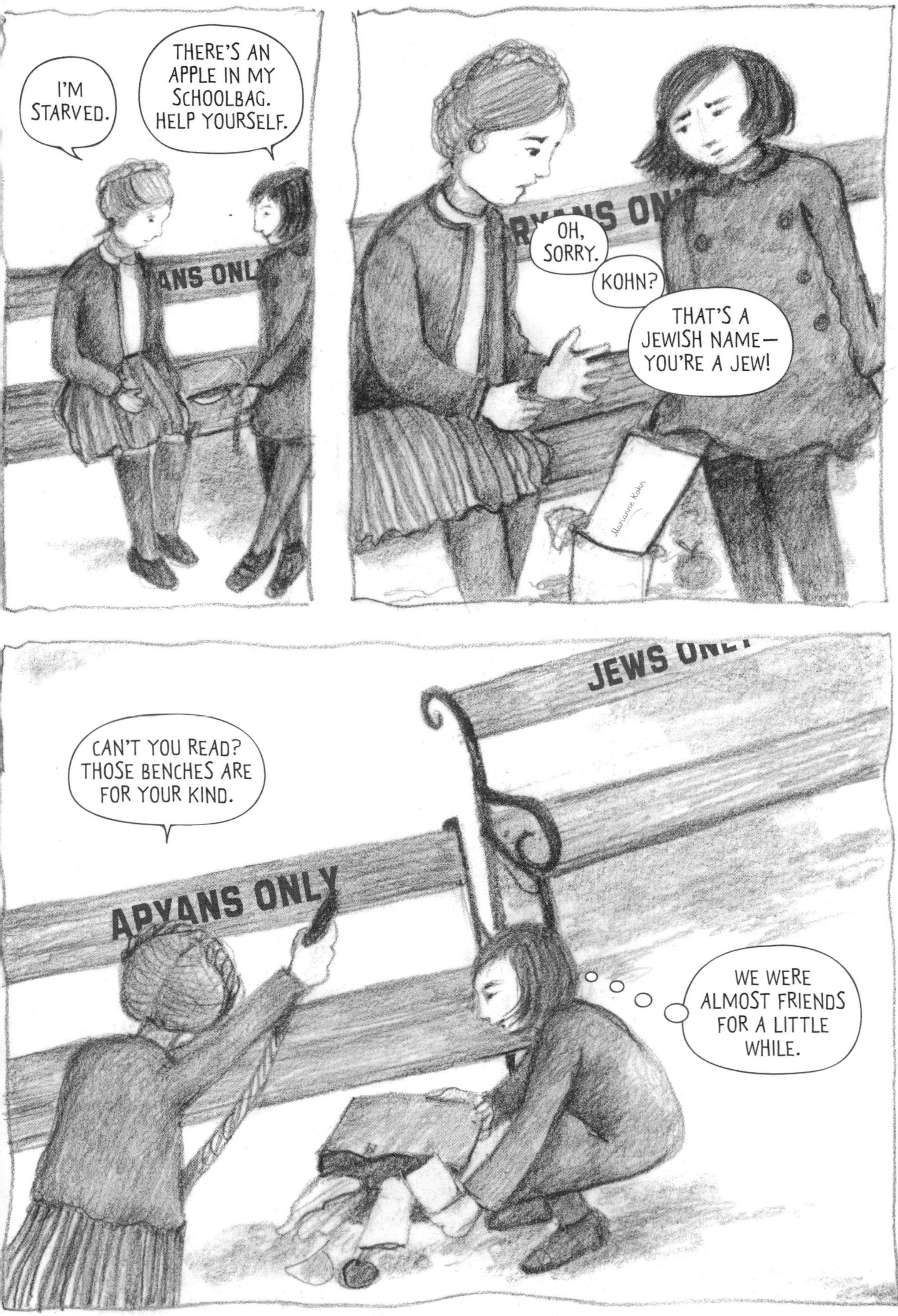
I'M STARVED.
THERE'S AN APPLE IN MY SCHOOLBAG. HELP YOURSELF.
OH, SORRY.
KOHN?
THAT'S A JEWISH NAME—YOU'RE A JEW!
CAN'T YOU READ? THOSE BENCHES ARE FOR YOUR KIND.
ARYANS ONLY
WE WERE ALMOST FRIENDS FOR A LITTLE WHILE.

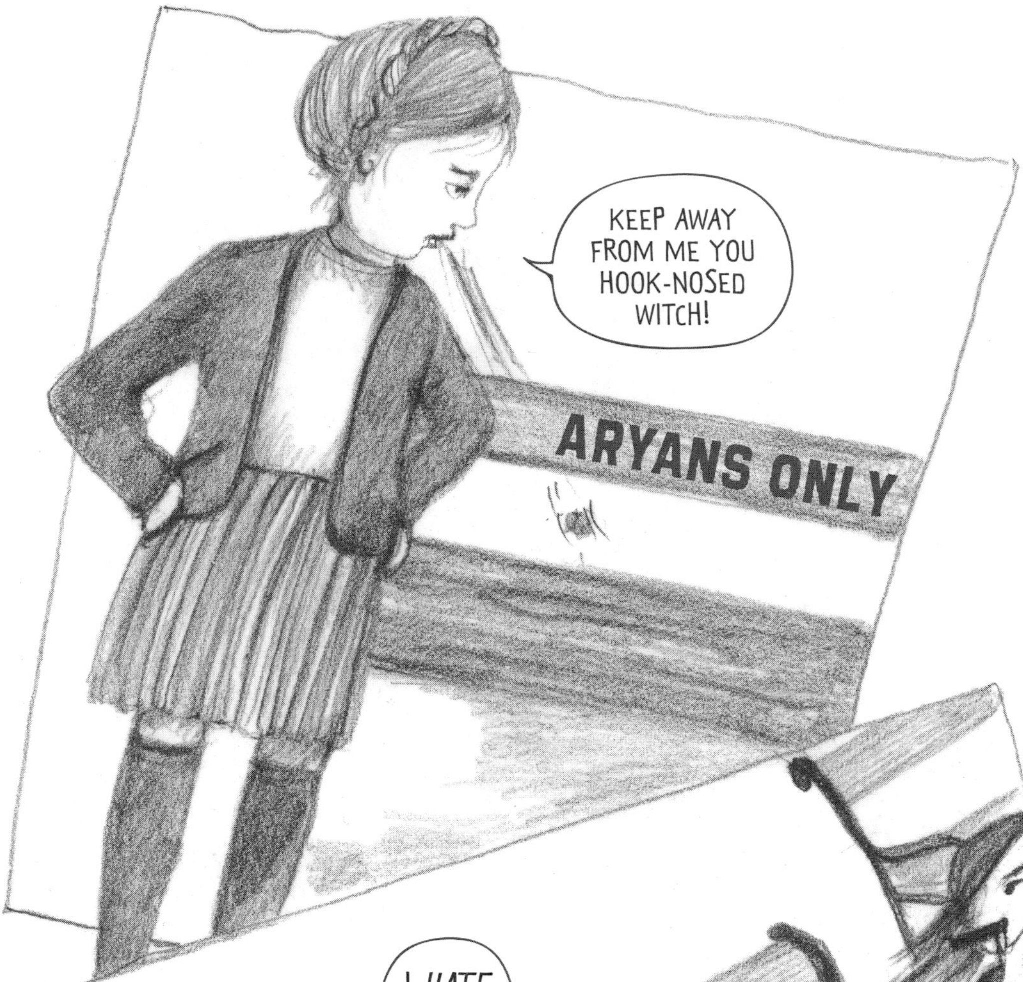
KEEP AWAY FROM ME YOU HOOK-NOSED WITCH!
ARYANS ONLY

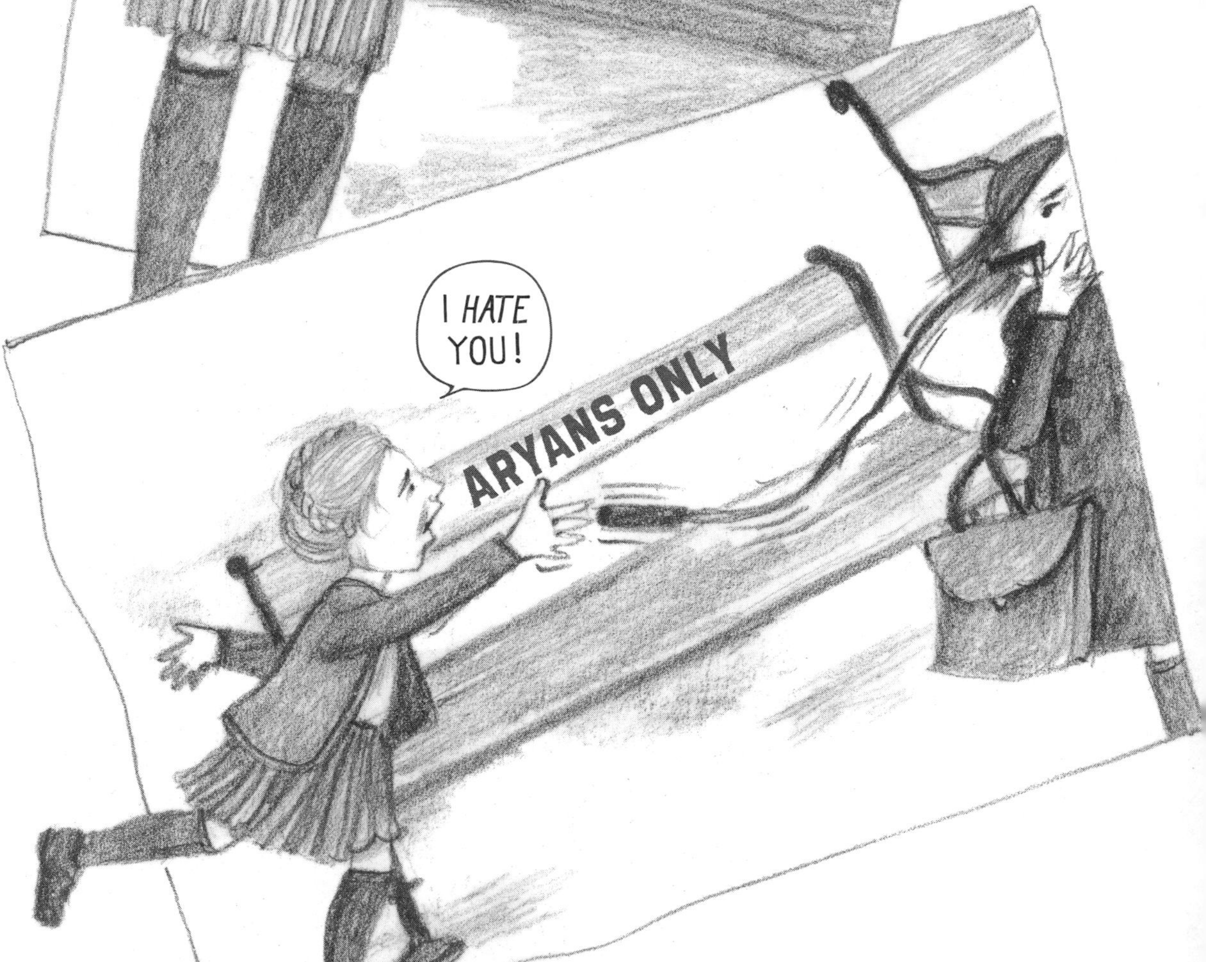
I *HATE* YOU!
ARYANS ONLY

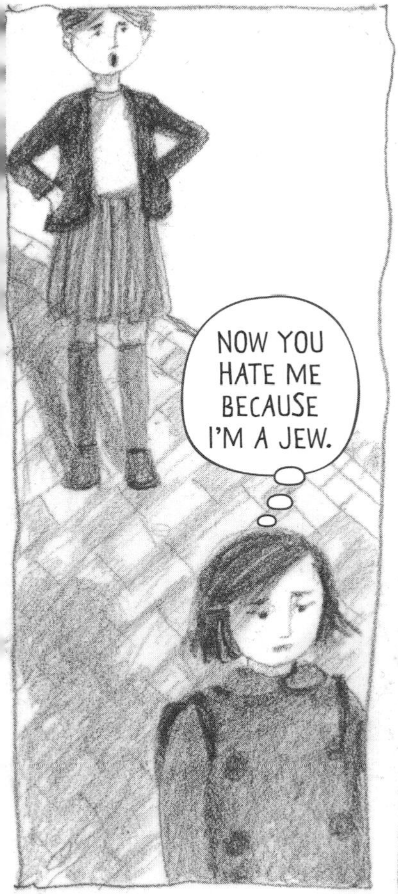
NOW YOU HATE ME BECAUSE I'M A JEW.

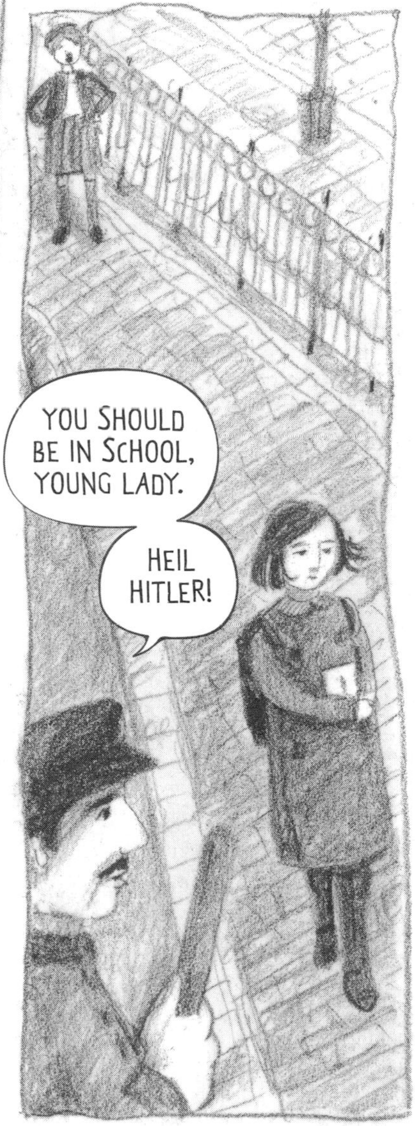
YOU SHOULD BE IN SCHOOL, YOUNG LADY.
HEIL HITLER!

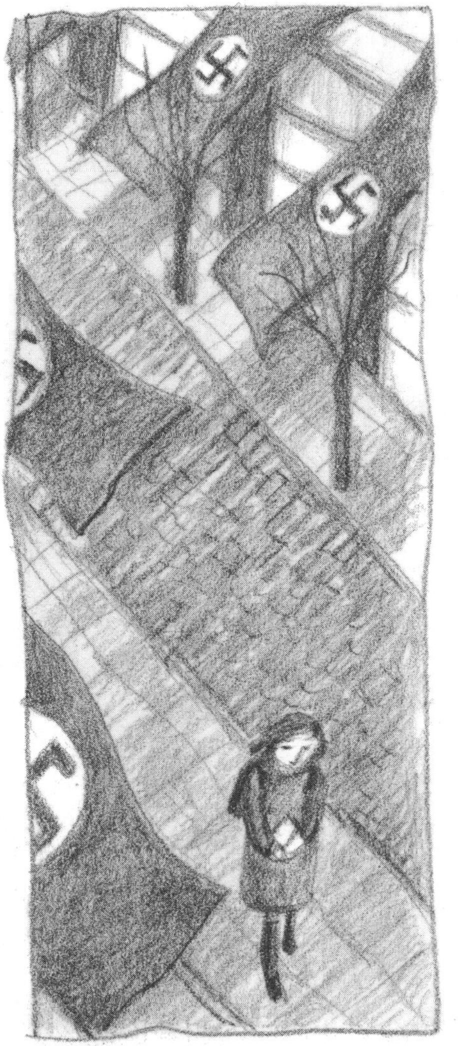

CHAPTER TWO

ERNEST

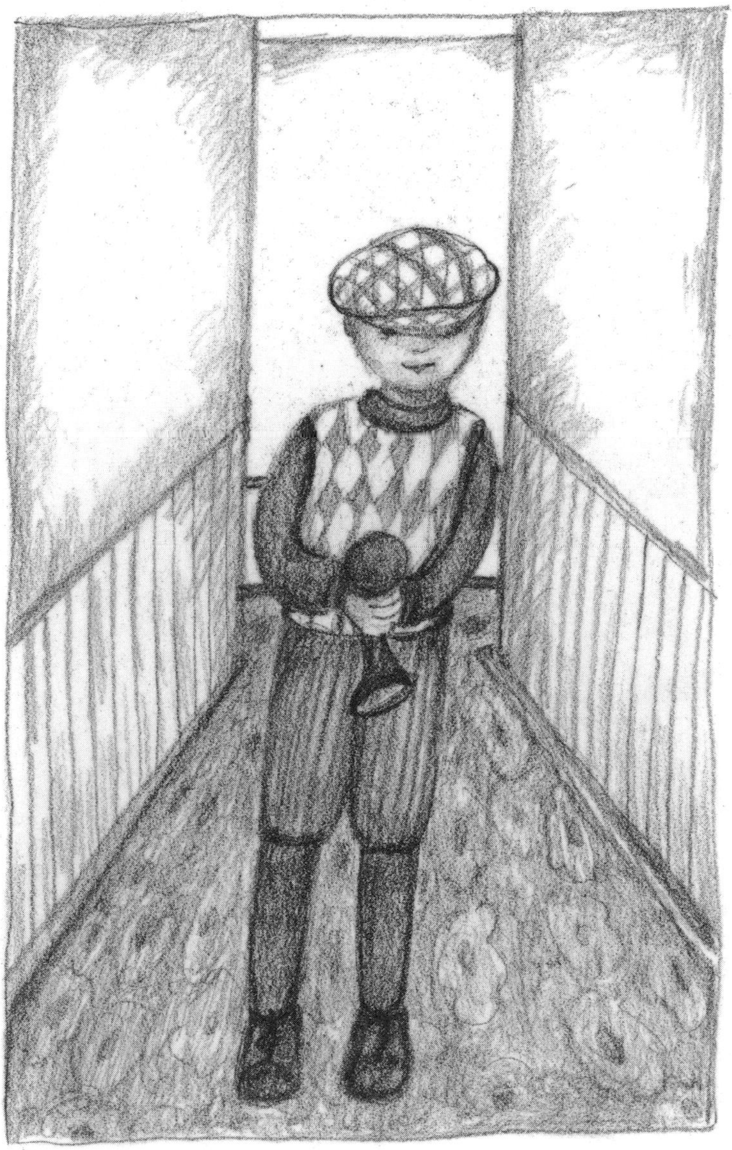

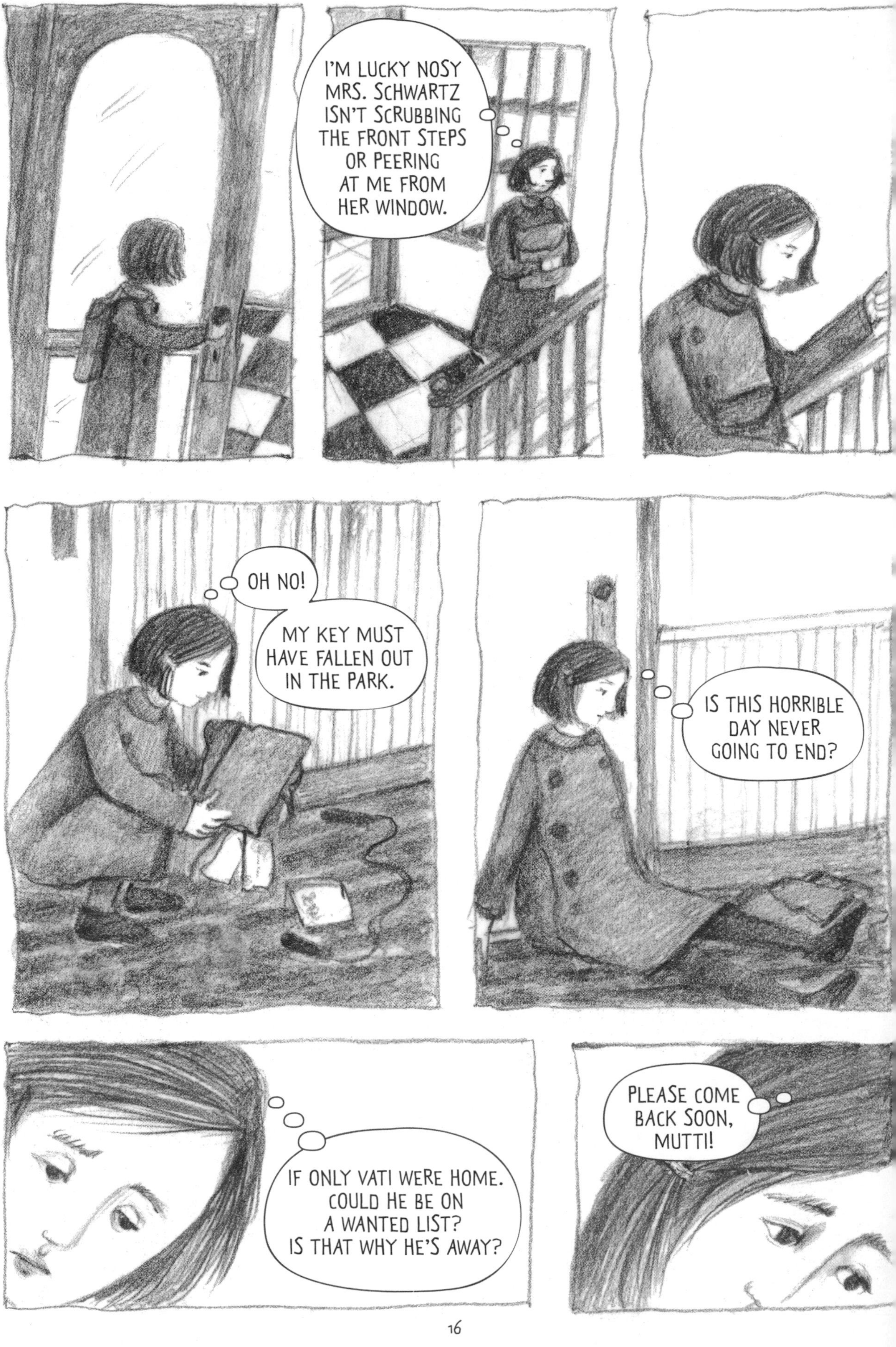
I'M LUCKY NOSY MRS. SCHWARTZ ISN'T SCRUBBING THE FRONT STEPS OR PEERING AT ME FROM HER WINDOW.
OH NO!
MY KEY MUST HAVE FALLEN OUT IN THE PARK.
IS THIS HORRIBLE DAY NEVER GOING TO END?
IF ONLY VATI WERE HOME. COULD HE BE ON A WANTED LIST? IS THAT WHY HE'S AWAY?
PLEASE COME BACK SOON, MUTTI!

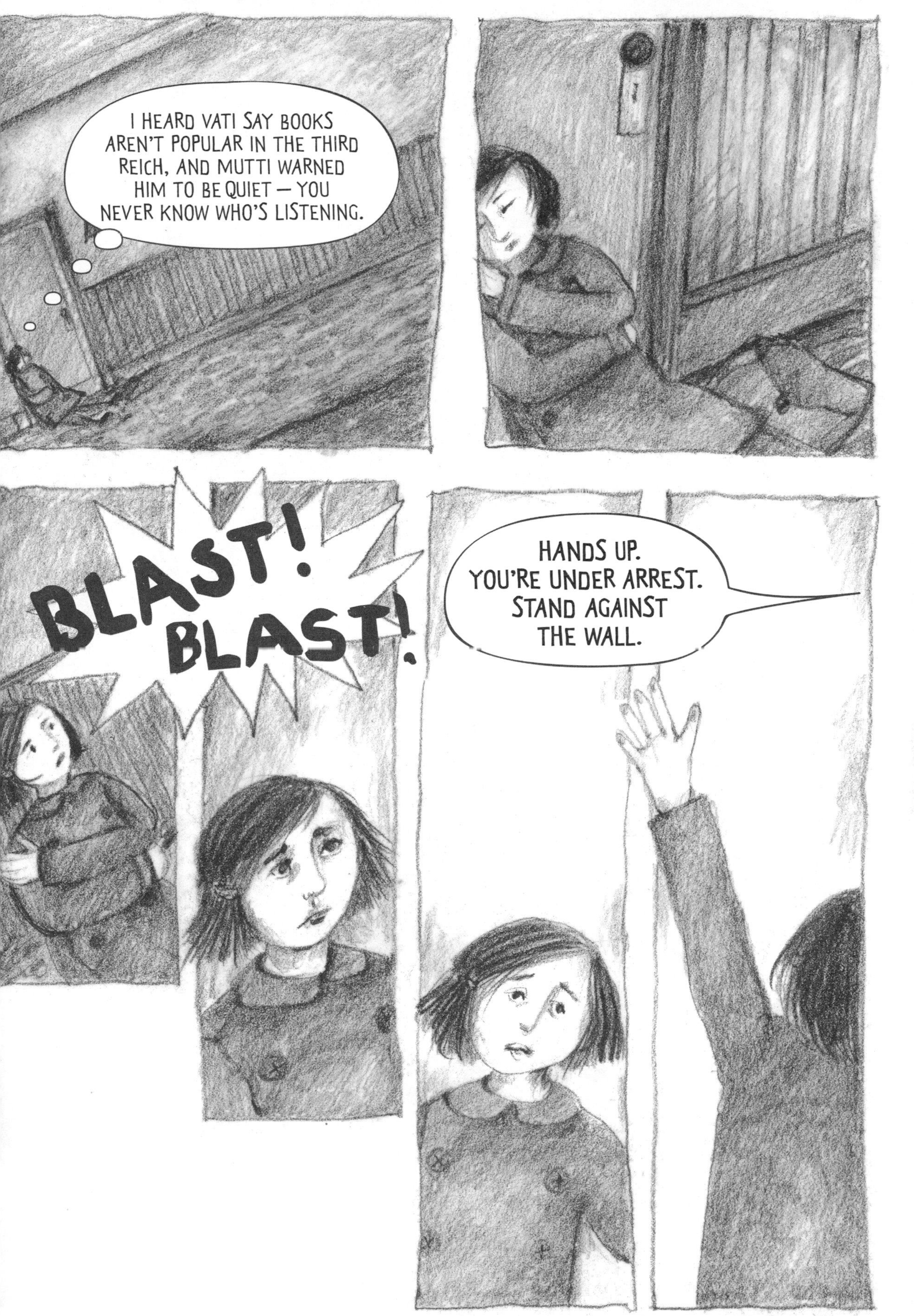

I HEARD VATI SAY BOOKS AREN'T POPULAR IN THE THIRD REICH, AND MUTTI WARNED HIM TO BE QUIET — YOU NEVER KNOW WHO'S LISTENING.
BLAST! BLAST!
HANDS UP. YOU'RE UNDER ARREST. STAND AGAINST THE WALL.

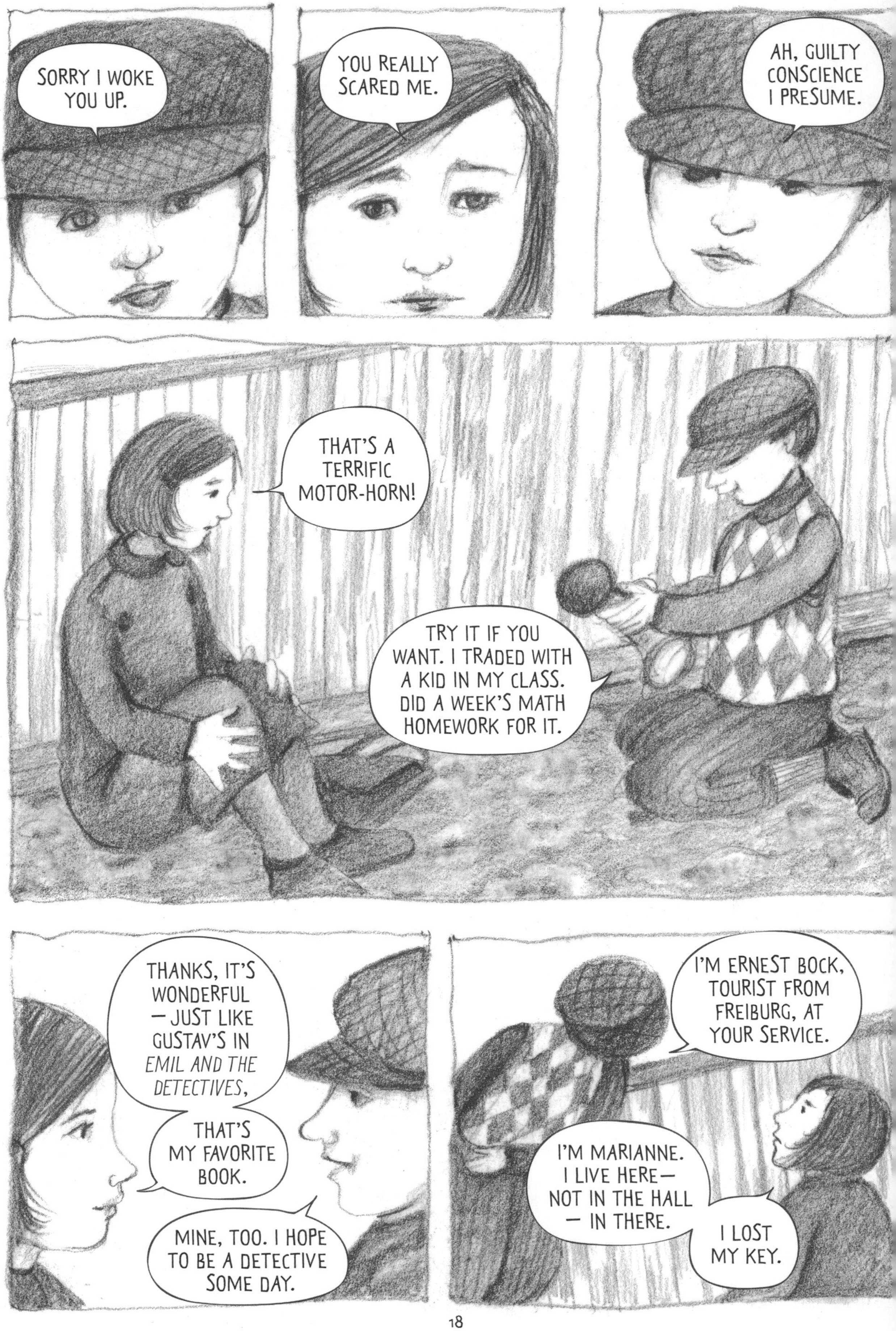
SORRY I WOKE YOU UP.
YOU REALLY SCARED ME.
AH, GUILTY CONSCIENCE I PRESUME.
THAT'S A TERRIFIC MOTOR-HORN!
TRY IT IF YOU WANT. I TRADED WITH A KID IN MY CLASS. DID A WEEK'S MATH HOMEWORK FOR IT.
THANKS, IT'S WONDERFUL — JUST LIKE GUSTAV'S IN *EMIL AND THE DETECTIVES*,
THAT'S MY FAVORITE BOOK.
MINE, TOO. I HOPE TO BE A DETECTIVE SOME DAY.
I'M ERNEST BOCK, TOURIST FROM FREIBURG, AT YOUR SERVICE.
I'M MARIANNE. I LIVE HERE— NOT IN THE HALL — IN THERE.
I LOST MY KEY.

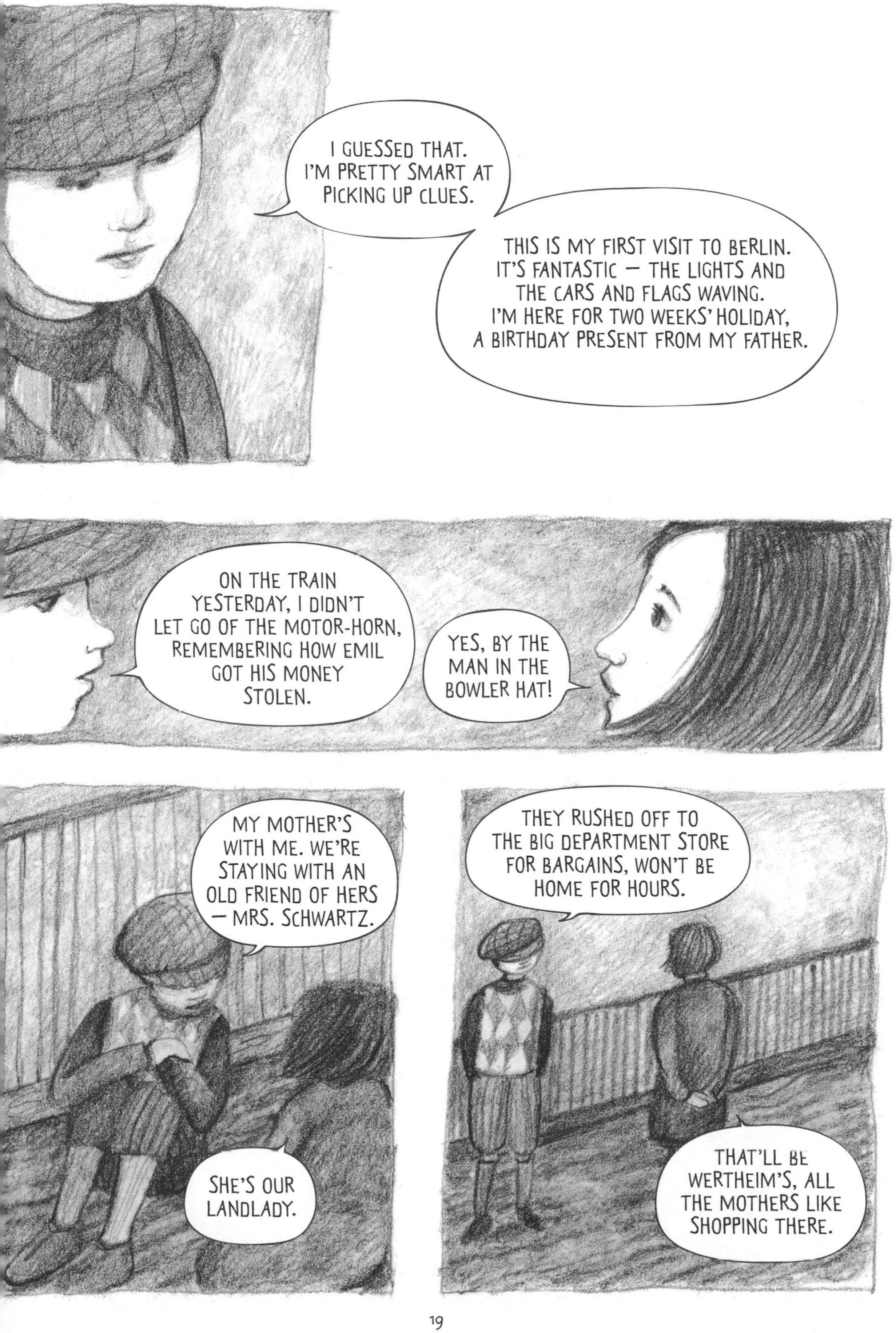
I GUESSED THAT. I'M PRETTY SMART AT PICKING UP CLUES.
THIS IS MY FIRST VISIT TO BERLIN. IT'S FANTASTIC — THE LIGHTS AND THE CARS AND FLAGS WAVING. I'M HERE FOR TWO WEEKS' HOLIDAY, A BIRTHDAY PRESENT FROM MY FATHER.
ON THE TRAIN YESTERDAY, I DIDN'T LET GO OF THE MOTOR-HORN, REMEMBERING HOW EMIL GOT HIS MONEY STOLEN.
YES, BY THE MAN IN THE BOWLER HAT!
MY MOTHER'S WITH ME. WE'RE STAYING WITH AN OLD FRIEND OF HERS — MRS. SCHWARTZ.
SHE'S OUR LANDLADY.
THEY RUSHED OFF TO THE BIG DEPARTMENT STORE FOR BARGAINS, WON'T BE HOME FOR HOURS.
THAT'LL BE WERTHEIM'S, ALL THE MOTHERS LIKE SHOPPING THERE.

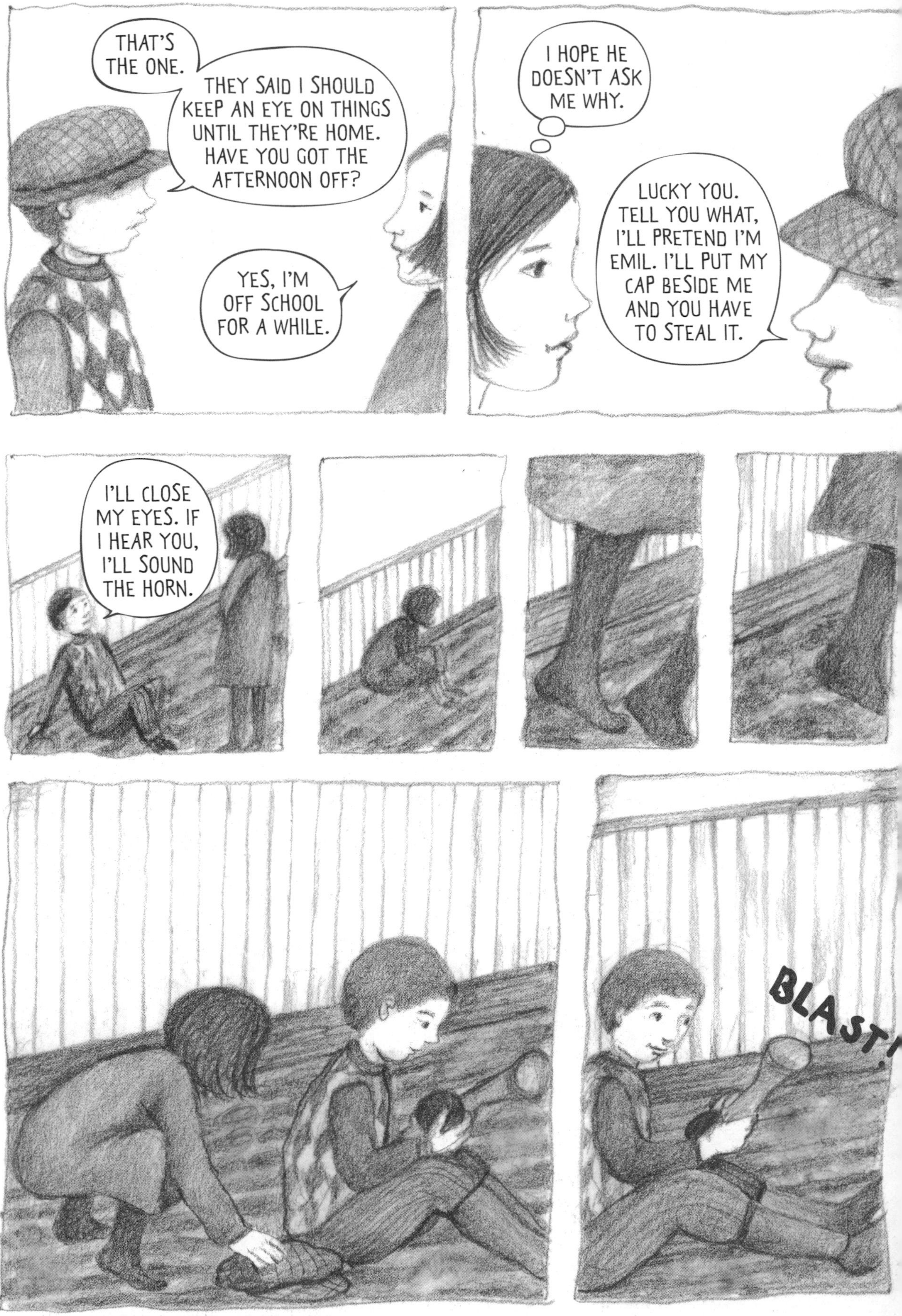
THAT'S THE ONE.
THEY SAID I SHOULD KEEP AN EYE ON THINGS UNTIL THEY'RE HOME. HAVE YOU GOT THE AFTERNOON OFF?
YES, I'M OFF SCHOOL FOR A WHILE.
I HOPE HE DOESN'T ASK ME WHY.
LUCKY YOU. TELL YOU WHAT, I'LL PRETEND I'M EMIL. I'LL PUT MY CAP BESIDE ME AND YOU HAVE TO STEAL IT.
I'LL CLOSE MY EYES. IF I HEAR YOU, I'LL SOUND THE HORN.
BLAST!

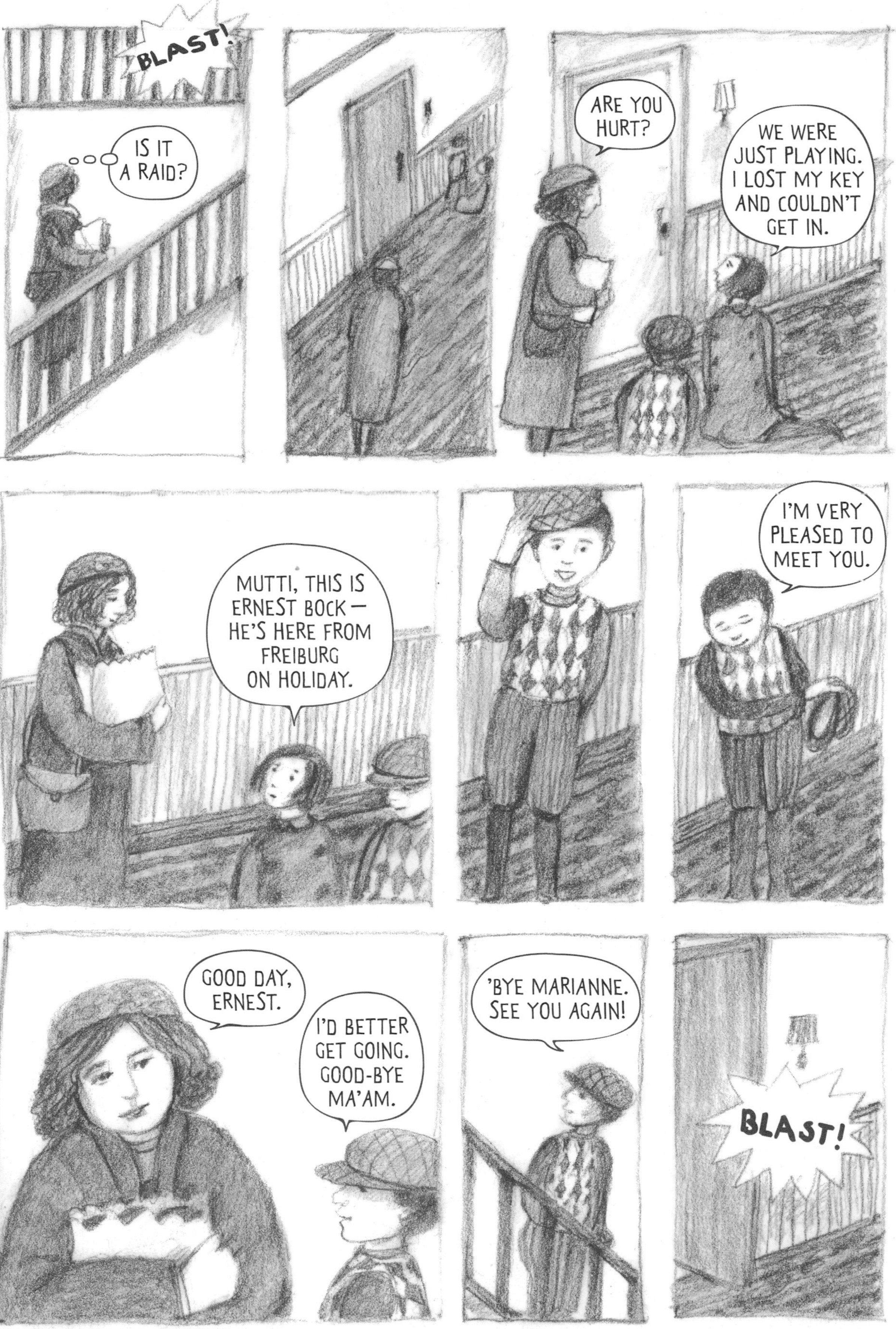
BLAST!
IS IT A RAID?
ARE YOU HURT?
WE WERE JUST PLAYING. I LOST MY KEY AND COULDN'T GET IN.
MUTTI, THIS IS ERNEST BOCK — HE'S HERE FROM FREIBURG ON HOLIDAY.
I'M VERY PLEASED TO MEET YOU.
GOOD DAY, ERNEST.
I'D BETTER GET GOING. GOOD-BYE MA'AM.
'BYE MARIANNE. SEE YOU AGAIN!
BLAST!

CHAPTER THREE

"NO JEW IS SAFE"

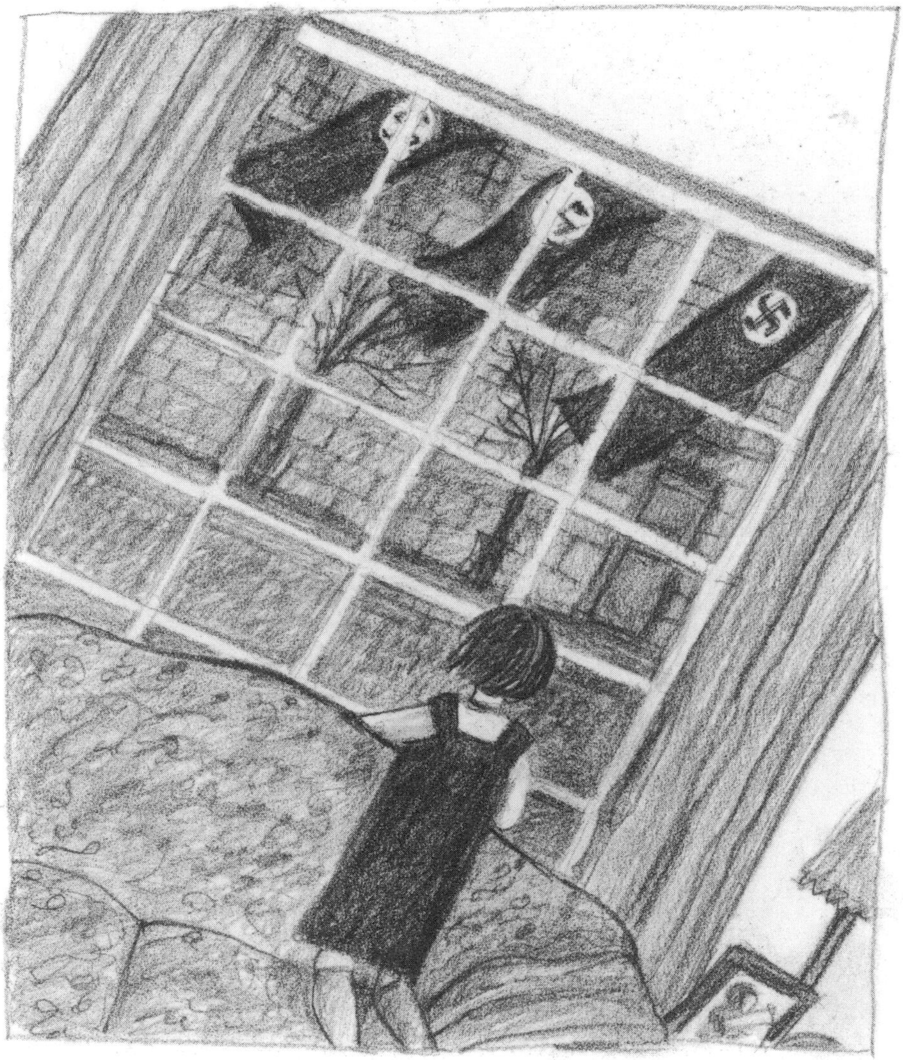

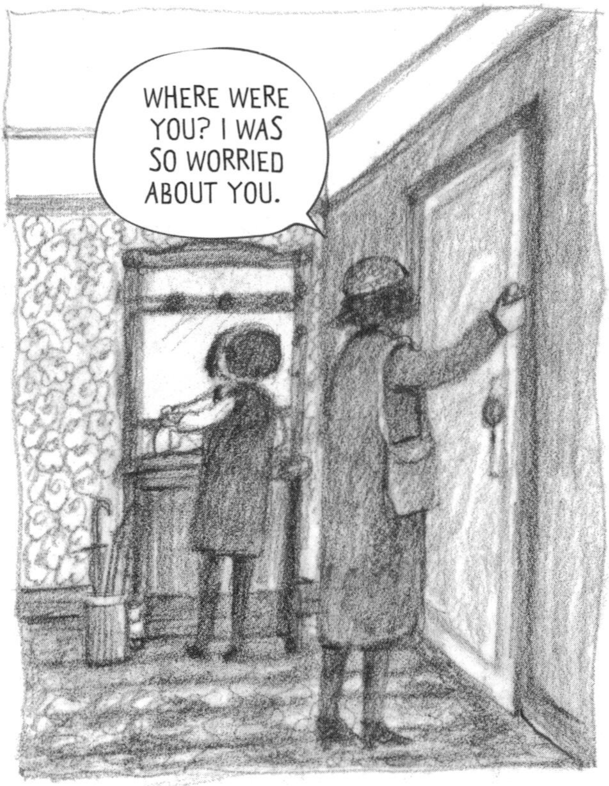
WHERE WERE YOU? I WAS SO WORRIED ABOUT YOU.
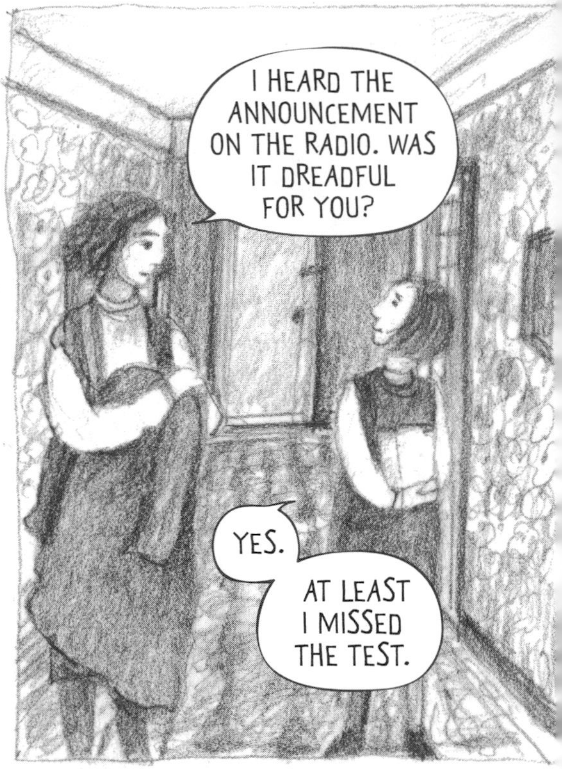
I HEARD THE ANNOUNCEMENT ON THE RADIO. WAS IT DREADFUL FOR YOU?
YES.
AT LEAST I MISSED THE TEST.
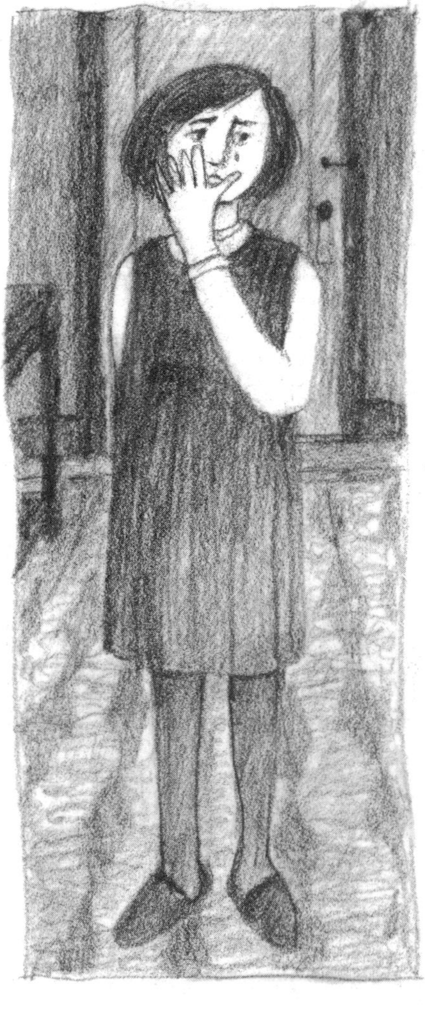
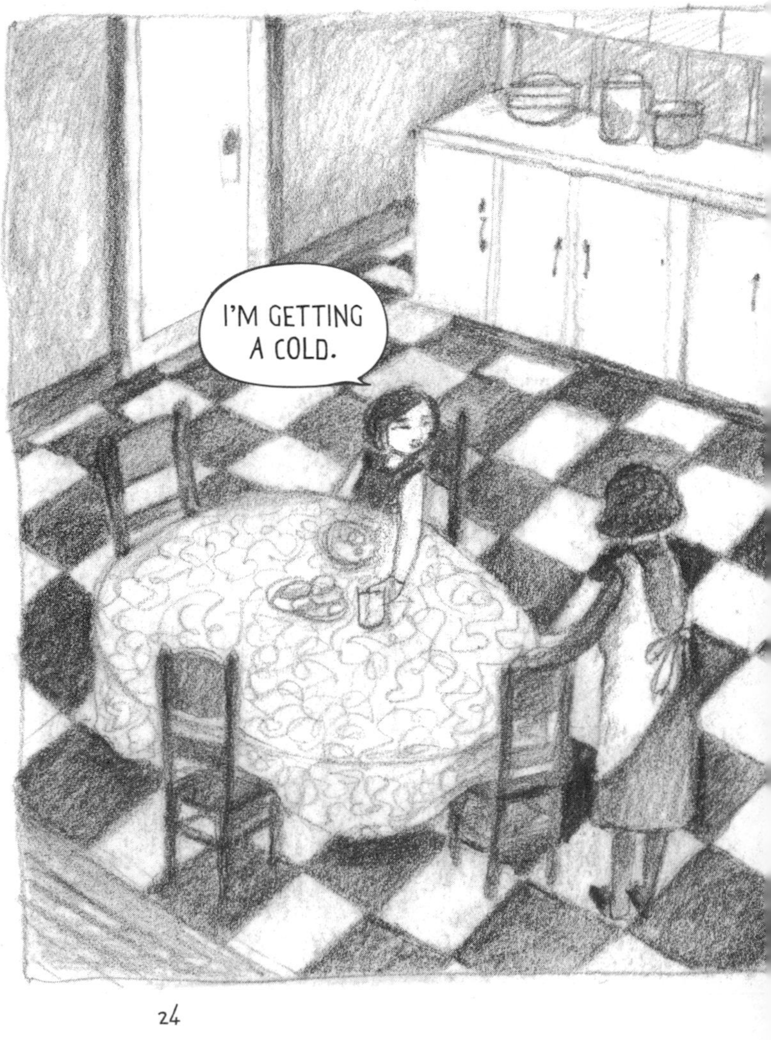
I'M GETTING A COLD.

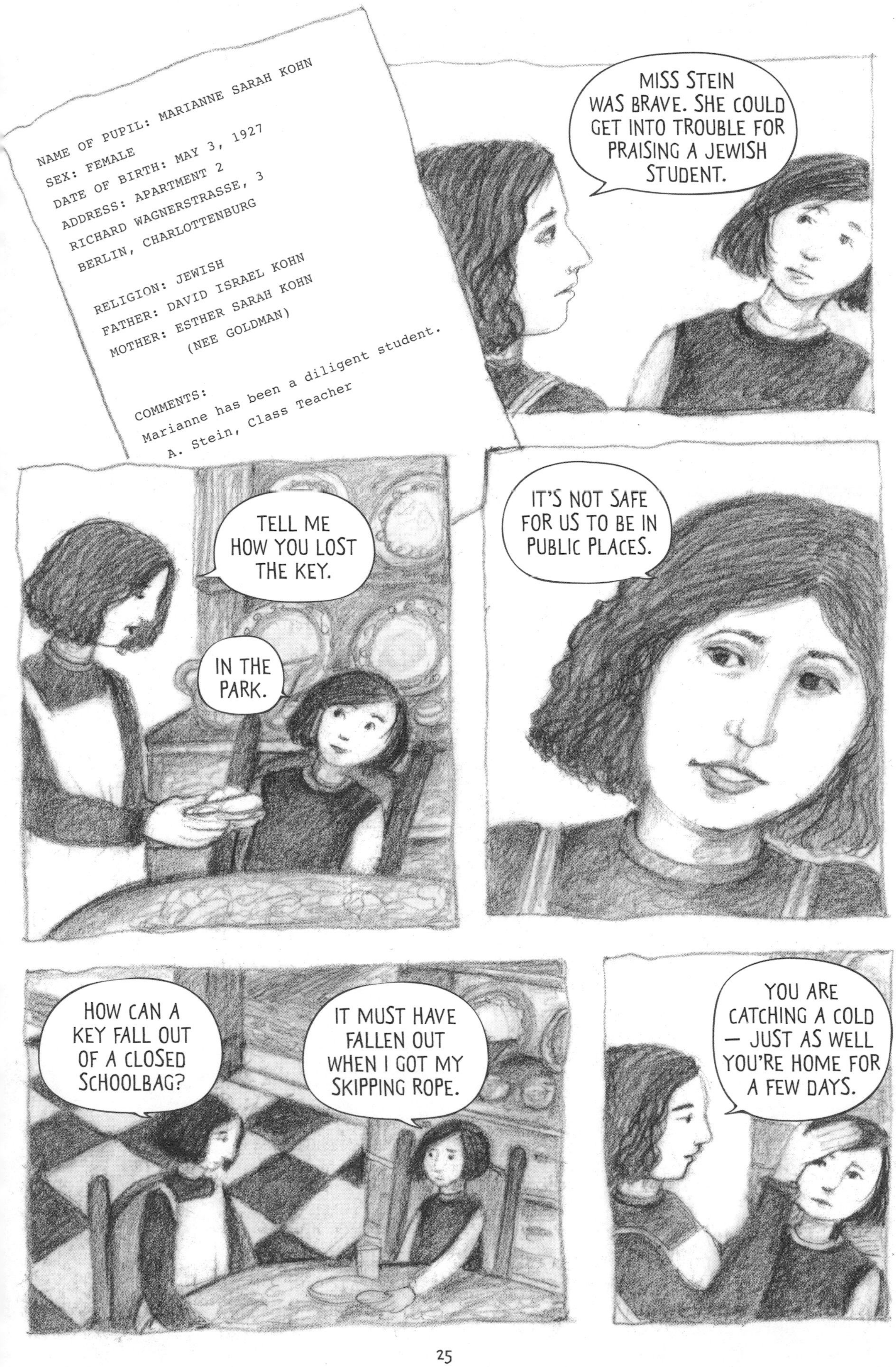
NAME OF PUPIL: MARIANNE SARAH KOHN
SEX: FEMALE
DATE OF BIRTH: MAY 3, 1927
ADDRESS: APARTMENT 2
RICHARD WAGNERSTRASSE, 3
BERLIN, CHARLOTTENBURG
RELIGION: JEWISH
FATHER: DAVID ISRAEL KOHN
MOTHER: ESTHER SARAH KOHN
(NEE GOLDMAN)
COMMENTS:
Marianne has been a diligent student.
A. Stein, Class Teacher
MISS STEIN WAS BRAVE. SHE COULD GET INTO TROUBLE FOR PRAISING A JEWISH STUDENT.
TELL ME HOW YOU LOST THE KEY.
IN THE PARK.
IT'S NOT SAFE FOR US TO BE IN PUBLIC PLACES.
HOW CAN A KEY FALL OUT OF A CLOSED SCHOOLBAG?
IT MUST HAVE FALLEN OUT WHEN I GOT MY SKIPPING ROPE.
YOU ARE CATCHING A COLD — JUST AS WELL YOU'RE HOME FOR A FEW DAYS.

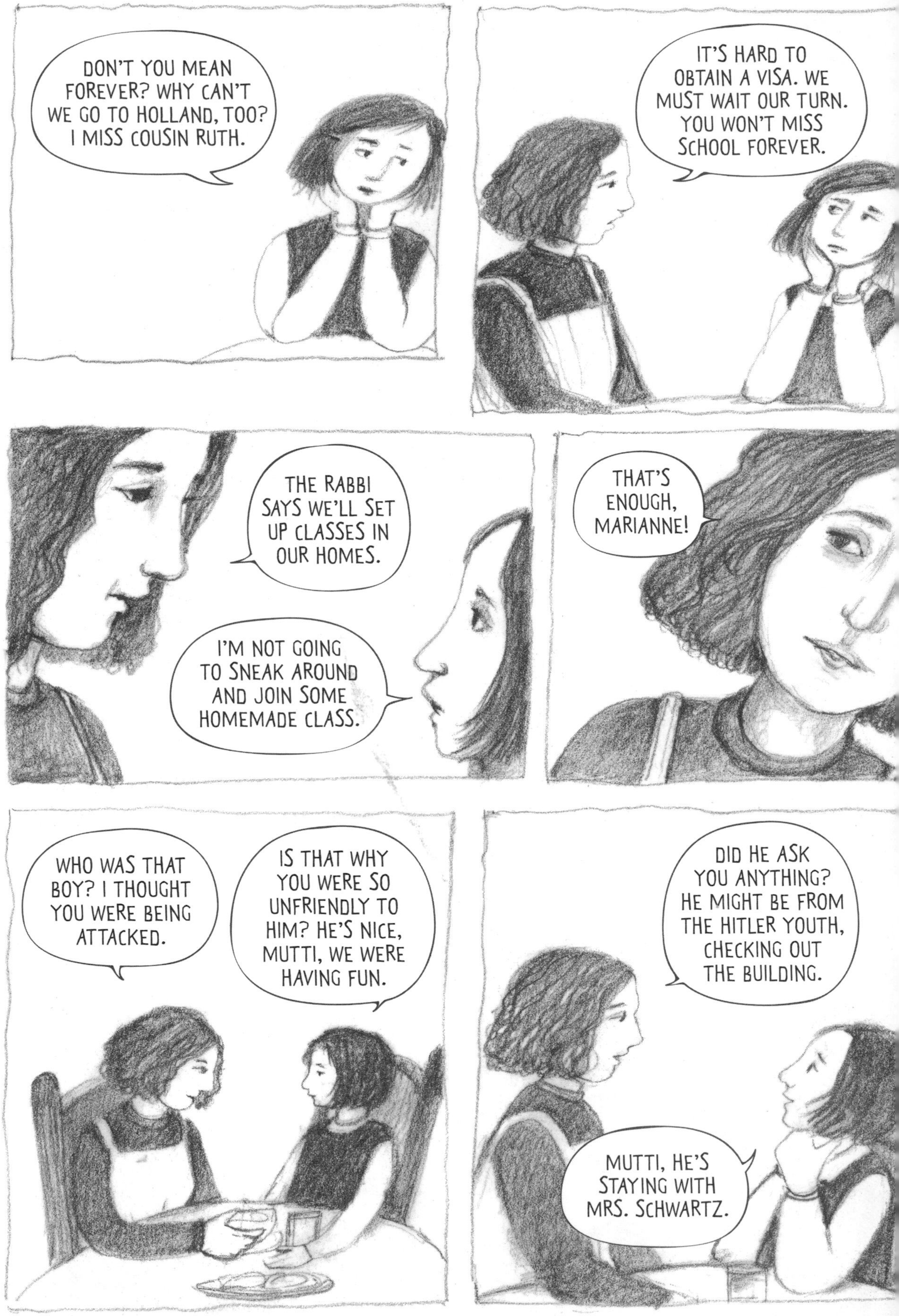
DON'T YOU MEAN FOREVER? WHY CAN'T WE GO TO HOLLAND, TOO? I MISS COUSIN RUTH.
IT'S HARD TO OBTAIN A VISA. WE MUST WAIT OUR TURN. YOU WON'T MISS SCHOOL FOREVER.
THE RABBI SAYS WE'LL SET UP CLASSES IN OUR HOMES.
I'M NOT GOING TO SNEAK AROUND AND JOIN SOME HOMEMADE CLASS.
THAT'S ENOUGH, MARIANNE!
WHO WAS THAT BOY? I THOUGHT YOU WERE BEING ATTACKED.
IS THAT WHY YOU WERE SO UNFRIENDLY TO HIM? HE'S NICE, MUTTI, WE WERE HAVING FUN.
DID HE ASK YOU ANYTHING? HE MIGHT BE FROM THE HITLER YOUTH, CHECKING OUT THE BUILDING.
MUTTI, HE'S STAYING WITH MRS. SCHWARTZ.

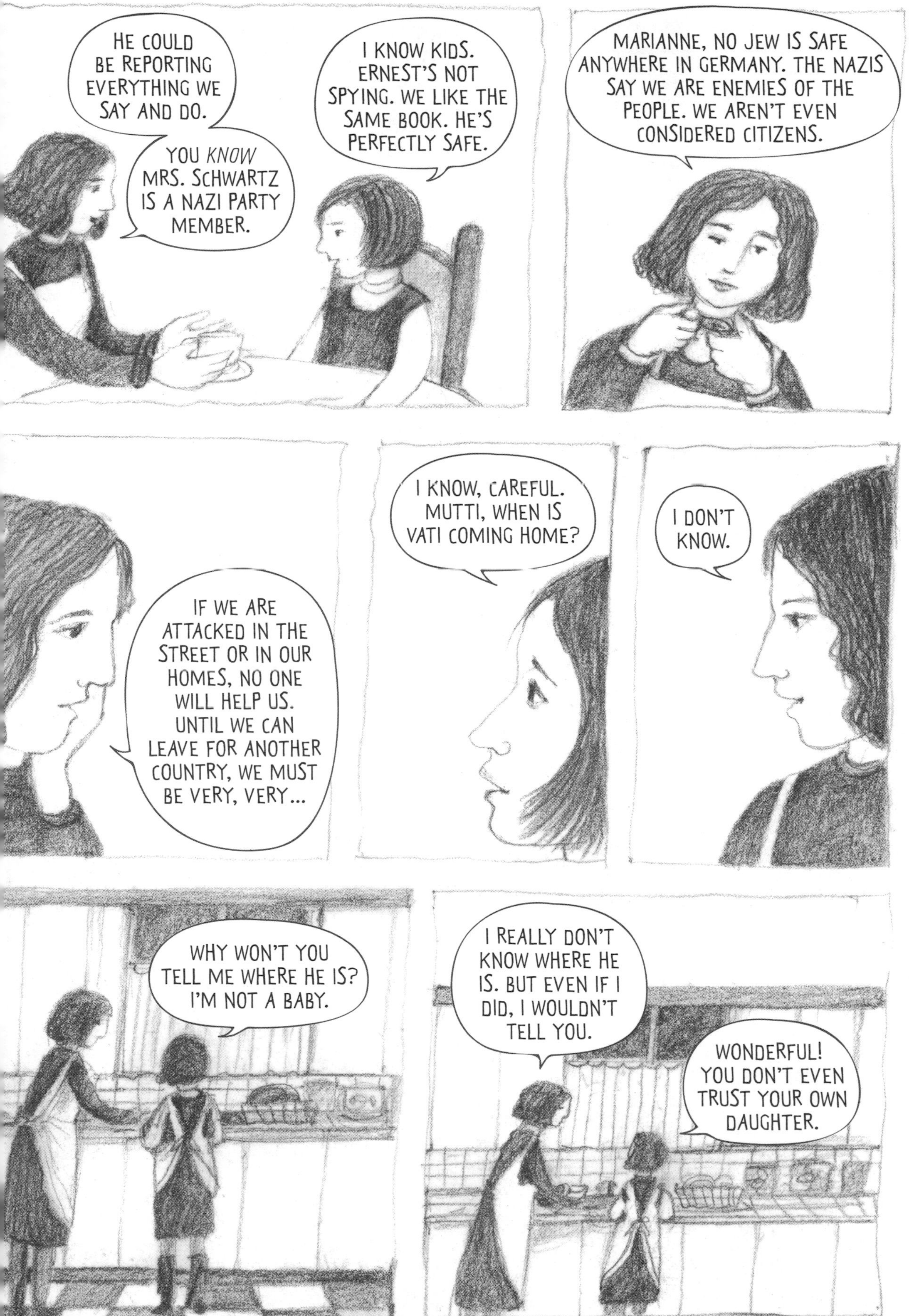
HE COULD BE REPORTING EVERYTHING WE SAY AND DO.
YOU *KNOW* MRS. SCHWARTZ IS A NAZI PARTY MEMBER.
I KNOW KIDS. ERNEST'S NOT SPYING. WE LIKE THE SAME BOOK. HE'S PERFECTLY SAFE.
MARIANNE, NO JEW IS SAFE ANYWHERE IN GERMANY. THE NAZIS SAY WE ARE ENEMIES OF THE PEOPLE. WE AREN'T EVEN CONSIDERED CITIZENS.
IF WE ARE ATTACKED IN THE STREET OR IN OUR HOMES, NO ONE WILL HELP US. UNTIL WE CAN LEAVE FOR ANOTHER COUNTRY, WE MUST BE VERY, VERY...
I KNOW, CAREFUL. MUTTI, WHEN IS VATI COMING HOME?
I DON'T KNOW.
WHY WON'T YOU TELL ME WHERE HE IS? I'M NOT A BABY.
I REALLY DON'T KNOW WHERE HE IS. BUT EVEN IF I DID, I WOULDN'T TELL YOU.
WONDERFUL! YOU DON'T EVEN TRUST YOUR OWN DAUGHTER.

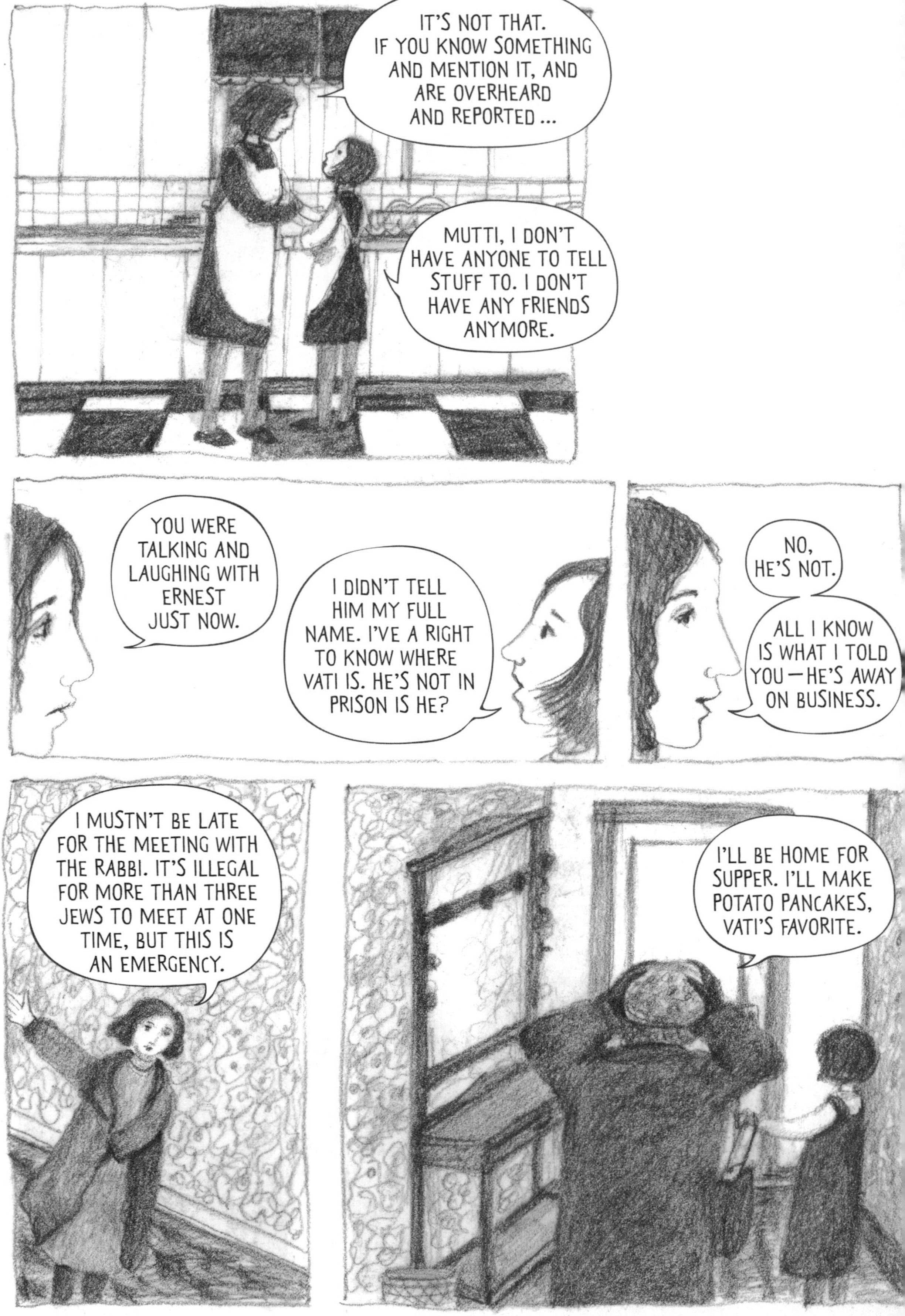
IT'S NOT THAT. IF YOU KNOW SOMETHING AND MENTION IT, AND ARE OVERHEARD AND REPORTED ...
MUTTI, I DON'T HAVE ANYONE TO TELL STUFF TO. I DON'T HAVE ANY FRIENDS ANYMORE.
YOU WERE TALKING AND LAUGHING WITH ERNEST JUST NOW.
I DIDN'T TELL HIM MY FULL NAME. I'VE A RIGHT TO KNOW WHERE VATI IS. HE'S NOT IN PRISON IS HE?
NO, HE'S NOT.
ALL I KNOW IS WHAT I TOLD YOU—HE'S AWAY ON BUSINESS.
I MUSTN'T BE LATE FOR THE MEETING WITH THE RABBI. IT'S ILLEGAL FOR MORE THAN THREE JEWS TO MEET AT ONE TIME, BUT THIS IS AN EMERGENCY.
I'LL BE HOME FOR SUPPER. I'LL MAKE POTATO PANCAKES, VATI'S FAVORITE.

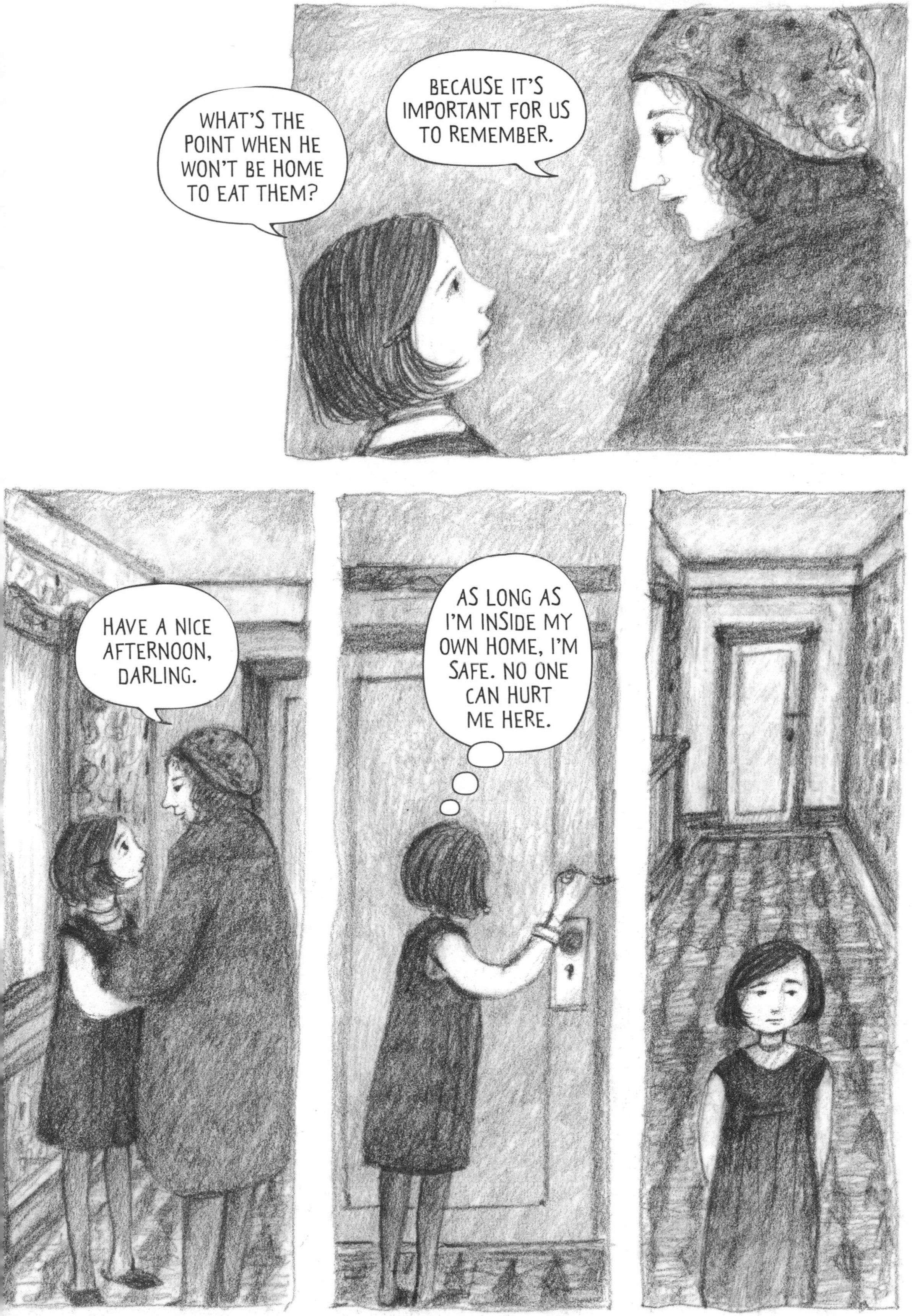
WHAT'S THE POINT WHEN HE WON'T BE HOME TO EAT THEM?
BECAUSE IT'S IMPORTANT FOR US TO REMEMBER.
HAVE A NICE AFTERNOON, DARLING.
AS LONG AS I'M INSIDE MY OWN HOME, I'M SAFE. NO ONE CAN HURT ME HERE.

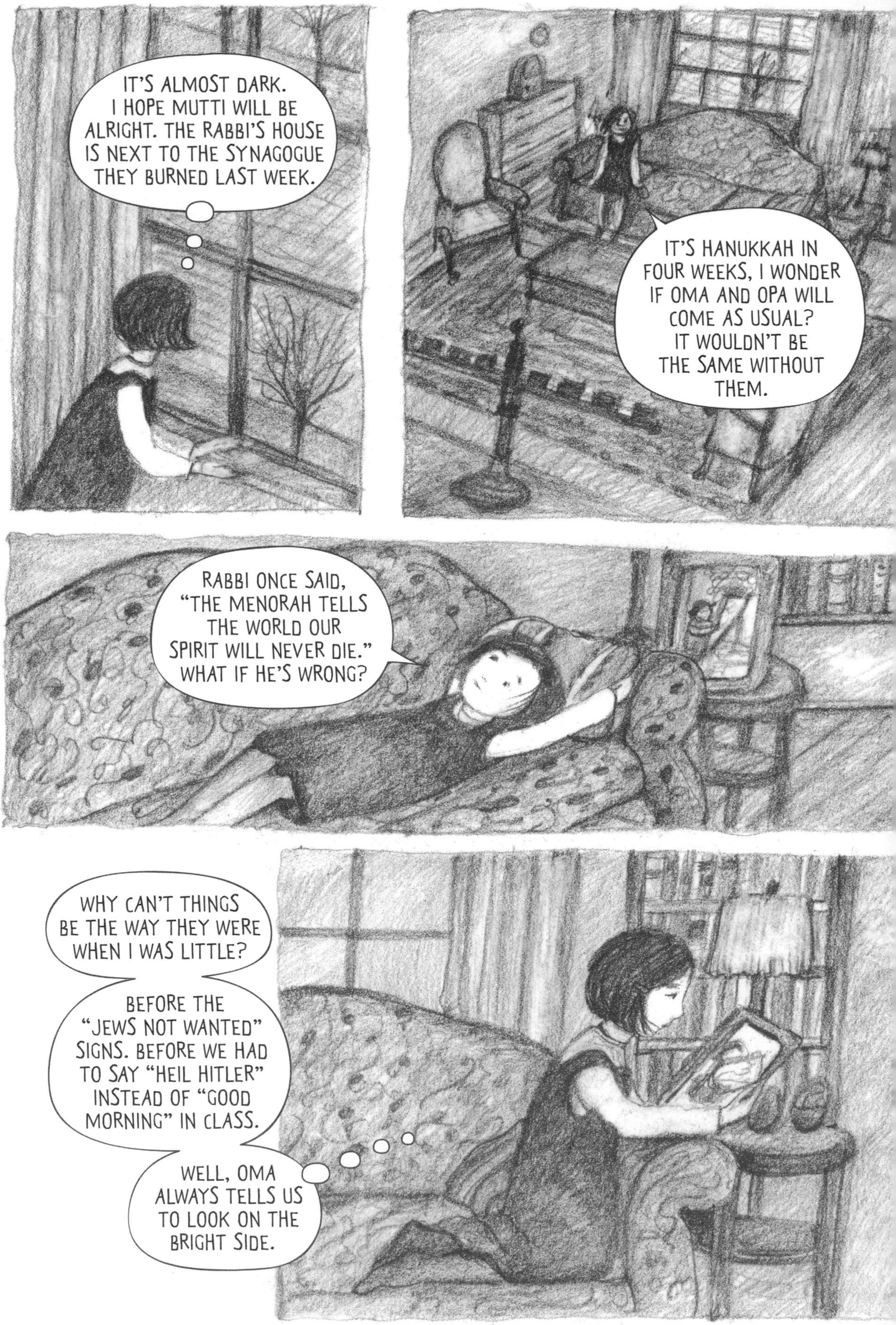
IT'S ALMOST DARK. I HOPE MUTTI WILL BE ALRIGHT. THE RABBI'S HOUSE IS NEXT TO THE SYNAGOGUE THEY BURNED LAST WEEK.
IT'S HANUKKAH IN FOUR WEEKS, I WONDER IF OMA AND OPA WILL COME AS USUAL? IT WOULDN'T BE THE SAME WITHOUT THEM.
RABBI ONCE SAID, "THE MENORAH TELLS THE WORLD OUR SPIRIT WILL NEVER DIE." WHAT IF HE'S WRONG?
WHY CAN'T THINGS BE THE WAY THEY WERE WHEN I WAS LITTLE?
BEFORE THE "JEWS NOT WANTED" SIGNS. BEFORE WE HAD TO SAY "HEIL HITLER" INSTEAD OF "GOOD MORNING" IN CLASS.
WELL, OMA ALWAYS TELLS US TO LOOK ON THE BRIGHT SIDE.

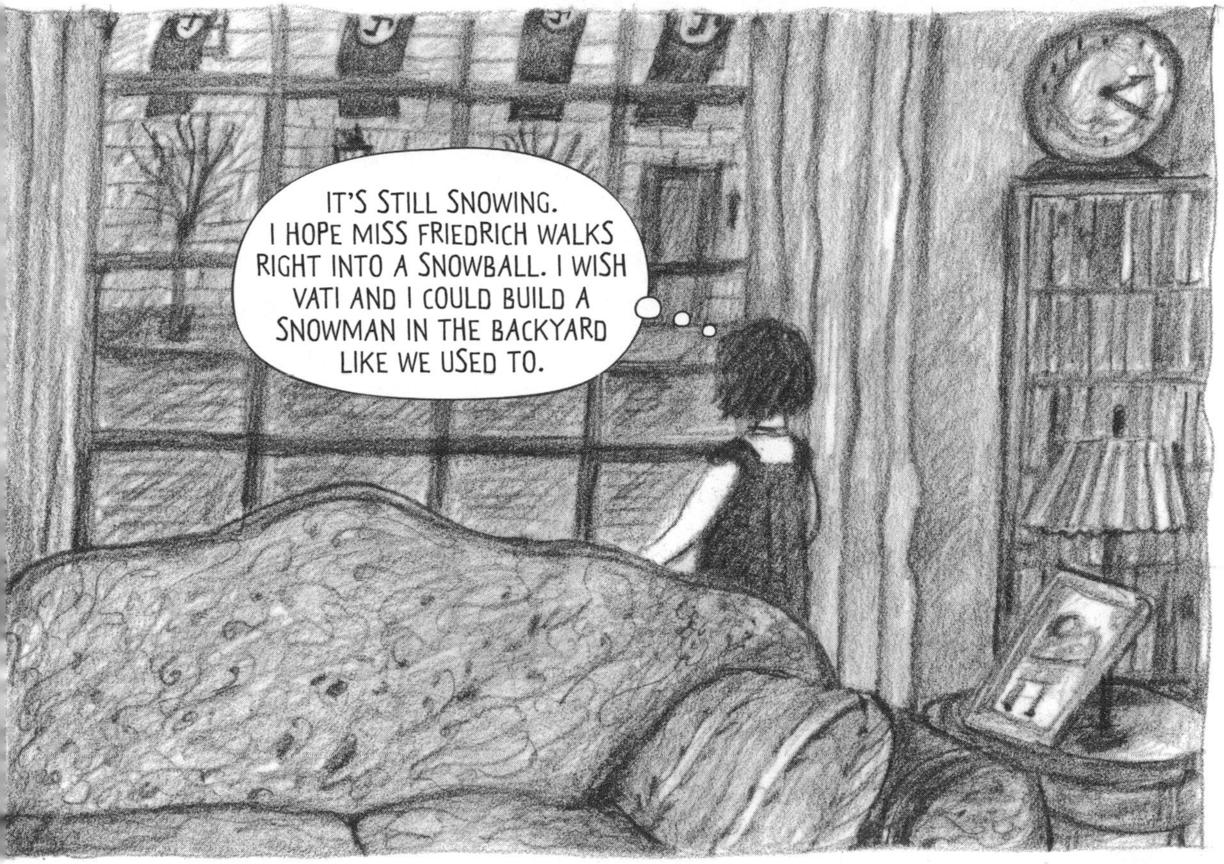
IT'S STILL SNOWING. I HOPE MISS FRIEDRICH WALKS RIGHT INTO A SNOWBALL. I WISH VATI AND I COULD BUILD A SNOWMAN IN THE BACKYARD LIKE WE USED TO.

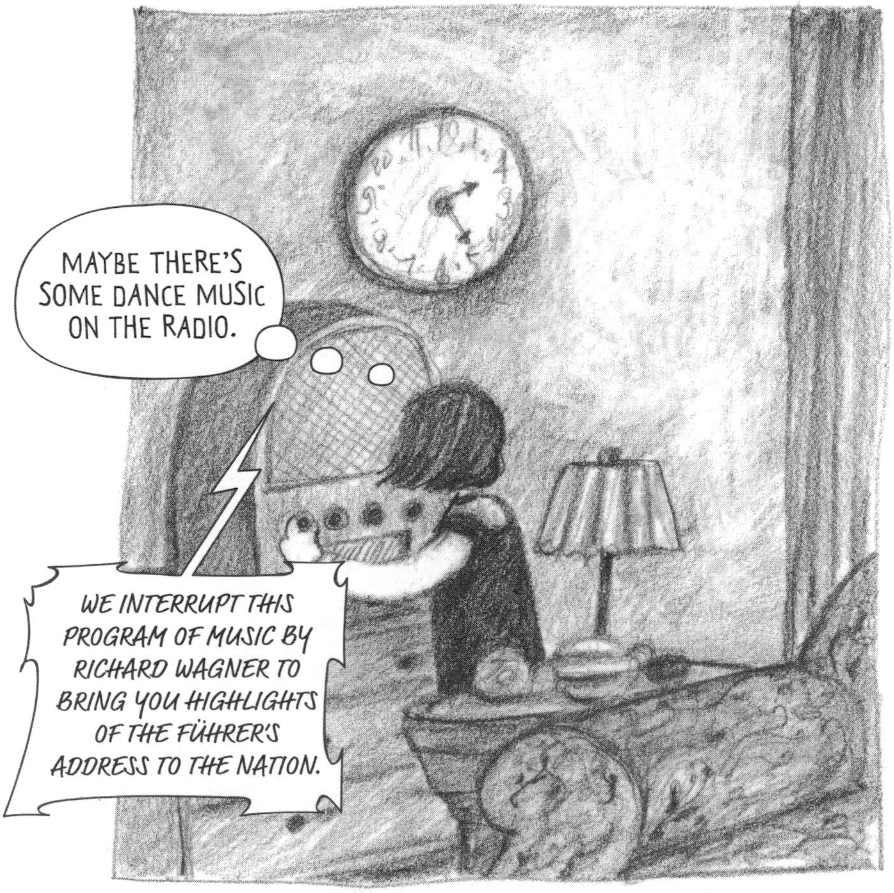
MAYBE THERE'S SOME DANCE MUSIC ON THE RADIO.
WE INTERRUPT THIS PROGRAM OF MUSIC BY RICHARD WAGNER TO BRING YOU HIGHLIGHTS OF THE FÜHRER'S ADDRESS TO THE NATION.

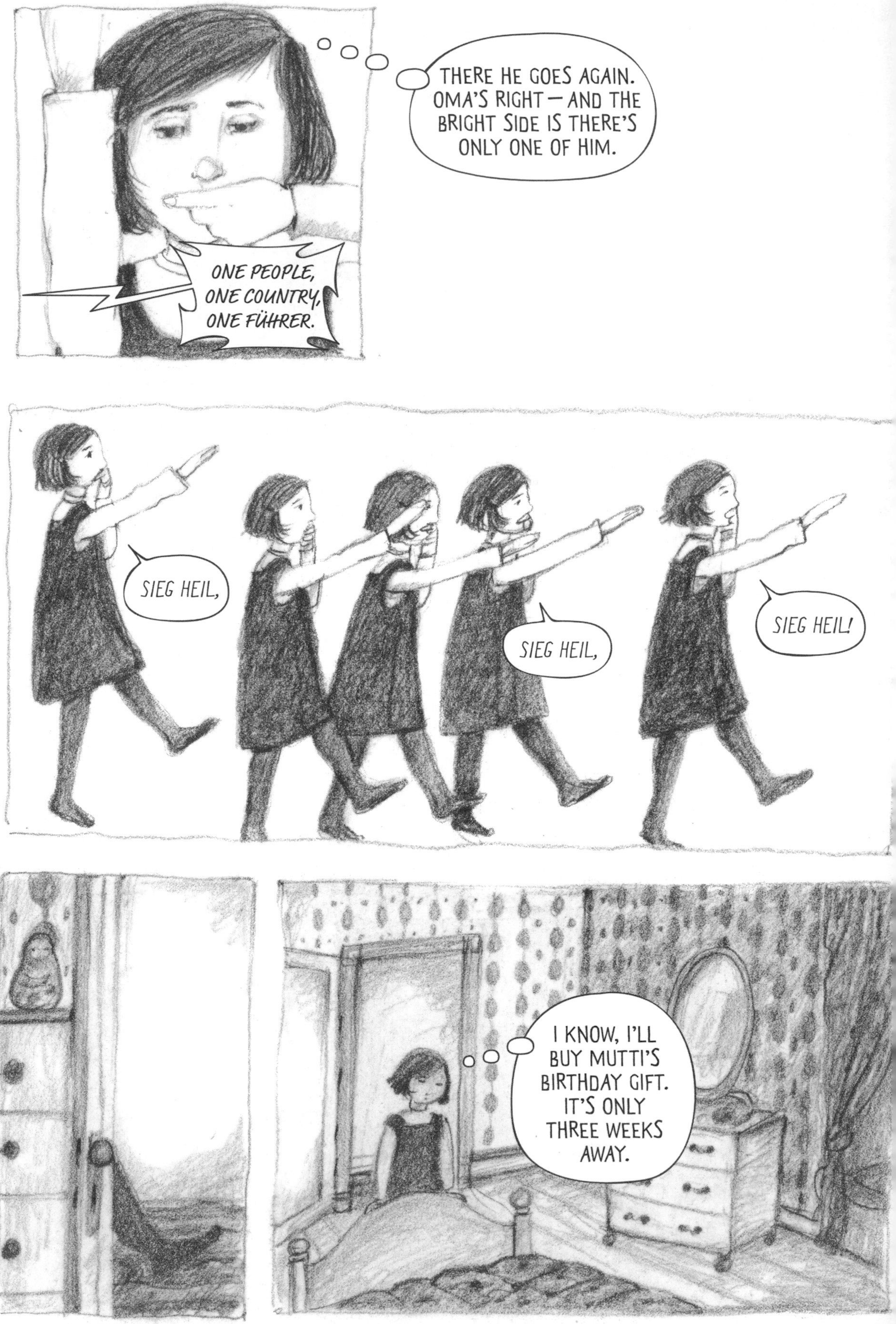
THERE HE GOES AGAIN. OMA'S RIGHT — AND THE BRIGHT SIDE IS THERE'S ONLY ONE OF HIM.
ONE PEOPLE, ONE COUNTRY, ONE FÜHRER.
SIEG HEIL,
SIEG HEIL,
SIEG HEIL!
I KNOW, I'LL BUY MUTTI'S BIRTHDAY GIFT. IT'S ONLY THREE WEEKS AWAY.

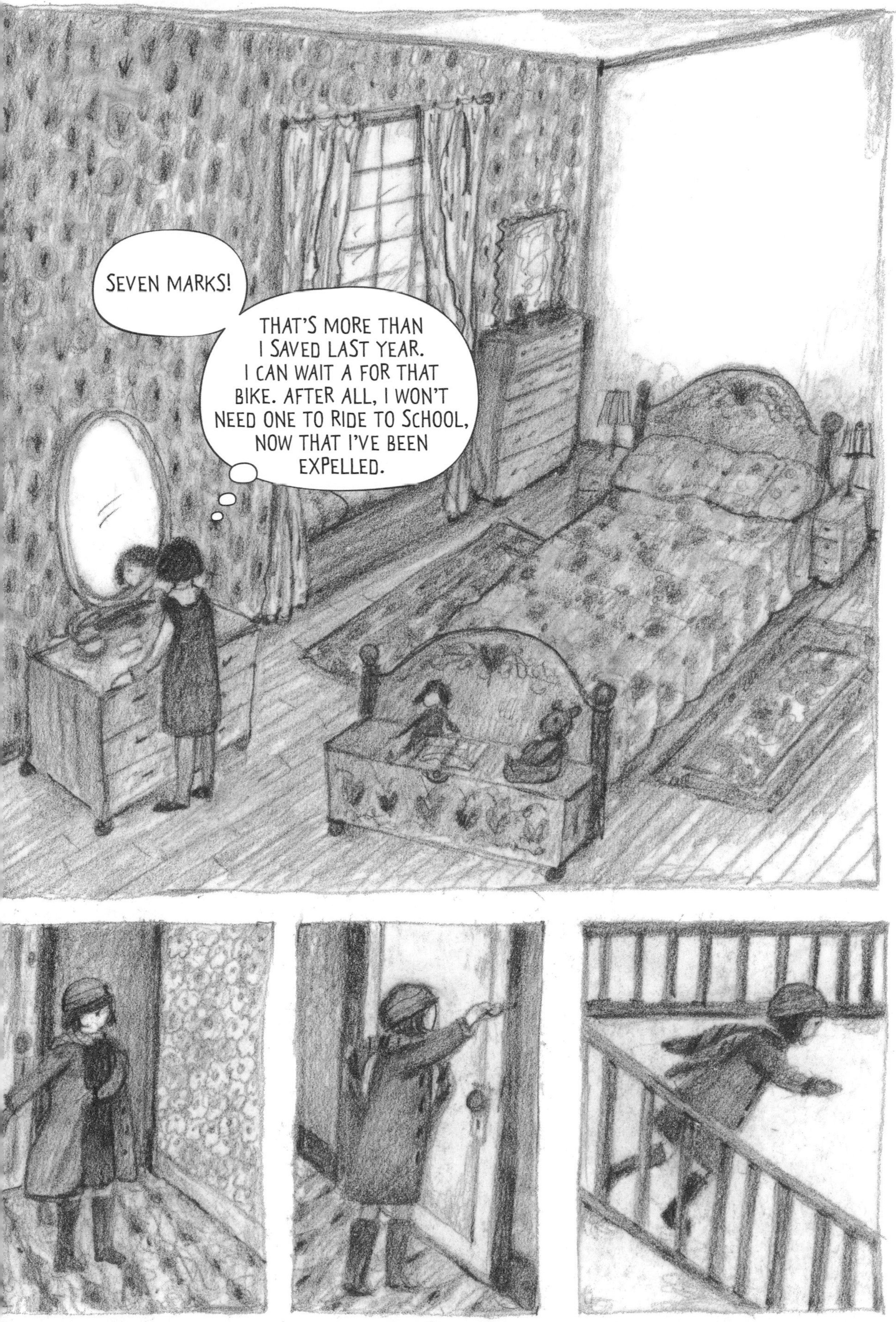
SEVEN MARKS!
THAT'S MORE THAN I SAVED LAST YEAR. I CAN WAIT A FOR THAT BIKE. AFTER ALL, I WON'T NEED ONE TO RIDE TO SCHOOL, NOW THAT I'VE BEEN EXPELLED.

CHAPTER FOUR

THE CHRISTMAS MARKET

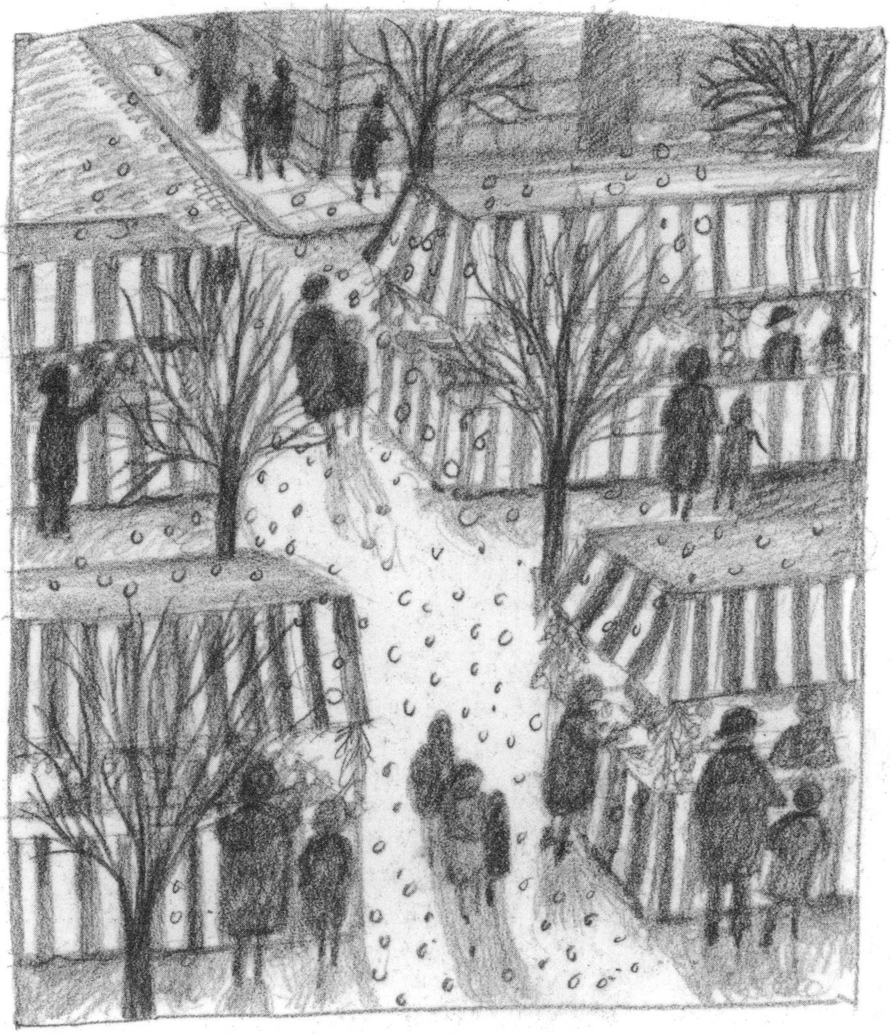

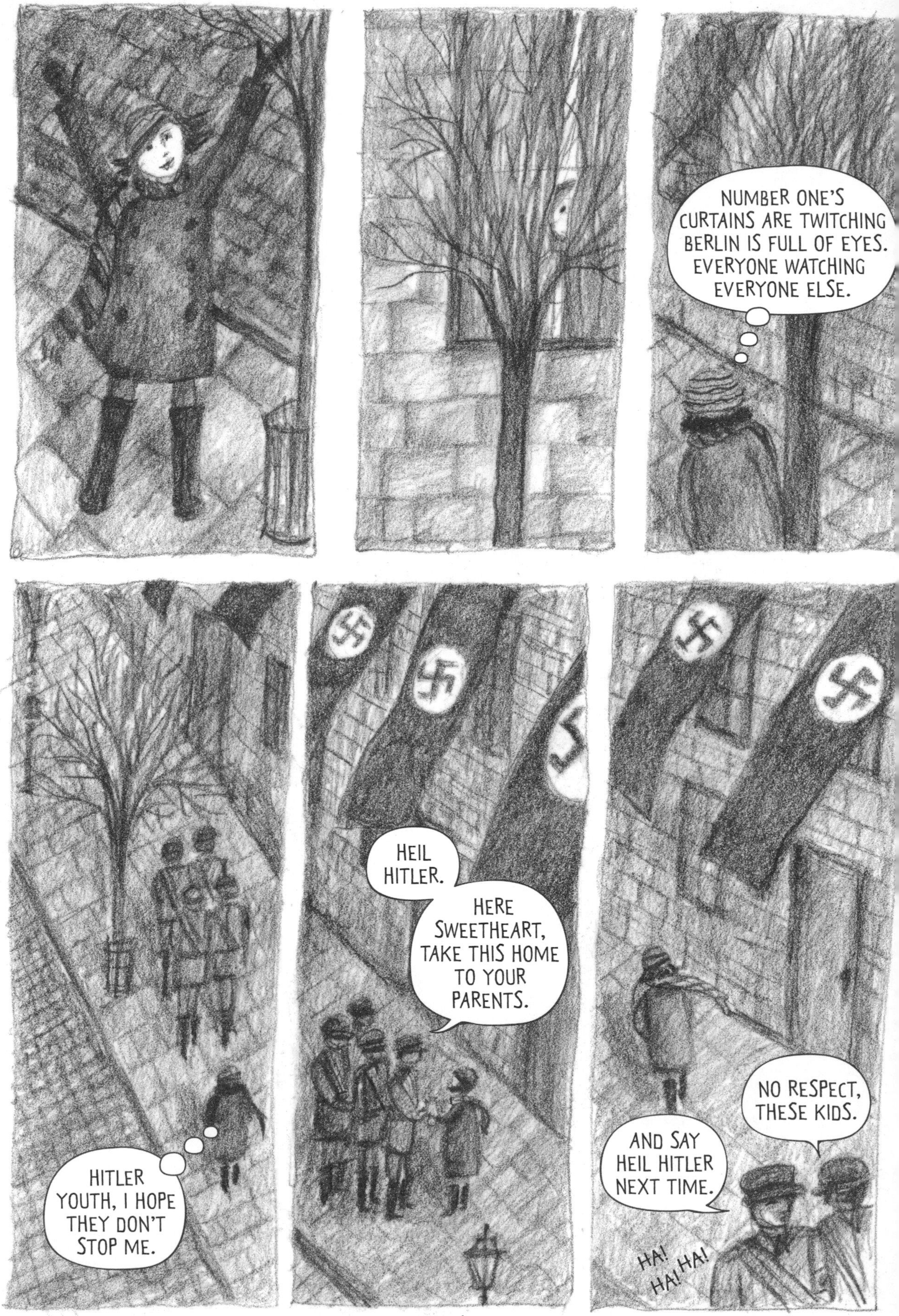
NUMBER ONE'S CURTAINS ARE TWITCHING BERLIN IS FULL OF EYES. EVERYONE WATCHING EVERYONE ELSE.
HITLER YOUTH, I HOPE THEY DON'T STOP ME.
HEIL HITLER.
HERE SWEETHEART, TAKE THIS HOME TO YOUR PARENTS.
NO RESPECT, THESE KIDS.
AND SAY HEIL HITLER NEXT TIME.
HA! HA! HA!

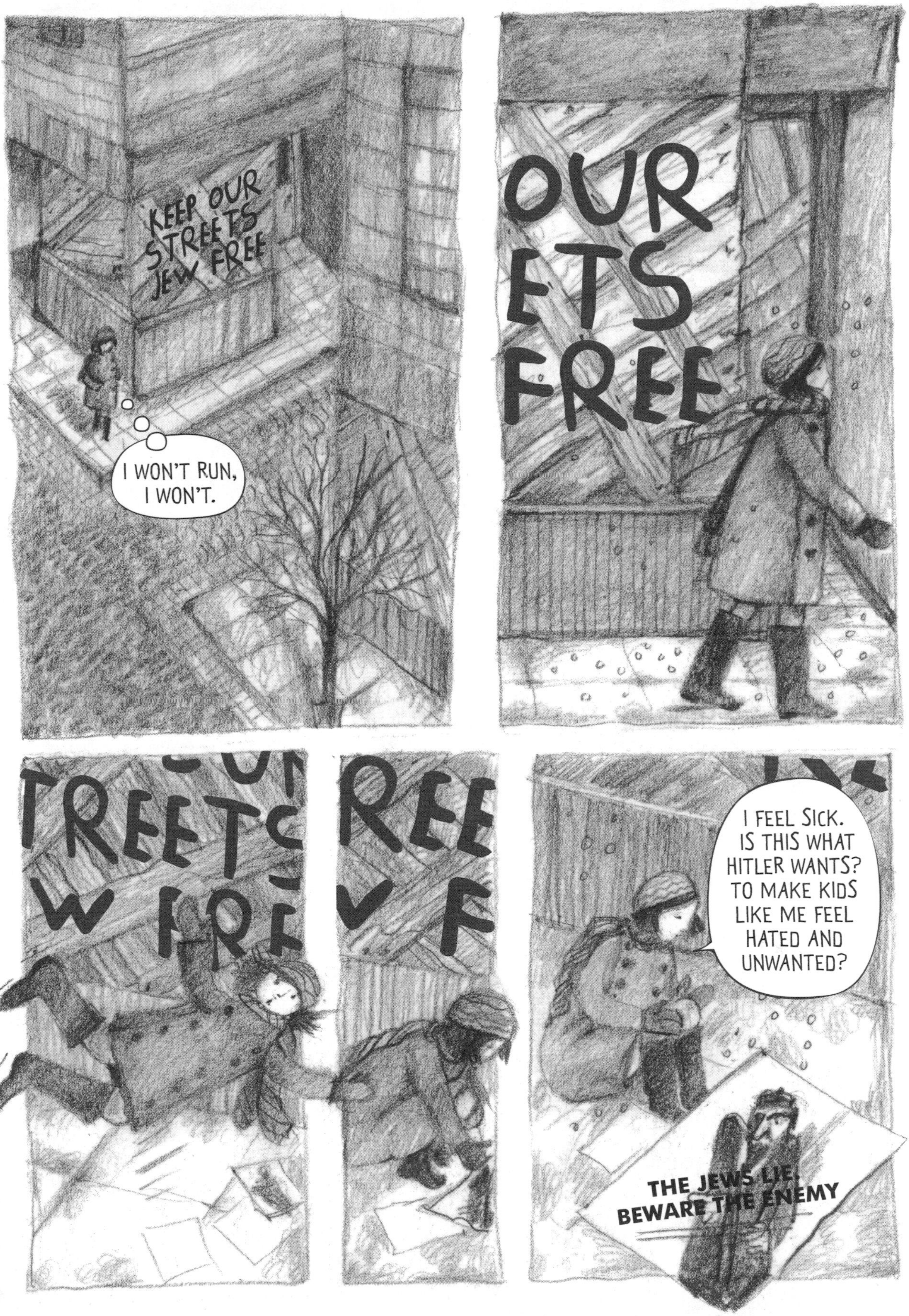
KEEP OUR STREETS JEW FREE
I WON'T RUN, I WON'T.
OUR ETS FREE
I FEEL SICK. IS THIS WHAT HITLER WANTS? TO MAKE KIDS LIKE ME FEEL HATED AND UNWANTED?
THE JEWS LIE. BEWARE THE ENEMY

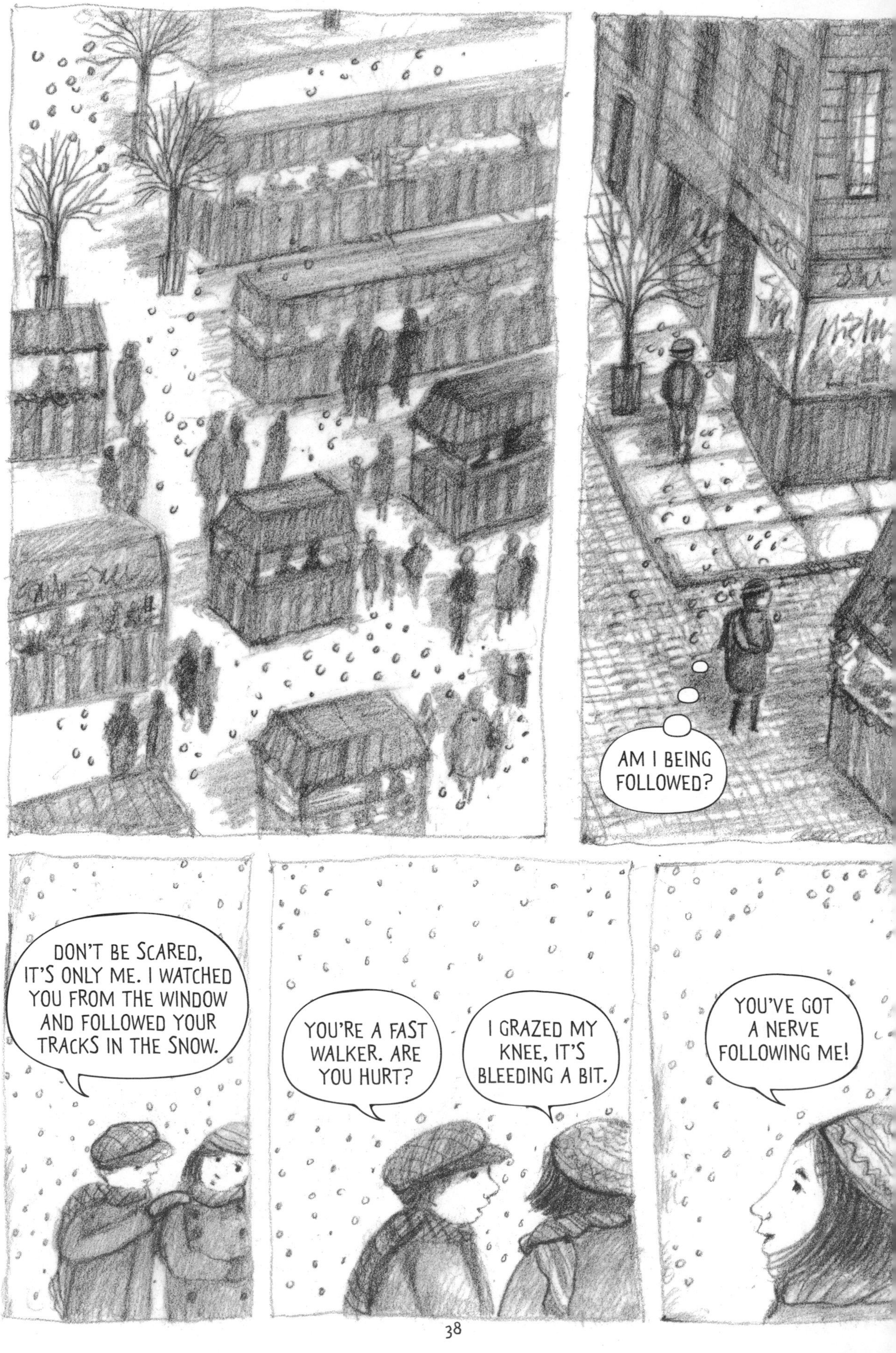
AM I BEING FOLLOWED?
DON'T BE SCARED, IT'S ONLY ME. I WATCHED YOU FROM THE WINDOW AND FOLLOWED YOUR TRACKS IN THE SNOW.
YOU'RE A FAST WALKER. ARE YOU HURT?
I GRAZED MY KNEE, IT'S BLEEDING A BIT.
YOU'VE GOT A NERVE FOLLOWING ME!

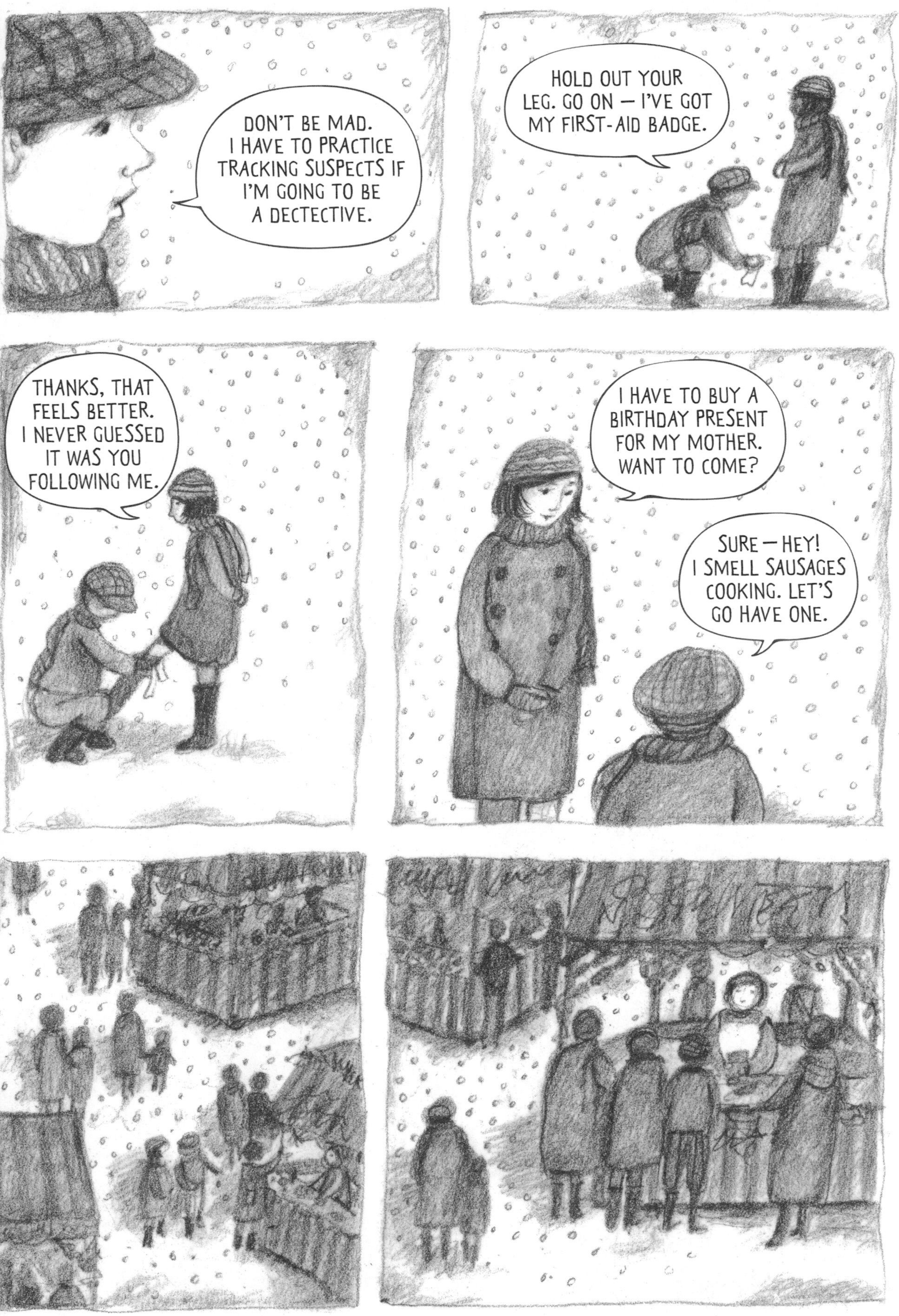
DON'T BE MAD. I HAVE TO PRACTICE TRACKING SUSPECTS IF I'M GOING TO BE A DECTECTIVE.
HOLD OUT YOUR LEG. GO ON — I'VE GOT MY FIRST-AID BADGE.
THANKS, THAT FEELS BETTER. I NEVER GUESSED IT WAS YOU FOLLOWING ME.
I HAVE TO BUY A BIRTHDAY PRESENT FOR MY MOTHER. WANT TO COME?
SURE — HEY! I SMELL SAUSAGES COOKING. LET'S GO HAVE ONE.

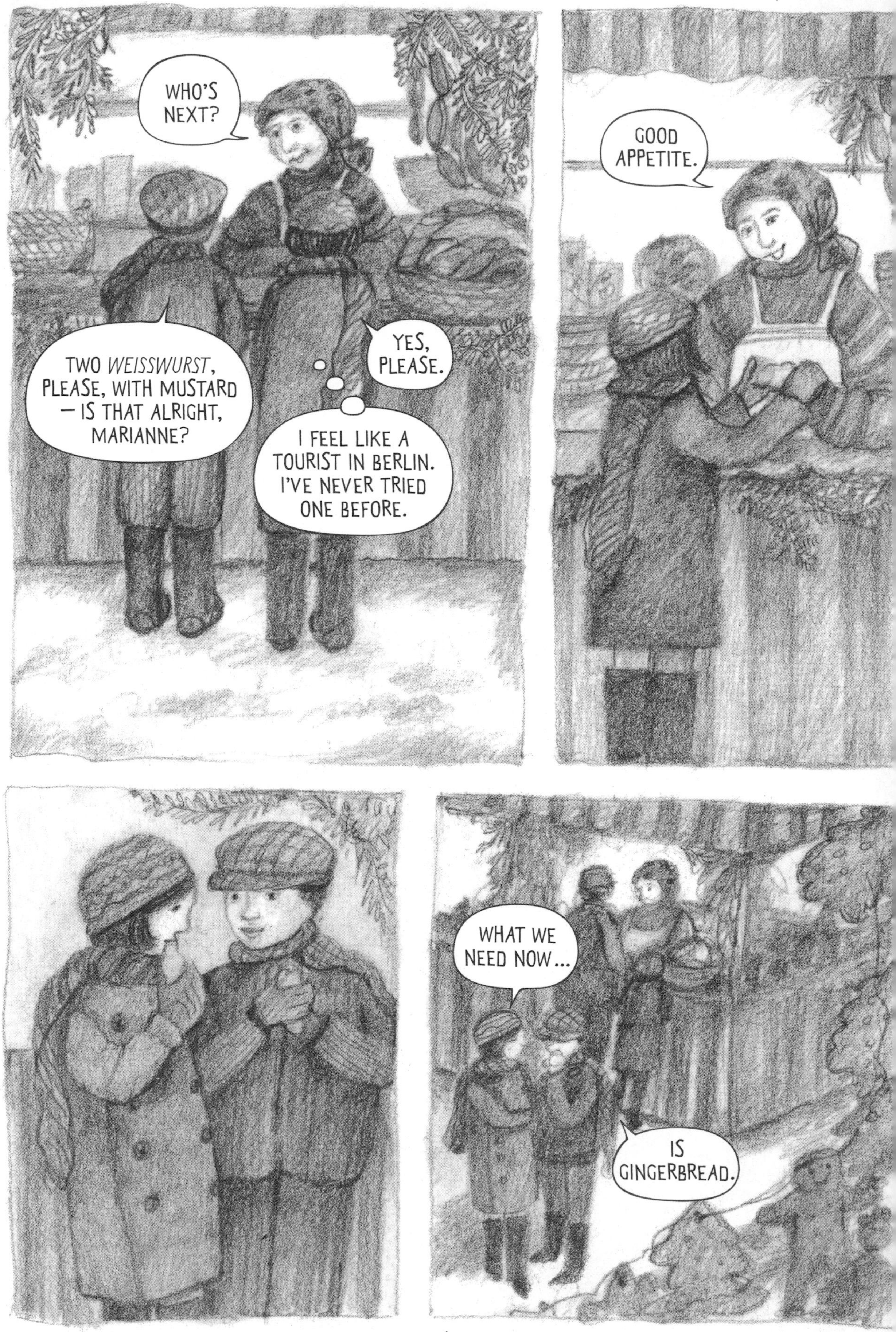
WHO'S NEXT?
TWO *WEISSWURST*, PLEASE, WITH MUSTARD — IS THAT ALRIGHT, MARIANNE?
YES, PLEASE.
I FEEL LIKE A TOURIST IN BERLIN. I'VE NEVER TRIED ONE BEFORE.
GOOD APPETITE.
WHAT WE NEED NOW...
IS GINGERBREAD.

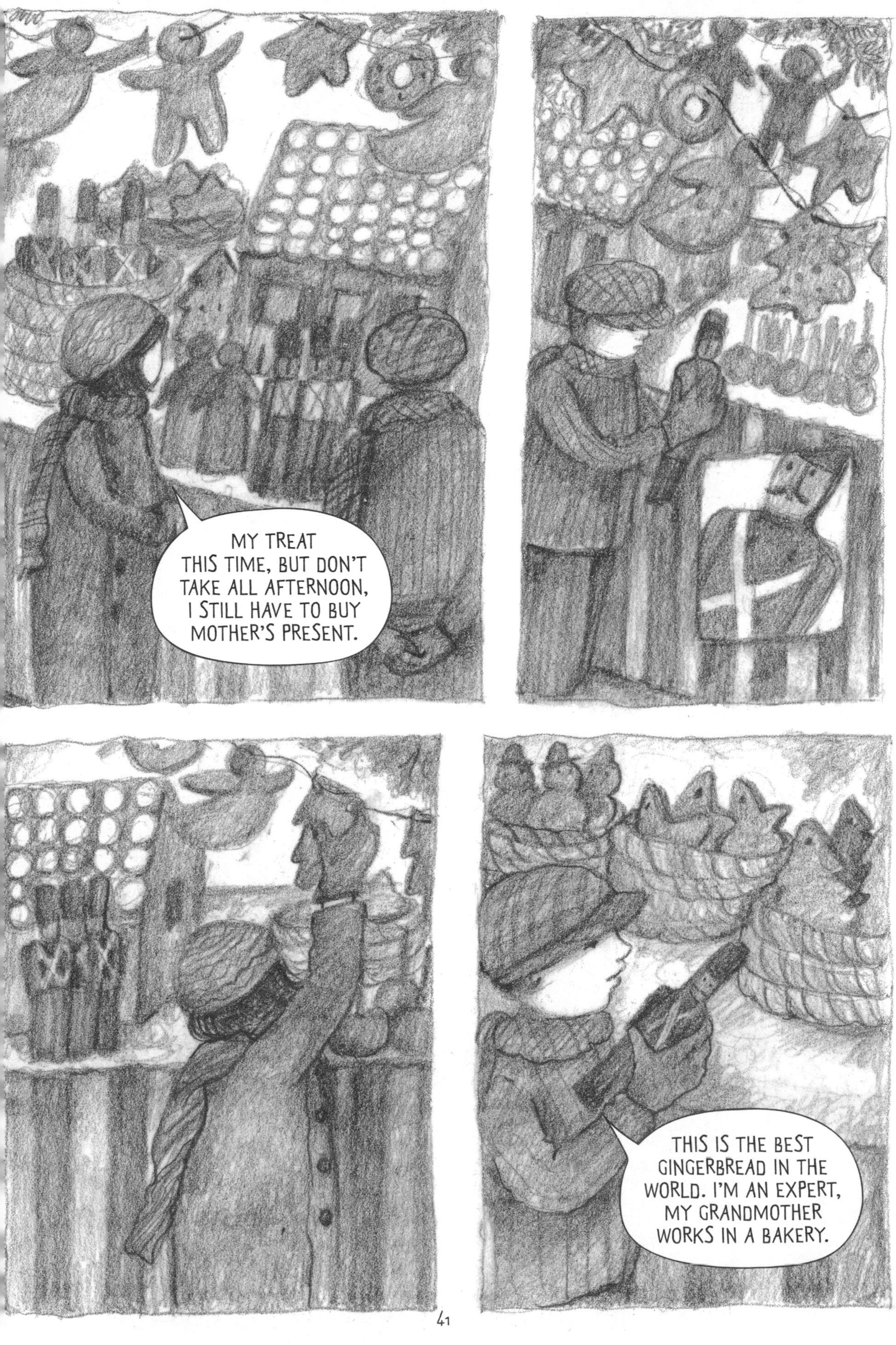
MY TREAT THIS TIME, BUT DON'T TAKE ALL AFTERNOON, I STILL HAVE TO BUY MOTHER'S PRESENT.
THIS IS THE BEST GINGERBREAD IN THE WORLD. I'M AN EXPERT, MY GRANDMOTHER WORKS IN A BAKERY.

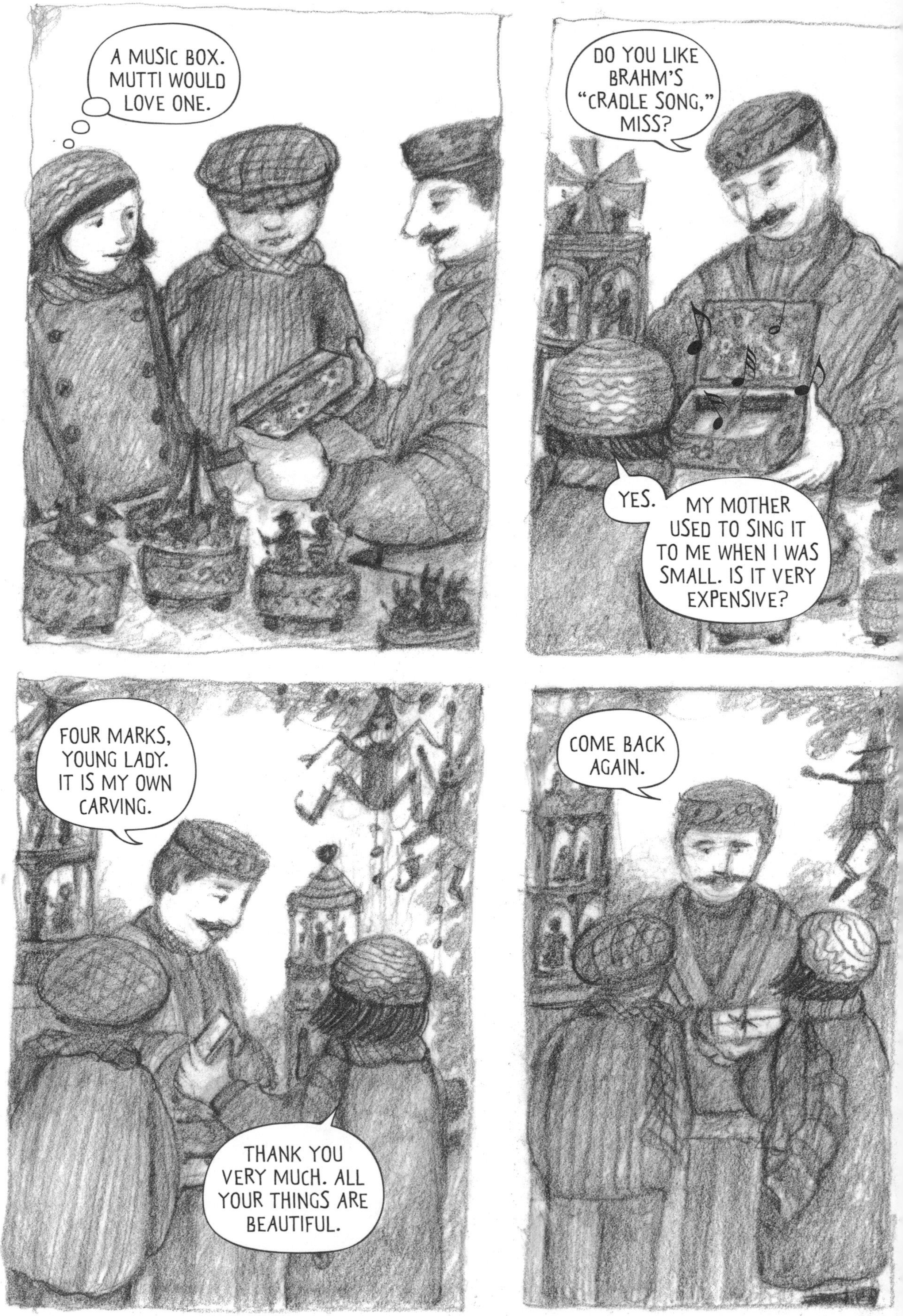
A MUSIC BOX. MUTTI WOULD LOVE ONE.
DO YOU LIKE BRAHM'S "CRADLE SONG," MISS?
YES.
MY MOTHER USED TO SING IT TO ME WHEN I WAS SMALL. IS IT VERY EXPENSIVE?
FOUR MARKS, YOUNG LADY. IT IS MY OWN CARVING.
THANK YOU VERY MUCH. ALL YOUR THINGS ARE BEAUTIFUL.
COME BACK AGAIN.

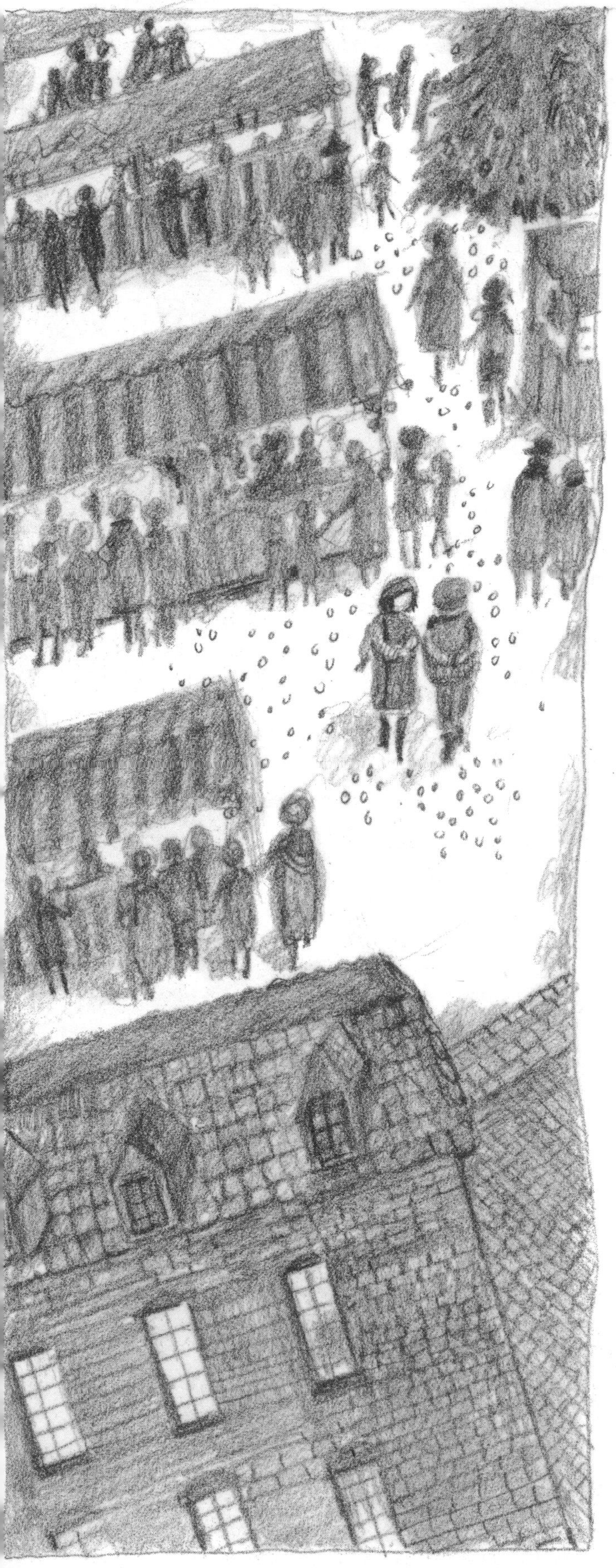

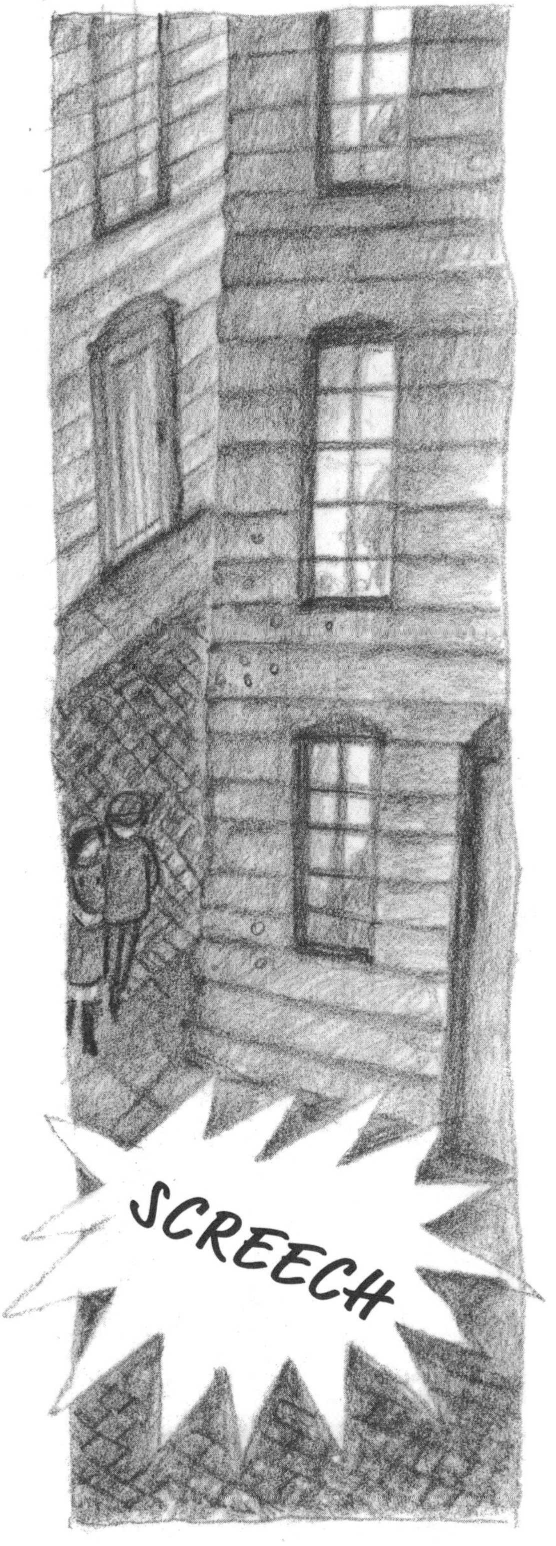
SCREECH

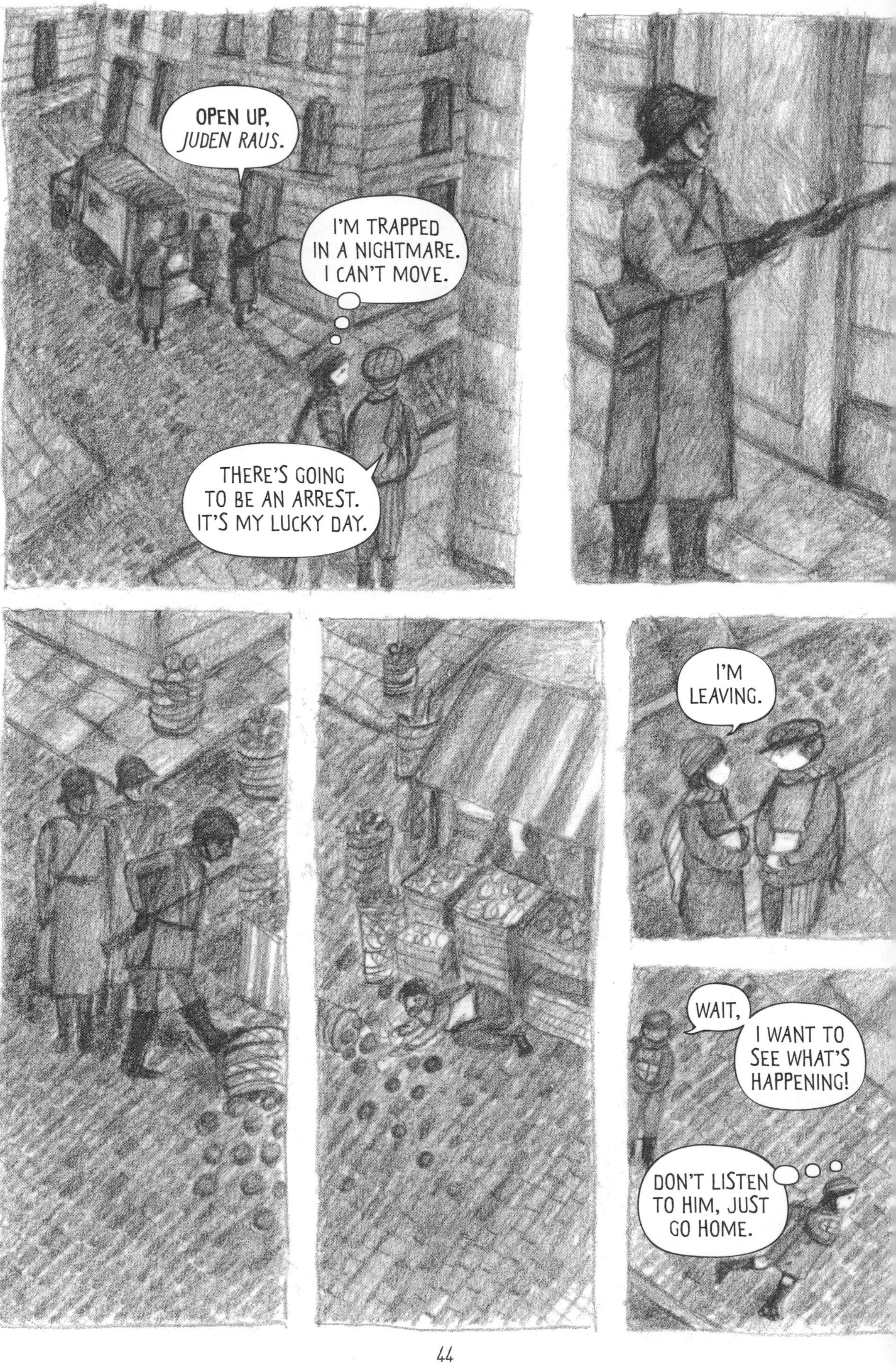
OPEN UP, *JUDEN RAUS*.
I'M TRAPPED IN A NIGHTMARE. I CAN'T MOVE.
THERE'S GOING TO BE AN ARREST. IT'S MY LUCKY DAY.
I'M LEAVING.
WAIT,
I WANT TO SEE WHAT'S HAPPENING!
DON'T LISTEN TO HIM, JUST GO HOME.

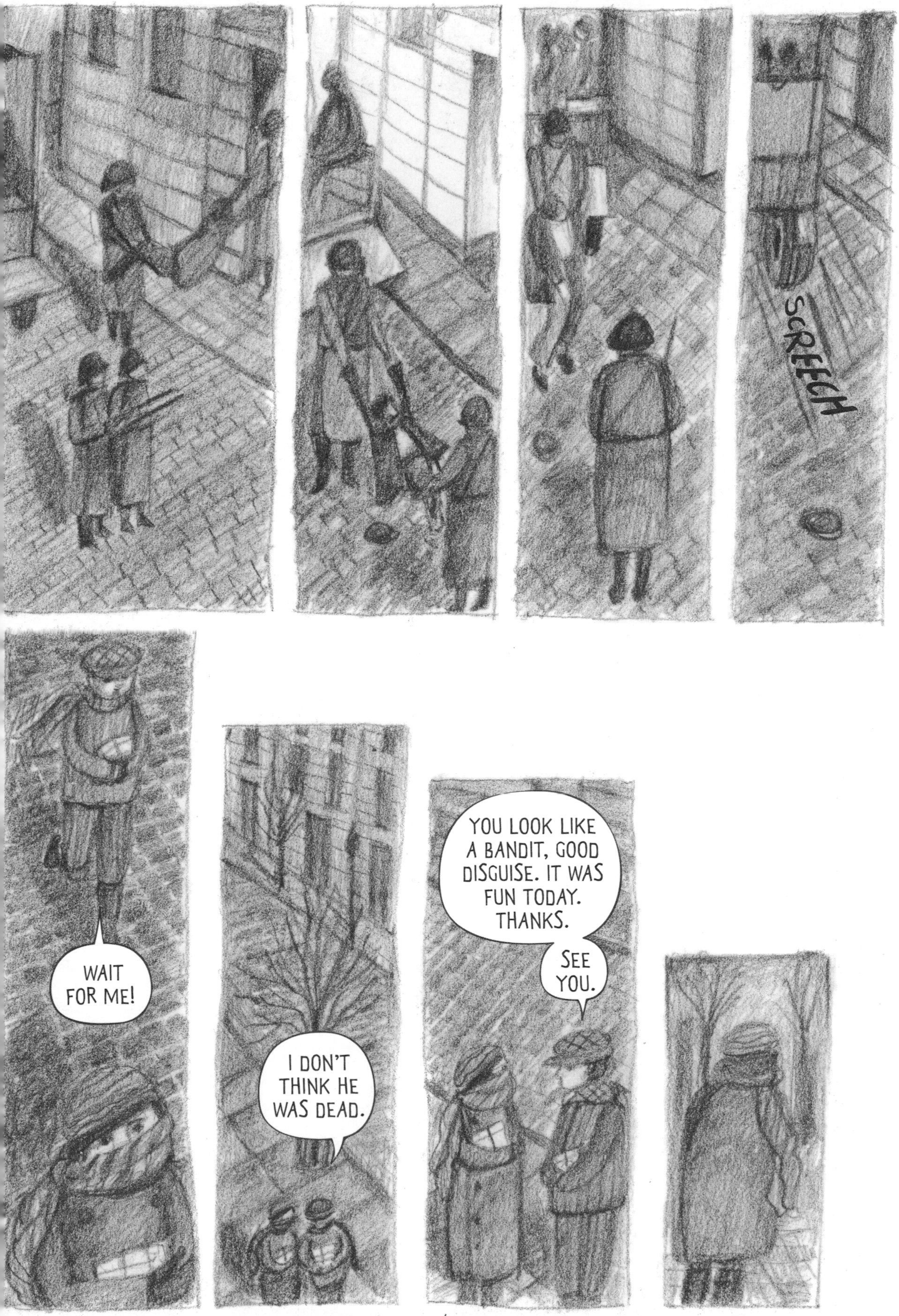
SCREECH
WAIT FOR ME!
I DON'T THINK HE WAS DEAD.
YOU LOOK LIKE A BANDIT, GOOD DISGUISE. IT WAS FUN TODAY. THANKS.
SEE YOU.

CHAPTER FIVE

A LETTER FROM RUTH

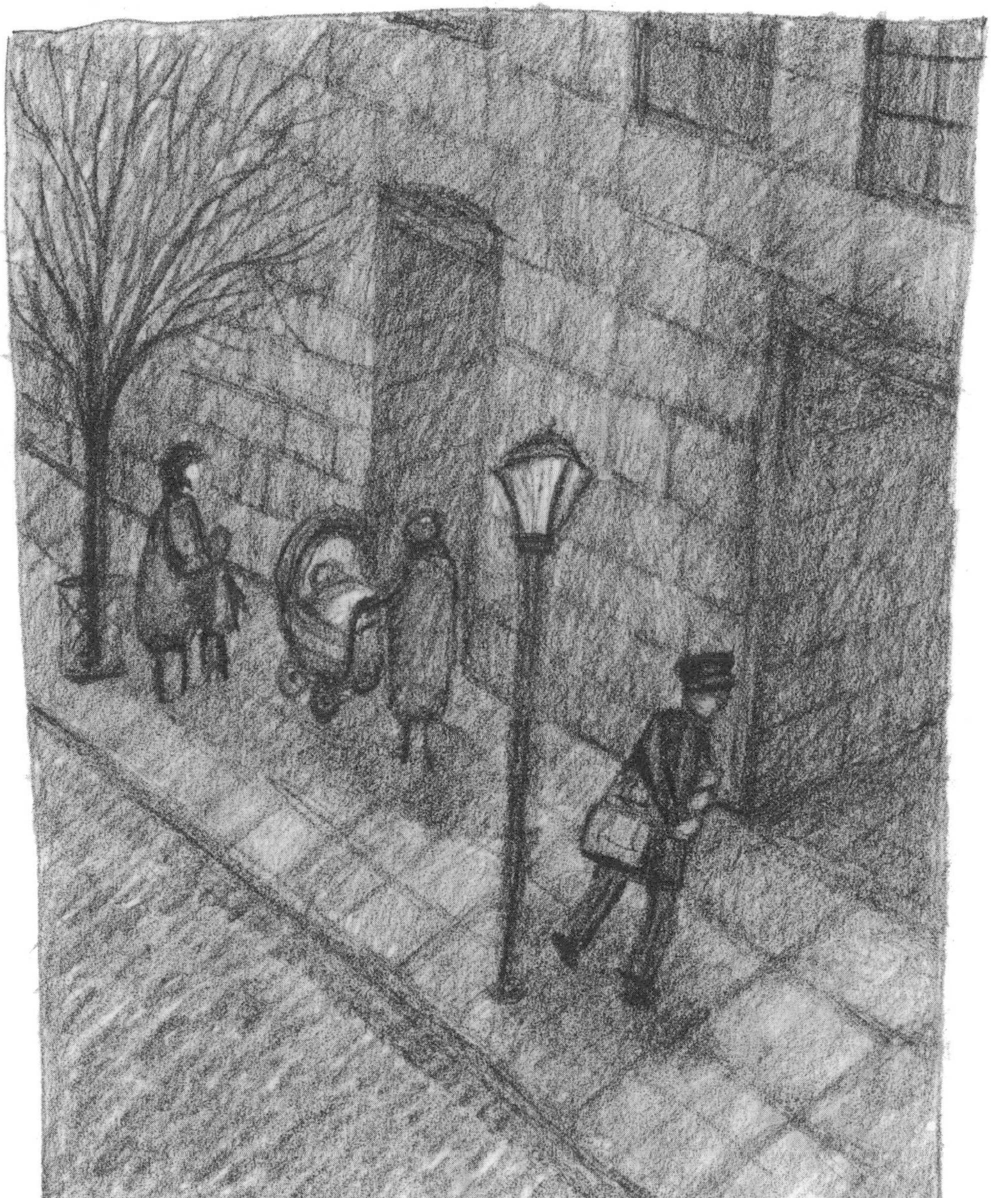

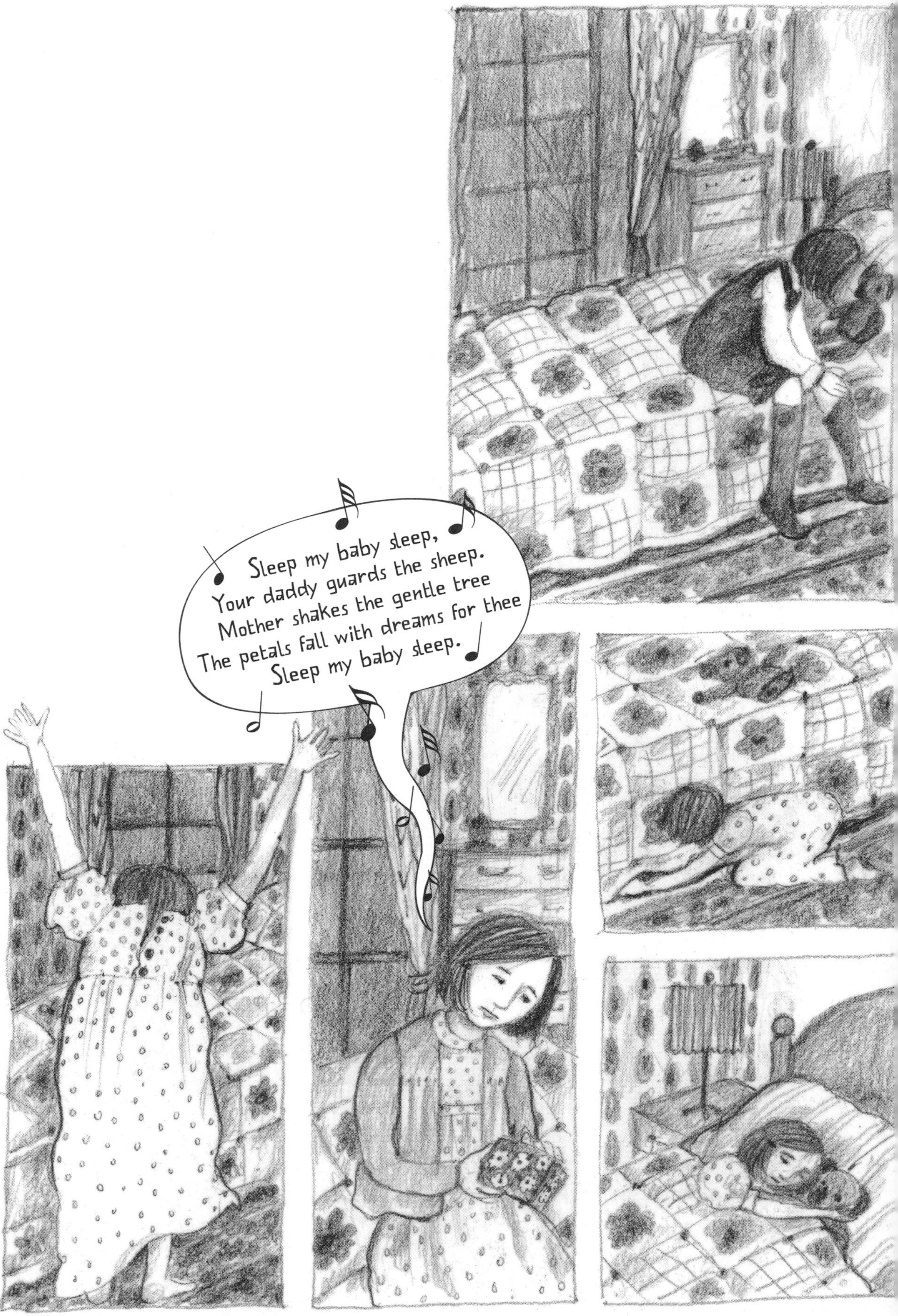
Sleep my baby sleep,
Your daddy guards the sheep.
Mother shakes the gentle tree
The petals fall with dreams for thee
Sleep my baby sleep.

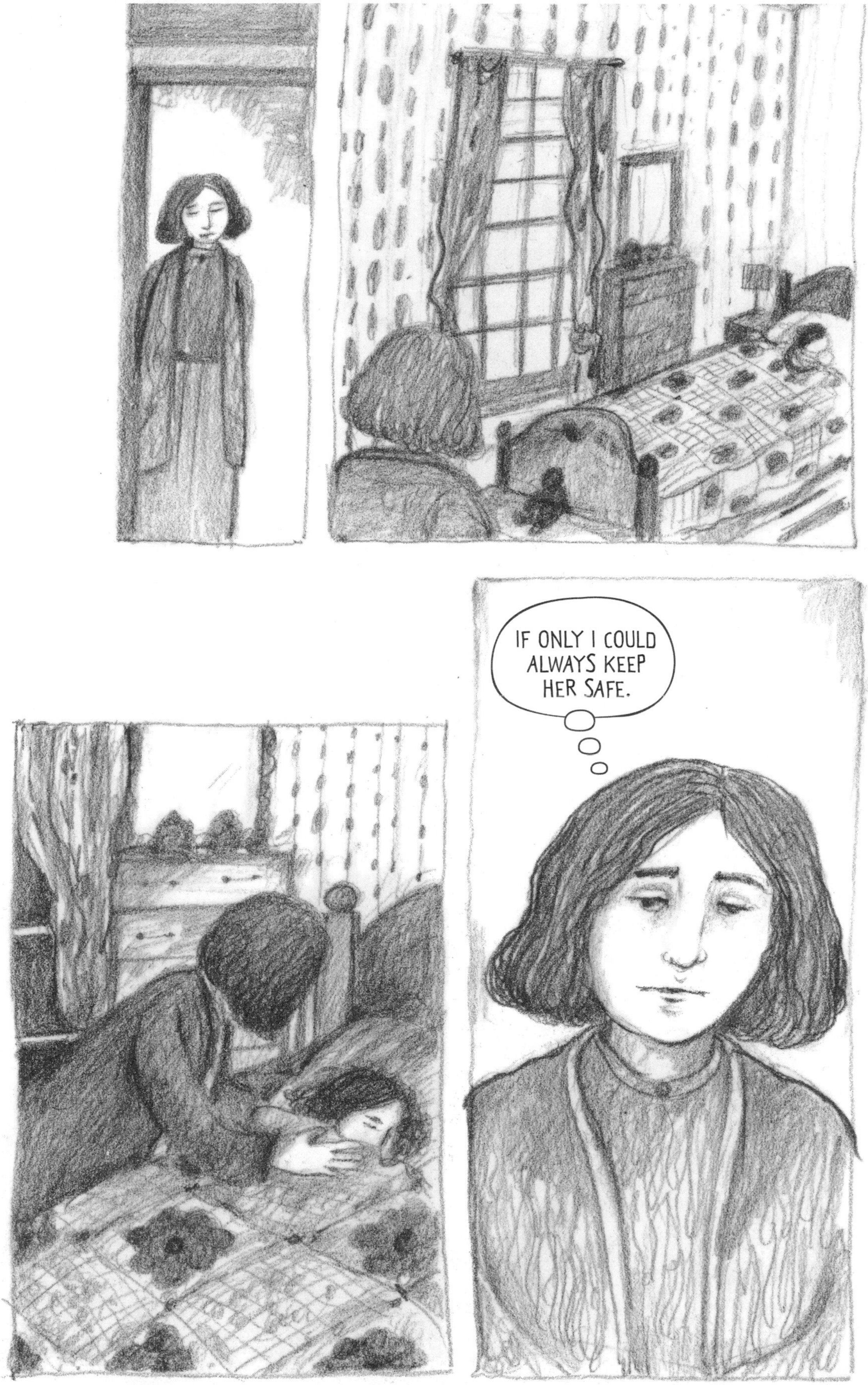
IF ONLY I COULD ALWAYS KEEP HER SAFE.

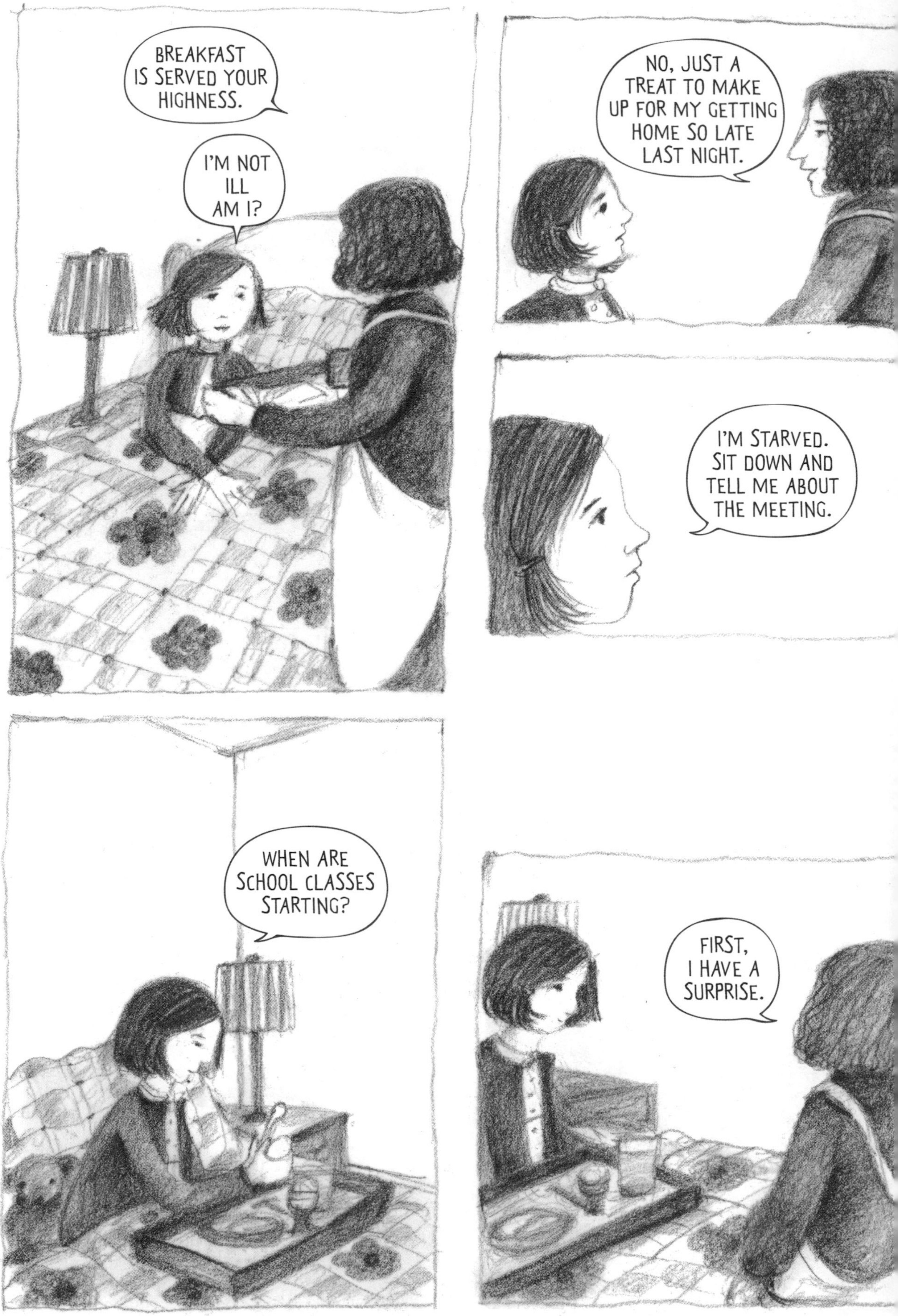
BREAKFAST IS SERVED YOUR HIGHNESS.
I'M NOT ILL AM I?
NO, JUST A TREAT TO MAKE UP FOR MY GETTING HOME SO LATE LAST NIGHT.
I'M STARVED. SIT DOWN AND TELL ME ABOUT THE MEETING.
WHEN ARE SCHOOL CLASSES STARTING?
FIRST, I HAVE A SURPRISE.

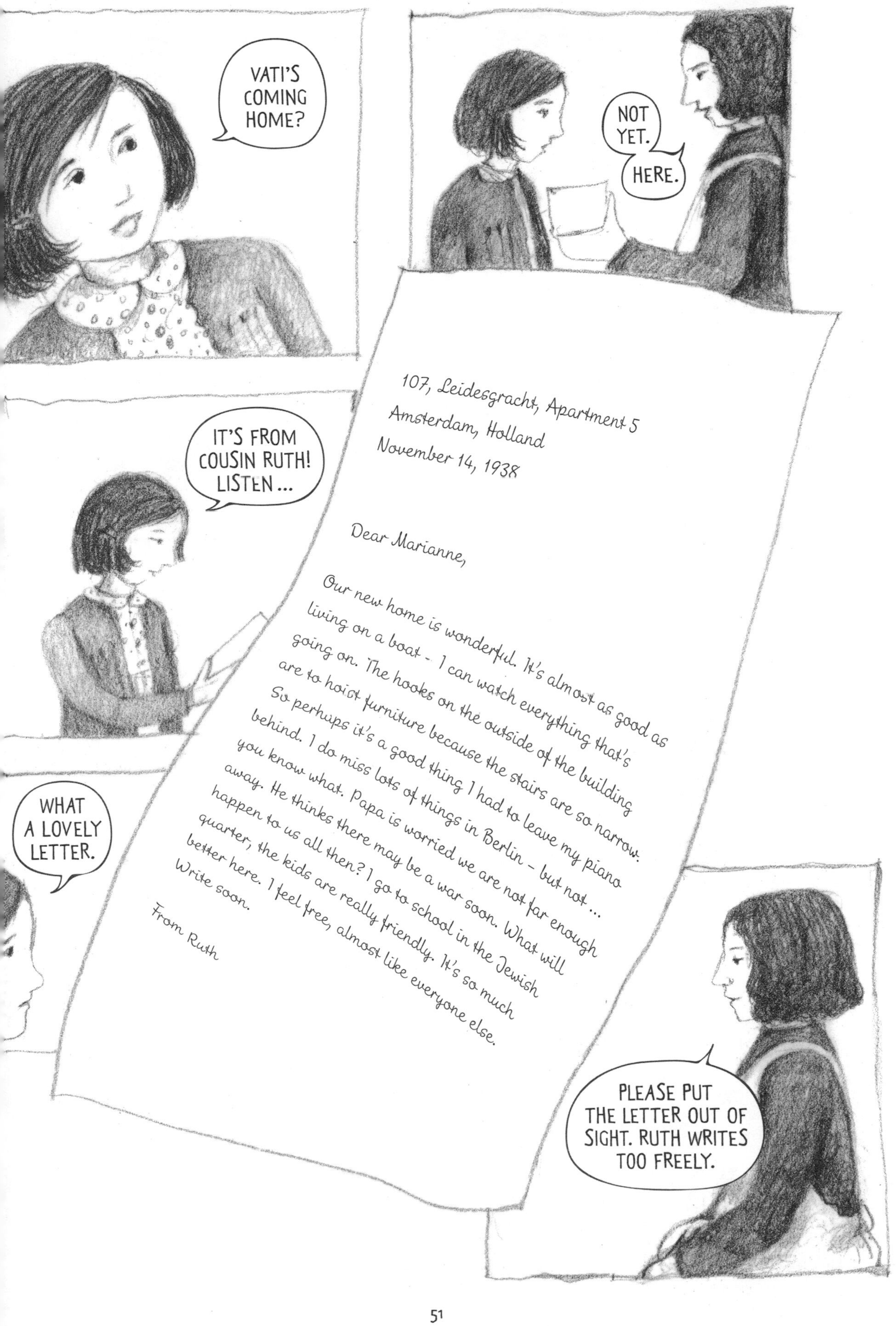
VATI'S COMING HOME?
NOT YET.
HERE.
IT'S FROM COUSIN RUTH! LISTEN...
107, Leidesgracht, Apartment 5
Amsterdam, Holland
November 14, 1938
Dear Marianne,
Our new home is wonderful. It's almost as good as
living on a boat - I can watch everything that's
going on. The hooks on the outside of the building
are to hoist furniture because the stairs are so narrow.
So perhaps it's a good thing I had to leave my piano
behind. I do miss lots of things in Berlin - but not ...
you know what. Papa is worried we are not far enough
away. He thinks there may be a war soon. What will
happen to us all then? I go to school in the Jewish
quarter, the kids are really friendly. It's so much
better here. I feel free, almost like everyone else.
Write soon.
From Ruth
WHAT A LOVELY LETTER.
PLEASE PUT THE LETTER OUT OF SIGHT. RUTH WRITES TOO FREELY.

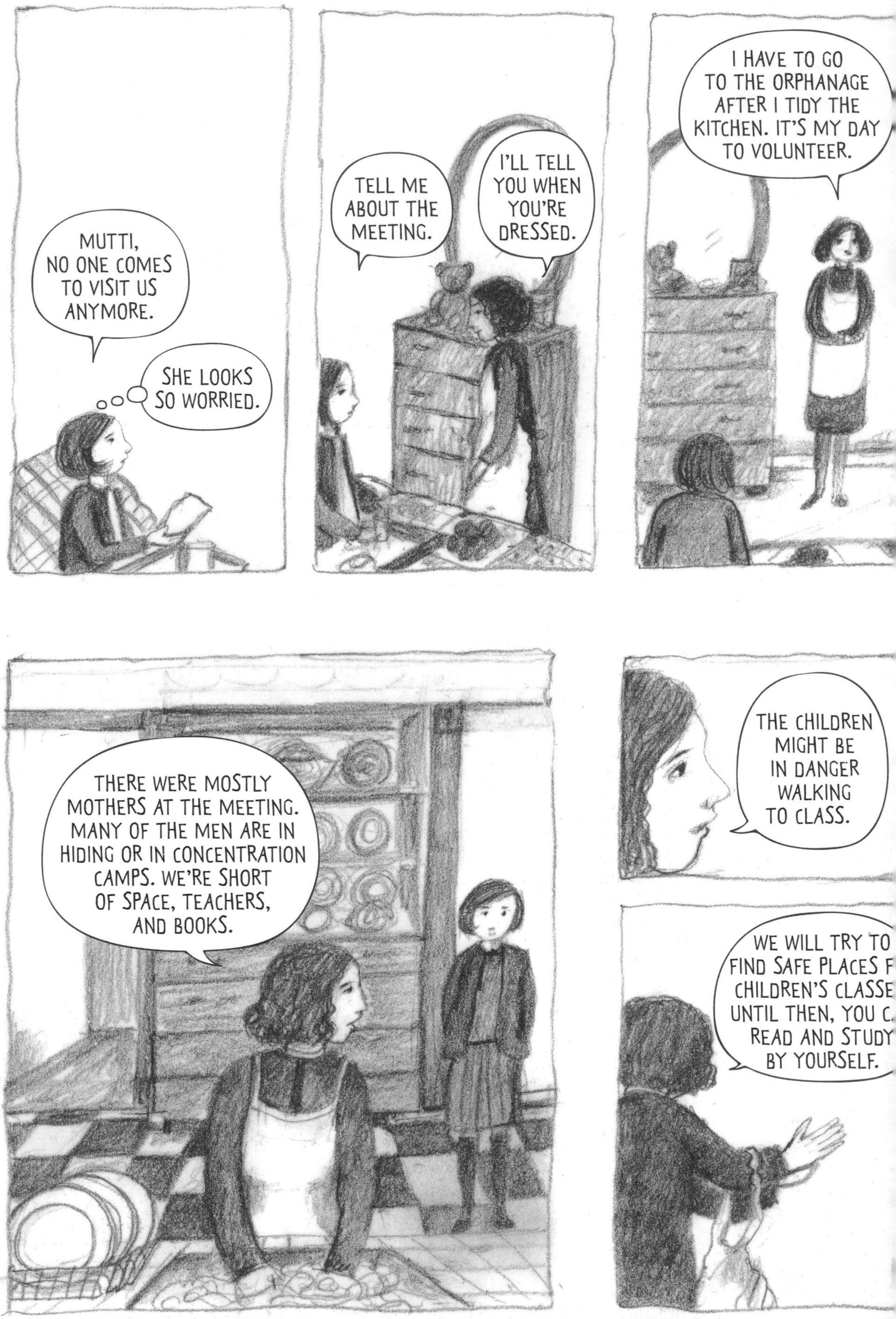
MUTTI, NO ONE COMES TO VISIT US ANYMORE.
SHE LOOKS SO WORRIED.
TELL ME ABOUT THE MEETING.
I'LL TELL YOU WHEN YOU'RE DRESSED.
I HAVE TO GO TO THE ORPHANAGE AFTER I TIDY THE KITCHEN. IT'S MY DAY TO VOLUNTEER.
THERE WERE MOSTLY MOTHERS AT THE MEETING. MANY OF THE MEN ARE IN HIDING OR IN CONCENTRATION CAMPS. WE'RE SHORT OF SPACE, TEACHERS, AND BOOKS.
THE CHILDREN MIGHT BE IN DANGER WALKING TO CLASS.
WE WILL TRY TO FIND SAFE PLACES F
CHILDREN'S CLASSE
UNTIL THEN, YOU C
READ AND STUDY
BY YOURSELF.

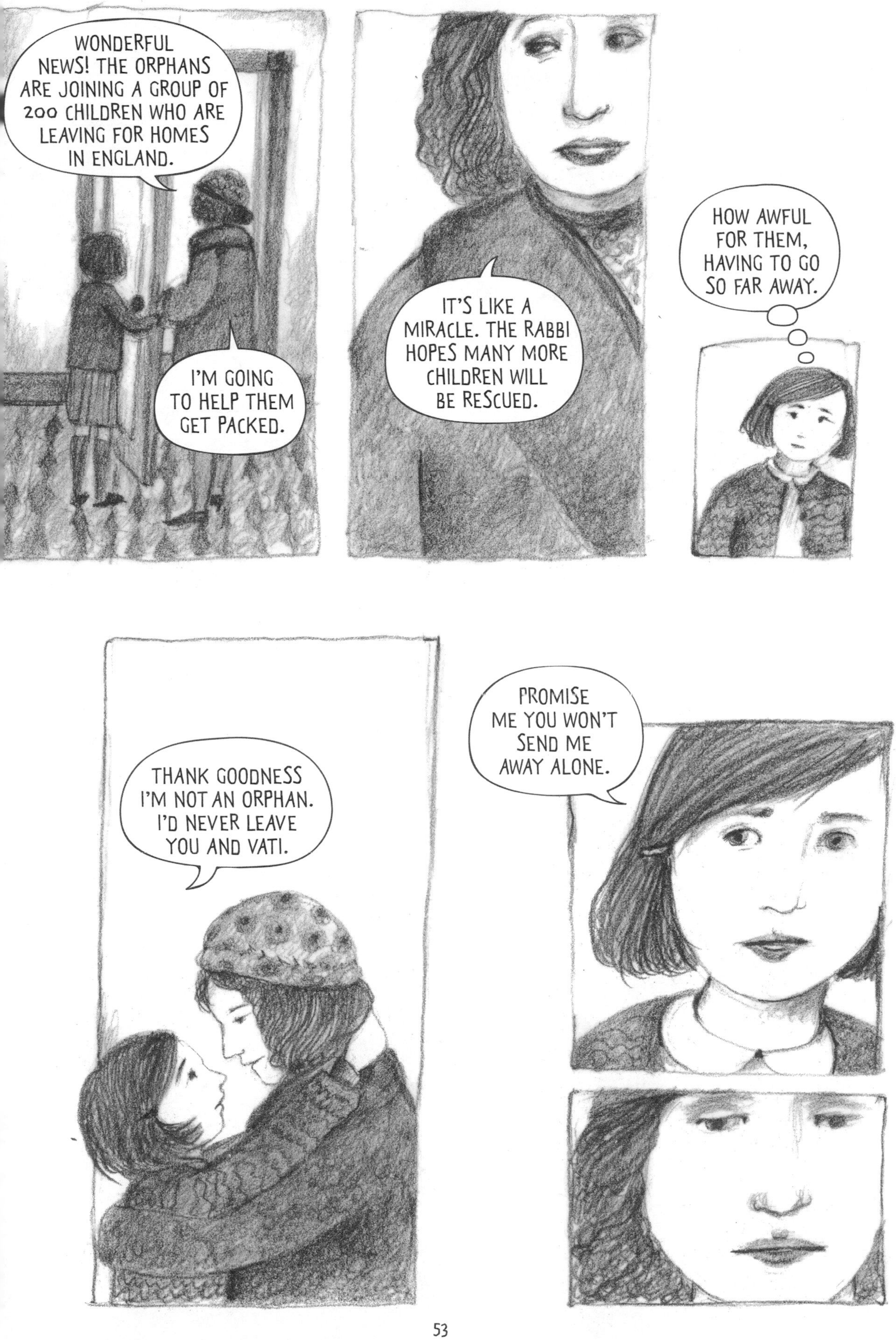
WONDERFUL NEWS! THE ORPHANS ARE JOINING A GROUP OF 200 CHILDREN WHO ARE LEAVING FOR HOMES IN ENGLAND.
I'M GOING TO HELP THEM GET PACKED.
IT'S LIKE A MIRACLE. THE RABBI HOPES MANY MORE CHILDREN WILL BE RESCUED.
HOW AWFUL FOR THEM, HAVING TO GO SO FAR AWAY.
THANK GOODNESS I'M NOT AN ORPHAN. I'D NEVER LEAVE YOU AND VATI.
PROMISE ME YOU WON'T SEND ME AWAY ALONE.

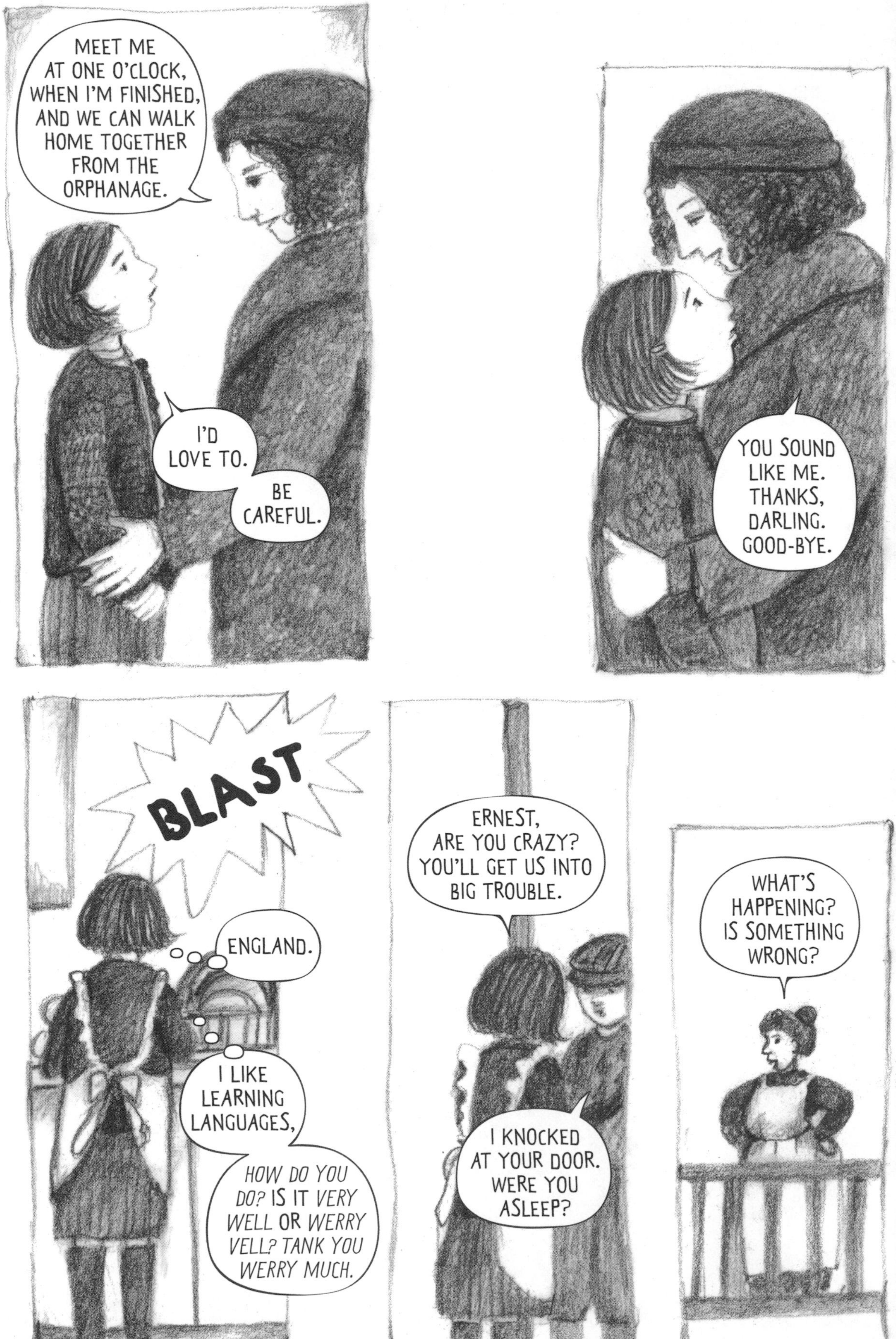
MEET ME AT ONE O'CLOCK, WHEN I'M FINISHED, AND WE CAN WALK HOME TOGETHER FROM THE ORPHANAGE.
I'D LOVE TO.
BE CAREFUL.
YOU SOUND LIKE ME. THANKS, DARLING. GOOD-BYE.
BLAST
ENGLAND.
I LIKE LEARNING LANGUAGES,
HOW DO YOU DO? IS IT VERY WELL OR WERRY VELL? TANK YOU WERRY MUCH.
ERNEST, ARE YOU CRAZY? YOU'LL GET US INTO BIG TROUBLE.
I KNOCKED AT YOUR DOOR. WERE YOU ASLEEP?
WHAT'S HAPPENING? IS SOMETHING WRONG?

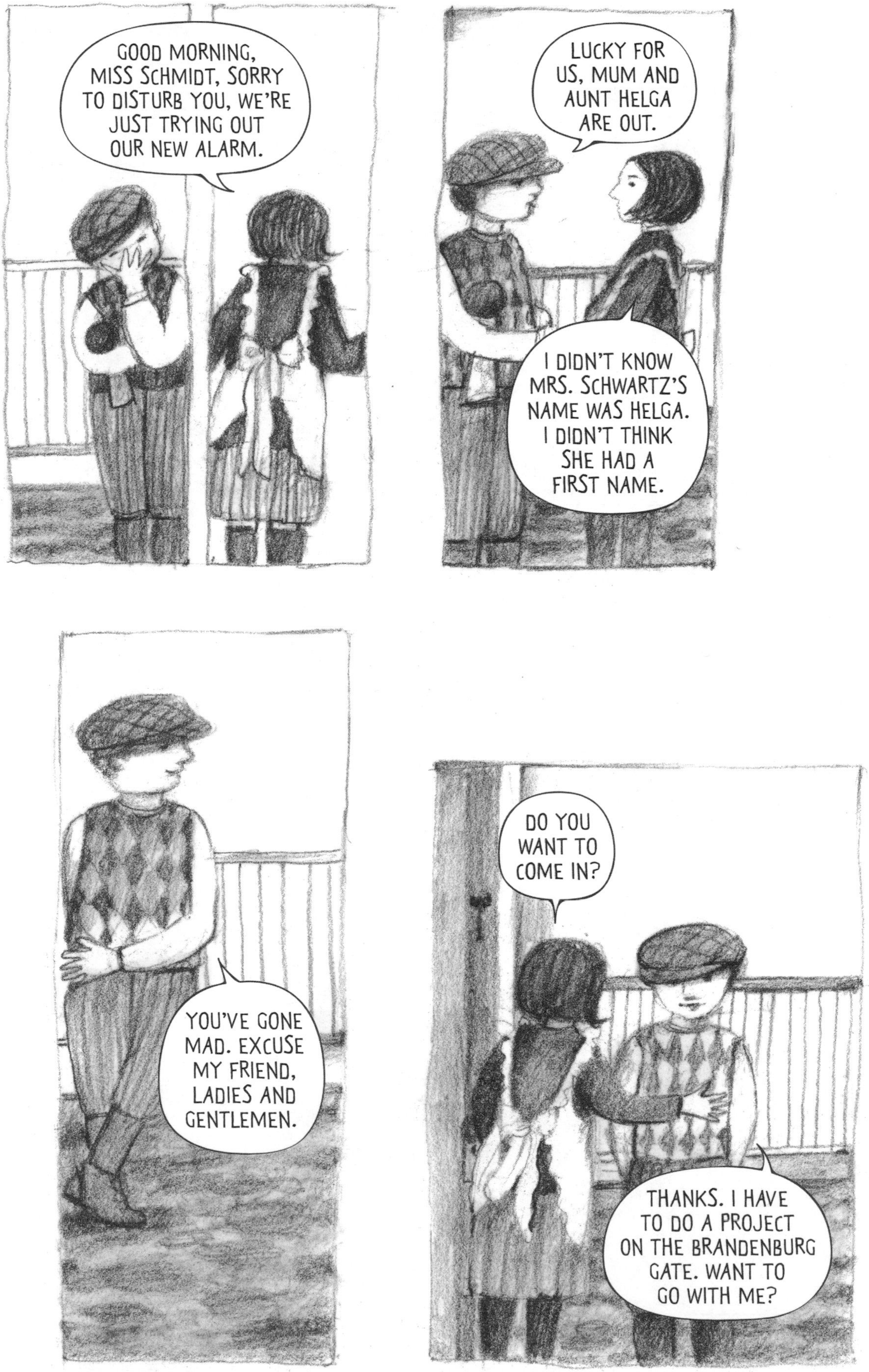
GOOD MORNING, MISS SCHMIDT, SORRY TO DISTURB YOU, WE'RE JUST TRYING OUT OUR NEW ALARM.
LUCKY FOR US, MUM AND AUNT HELGA ARE OUT.
I DIDN'T KNOW MRS. SCHWARTZ'S NAME WAS HELGA. I DIDN'T THINK SHE HAD A FIRST NAME.
YOU'VE GONE MAD. EXCUSE MY FRIEND, LADIES AND GENTLEMEN.
DO YOU WANT TO COME IN?
THANKS. I HAVE TO DO A PROJECT ON THE BRANDENBURG GATE. WANT TO GO WITH ME?

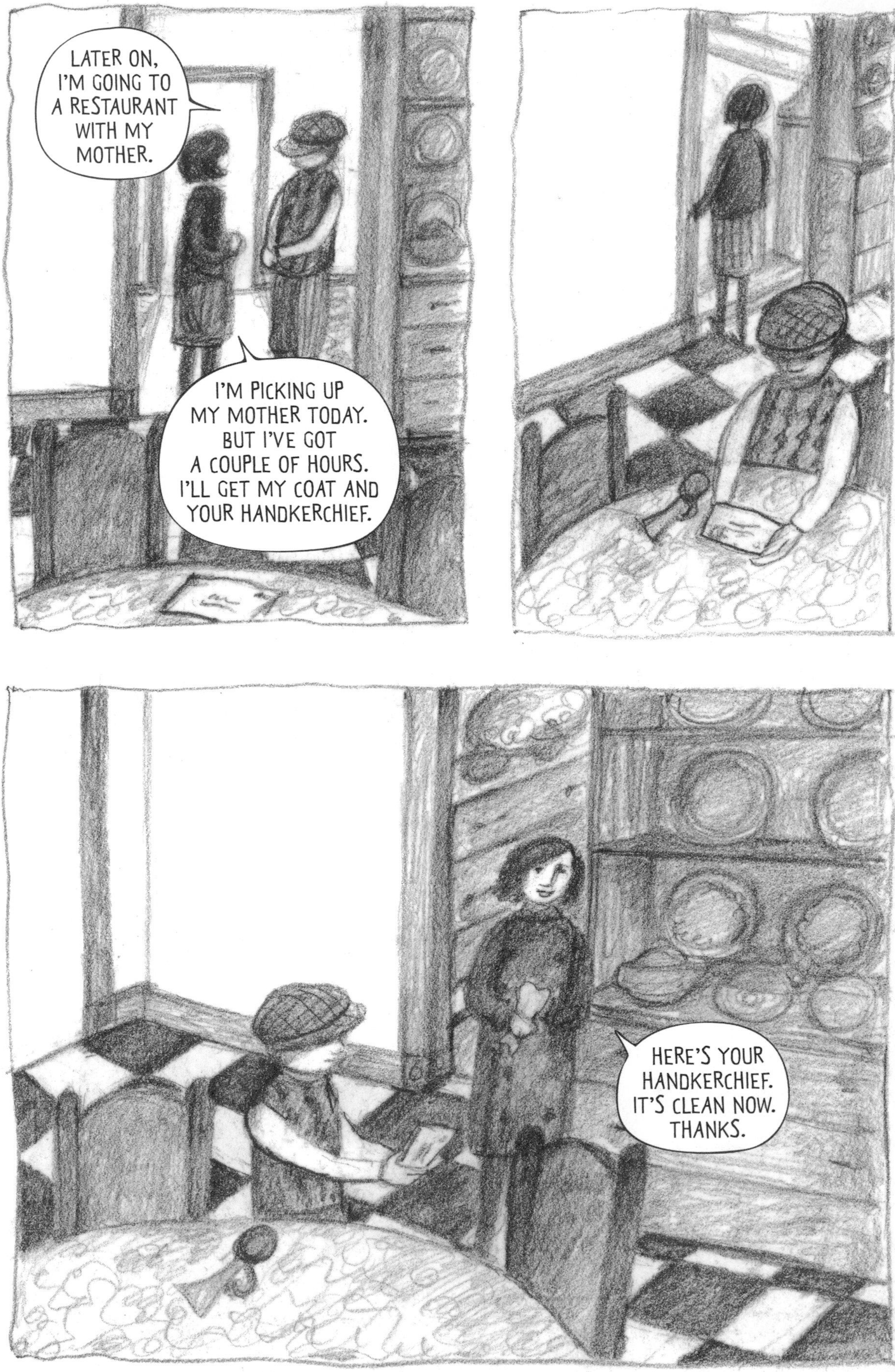
LATER ON, I'M GOING TO A RESTAURANT WITH MY MOTHER.
I'M PICKING UP MY MOTHER TODAY. BUT I'VE GOT A COUPLE OF HOURS. I'LL GET MY COAT AND YOUR HANDKERCHIEF.
HERE'S YOUR HANDKERCHIEF. IT'S CLEAN NOW. THANKS.

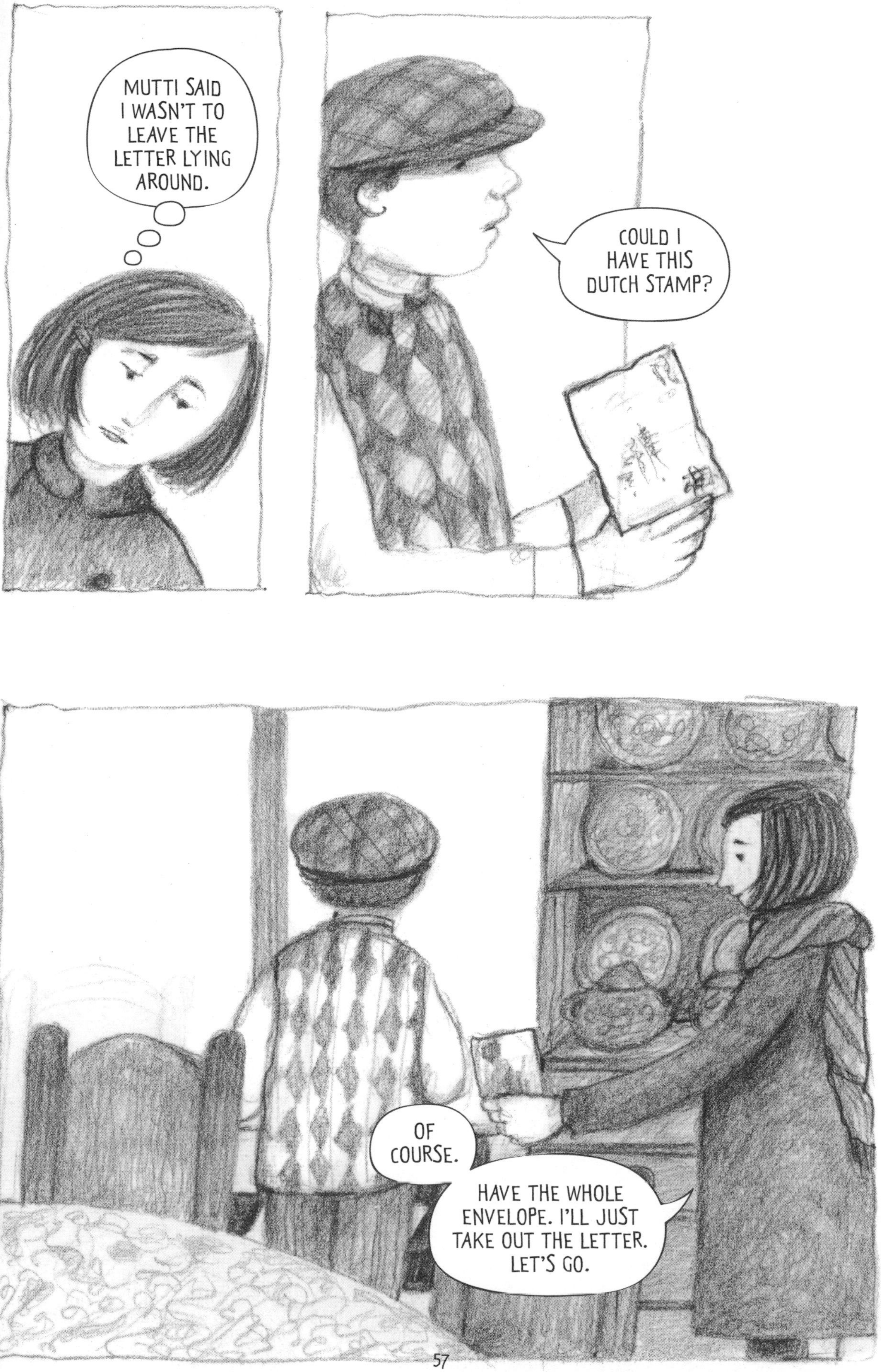
MUTTI SAID I WASN'T TO LEAVE THE LETTER LYING AROUND.
COULD I HAVE THIS DUTCH STAMP?
OF COURSE.
HAVE THE WHOLE ENVELOPE. I'LL JUST TAKE OUT THE LETTER. LET'S GO.

CHAPTER SIX

PARADE

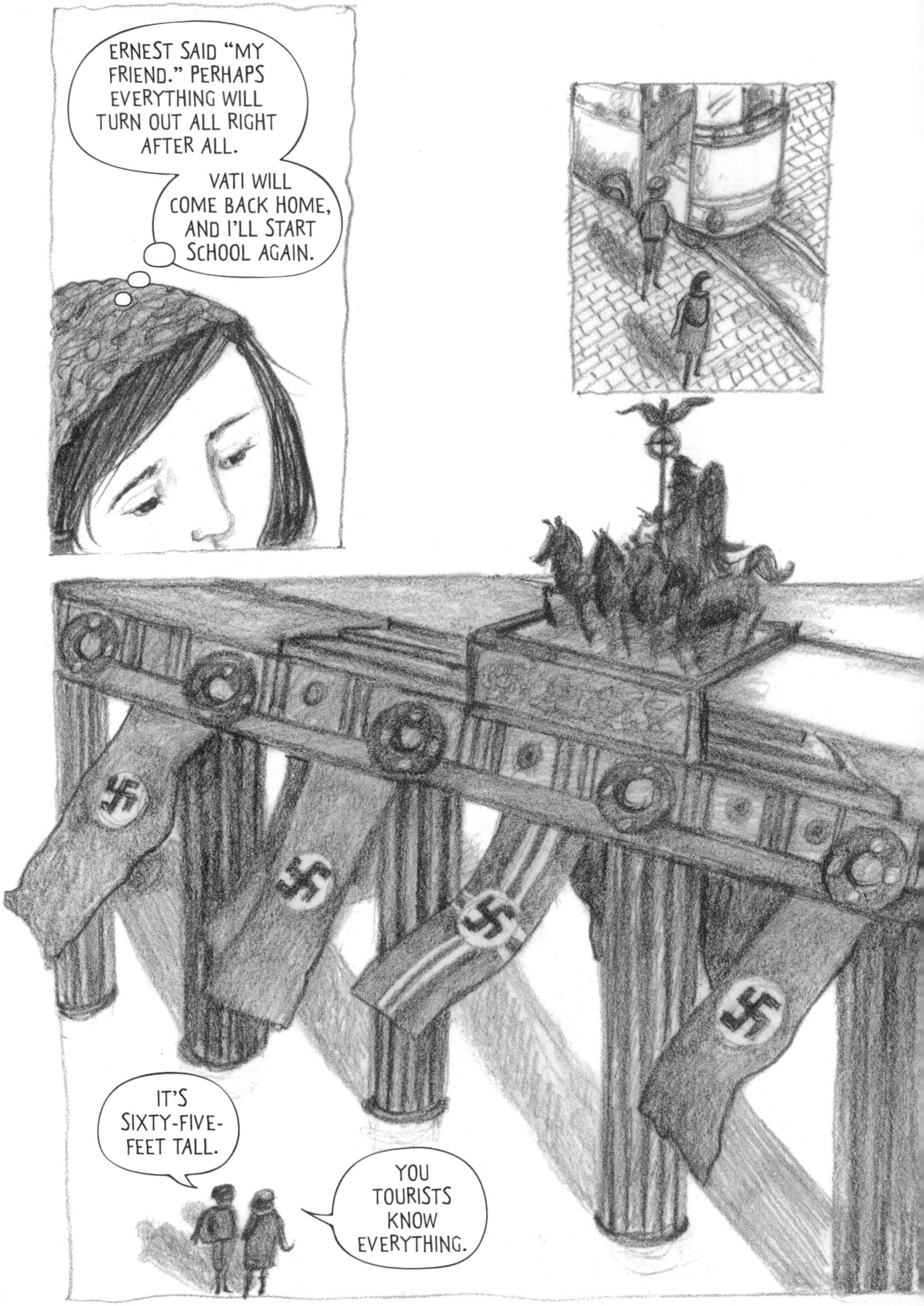
ERNEST SAID "MY FRIEND." PERHAPS EVERYTHING WILL TURN OUT ALL RIGHT AFTER ALL.
VATI WILL COME BACK HOME, AND I'LL START SCHOOL AGAIN.
IT'S SIXTY-FIVE-FEET TALL.
YOU TOURISTS KNOW EVERYTHING.

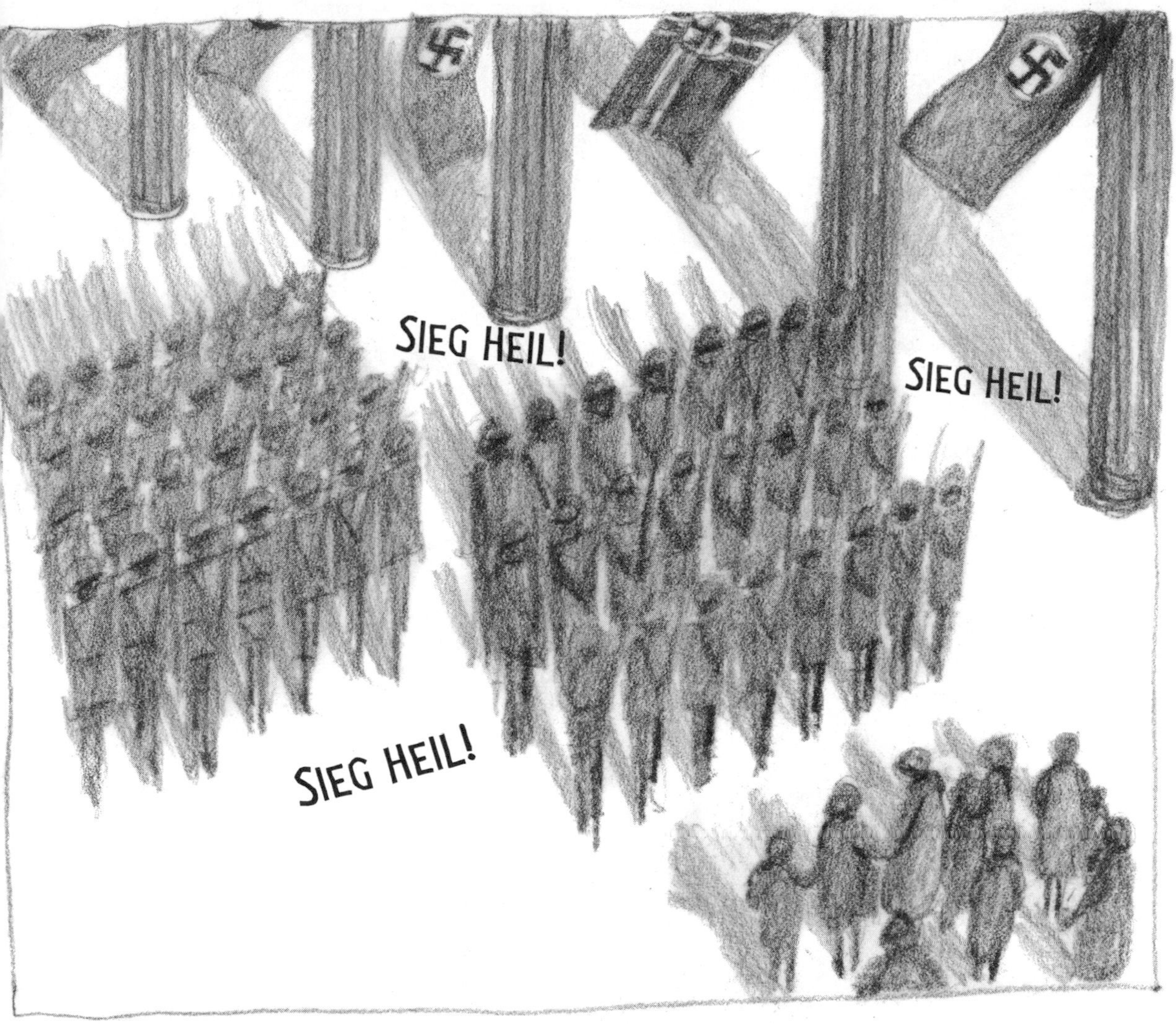
SIEG HEIL!
SIEG HEIL!
SIEG HEIL!

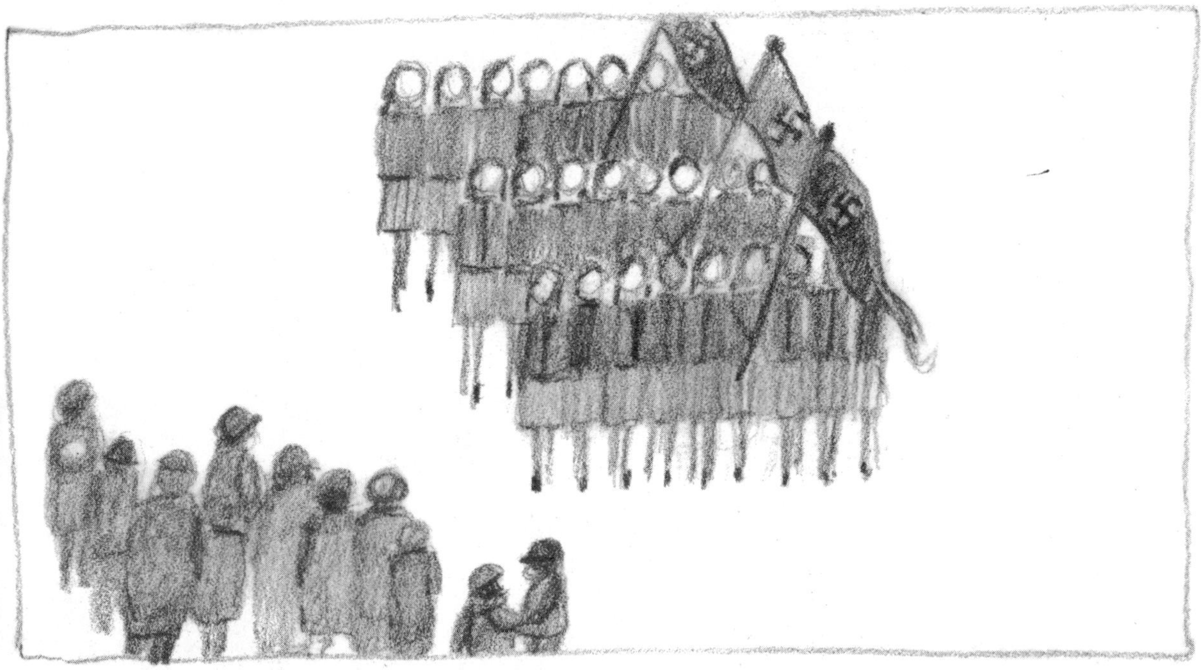

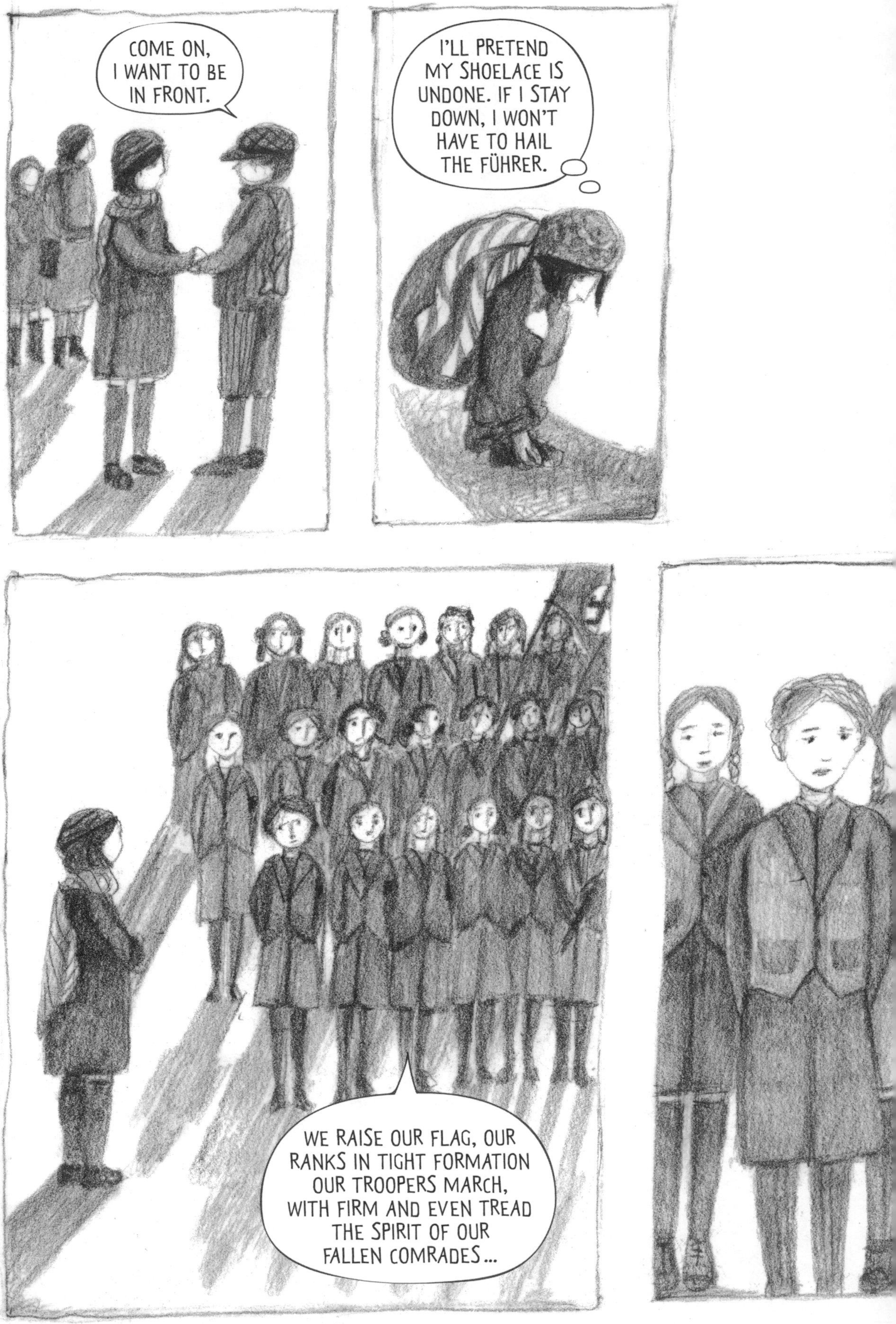
COME ON, I WANT TO BE IN FRONT.
I'LL PRETEND MY SHOELACE IS UNDONE. IF I STAY DOWN, I WON'T HAVE TO HAIL THE FÜHRER.
WE RAISE OUR FLAG, OUR RANKS IN TIGHT FORMATION OUR TROOPERS MARCH, WITH FIRM AND EVEN TREAD THE SPIRIT OF OUR FALLEN COMRADES...

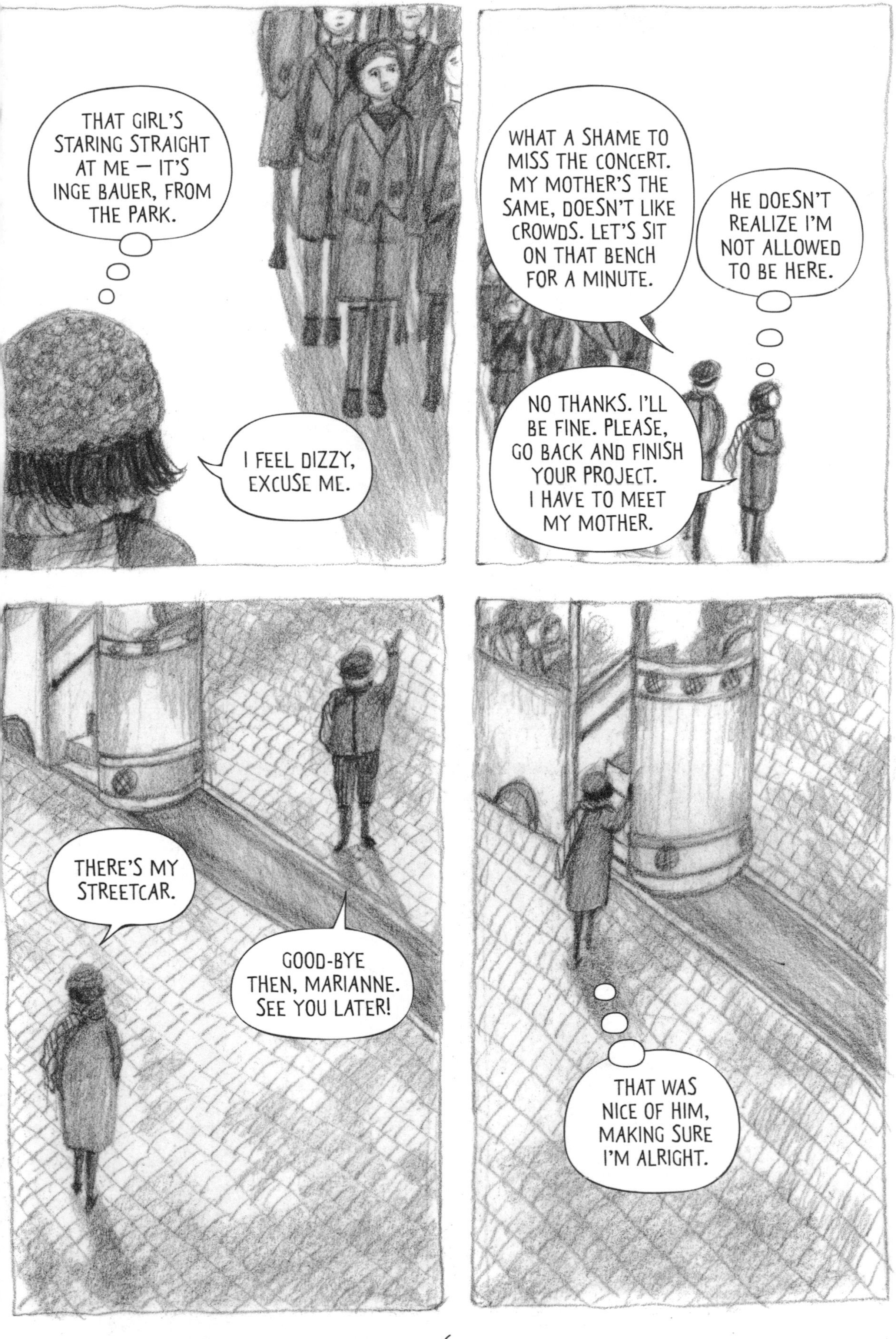
THAT GIRL'S STARING STRAIGHT AT ME — IT'S INGE BAUER, FROM THE PARK.
I FEEL DIZZY, EXCUSE ME.
WHAT A SHAME TO MISS THE CONCERT. MY MOTHER'S THE SAME, DOESN'T LIKE CROWDS. LET'S SIT ON THAT BENCH FOR A MINUTE.
HE DOESN'T REALIZE I'M NOT ALLOWED TO BE HERE.
NO THANKS. I'LL BE FINE. PLEASE, GO BACK AND FINISH YOUR PROJECT. I HAVE TO MEET MY MOTHER.
THERE'S MY STREETCAR.
GOOD-BYE THEN, MARIANNE. SEE YOU LATER!
THAT WAS NICE OF HIM, MAKING SURE I'M ALRIGHT.

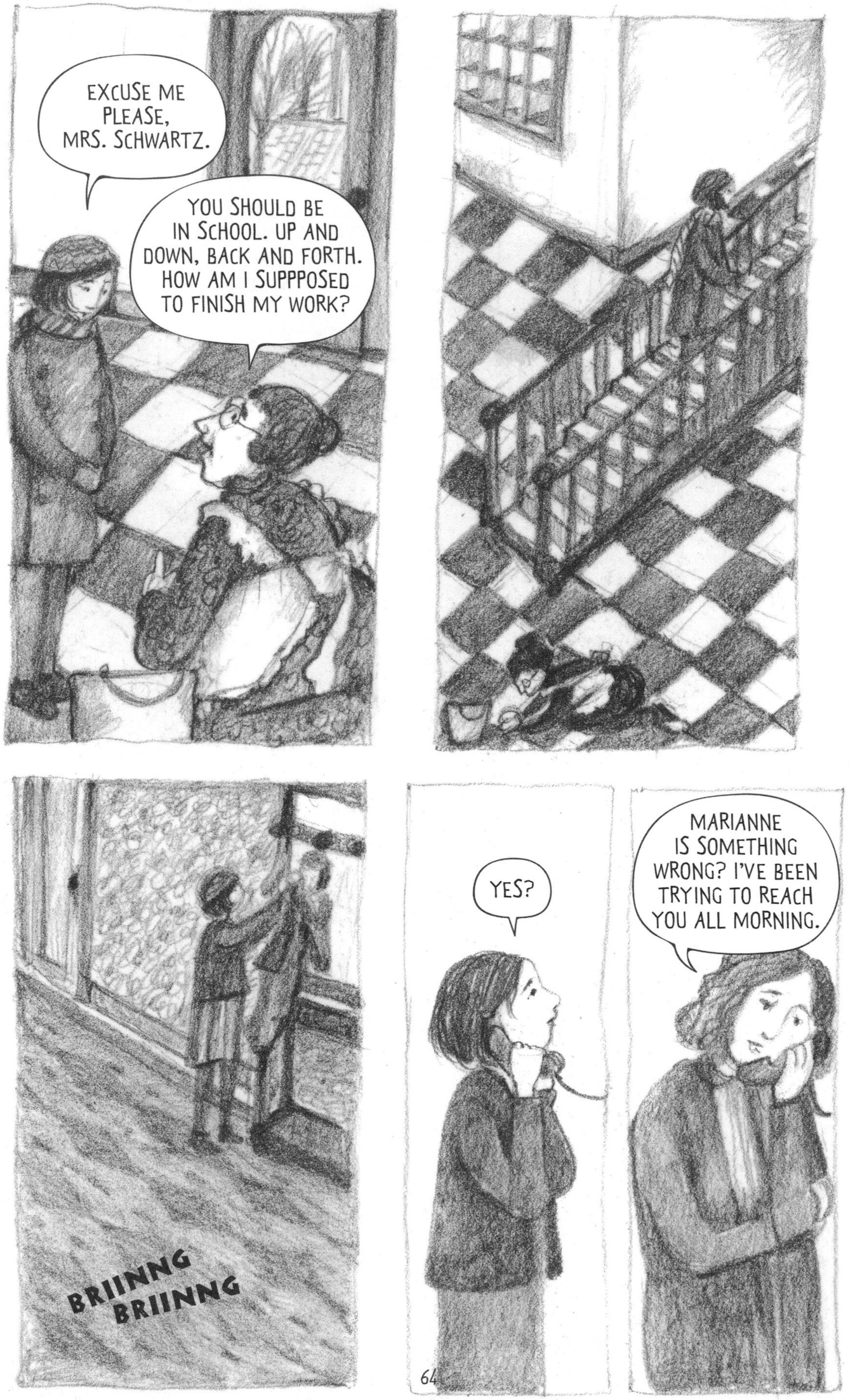
EXCUSE ME PLEASE, MRS. SCHWARTZ.
YOU SHOULD BE IN SCHOOL. UP AND DOWN, BACK AND FORTH. HOW AM I SUPPPOSED TO FINISH MY WORK?
BRIINNG BRIINNG
YES?
MARIANNE IS SOMETHING WRONG? I'VE BEEN TRYING TO REACH YOU ALL MORNING.

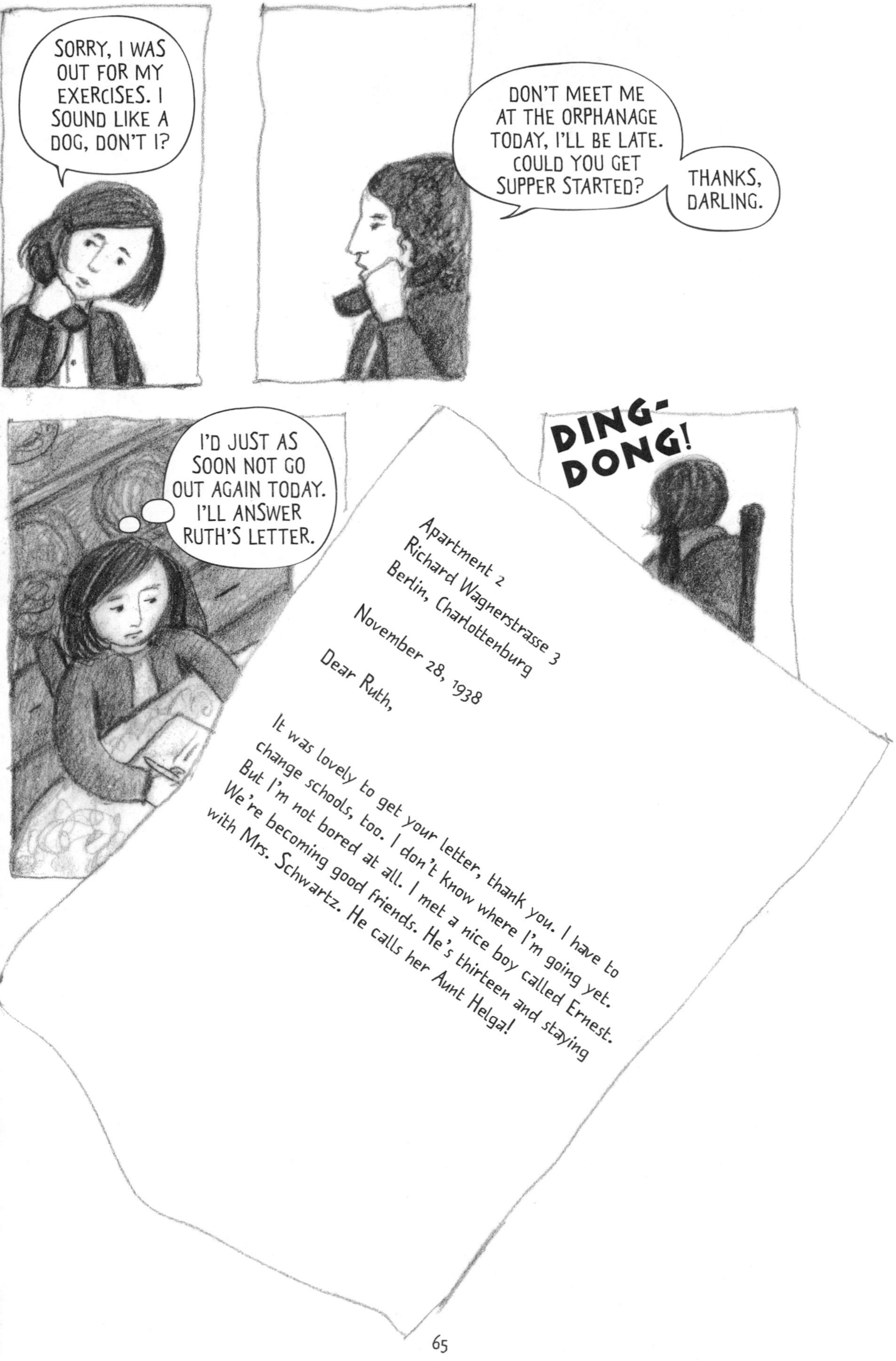
SORRY, I WAS OUT FOR MY EXERCISES. I SOUND LIKE A DOG, DON'T I?
DON'T MEET ME AT THE ORPHANAGE TODAY, I'LL BE LATE. COULD YOU GET SUPPER STARTED?
THANKS, DARLING.
I'D JUST AS SOON NOT GO OUT AGAIN TODAY. I'LL ANSWER RUTH'S LETTER.
Apartment 2
Richard Wagnerstrasse 3
Berlin, Charlottenburg
November 28, 1938
Dear Ruth,
It was lovely to get your letter, thank you. I have to change schools, too. I don't know where I'm going yet. But I'm not bored at all. I met a nice boy called Ernest. We're becoming good friends. He's thirteen and staying with Mrs. Schwartz. He calls her Aunt Helga!
DING-DONG!

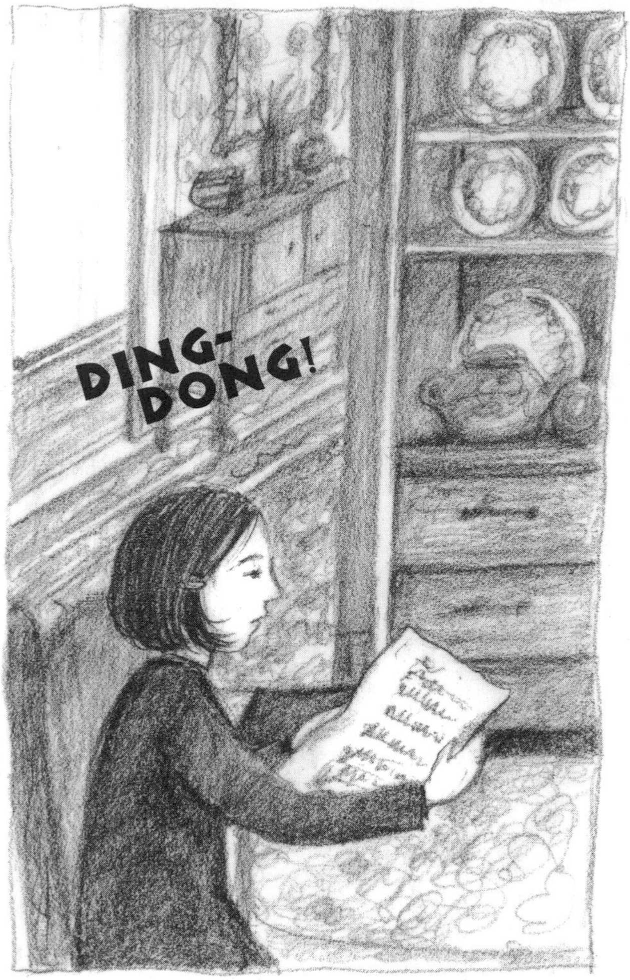
DING-DONG!

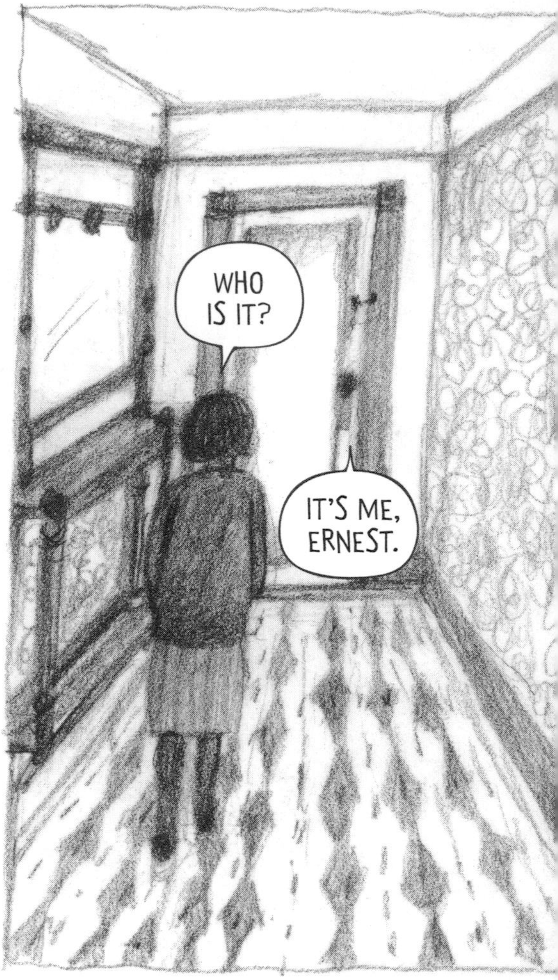
WHO IS IT?
IT'S ME, ERNEST.

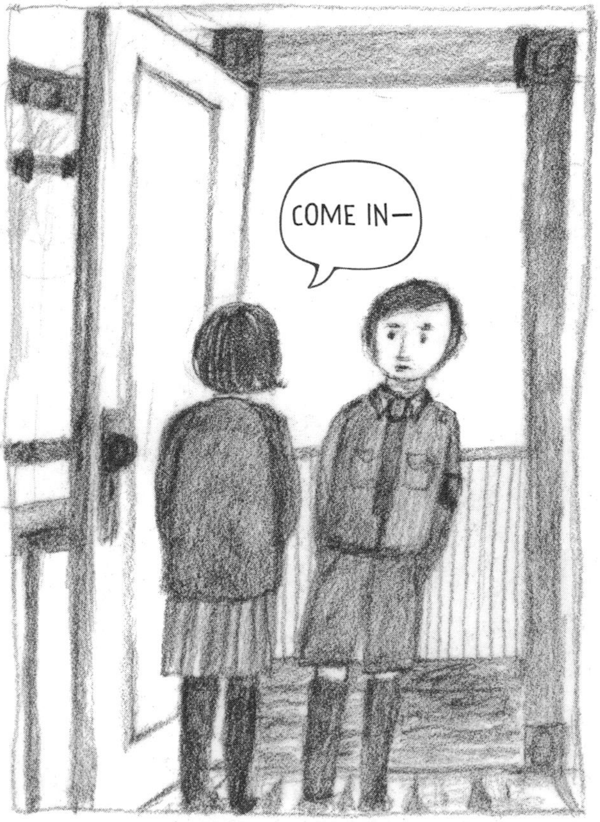
COME IN—

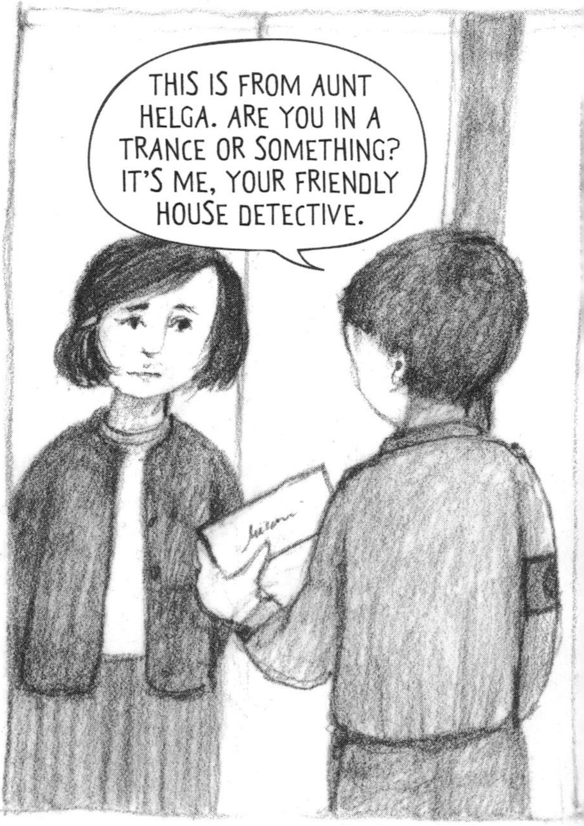
THIS IS FROM AUNT HELGA. ARE YOU IN A TRANCE OR SOMETHING? IT'S ME, YOUR FRIENDLY HOUSE DETECTIVE.

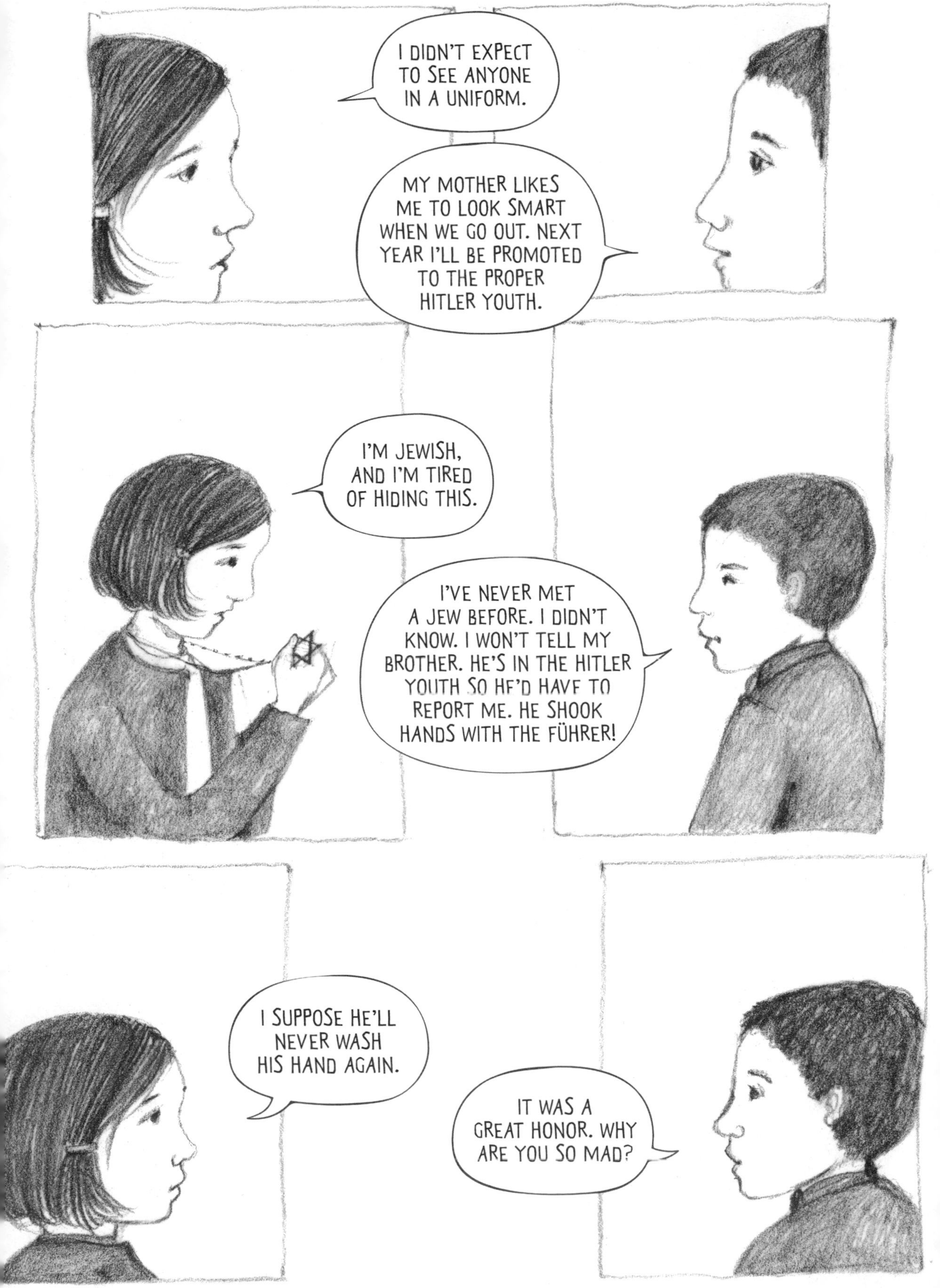
I DIDN'T EXPECT TO SEE ANYONE IN A UNIFORM.
MY MOTHER LIKES ME TO LOOK SMART WHEN WE GO OUT. NEXT YEAR I'LL BE PROMOTED TO THE PROPER HITLER YOUTH.
I'M JEWISH, AND I'M TIRED OF HIDING THIS.
I'VE NEVER MET A JEW BEFORE. I DIDN'T KNOW. I WON'T TELL MY BROTHER. HE'S IN THE HITLER YOUTH SO HE'D HAVE TO REPORT ME. HE SHOOK HANDS WITH THE FÜHRER!
I SUPPOSE HE'LL NEVER WASH HIS HAND AGAIN.
IT WAS A GREAT HONOR. WHY ARE YOU SO MAD?

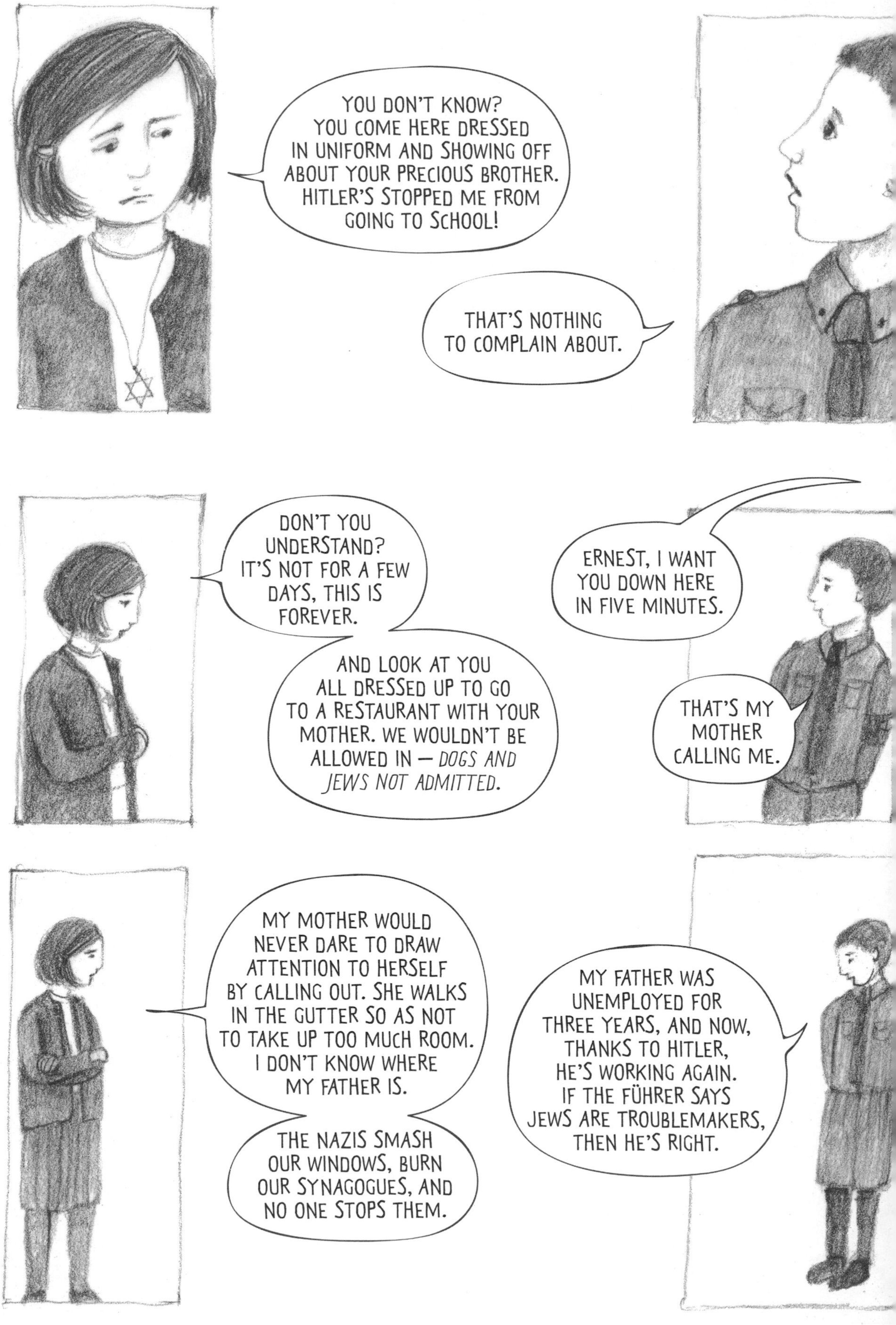
YOU DON'T KNOW? YOU COME HERE DRESSED IN UNIFORM AND SHOWING OFF ABOUT YOUR PRECIOUS BROTHER. HITLER'S STOPPED ME FROM GOING TO SCHOOL!
THAT'S NOTHING TO COMPLAIN ABOUT.
DON'T YOU UNDERSTAND? IT'S NOT FOR A FEW DAYS, THIS IS FOREVER.
AND LOOK AT YOU ALL DRESSED UP TO GO TO A RESTAURANT WITH YOUR MOTHER. WE WOULDN'T BE ALLOWED IN – *DOGS AND JEWS NOT ADMITTED*.
ERNEST, I WANT YOU DOWN HERE IN FIVE MINUTES.
THAT'S MY MOTHER CALLING ME.
MY MOTHER WOULD NEVER DARE TO DRAW ATTENTION TO HERSELF BY CALLING OUT. SHE WALKS IN THE GUTTER SO AS NOT TO TAKE UP TOO MUCH ROOM. I DON'T KNOW WHERE MY FATHER IS.
THE NAZIS SMASH OUR WINDOWS, BURN OUR SYNAGOGUES, AND NO ONE STOPS THEM.
MY FATHER WAS UNEMPLOYED FOR THREE YEARS, AND NOW, THANKS TO HITLER, HE'S WORKING AGAIN. IF THE FÜHRER SAYS JEWS ARE TROUBLEMAKERS, THEN HE'S RIGHT.

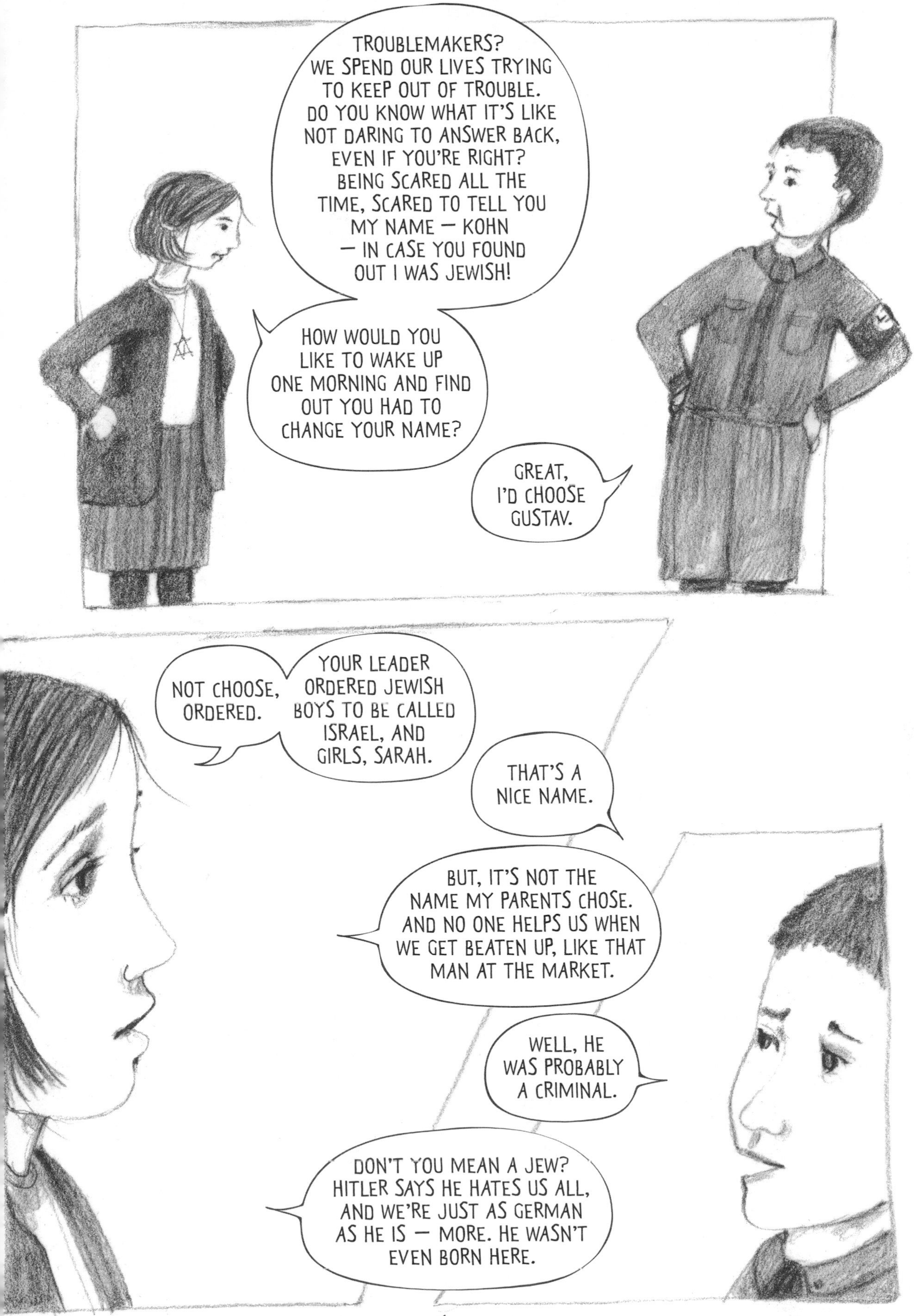
TROUBLEMAKERS? WE SPEND OUR LIVES TRYING TO KEEP OUT OF TROUBLE. DO YOU KNOW WHAT IT'S LIKE NOT DARING TO ANSWER BACK, EVEN IF YOU'RE RIGHT? BEING SCARED ALL THE TIME, SCARED TO TELL YOU MY NAME — KOHN — IN CASE YOU FOUND OUT I WAS JEWISH!
HOW WOULD YOU LIKE TO WAKE UP ONE MORNING AND FIND OUT YOU HAD TO CHANGE YOUR NAME?
GREAT, I'D CHOOSE GUSTAV.
NOT CHOOSE, ORDERED.
YOUR LEADER ORDERED JEWISH BOYS TO BE CALLED ISRAEL, AND GIRLS, SARAH.
THAT'S A NICE NAME.
BUT, IT'S NOT THE NAME MY PARENTS CHOSE. AND NO ONE HELPS US WHEN WE GET BEATEN UP, LIKE THAT MAN AT THE MARKET.
WELL, HE WAS PROBABLY A CRIMINAL.
DON'T YOU MEAN A JEW? HITLER SAYS HE HATES US ALL, AND WE'RE JUST AS GERMAN AS HE IS — MORE. HE WASN'T EVEN BORN HERE.

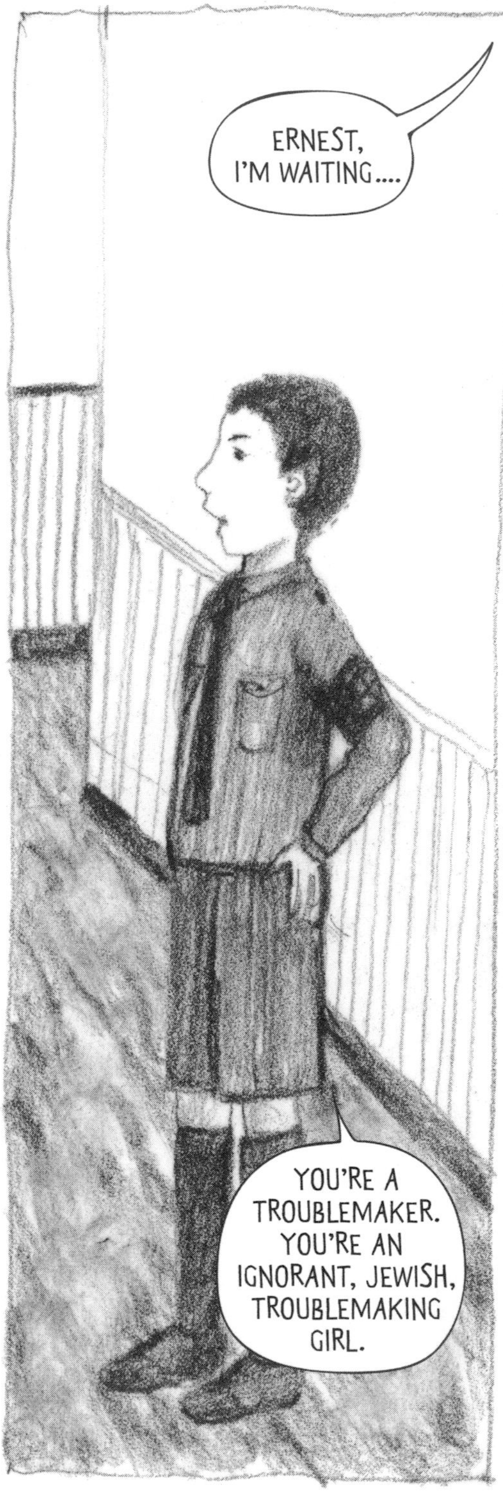
ERNEST, I'M WAITING....
YOU'RE A TROUBLEMAKER. YOU'RE AN IGNORANT, JEWISH, TROUBLEMAKING GIRL.

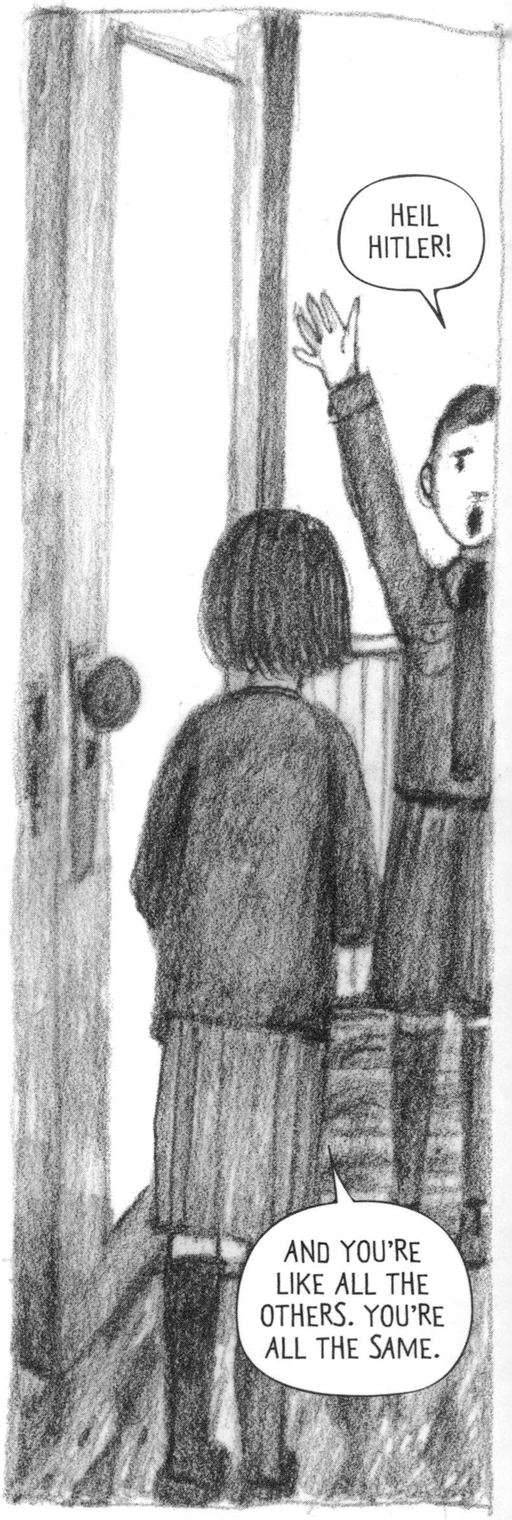
HEIL HITLER!
AND YOU'RE LIKE ALL THE OTHERS. YOU'RE ALL THE SAME.

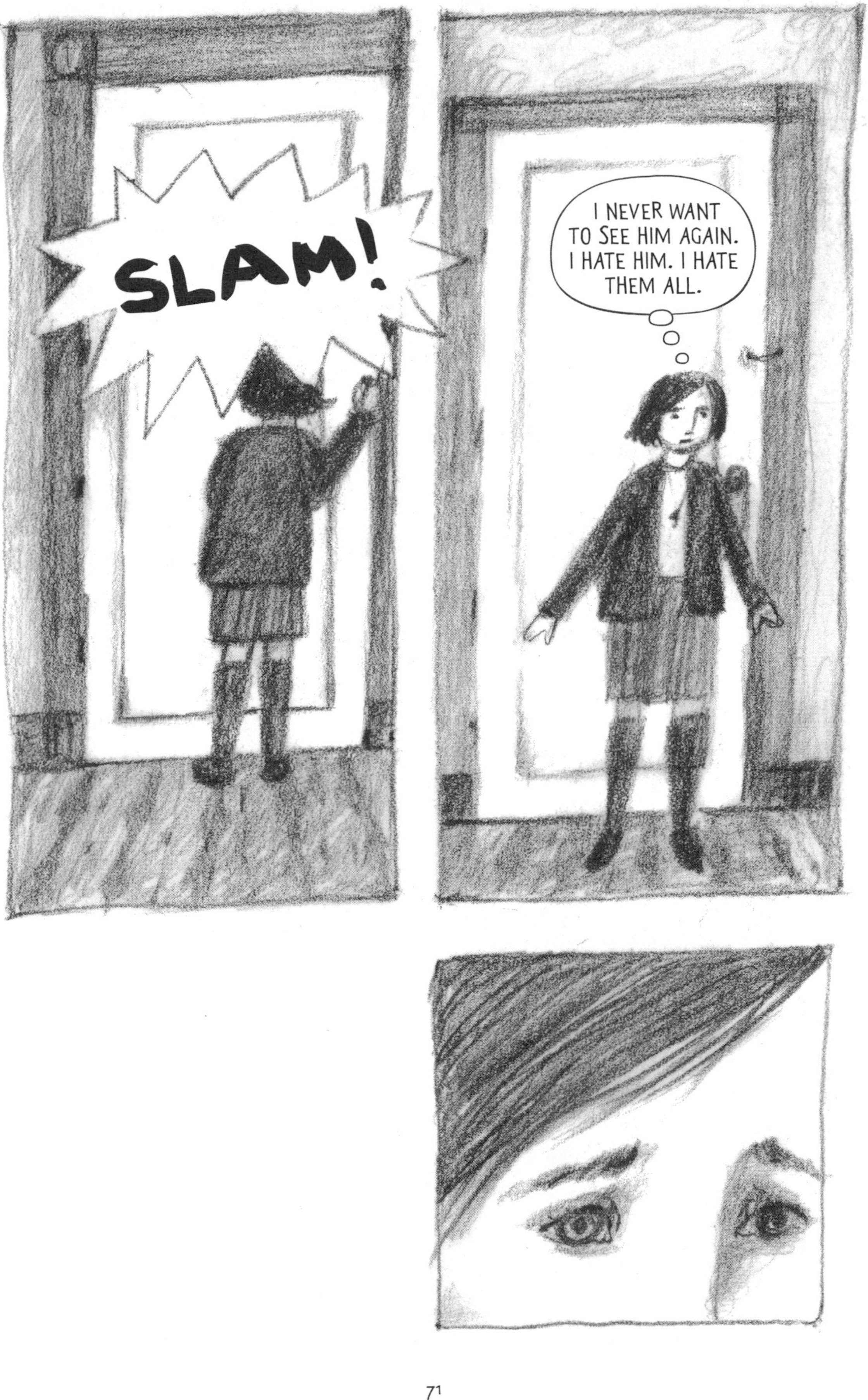
SLAM!
I NEVER WANT TO SEE HIM AGAIN. I HATE HIM. I HATE THEM ALL.

CHAPTER SEVEN

VISITORS

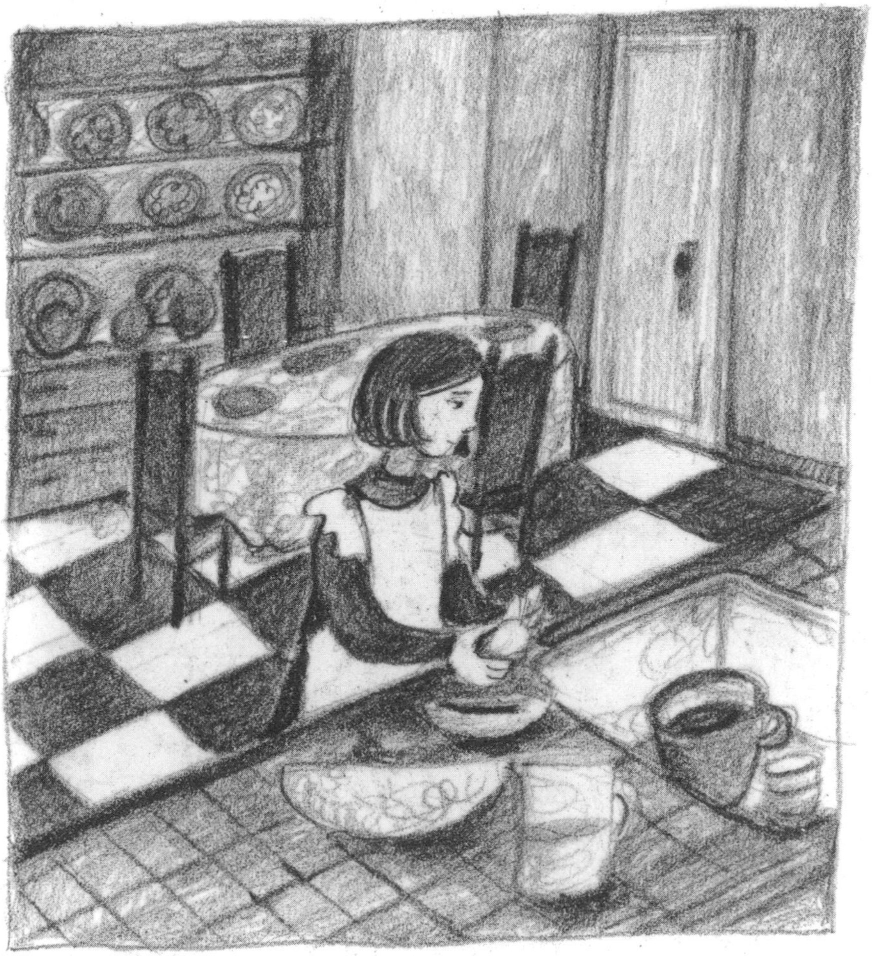

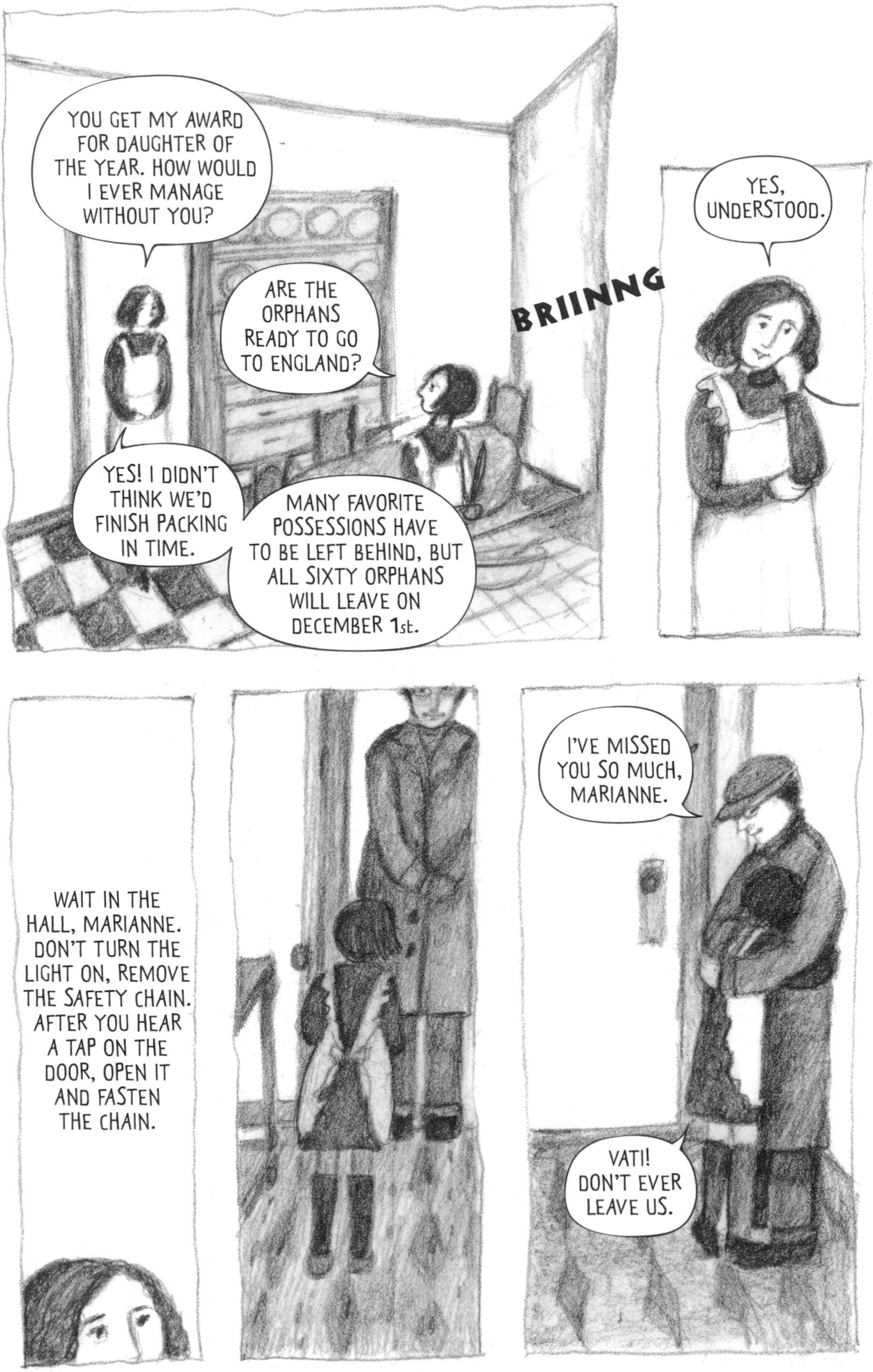
YOU GET MY AWARD FOR DAUGHTER OF THE YEAR. HOW WOULD I EVER MANAGE WITHOUT YOU?
YES! I DIDN'T THINK WE'D FINISH PACKING IN TIME.
ARE THE ORPHANS READY TO GO TO ENGLAND?
MANY FAVORITE POSSESSIONS HAVE TO BE LEFT BEHIND, BUT ALL SIXTY ORPHANS WILL LEAVE ON DECEMBER 1st.
BRIINNG
YES, UNDERSTOOD.
WAIT IN THE HALL, MARIANNE. DON'T TURN THE LIGHT ON, REMOVE THE SAFETY CHAIN. AFTER YOU HEAR A TAP ON THE DOOR, OPEN IT AND FASTEN THE CHAIN.
I'VE MISSED YOU SO MUCH, MARIANNE.
VATI! DON'T EVER LEAVE US.

CHAPTER SEVEN

VISITORS

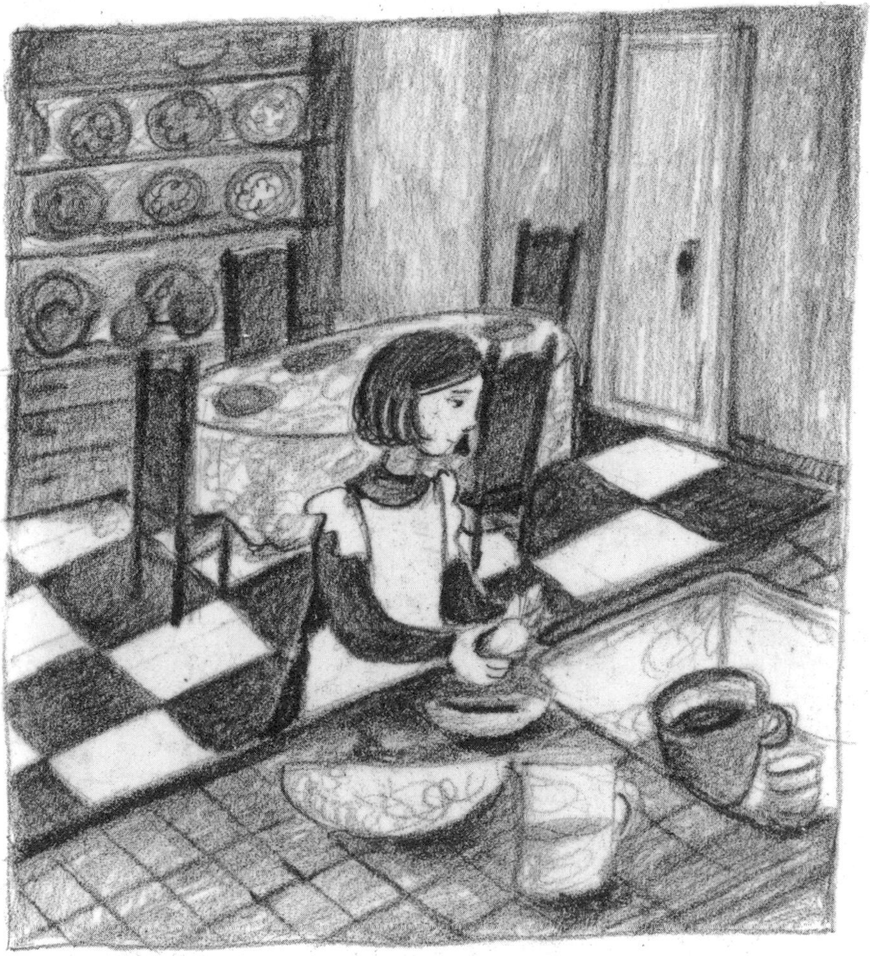

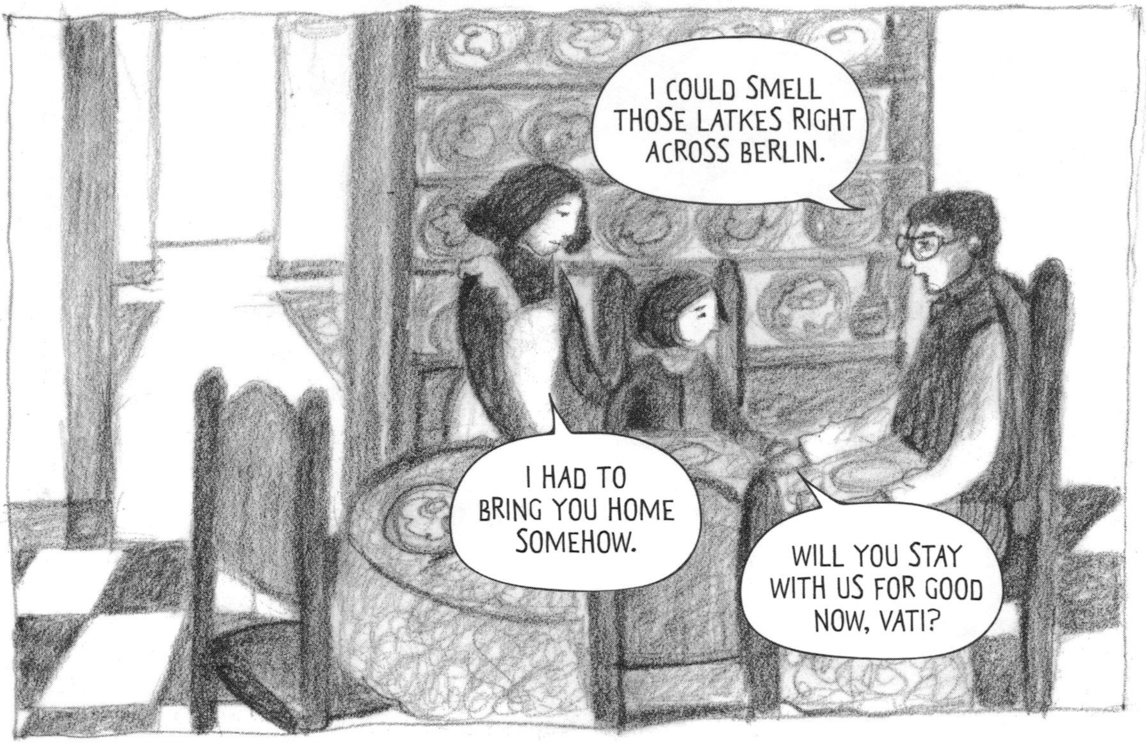
I COULD SMELL THOSE LATKES RIGHT ACROSS BERLIN.
I HAD TO BRING YOU HOME SOMEHOW.
WILL YOU STAY WITH US FOR GOOD NOW, VATI?

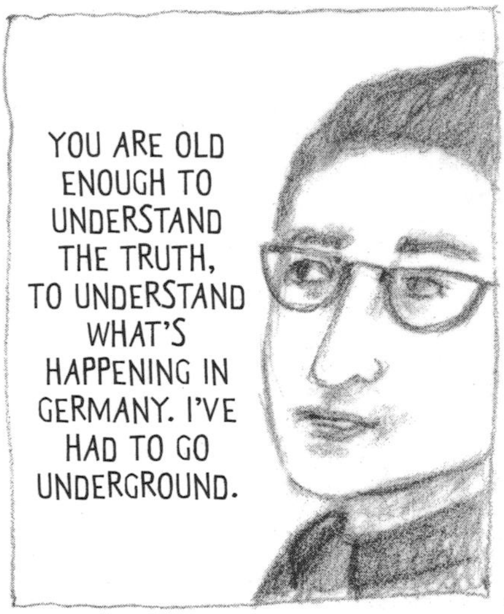
YOU ARE OLD ENOUGH TO UNDERSTAND THE TRUTH, TO UNDERSTAND WHAT'S HAPPENING IN GERMANY. I'VE HAD TO GO UNDERGROUND.

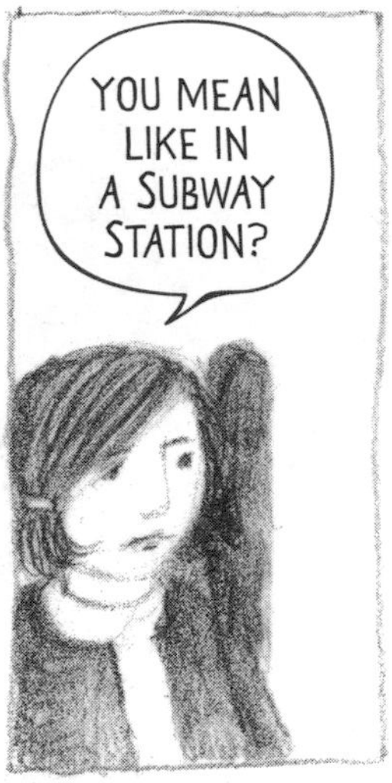
YOU MEAN LIKE IN A SUBWAY STATION?

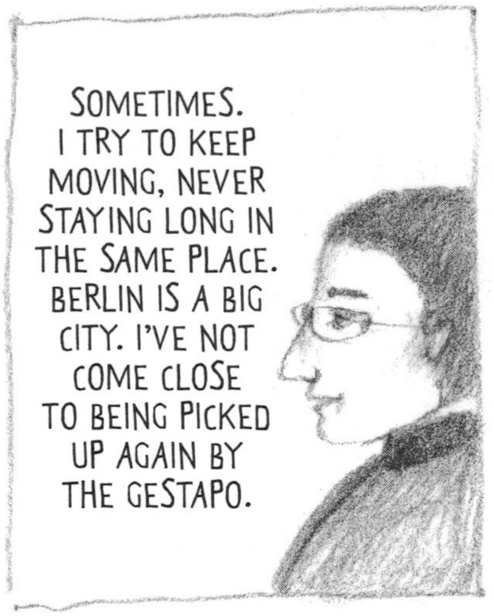
SOMETIMES. I TRY TO KEEP MOVING, NEVER STAYING LONG IN THE SAME PLACE. BERLIN IS A BIG CITY. I'VE NOT COME CLOSE TO BEING PICKED UP AGAIN BY THE GESTAPO.

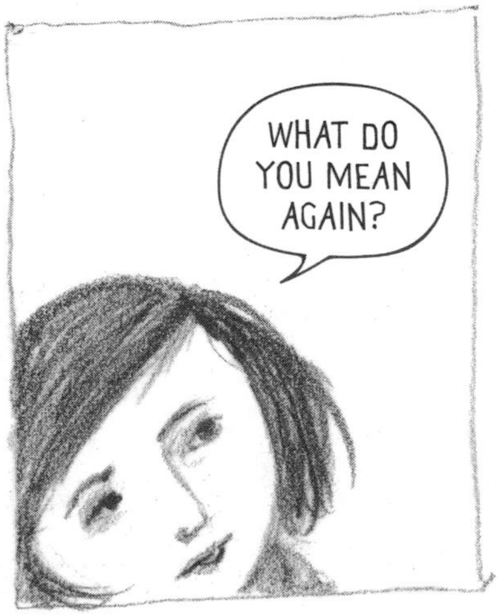
WHAT DO YOU MEAN AGAIN?

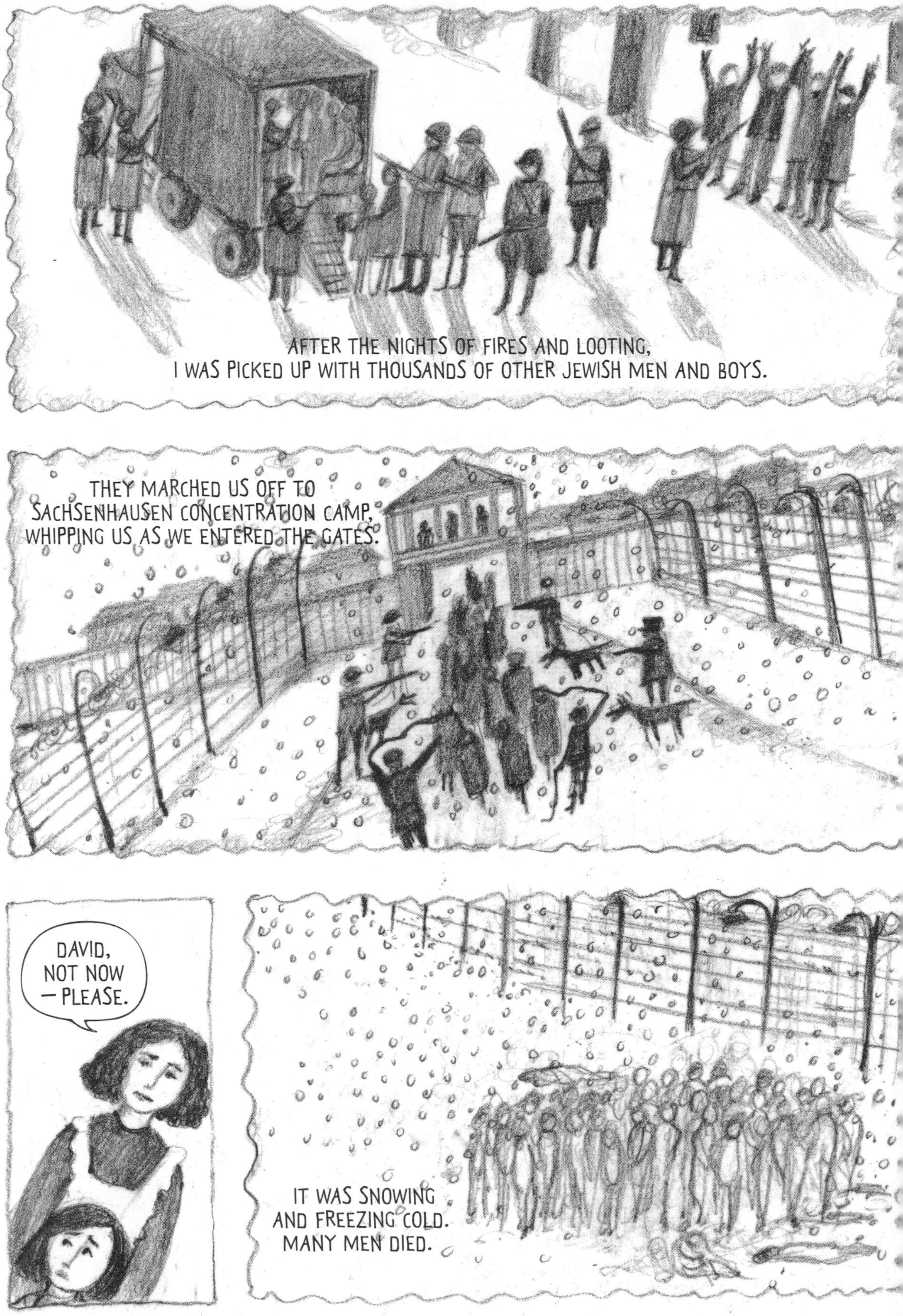
AFTER THE NIGHTS OF FIRES AND LOOTING,
I WAS PICKED UP WITH THOUSANDS OF OTHER JEWISH MEN AND BOYS.
THEY MARCHED US OFF TO
SACHSENHAUSEN CONCENTRATION CAMP,
WHIPPING US AS WE ENTERED THE GATES.
DAVID,
NOT NOW
— PLEASE.
IT WAS SNOWING
AND FREEZING COLD.
MANY MEN DIED.

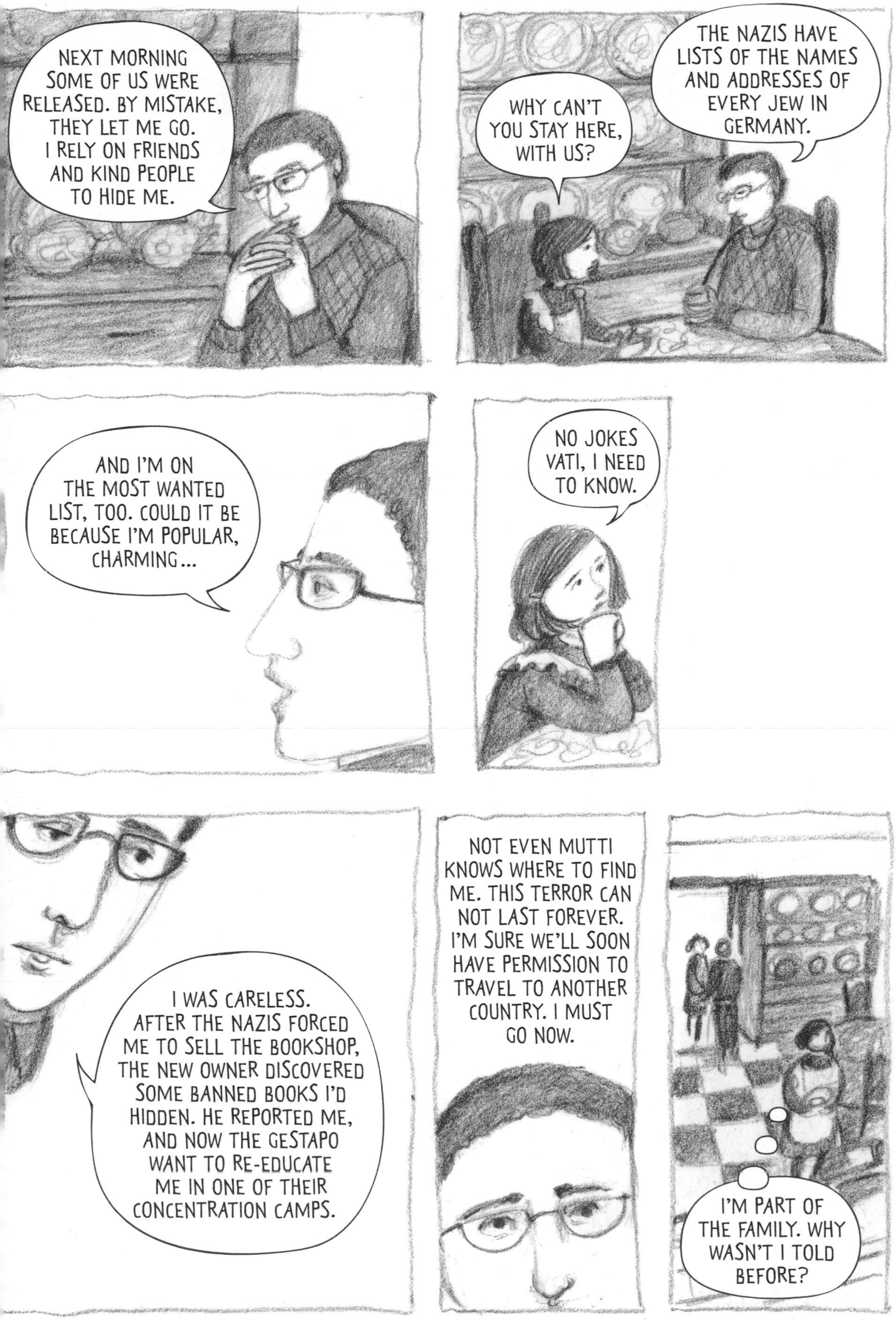
NEXT MORNING SOME OF US WERE RELEASED. BY MISTAKE, THEY LET ME GO. I RELY ON FRIENDS AND KIND PEOPLE TO HIDE ME.
WHY CAN'T YOU STAY HERE, WITH US?
THE NAZIS HAVE LISTS OF THE NAMES AND ADDRESSES OF EVERY JEW IN GERMANY.
AND I'M ON THE MOST WANTED LIST, TOO. COULD IT BE BECAUSE I'M POPULAR, CHARMING...
NO JOKES VATI, I NEED TO KNOW.
I WAS CARELESS. AFTER THE NAZIS FORCED ME TO SELL THE BOOKSHOP, THE NEW OWNER DISCOVERED SOME BANNED BOOKS I'D HIDDEN. HE REPORTED ME, AND NOW THE GESTAPO WANT TO RE-EDUCATE ME IN ONE OF THEIR CONCENTRATION CAMPS.
NOT EVEN MUTTI KNOWS WHERE TO FIND ME. THIS TERROR CAN NOT LAST FOREVER. I'M SURE WE'LL SOON HAVE PERMISSION TO TRAVEL TO ANOTHER COUNTRY. I MUST GO NOW.
I'M PART OF THE FAMILY. WHY WASN'T I TOLD BEFORE?

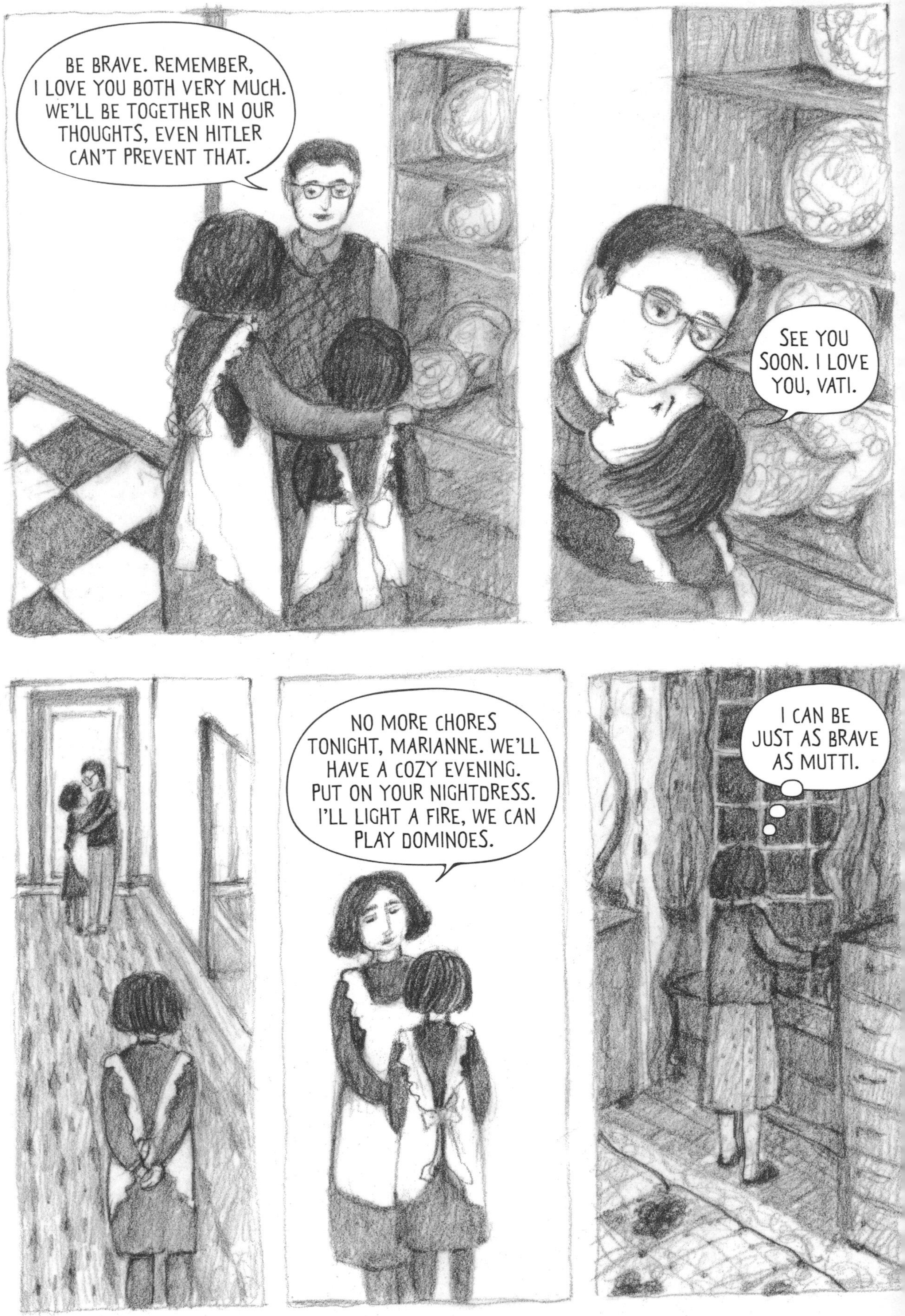
BE BRAVE. REMEMBER, I LOVE YOU BOTH VERY MUCH. WE'LL BE TOGETHER IN OUR THOUGHTS, EVEN HITLER CAN'T PREVENT THAT.
SEE YOU SOON. I LOVE YOU, VATI.
NO MORE CHORES TONIGHT, MARIANNE. WE'LL HAVE A COZY EVENING. PUT ON YOUR NIGHTDRESS. I'LL LIGHT A FIRE, WE CAN PLAY DOMINOES.
I CAN BE JUST AS BRAVE AS MUTTI.

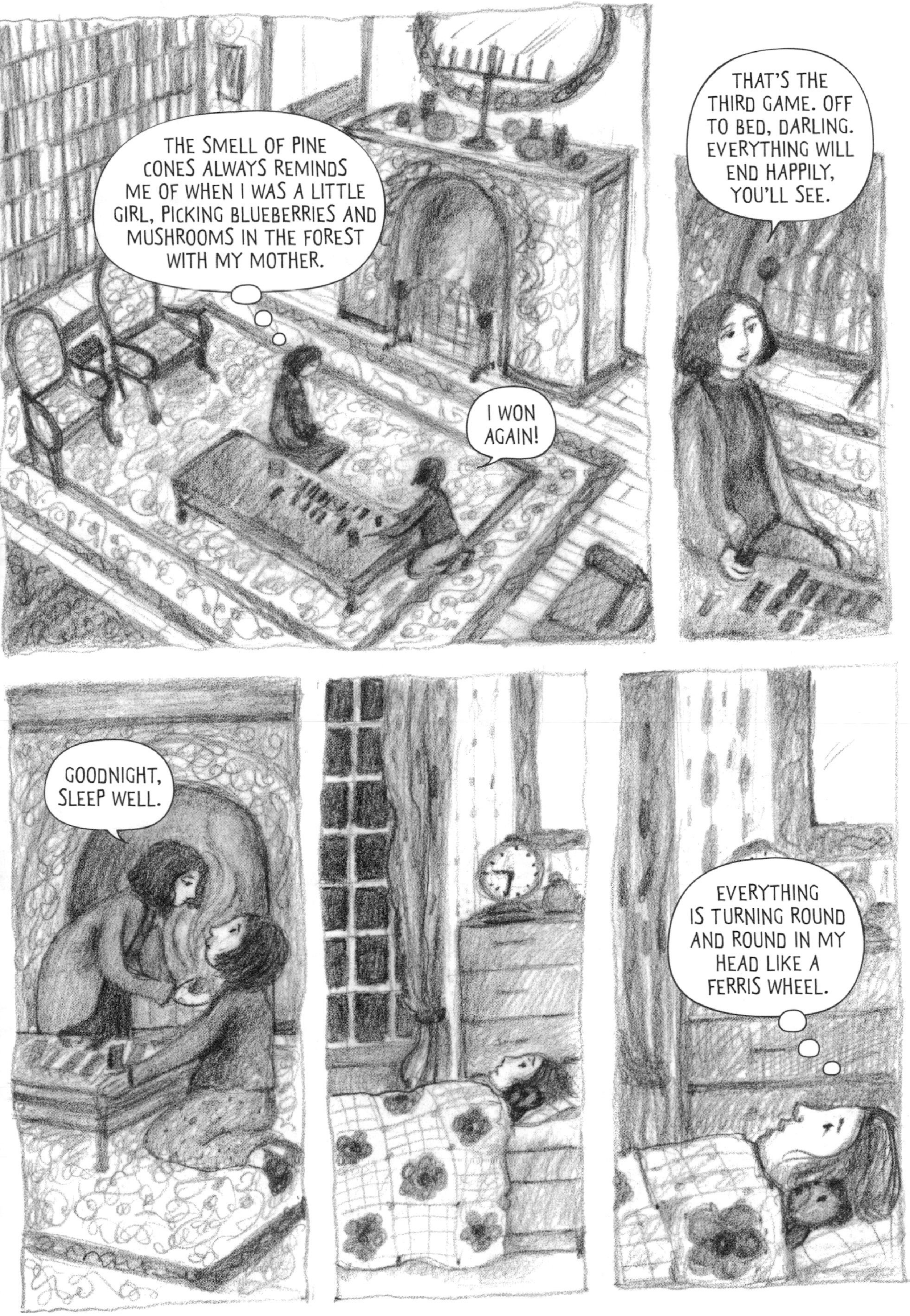
THE SMELL OF PINE CONES ALWAYS REMINDS ME OF WHEN I WAS A LITTLE GIRL, PICKING BLUEBERRIES AND MUSHROOMS IN THE FOREST WITH MY MOTHER.
I WON AGAIN!
THAT'S THE THIRD GAME. OFF TO BED, DARLING. EVERYTHING WILL END HAPPILY, YOU'LL SEE.
GOODNIGHT, SLEEP WELL.
EVERYTHING IS TURNING ROUND AND ROUND IN MY HEAD LIKE A FERRIS WHEEL.

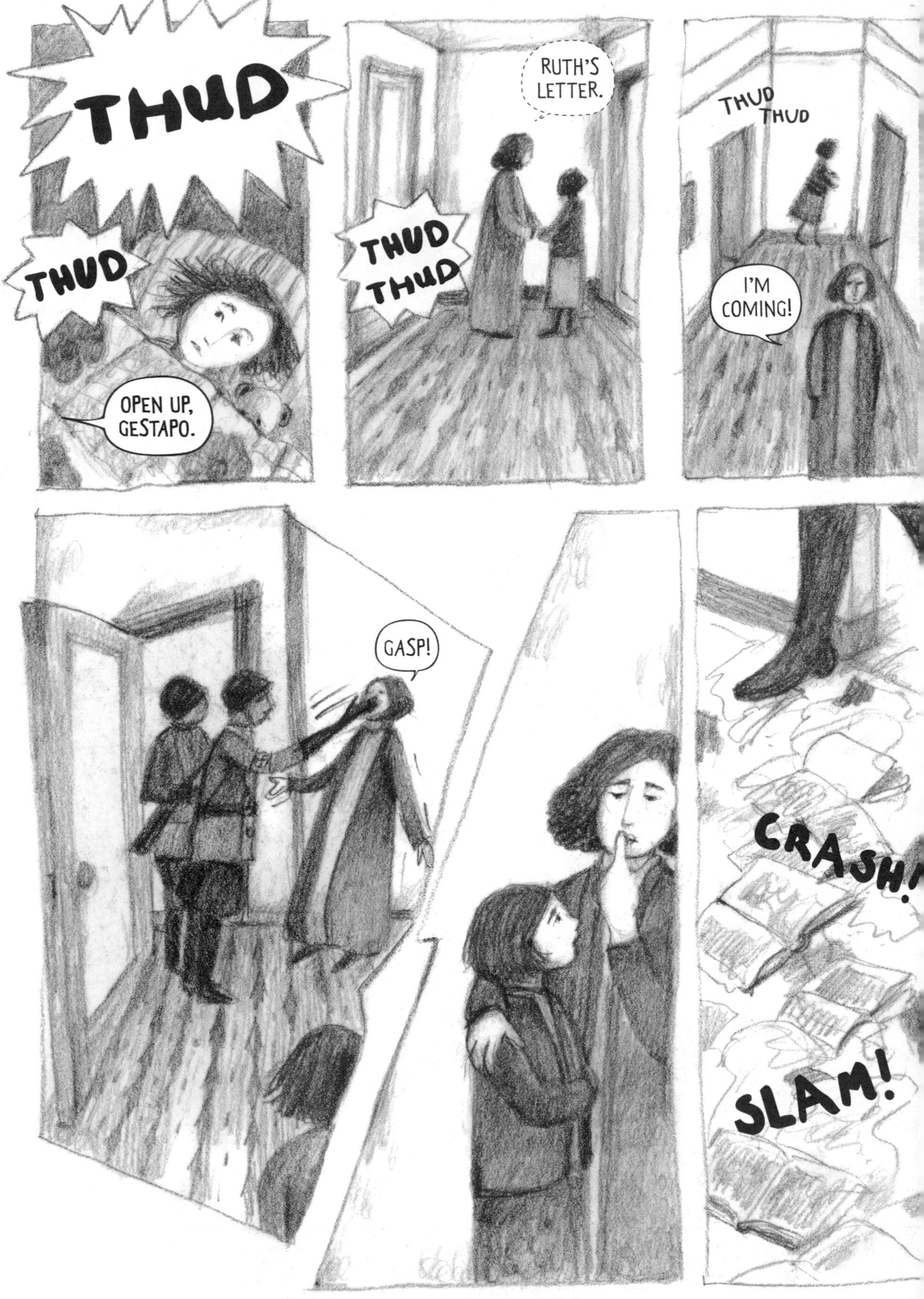
THUD
THUD
OPEN UP, GESTAPO.
THUD THUD
RUTH'S LETTER.
THUD THUD
I'M COMING!
GASP!
CRASH!
SLAM!

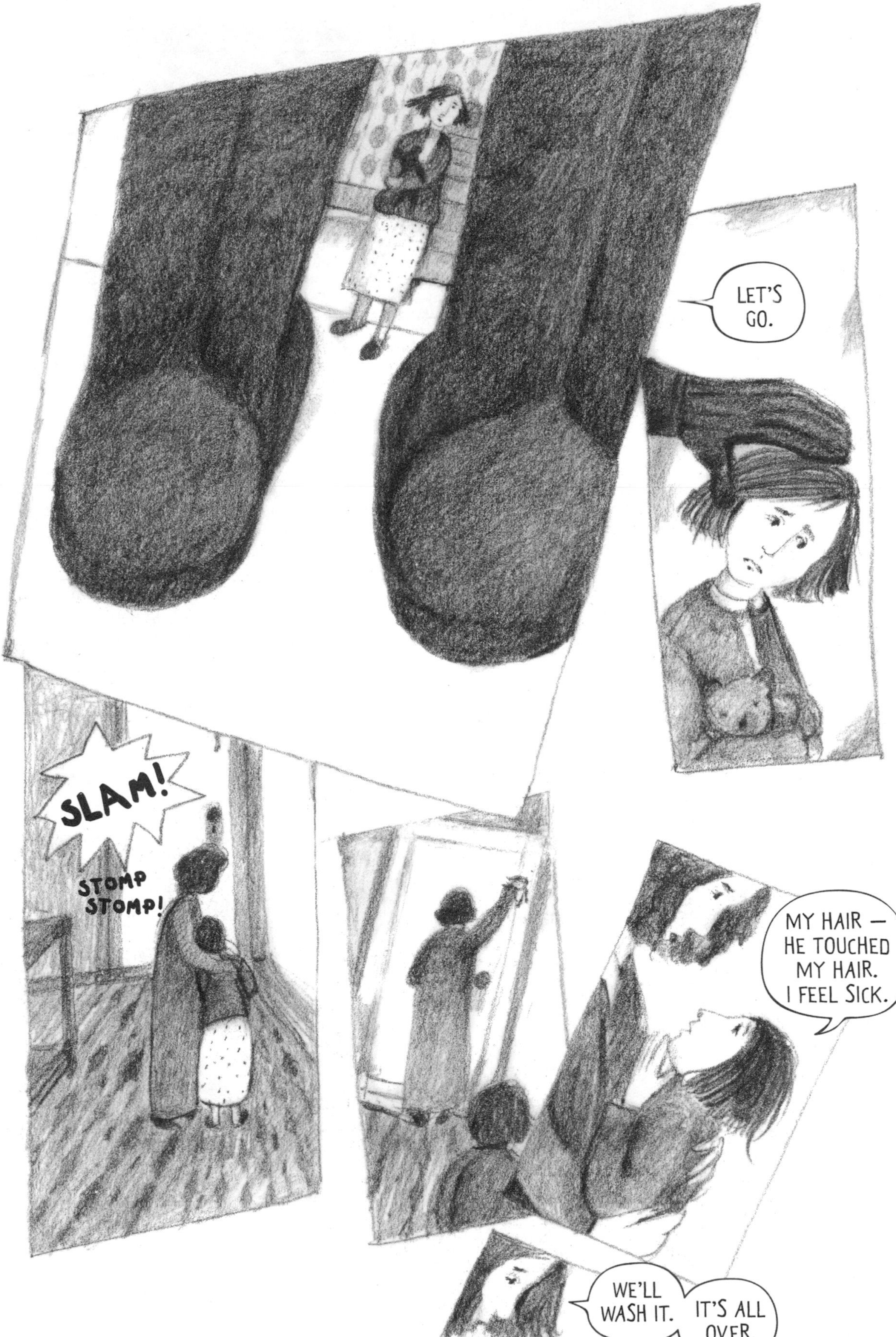
LET'S GO.
SLAM!
STOMP STOMP!
MY HAIR — HE TOUCHED MY HAIR. I FEEL SICK.
WE'LL WASH IT.
IT'S ALL OVER.

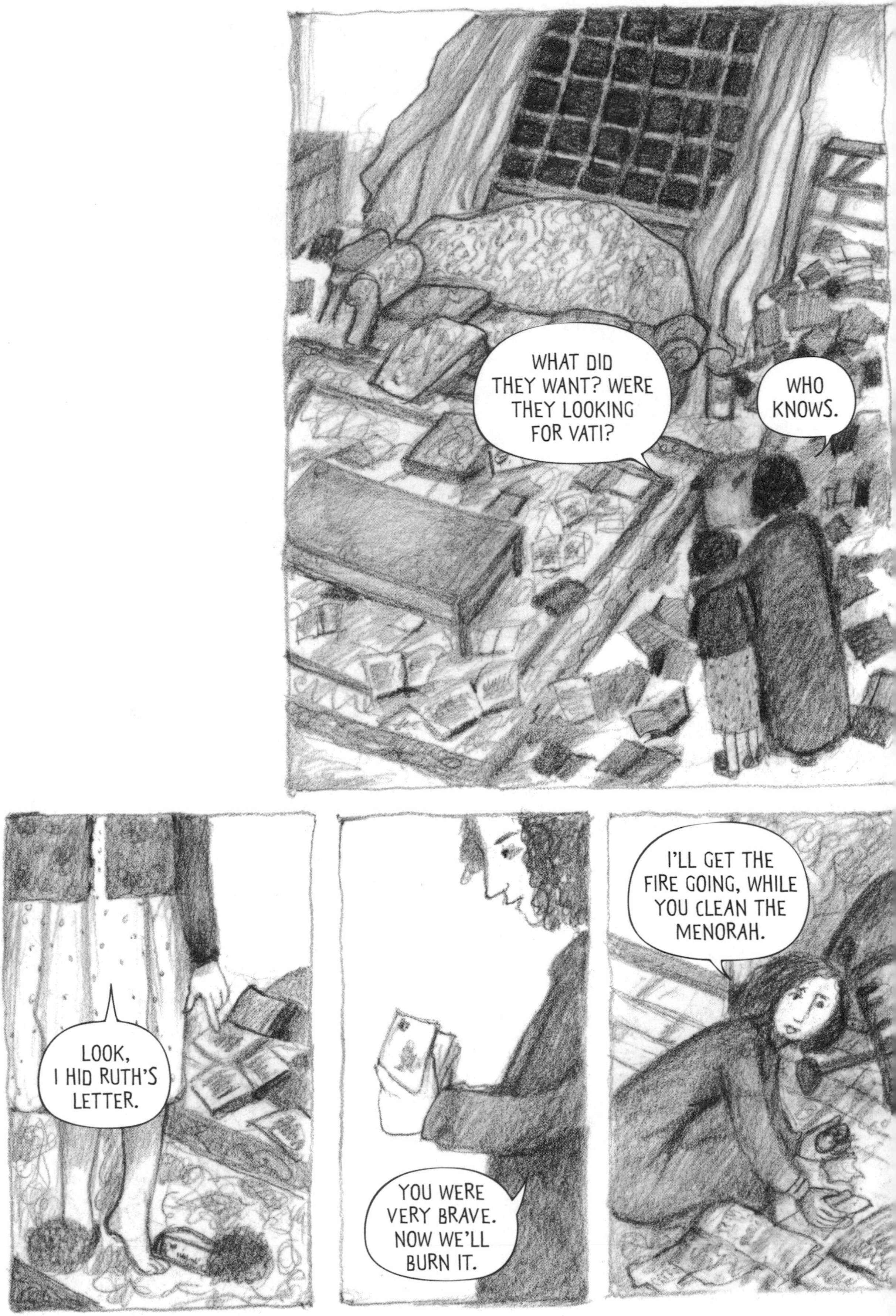
WHAT DID THEY WANT? WERE THEY LOOKING FOR VATI?
WHO KNOWS.
LOOK, I HID RUTH'S LETTER.
YOU WERE VERY BRAVE. NOW WE'LL BURN IT.
I'LL GET THE FIRE GOING, WHILE YOU CLEAN THE MENORAH.

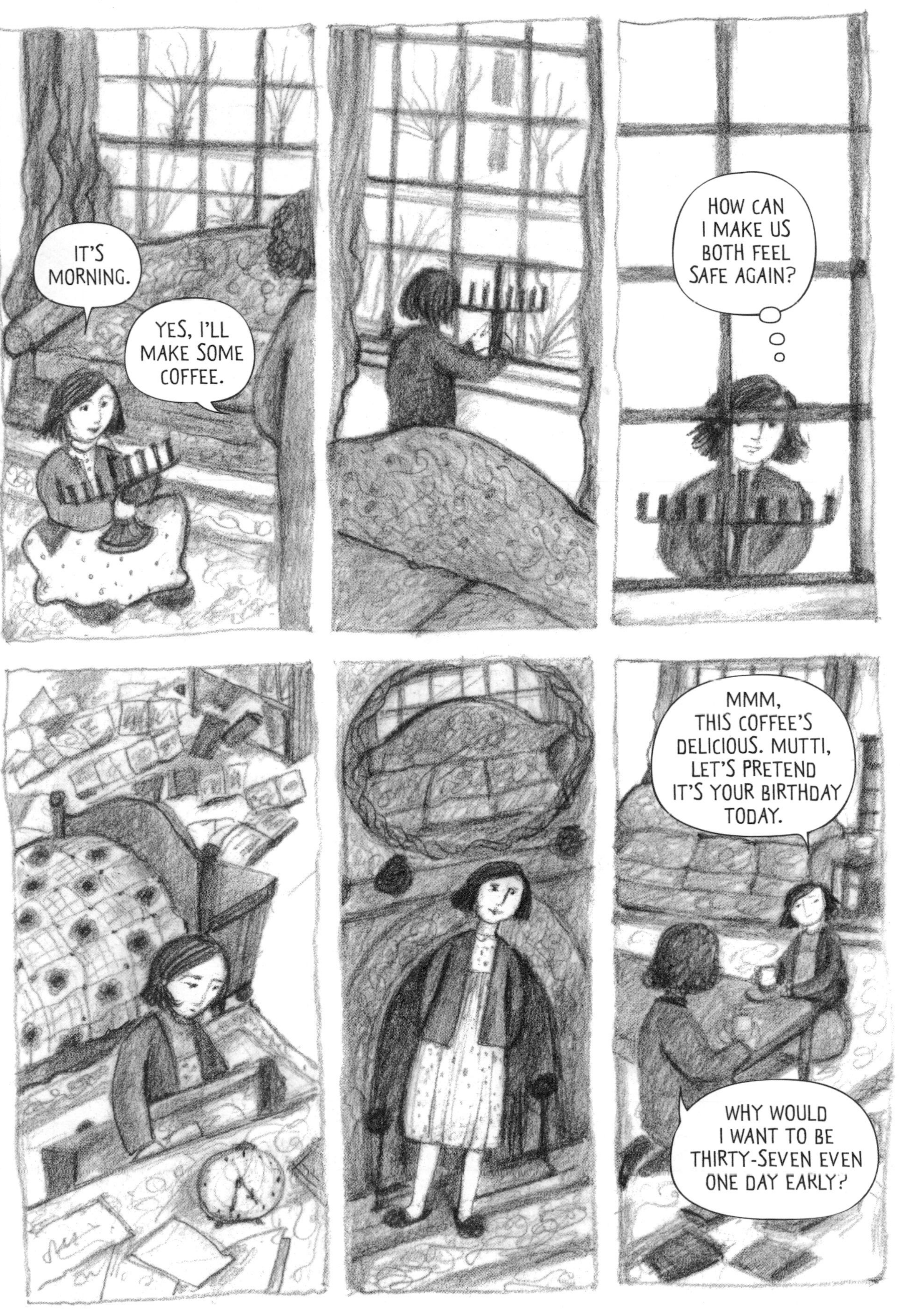

IT'S MORNING.
YES, I'LL MAKE SOME COFFEE.
HOW CAN I MAKE US BOTH FEEL SAFE AGAIN?
MMM, THIS COFFEE'S DELICIOUS. MUTTI, LET'S PRETEND IT'S YOUR BIRTHDAY TODAY.
WHY WOULD I WANT TO BE THIRTY-SEVEN EVEN ONE DAY EARLY?

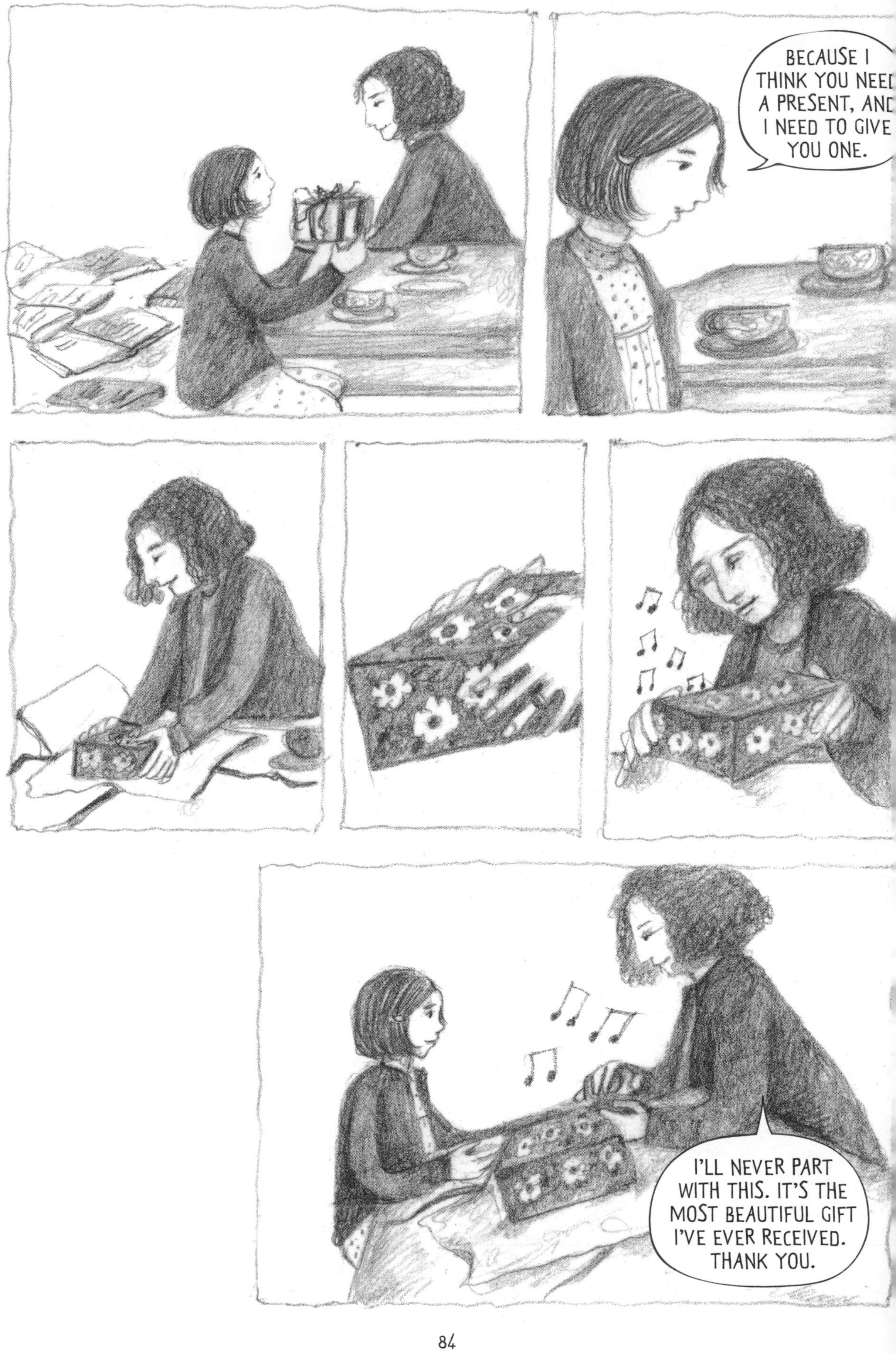
BECAUSE I THINK YOU NEED A PRESENT, AND I NEED TO GIVE YOU ONE.
I'LL NEVER PART WITH THIS. IT'S THE MOST BEAUTIFUL GIFT I'VE EVER RECEIVED. THANK YOU.

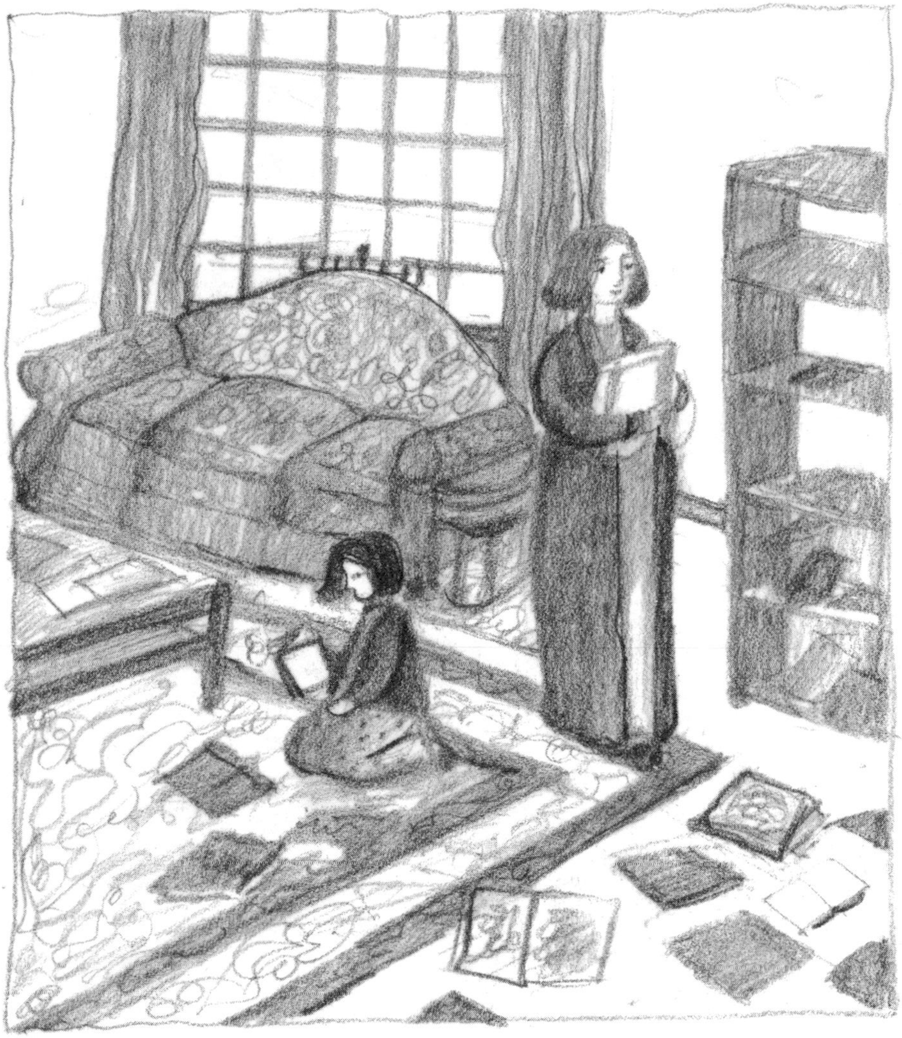

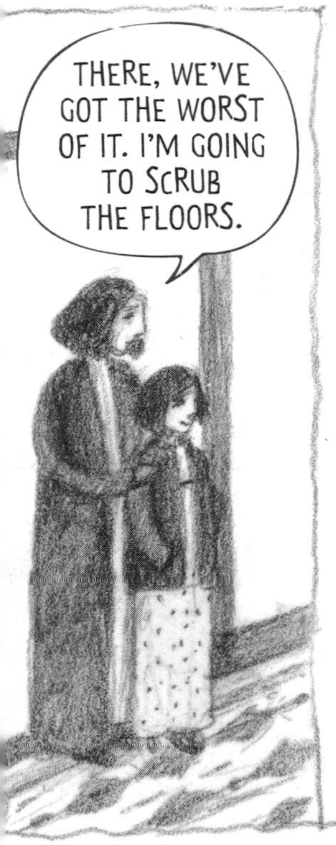
THERE, WE'VE GOT THE WORST OF IT. I'M GOING TO SCRUB THE FLOORS.

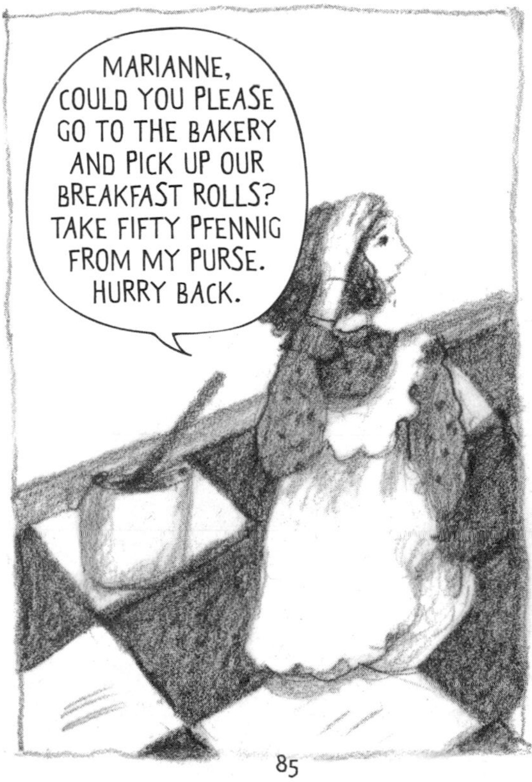
MARIANNE, COULD YOU PLEASE GO TO THE BAKERY AND PICK UP OUR BREAKFAST ROLLS? TAKE FIFTY PFENNIG FROM MY PURSE. HURRY BACK.

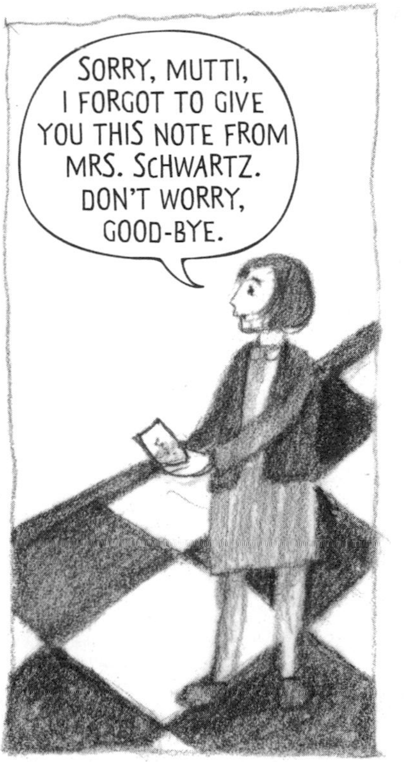
SORRY, MUTTI, I FORGOT TO GIVE YOU THIS NOTE FROM MRS. SCHWARTZ. DON'T WORRY, GOOD-BYE.

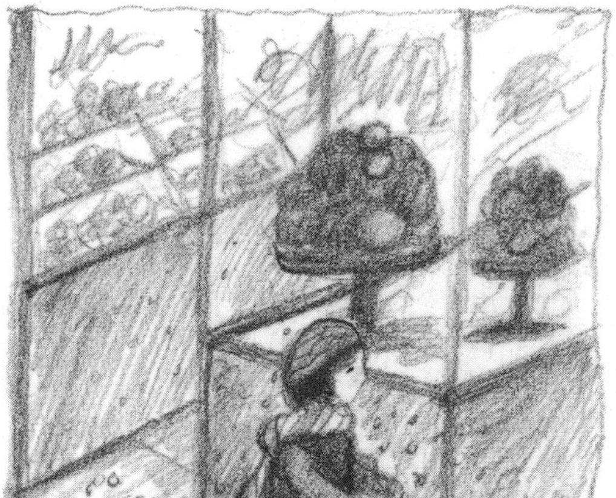

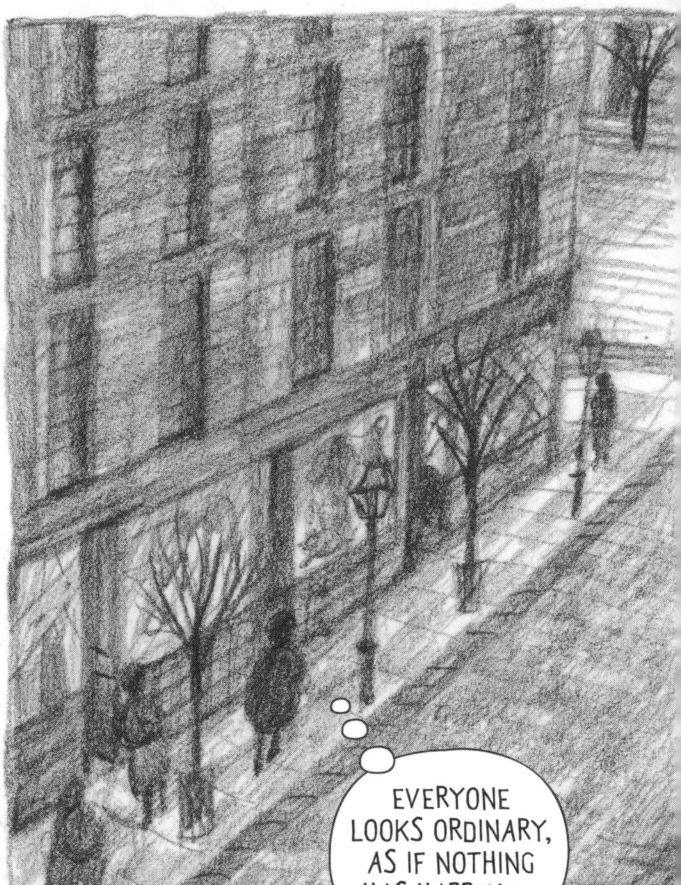
EVERYONE LOOKS ORDINARY, AS IF NOTHING HAS HAPPENED.

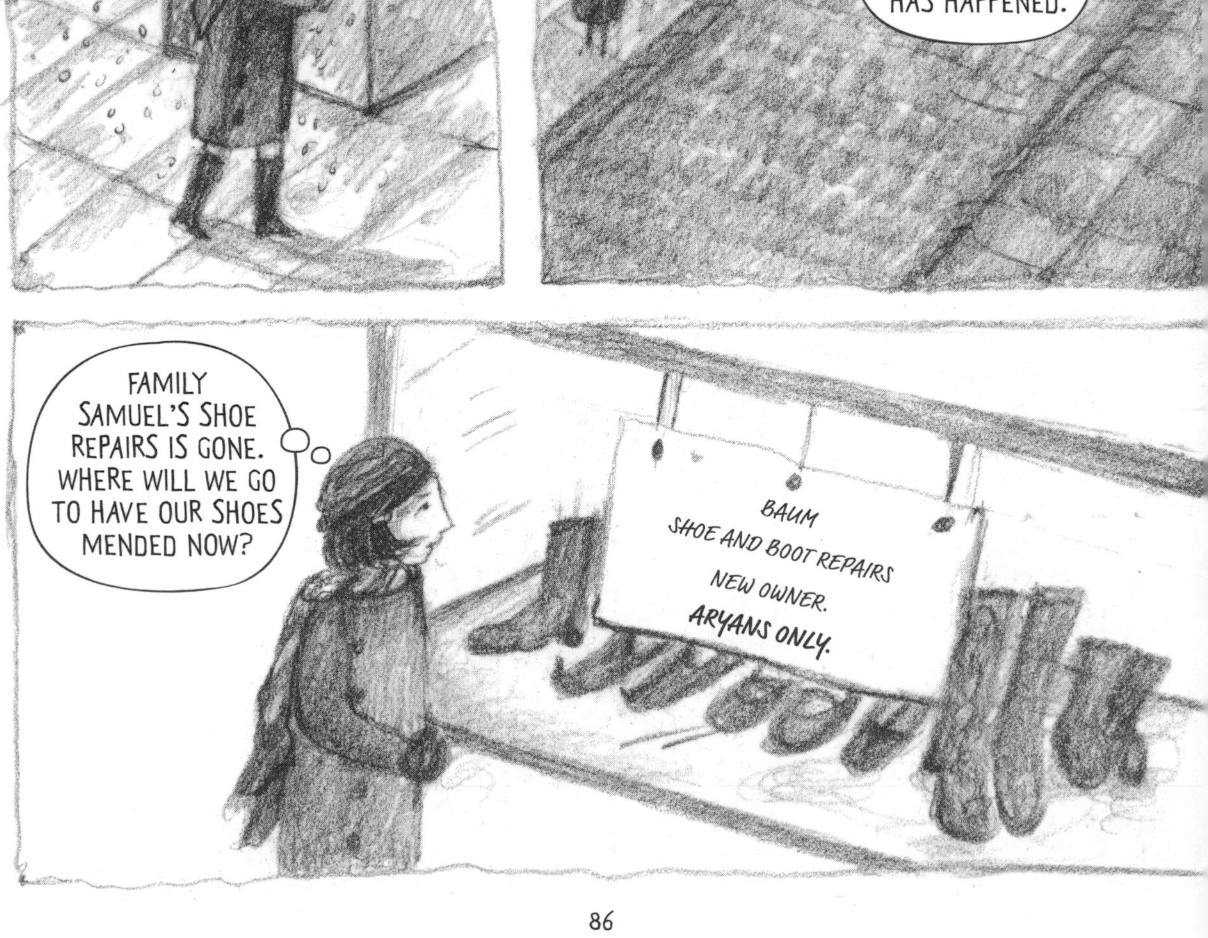
FAMILY SAMUEL'S SHOE REPAIRS IS GONE. WHERE WILL WE GO TO HAVE OUR SHOES MENDED NOW?
BAUM
SHOE AND BOOT REPAIRS
NEW OWNER.
ARYANS ONLY.

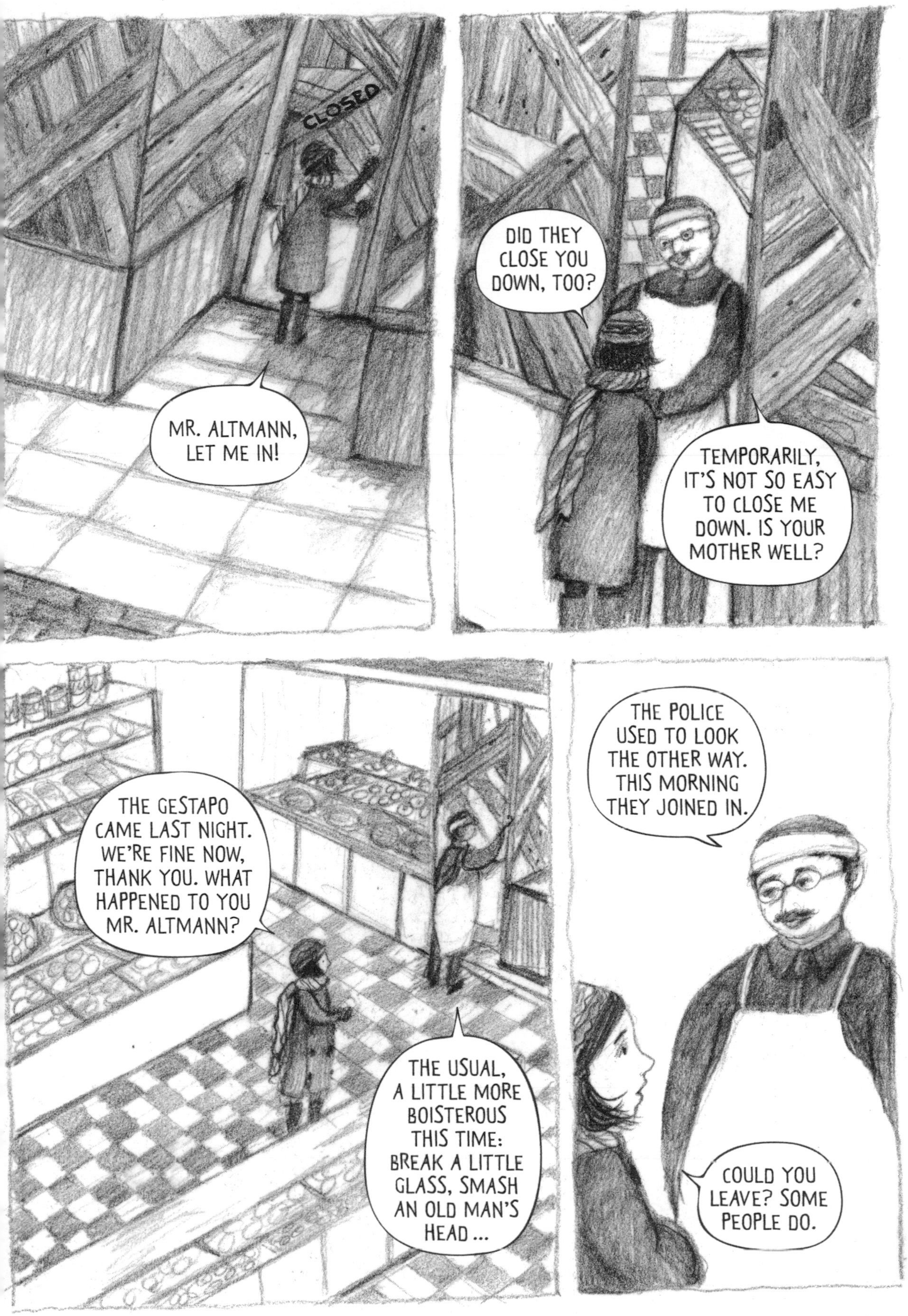
CLOSED
MR. ALTMANN, LET ME IN!
DID THEY CLOSE YOU DOWN, TOO?
TEMPORARILY, IT'S NOT SO EASY TO CLOSE ME DOWN. IS YOUR MOTHER WELL?
THE GESTAPO CAME LAST NIGHT. WE'RE FINE NOW, THANK YOU. WHAT HAPPENED TO YOU MR. ALTMANN?
THE USUAL, A LITTLE MORE BOISTEROUS THIS TIME: BREAK A LITTLE GLASS, SMASH AN OLD MAN'S HEAD ...
THE POLICE USED TO LOOK THE OTHER WAY. THIS MORNING THEY JOINED IN.
COULD YOU LEAVE? SOME PEOPLE DO.

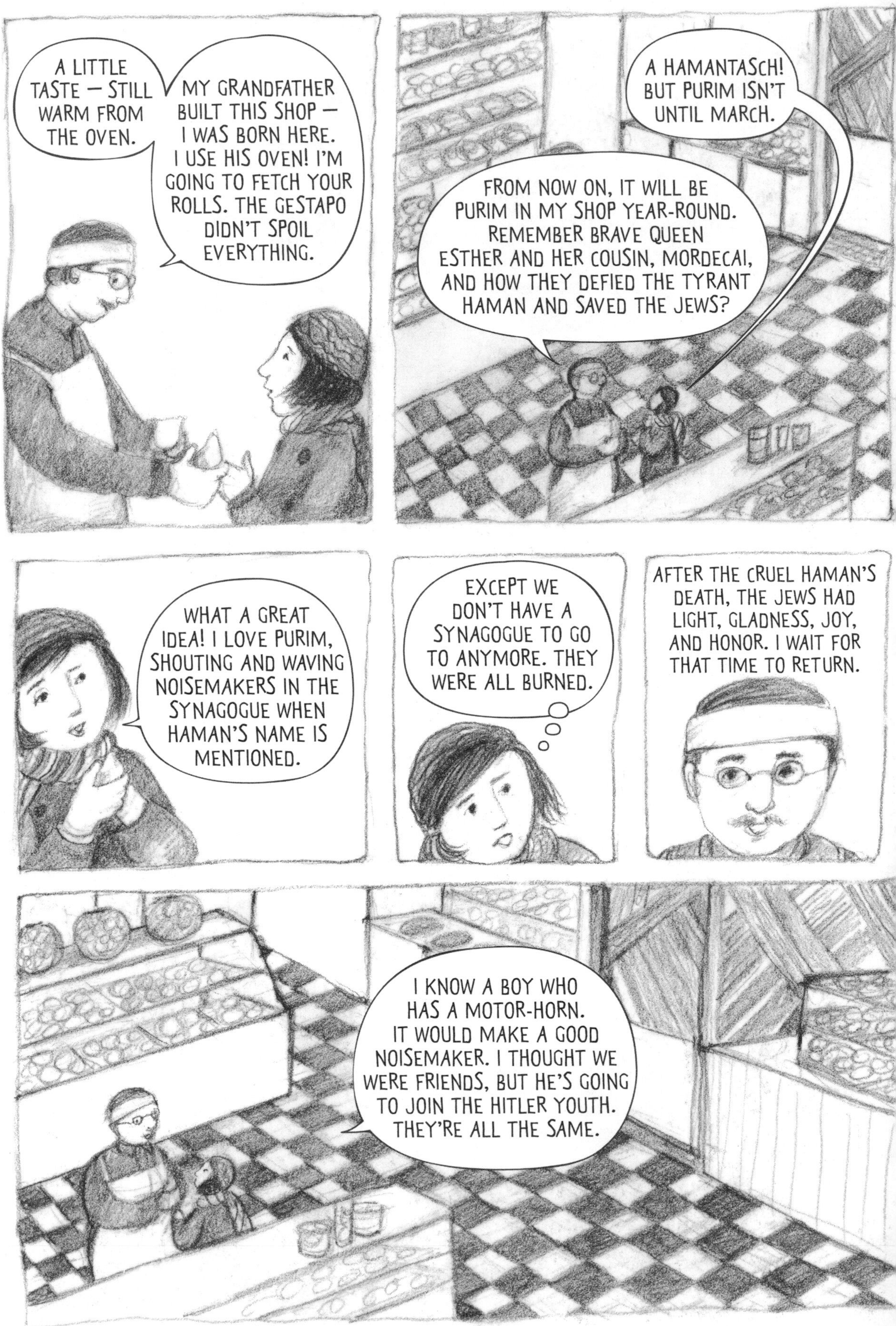
A LITTLE TASTE — STILL WARM FROM THE OVEN.
MY GRANDFATHER BUILT THIS SHOP — I WAS BORN HERE. I USE HIS OVEN! I'M GOING TO FETCH YOUR ROLLS. THE GESTAPO DIDN'T SPOIL EVERYTHING.
A HAMANTASCH! BUT PURIM ISN'T UNTIL MARCH.
FROM NOW ON, IT WILL BE PURIM IN MY SHOP YEAR-ROUND. REMEMBER BRAVE QUEEN ESTHER AND HER COUSIN, MORDECAI, AND HOW THEY DEFIED THE TYRANT HAMAN AND SAVED THE JEWS?
WHAT A GREAT IDEA! I LOVE PURIM, SHOUTING AND WAVING NOISEMAKERS IN THE SYNAGOGUE WHEN HAMAN'S NAME IS MENTIONED.
EXCEPT WE DON'T HAVE A SYNAGOGUE TO GO TO ANYMORE. THEY WERE ALL BURNED.
AFTER THE CRUEL HAMAN'S DEATH, THE JEWS HAD LIGHT, GLADNESS, JOY, AND HONOR. I WAIT FOR THAT TIME TO RETURN.
I KNOW A BOY WHO HAS A MOTOR-HORN. IT WOULD MAKE A GOOD NOISEMAKER. I THOUGHT WE WERE FRIENDS, BUT HE'S GOING TO JOIN THE HITLER YOUTH. THEY'RE ALL THE SAME.

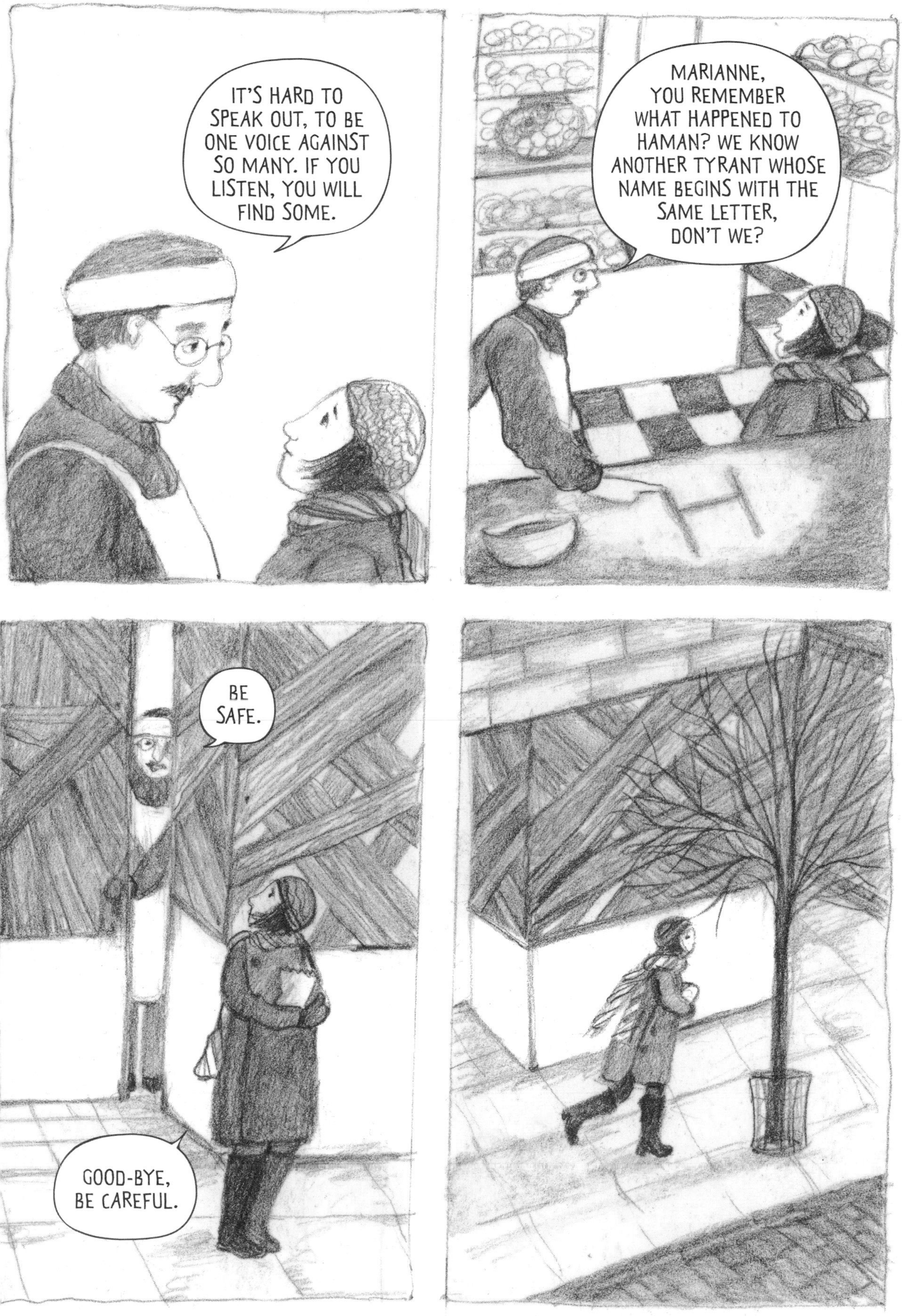
IT'S HARD TO SPEAK OUT, TO BE ONE VOICE AGAINST SO MANY. IF YOU LISTEN, YOU WILL FIND SOME.
MARIANNE, YOU REMEMBER WHAT HAPPENED TO HAMAN? WE KNOW ANOTHER TYRANT WHOSE NAME BEGINS WITH THE SAME LETTER, DON'T WE?
BE SAFE.
GOOD-BYE, BE CAREFUL.

CHAPTER EIGHT

LEAVING

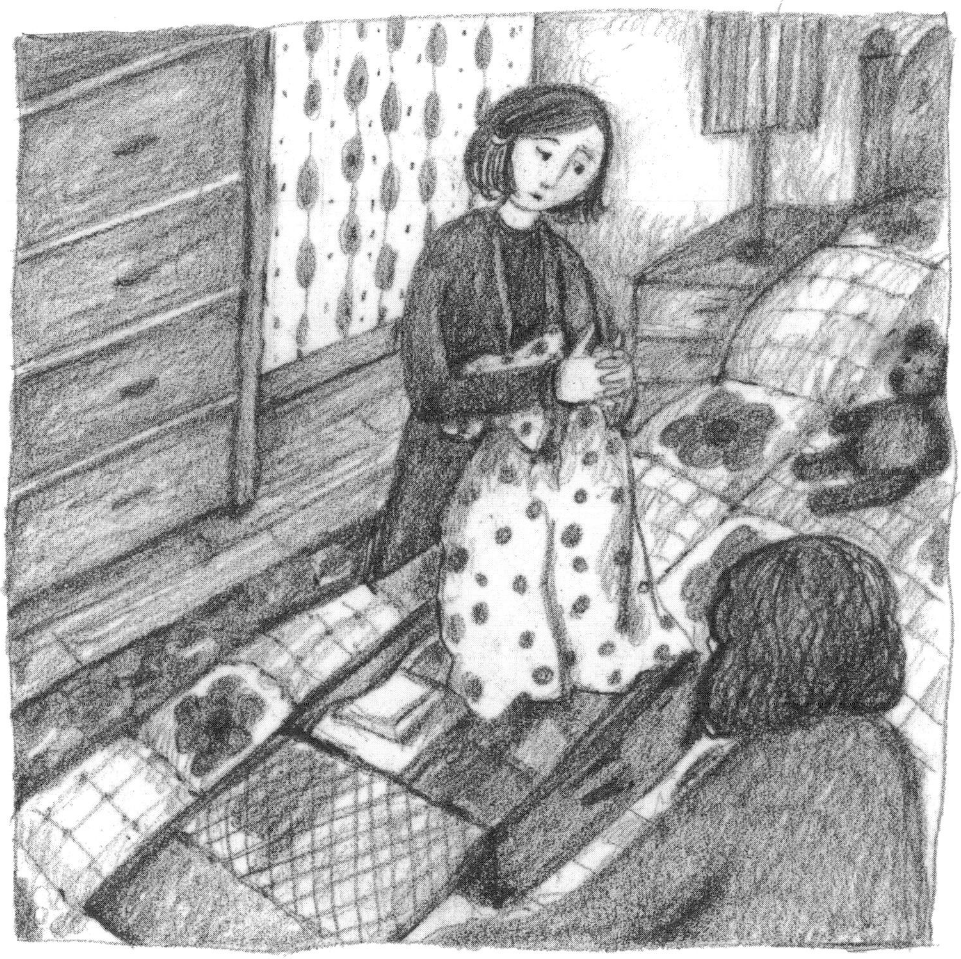

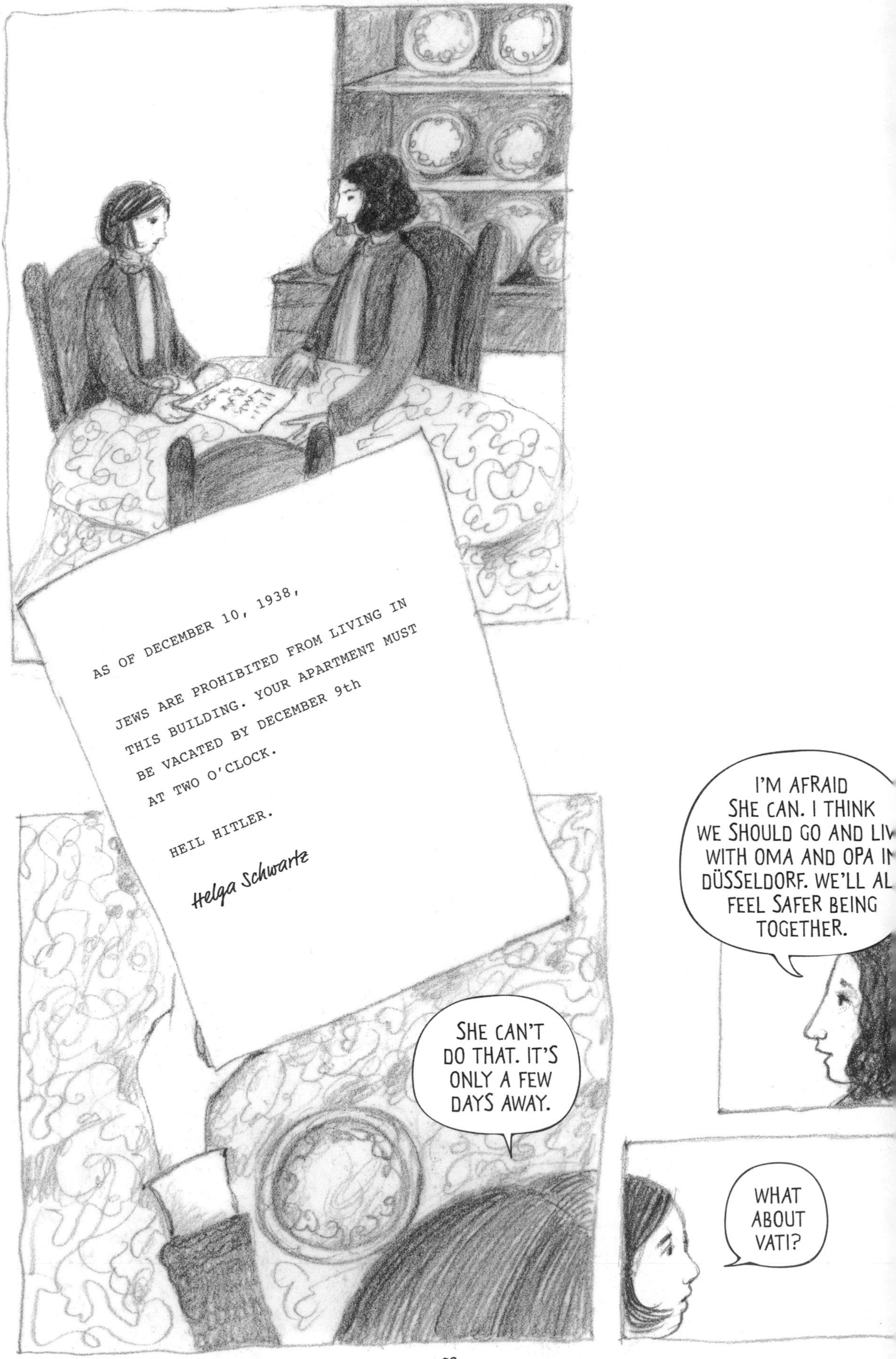
AS OF DECEMBER 10, 1938,
JEWS ARE PROHIBITED FROM LIVING IN THIS BUILDING. YOUR APARTMENT MUST BE VACATED BY DECEMBER 9th AT TWO O'CLOCK.
HEIL HITLER.
Helga Schwartz
SHE CAN'T DO THAT. IT'S ONLY A FEW DAYS AWAY.
I'M AFRAID SHE CAN. I THINK WE SHOULD GO AND LIV WITH OMA AND OPA IN DÜSSELDORF. WE'LL AL FEEL SAFER BEING TOGETHER.
WHAT ABOUT VATI?

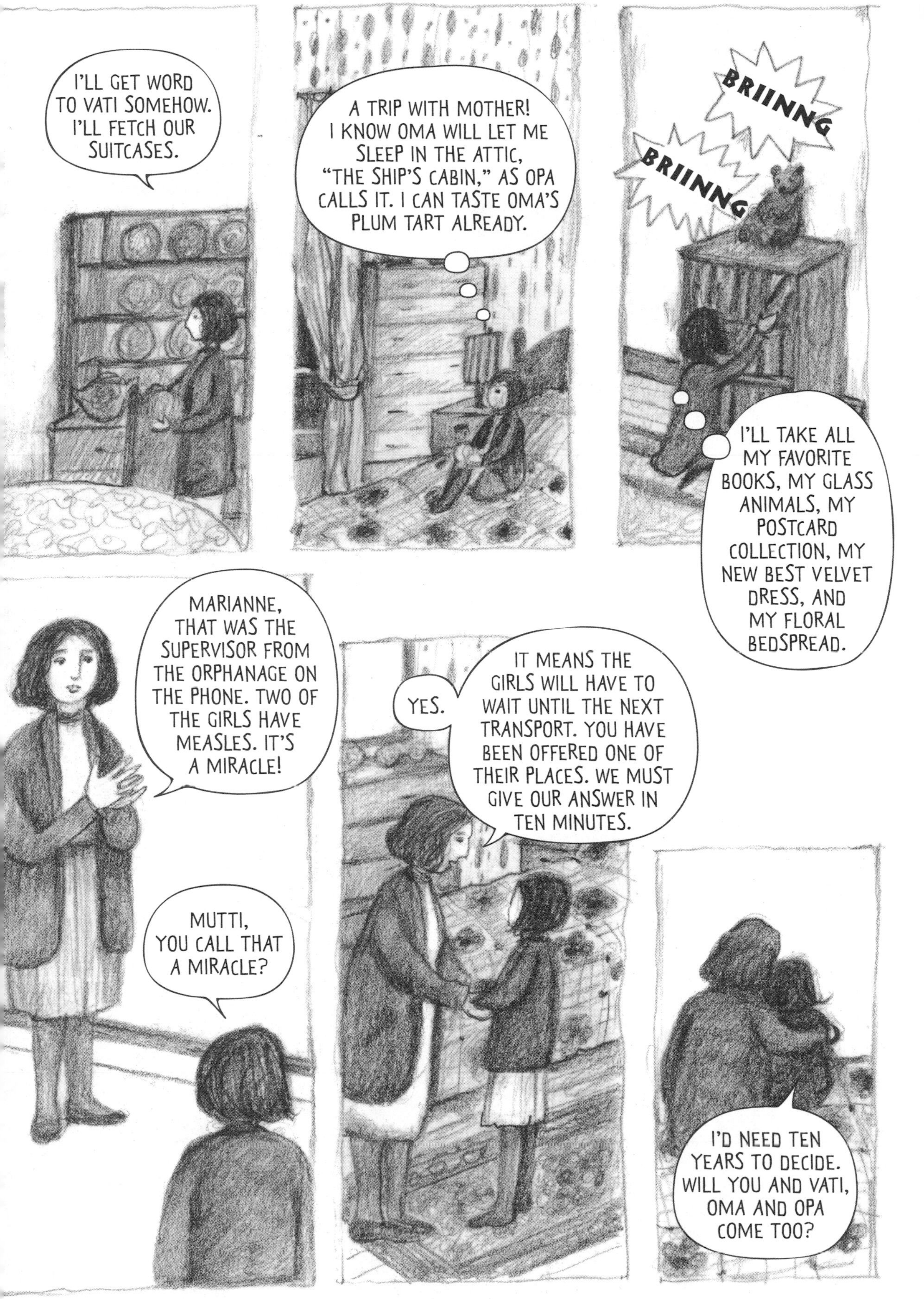

I'LL GET WORD TO VATI SOMEHOW. I'LL FETCH OUR SUITCASES.
A TRIP WITH MOTHER! I KNOW OMA WILL LET ME SLEEP IN THE ATTIC, "THE SHIP'S CABIN," AS OPA CALLS IT. I CAN TASTE OMA'S PLUM TART ALREADY.
BRIINNG
BRIINNG
I'LL TAKE ALL MY FAVORITE BOOKS, MY GLASS ANIMALS, MY POSTCARD COLLECTION, MY NEW BEST VELVET DRESS, AND MY FLORAL BEDSPREAD.
MARIANNE, THAT WAS THE SUPERVISOR FROM THE ORPHANAGE ON THE PHONE. TWO OF THE GIRLS HAVE MEASLES. IT'S A MIRACLE!
MUTTI, YOU CALL THAT A MIRACLE?
YES.
IT MEANS THE GIRLS WILL HAVE TO WAIT UNTIL THE NEXT TRANSPORT. YOU HAVE BEEN OFFERED ONE OF THEIR PLACES. WE MUST GIVE OUR ANSWER IN TEN MINUTES.
I'D NEED TEN YEARS TO DECIDE. WILL YOU AND VATI, OMA AND OPA COME TOO?

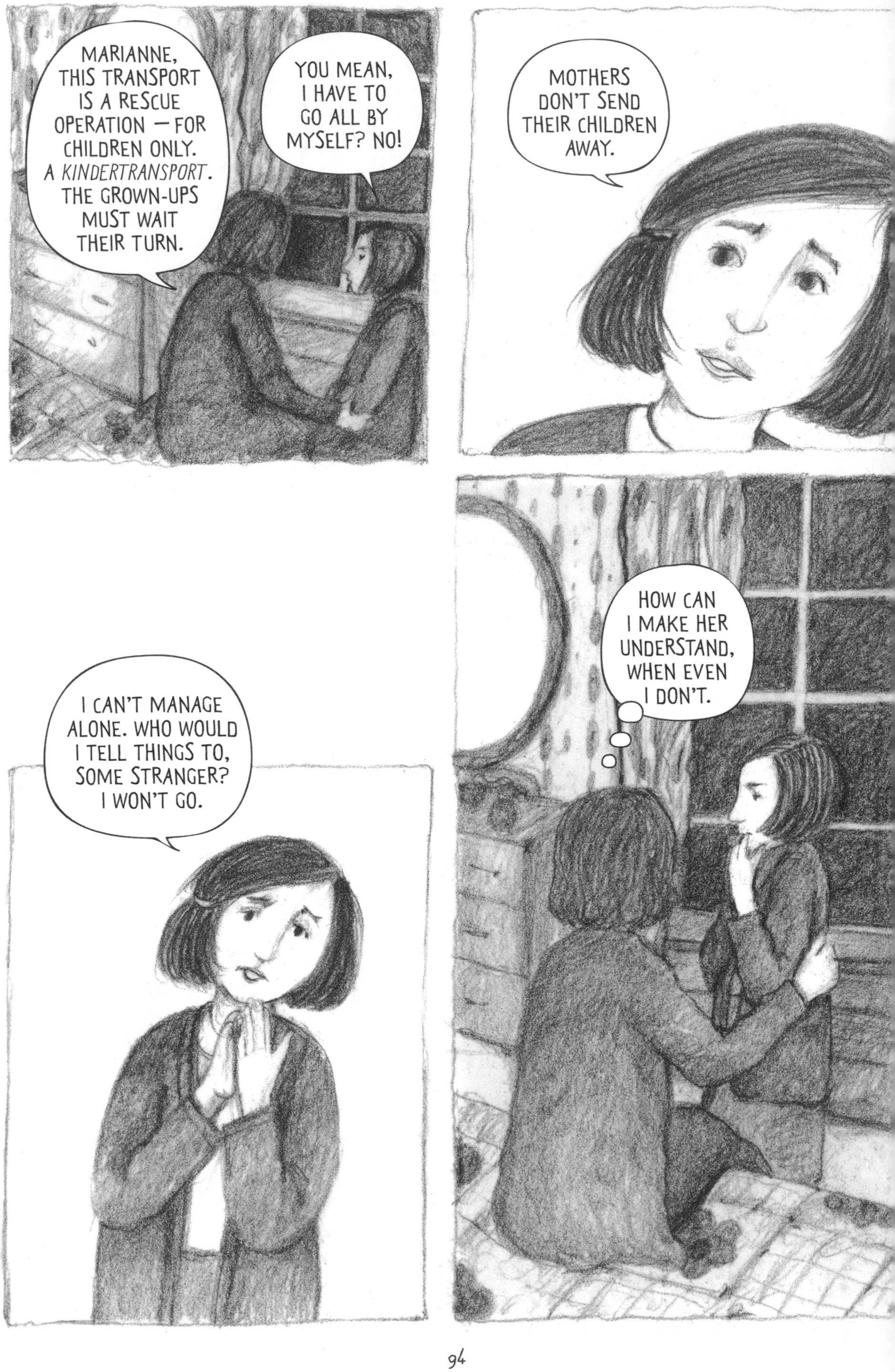
MARIANNE, THIS TRANSPORT IS A RESCUE OPERATION — FOR CHILDREN ONLY. A *KINDERTRANSPORT*. THE GROWN-UPS MUST WAIT THEIR TURN.
YOU MEAN, I HAVE TO GO ALL BY MYSELF? NO!
MOTHERS DON'T SEND THEIR CHILDREN AWAY.
I CAN'T MANAGE ALONE. WHO WOULD I TELL THINGS TO, SOME STRANGER? I WON'T GO.
HOW CAN I MAKE HER UNDERSTAND, WHEN EVEN I DON'T.

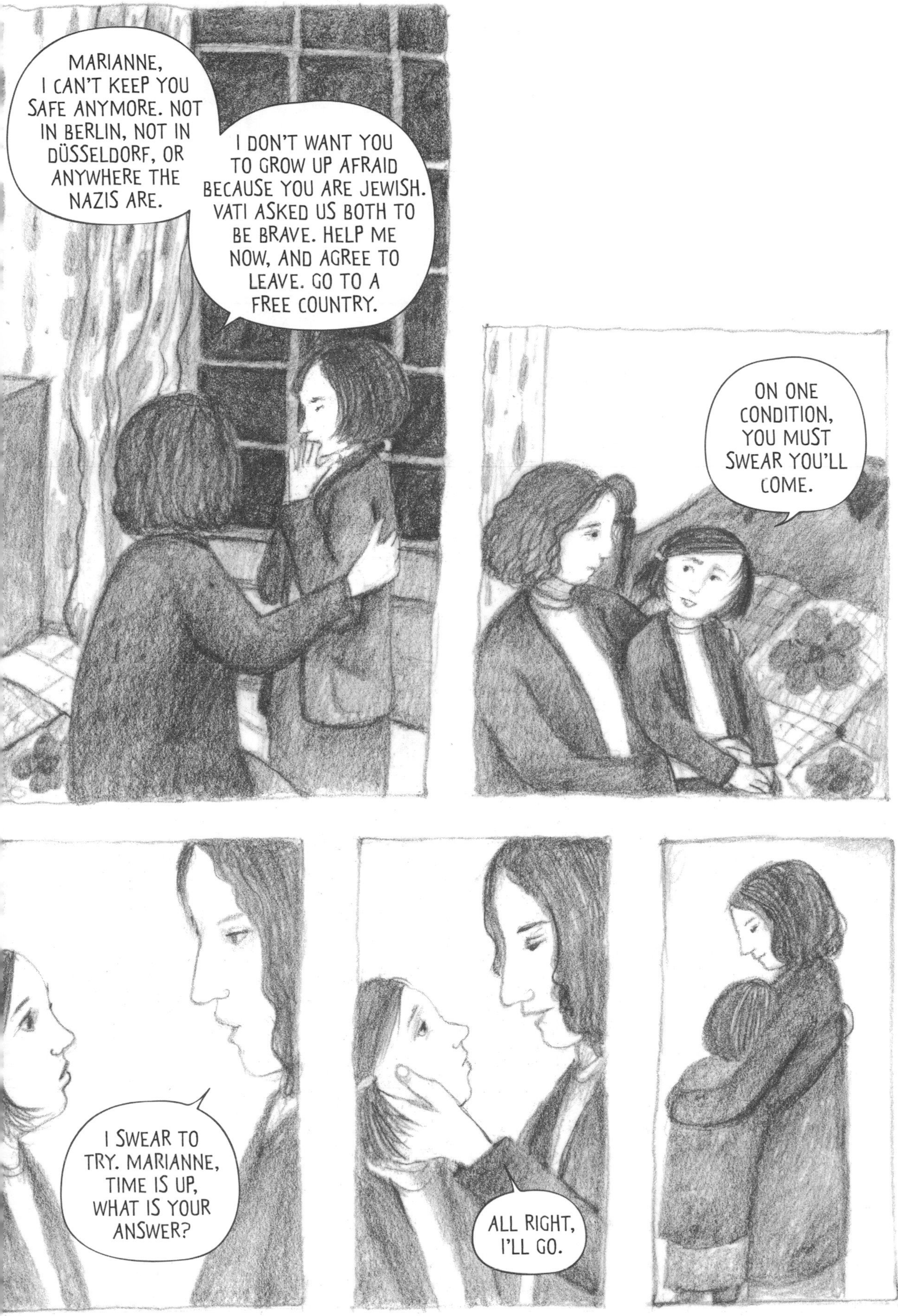
MARIANNE, I CAN'T KEEP YOU SAFE ANYMORE. NOT IN BERLIN, NOT IN DÜSSELDORF, OR ANYWHERE THE NAZIS ARE.
I DON'T WANT YOU TO GROW UP AFRAID BECAUSE YOU ARE JEWISH. VATI ASKED US BOTH TO BE BRAVE. HELP ME NOW, AND AGREE TO LEAVE. GO TO A FREE COUNTRY.
ON ONE CONDITION, YOU MUST SWEAR YOU'LL COME.
I SWEAR TO TRY. MARIANNE, TIME IS UP, WHAT IS YOUR ANSWER?
ALL RIGHT, I'LL GO.

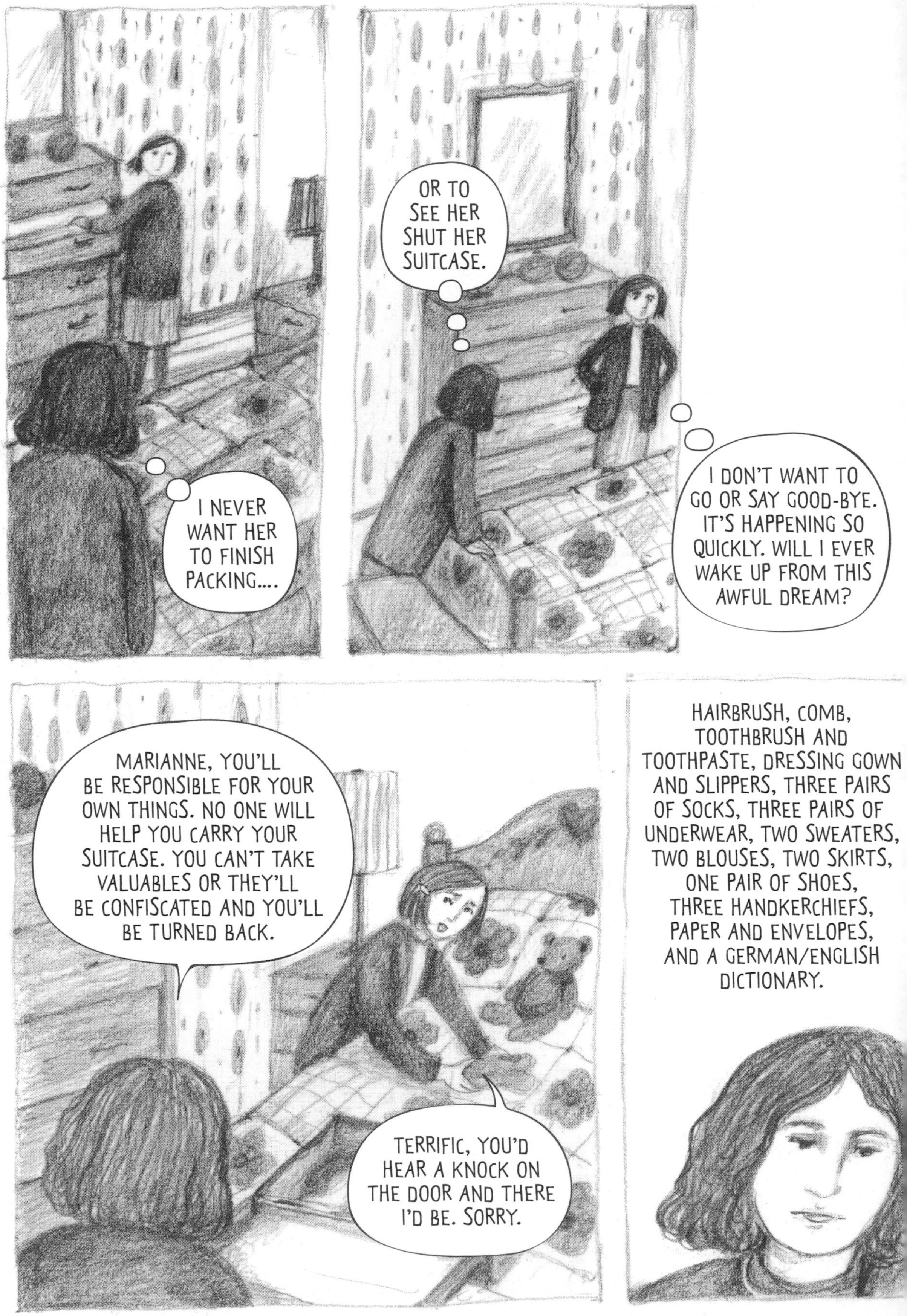
I NEVER WANT HER TO FINISH PACKING....
OR TO SEE HER SHUT HER SUITCASE.
I DON'T WANT TO GO OR SAY GOOD-BYE. IT'S HAPPENING SO QUICKLY. WILL I EVER WAKE UP FROM THIS AWFUL DREAM?
MARIANNE, YOU'LL BE RESPONSIBLE FOR YOUR OWN THINGS. NO ONE WILL HELP YOU CARRY YOUR SUITCASE. YOU CAN'T TAKE VALUABLES OR THEY'LL BE CONFISCATED AND YOU'LL BE TURNED BACK.
TERRIFIC, YOU'D HEAR A KNOCK ON THE DOOR AND THERE I'D BE. SORRY.
HAIRBRUSH, COMB, TOOTHBRUSH AND TOOTHPASTE, DRESSING GOWN AND SLIPPERS, THREE PAIRS OF SOCKS, THREE PAIRS OF UNDERWEAR, TWO SWEATERS, TWO BLOUSES, TWO SKIRTS, ONE PAIR OF SHOES, THREE HANDKERCHIEFS, PAPER AND ENVELOPES, AND A GERMAN/ENGLISH DICTIONARY.

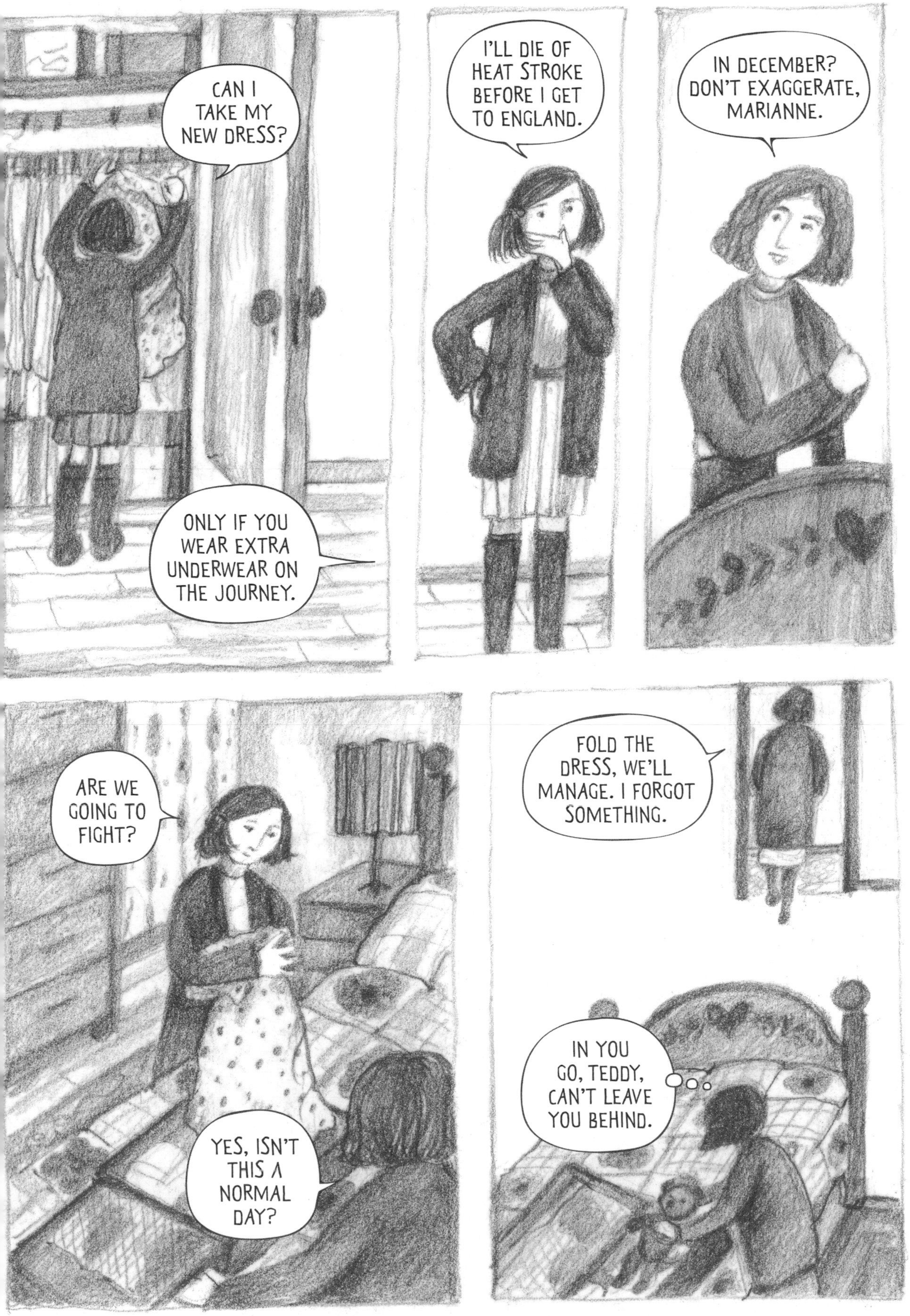
CAN I TAKE MY NEW DRESS?
ONLY IF YOU WEAR EXTRA UNDERWEAR ON THE JOURNEY.
I'LL DIE OF HEAT STROKE BEFORE I GET TO ENGLAND.
IN DECEMBER? DON'T EXAGGERATE, MARIANNE.
ARE WE GOING TO FIGHT?
YES, ISN'T THIS A NORMAL DAY?
FOLD THE DRESS, WE'LL MANAGE. I FORGOT SOMETHING.
IN YOU GO, TEDDY, CAN'T LEAVE YOU BEHIND.

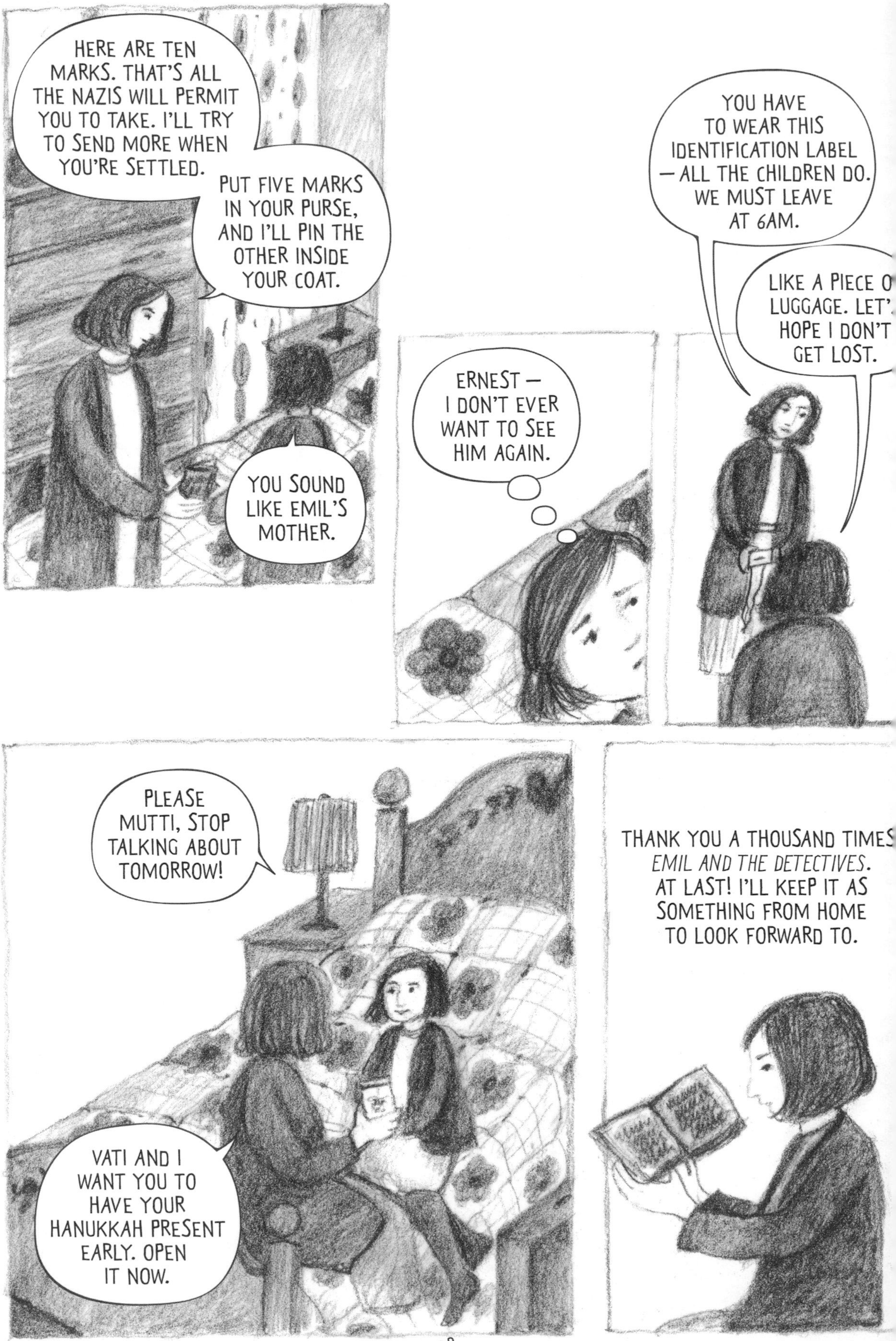
HERE ARE TEN MARKS. THAT'S ALL THE NAZIS WILL PERMIT YOU TO TAKE. I'LL TRY TO SEND MORE WHEN YOU'RE SETTLED.
PUT FIVE MARKS IN YOUR PURSE, AND I'LL PIN THE OTHER INSIDE YOUR COAT.
YOU SOUND LIKE EMIL'S MOTHER.
ERNEST — I DON'T EVER WANT TO SEE HIM AGAIN.
YOU HAVE TO WEAR THIS IDENTIFICATION LABEL — ALL THE CHILDREN DO. WE MUST LEAVE AT 6AM.
LIKE A PIECE O LUGGAGE. LET' HOPE I DON'T GET LOST.
PLEASE MUTTI, STOP TALKING ABOUT TOMORROW!
VATI AND I WANT YOU TO HAVE YOUR HANUKKAH PRESENT EARLY. OPEN IT NOW.
THANK YOU A THOUSAND TIMES *EMIL AND THE DETECTIVES.* AT LAST! I'LL KEEP IT AS SOMETHING FROM HOME TO LOOK FORWARD TO.

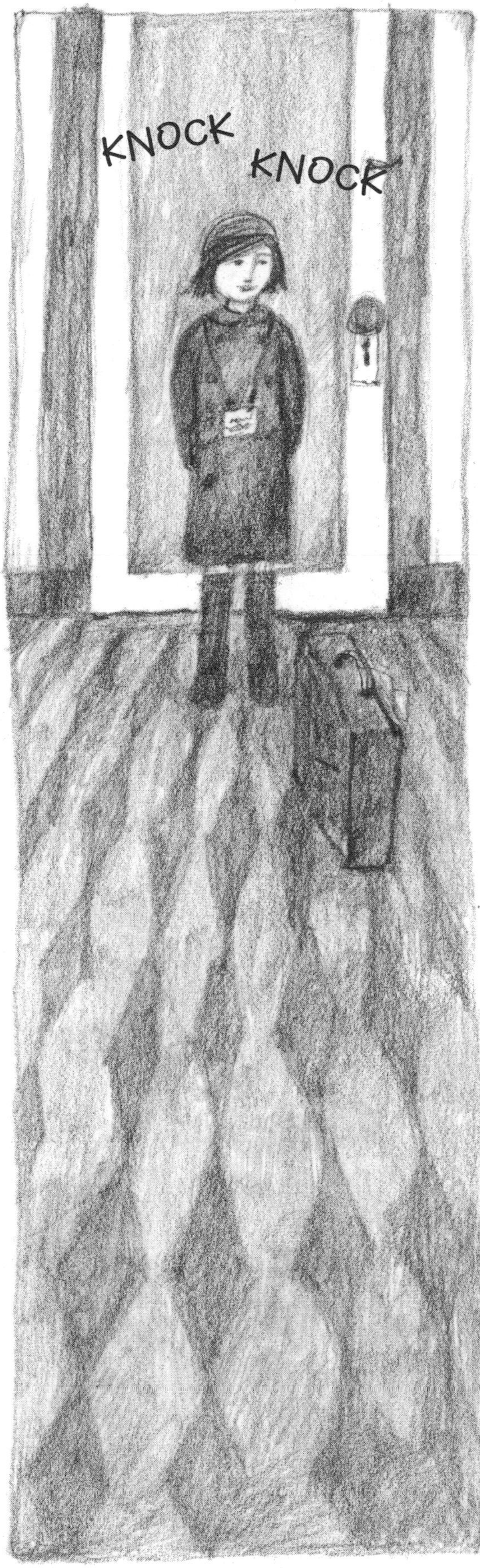
KNOCK
KNOCK

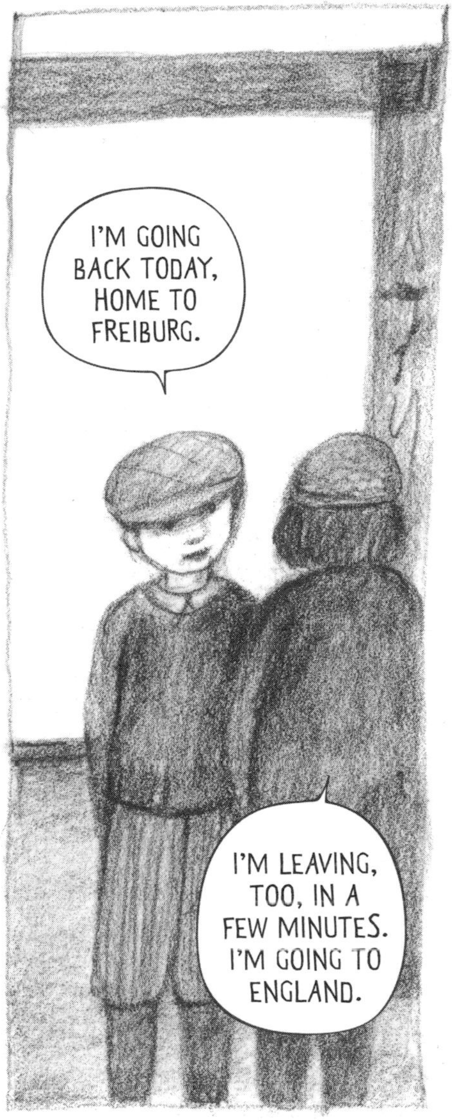
I'M GOING BACK TODAY, HOME TO FREIBURG.
I'M LEAVING, TOO, IN A FEW MINUTES. I'M GOING TO ENGLAND.

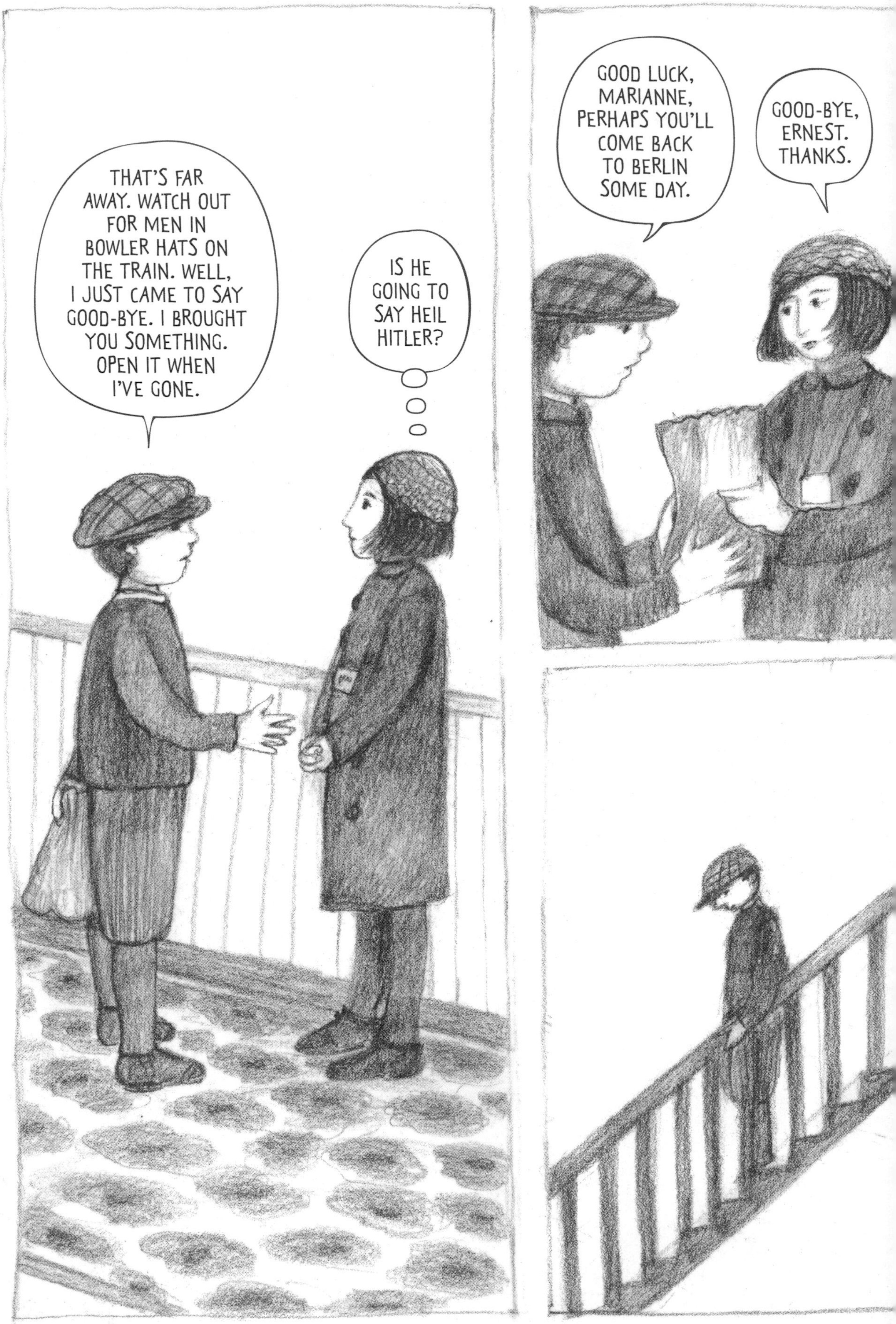
THAT'S FAR AWAY. WATCH OUT FOR MEN IN BOWLER HATS ON THE TRAIN. WELL, I JUST CAME TO SAY GOOD-BYE. I BROUGHT YOU SOMETHING. OPEN IT WHEN I'VE GONE.
IS HE GOING TO SAY HEIL HITLER?
GOOD LUCK, MARIANNE, PERHAPS YOU'LL COME BACK TO BERLIN SOME DAY.
GOOD-BYE, ERNEST. THANKS.

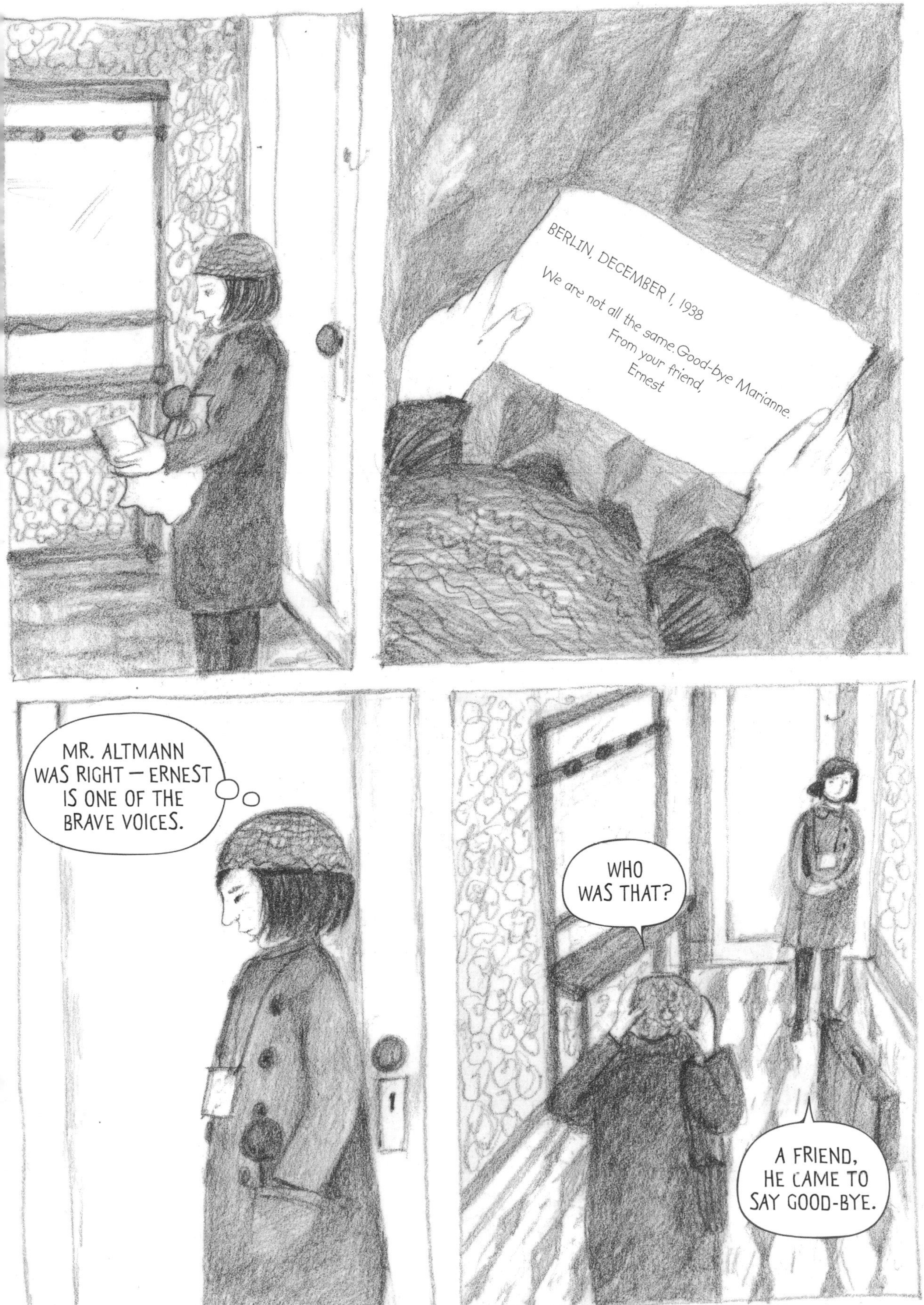
BERLIN, DECEMBER 1, 1938
We are not all the same. Good-bye Marianne.
From your friend,
Ernest
MR. ALTMANN WAS RIGHT — ERNEST IS ONE OF THE BRAVE VOICES.
WHO WAS THAT?
A FRIEND, HE CAME TO SAY GOOD-BYE.

CHAPTER NINE

THE TRAIN

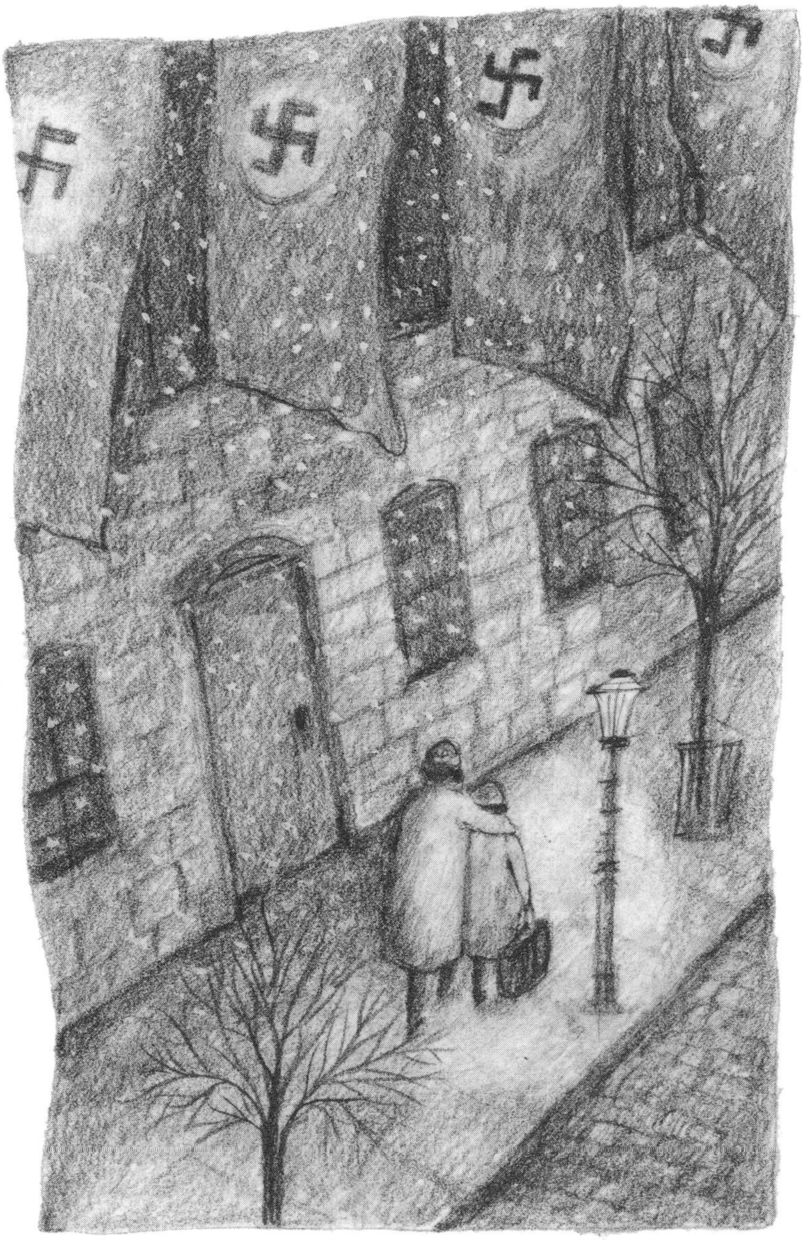

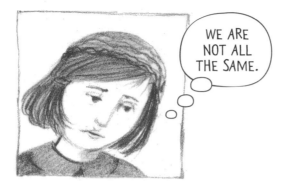

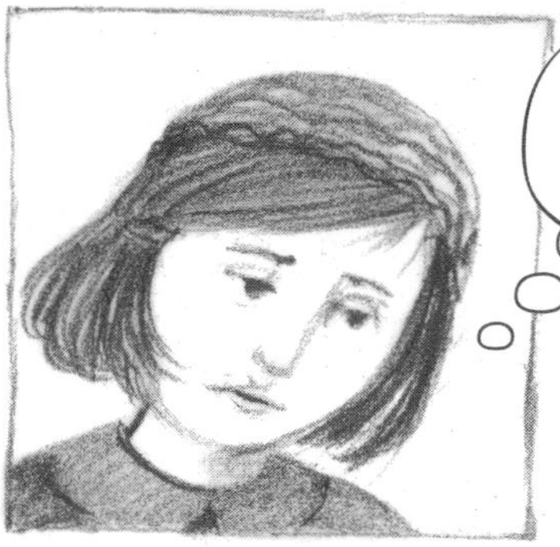
WE ARE NOT ALL THE SAME.

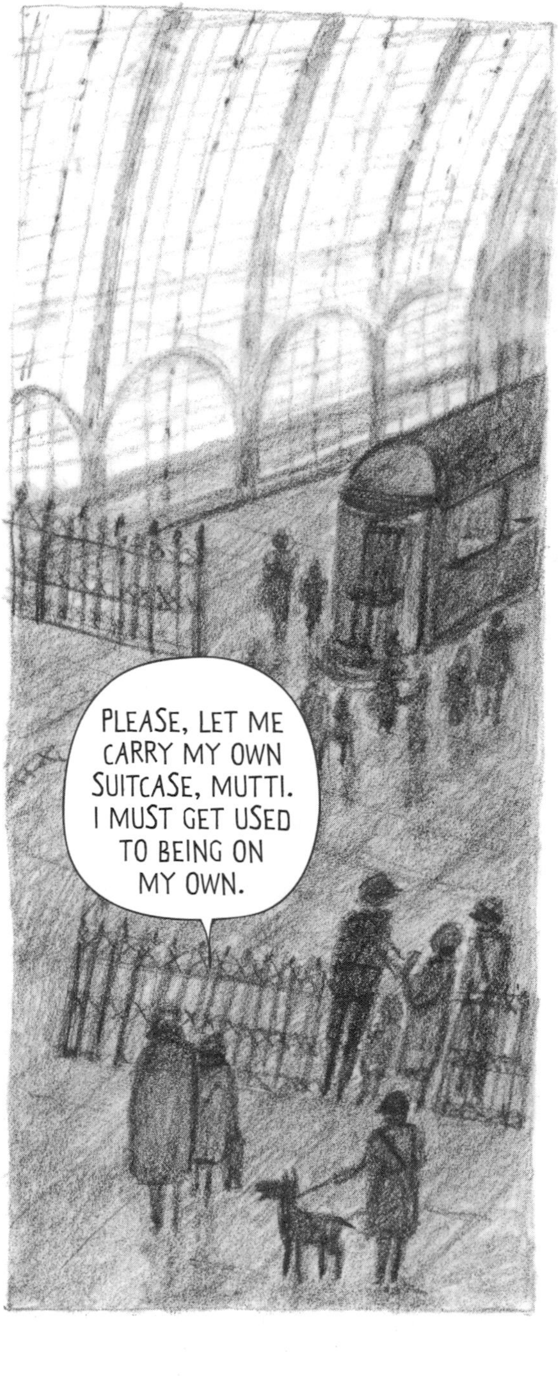
PLEASE, LET ME CARRY MY OWN SUITCASE, MUTTI. I MUST GET USED TO BEING ON MY OWN.

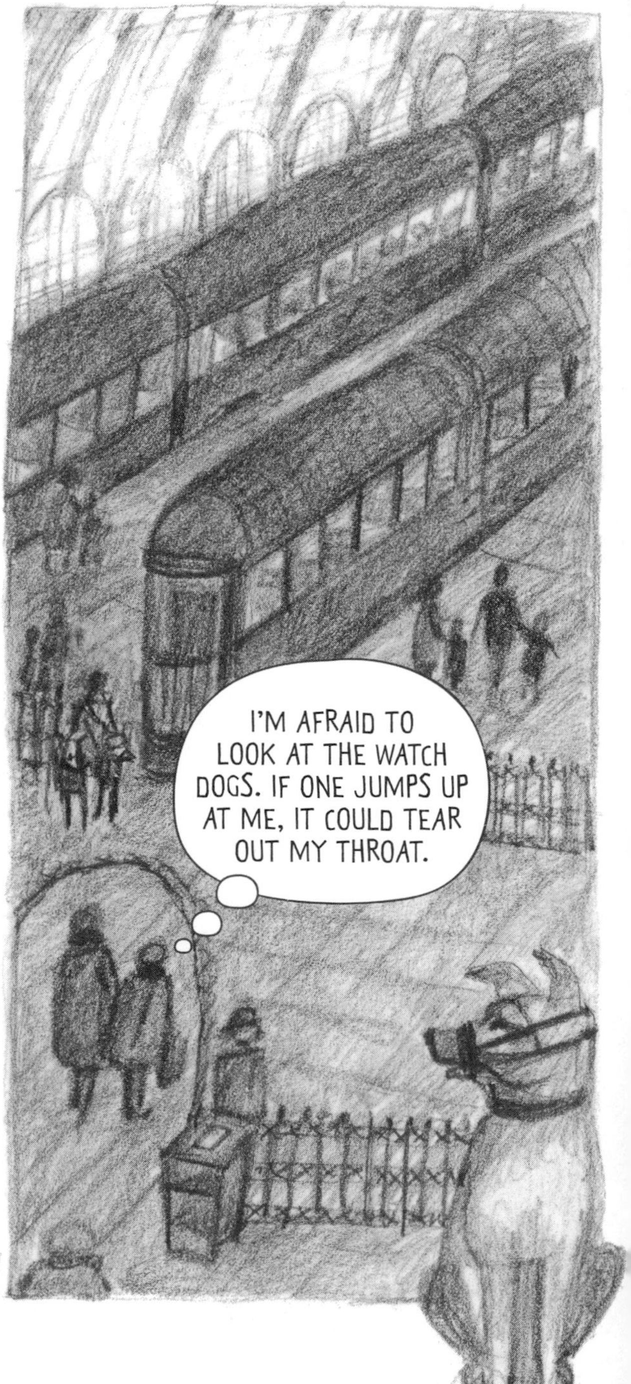
I'M AFRAID TO LOOK AT THE WATCH DOGS. IF ONE JUMPS UP AT ME, IT COULD TEAR OUT MY THROAT.

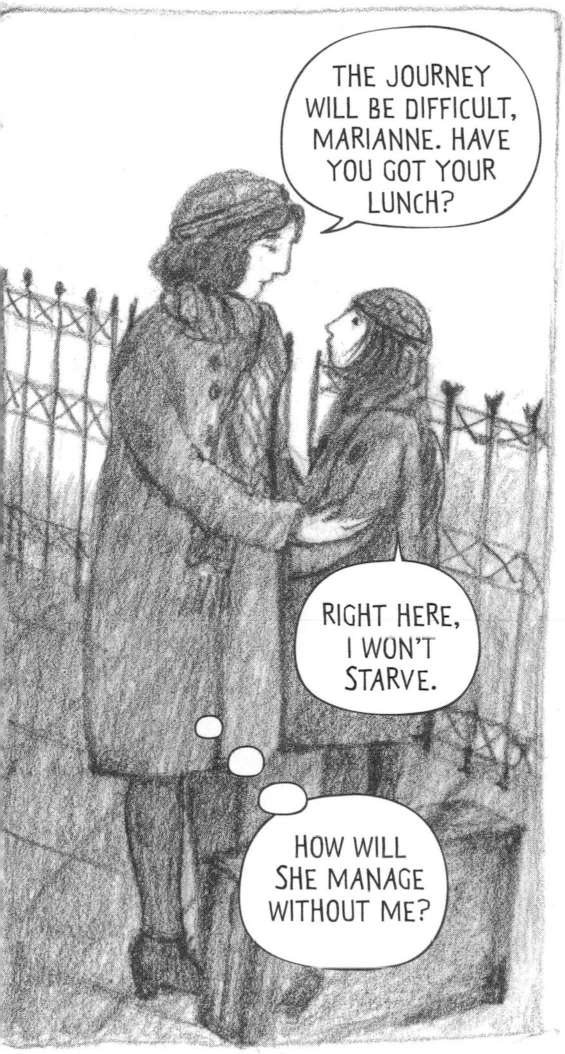
THE JOURNEY WILL BE DIFFICULT, MARIANNE. HAVE YOU GOT YOUR LUNCH?
RIGHT HERE, I WON'T STARVE.
HOW WILL SHE MANAGE WITHOUT ME?

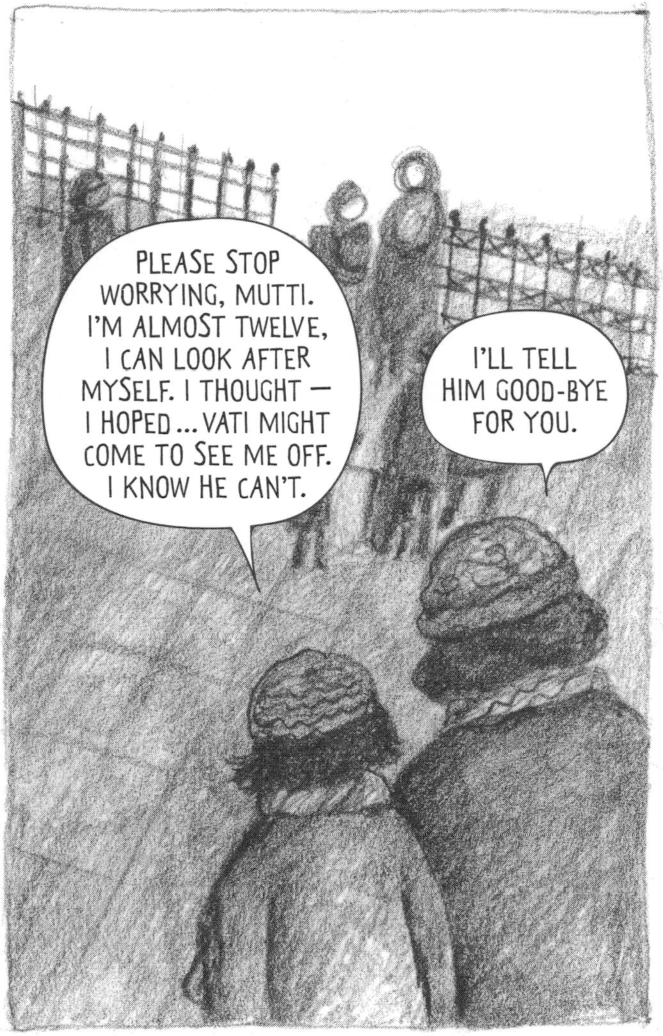
PLEASE STOP WORRYING, MUTTI. I'M ALMOST TWELVE, I CAN LOOK AFTER MYSELF. I THOUGHT — I HOPED ... VATI MIGHT COME TO SEE ME OFF. I KNOW HE CAN'T.
I'LL TELL HIM GOOD-BYE FOR YOU.

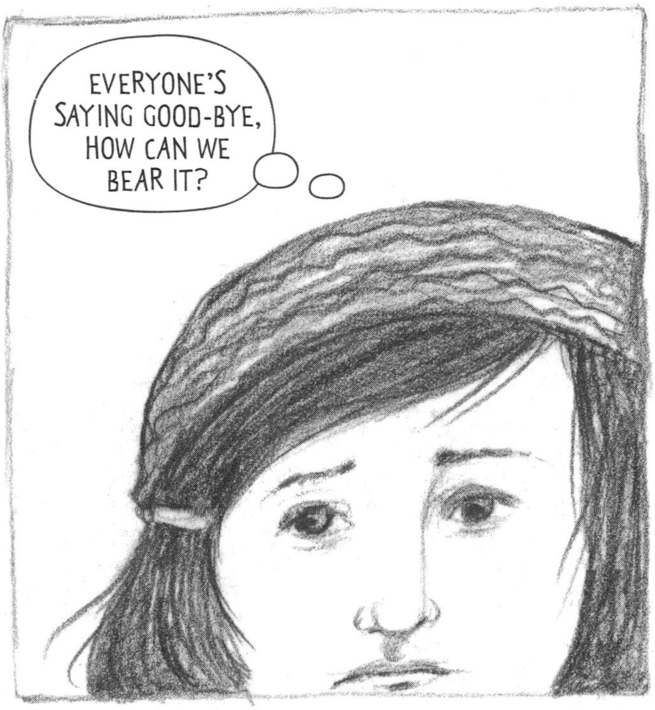
EVERYONE'S SAYING GOOD-BYE, HOW CAN WE BEAR IT?

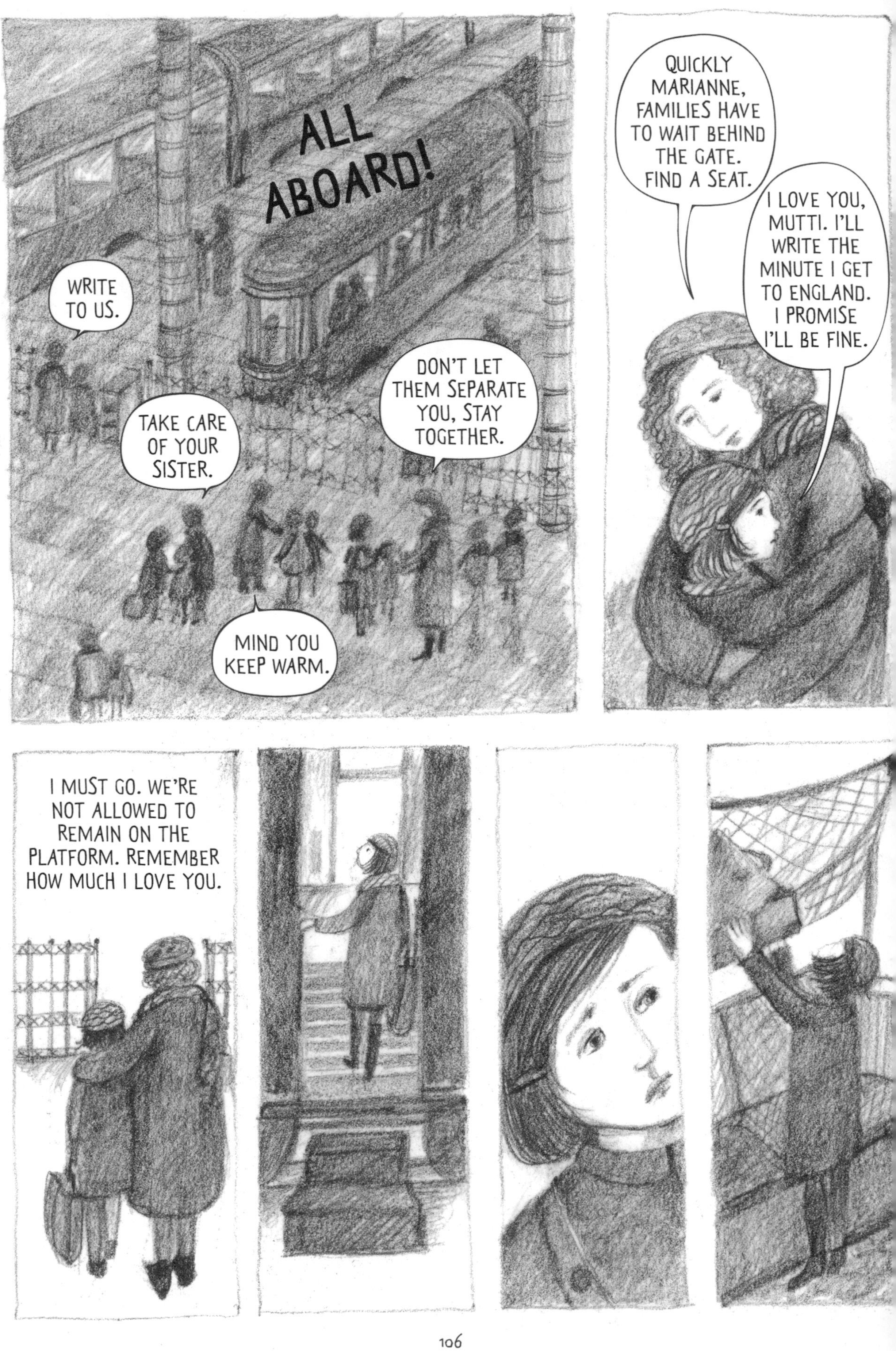
ALL ABOARD!
WRITE TO US.
TAKE CARE OF YOUR SISTER.
DON'T LET THEM SEPARATE YOU, STAY TOGETHER.
MIND YOU KEEP WARM.
QUICKLY MARIANNE, FAMILIES HAVE TO WAIT BEHIND THE GATE. FIND A SEAT.
I LOVE YOU, MUTTI. I'LL WRITE THE MINUTE I GET TO ENGLAND. I PROMISE I'LL BE FINE.
I MUST GO. WE'RE NOT ALLOWED TO REMAIN ON THE PLATFORM. REMEMBER HOW MUCH I LOVE YOU.

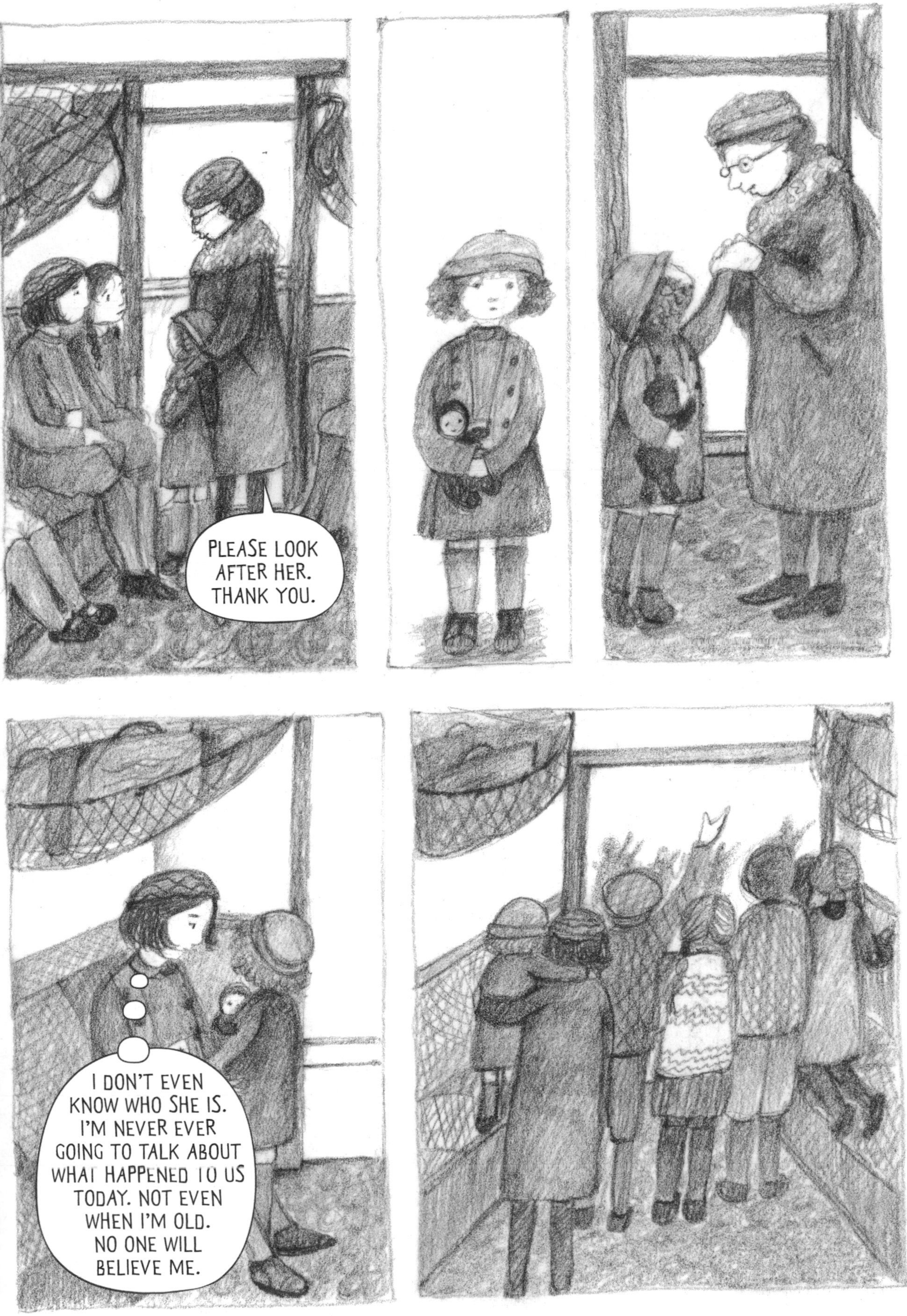
PLEASE LOOK AFTER HER. THANK YOU.
I DON'T EVEN KNOW WHO SHE IS. I'M NEVER EVER GOING TO TALK ABOUT WHAT HAPPENED TO US TODAY. NOT EVEN WHEN I'M OLD. NO ONE WILL BELIEVE ME.

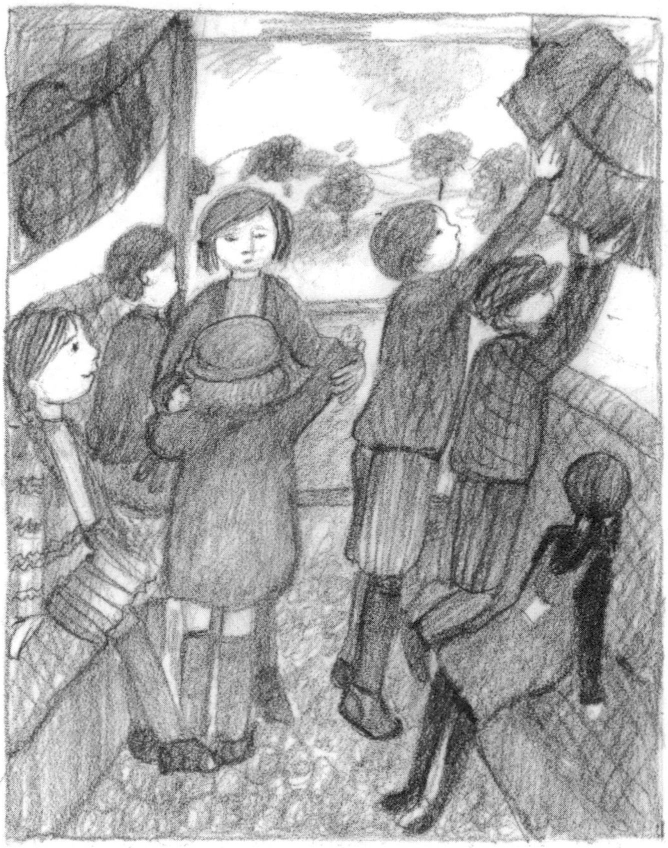

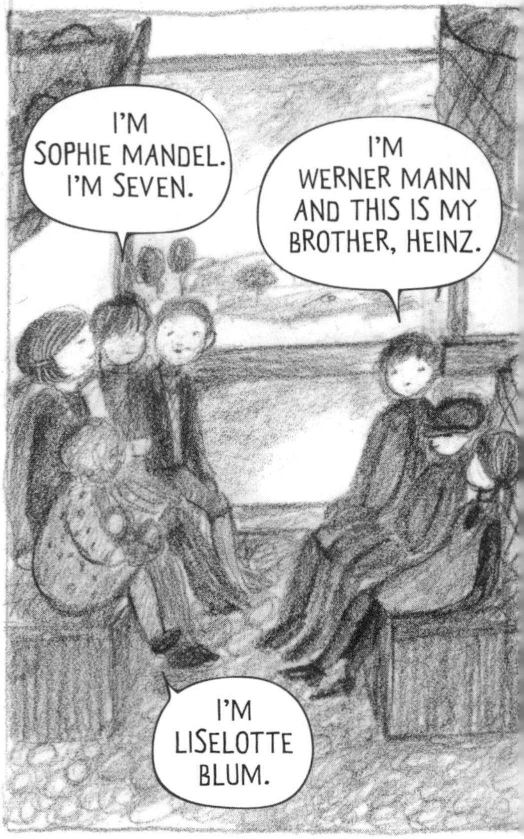
I'M SOPHIE MANDEL. I'M SEVEN.
I'M WERNER MANN AND THIS IS MY BROTHER, HEINZ.
I'M LISELOTTE BLUM.

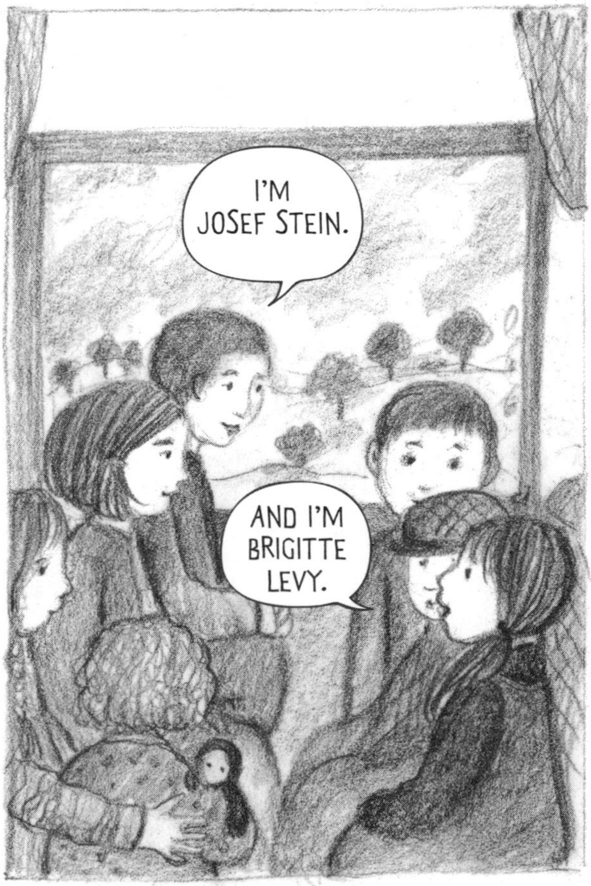
I'M JOSEF STEIN.
AND I'M BRIGITTE LEVY.

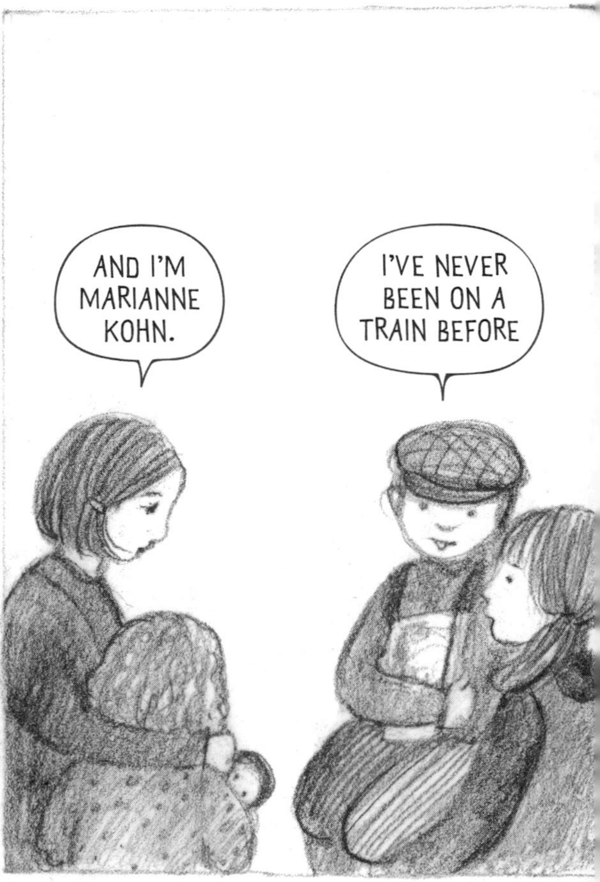
AND I'M MARIANNE KOHN.
I'VE NEVER BEEN ON A TRAIN BEFORE

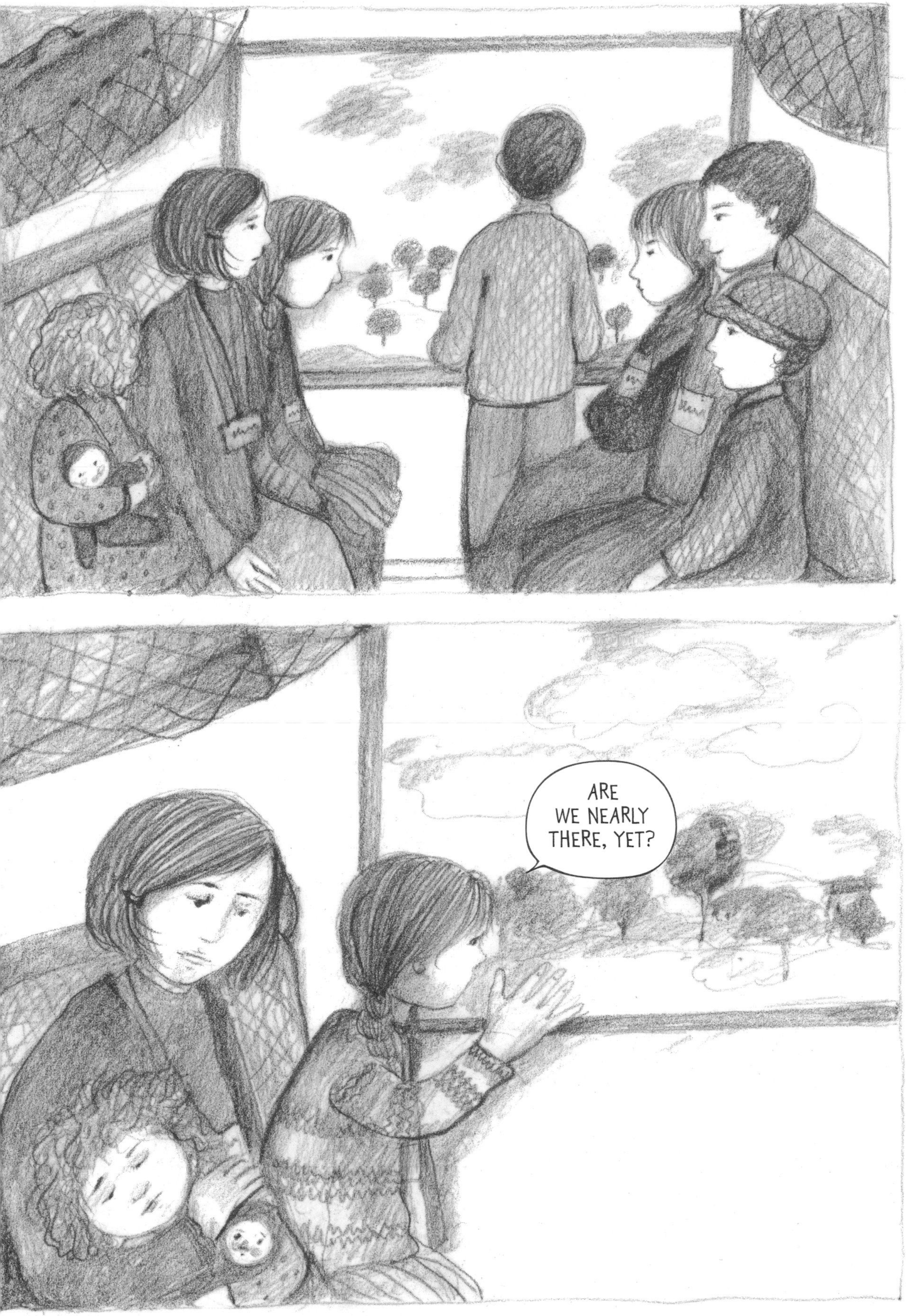
ARE WE NEARLY THERE, YET?

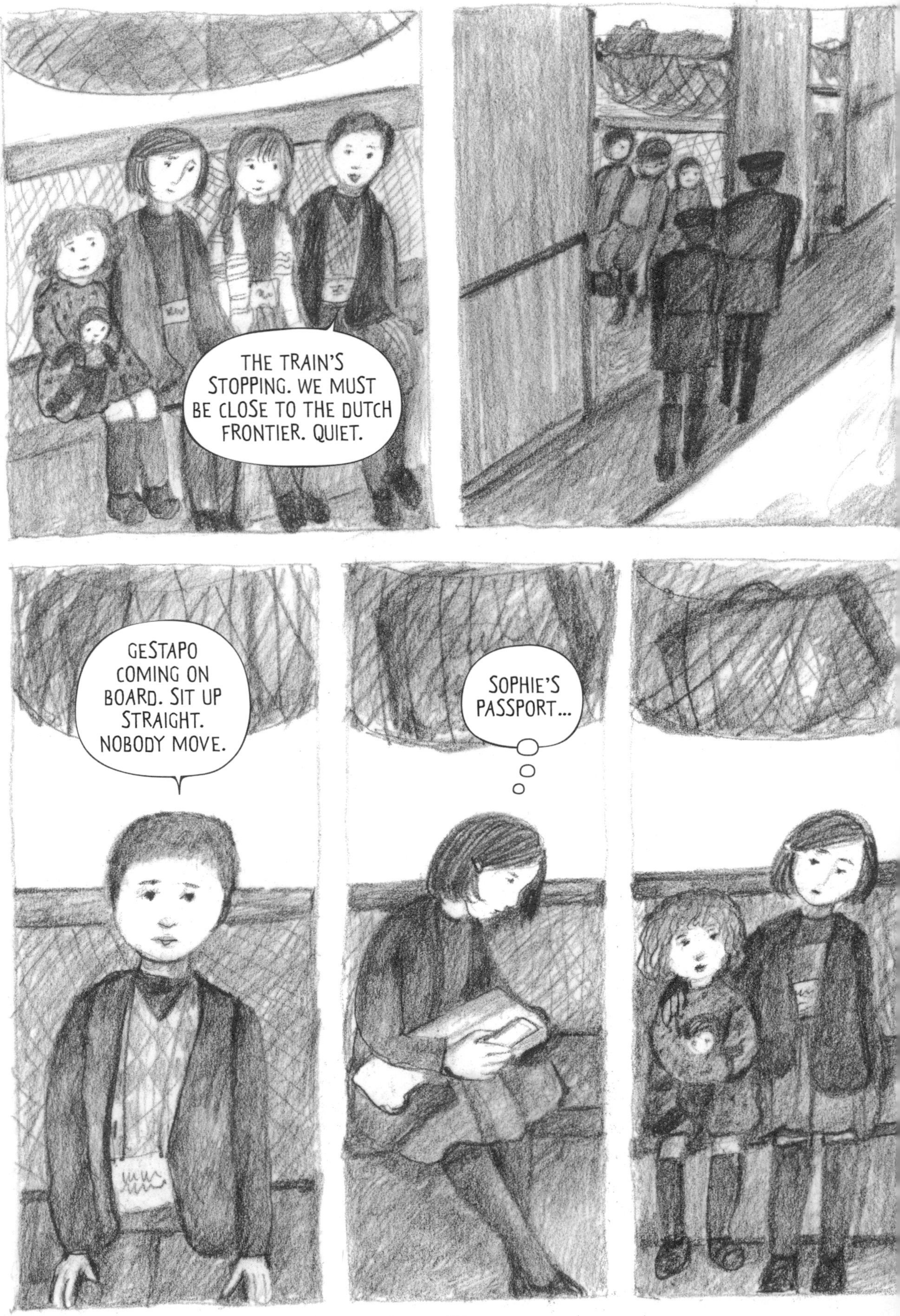
THE TRAIN'S STOPPING. WE MUST BE CLOSE TO THE DUTCH FRONTIER. QUIET.
GESTAPO COMING ON BOARD. SIT UP STRAIGHT. NOBODY MOVE.
SOPHIE'S PASSPORT...

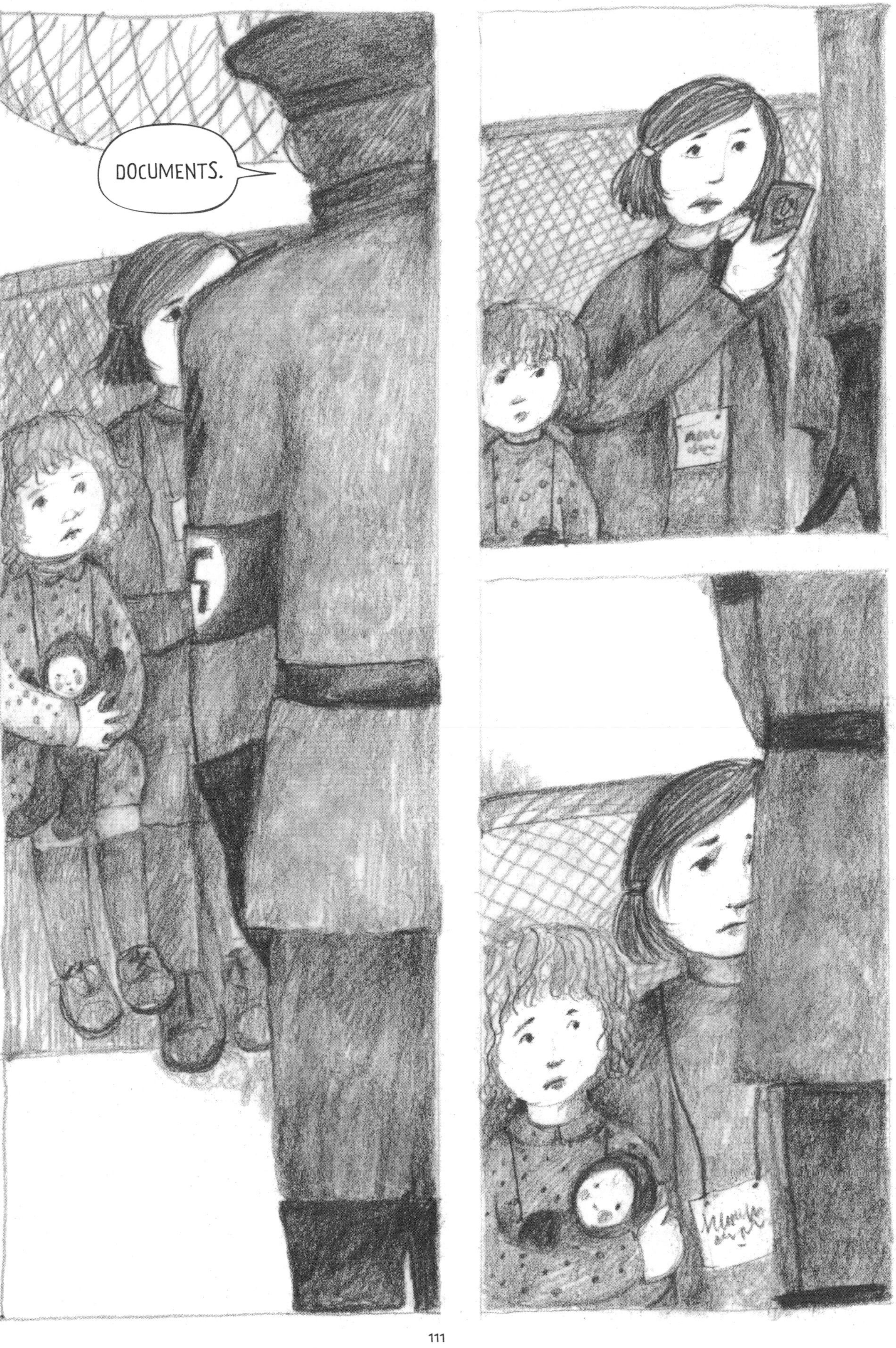
DOCUMENTS.

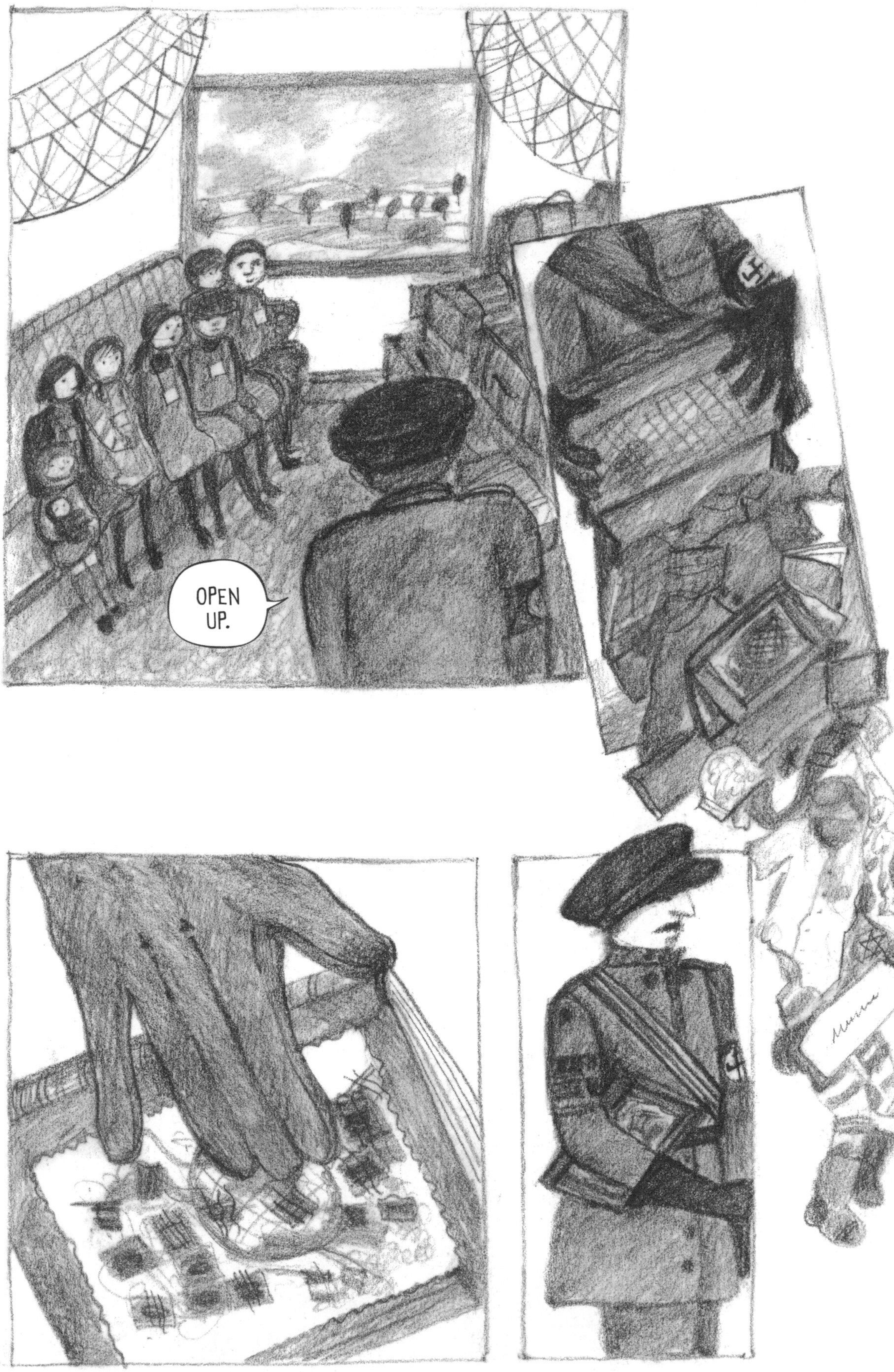
OPEN UP.

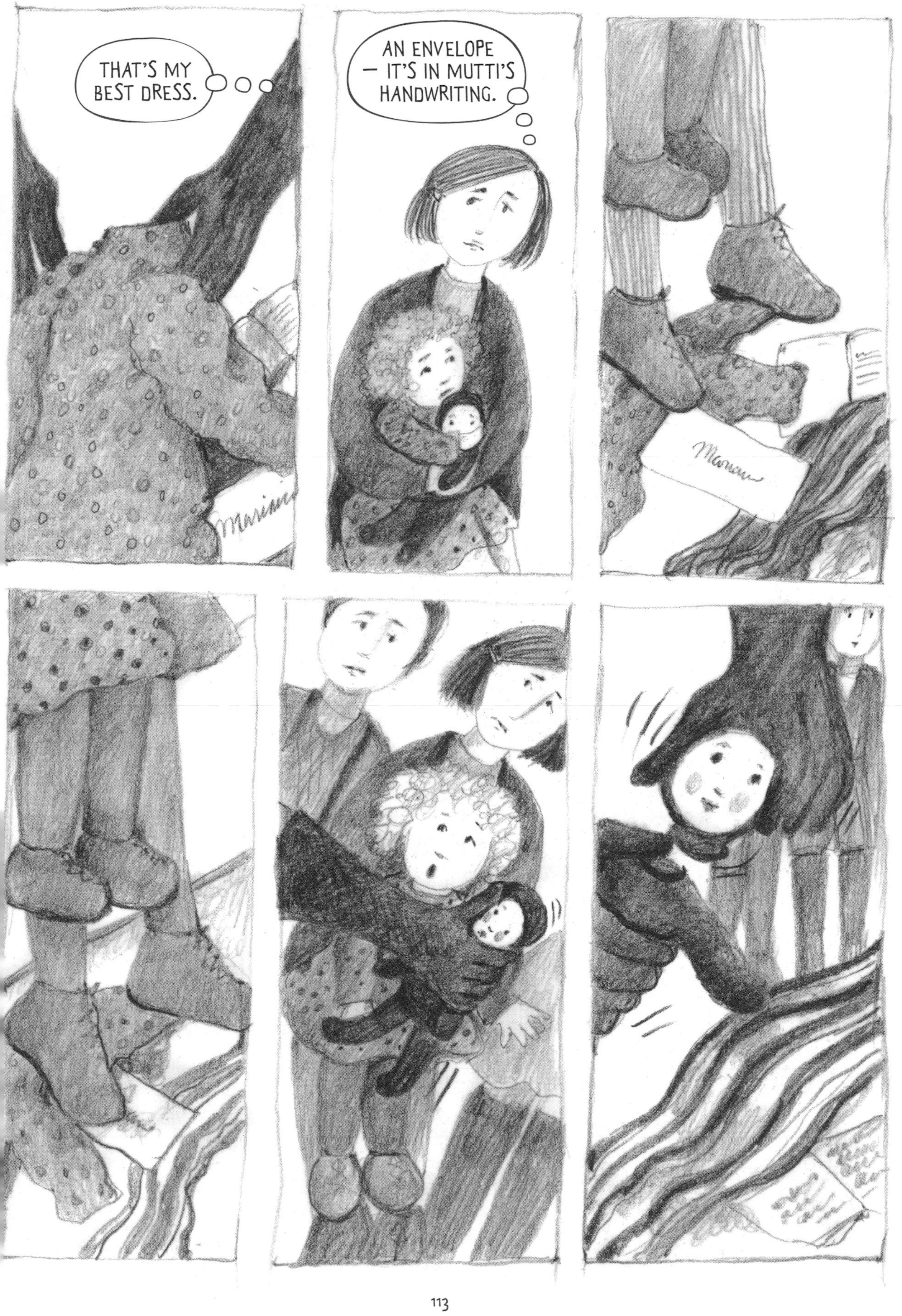
THAT'S MY BEST DRESS.
AN ENVELOPE — IT'S IN MUTTI'S HANDWRITING.

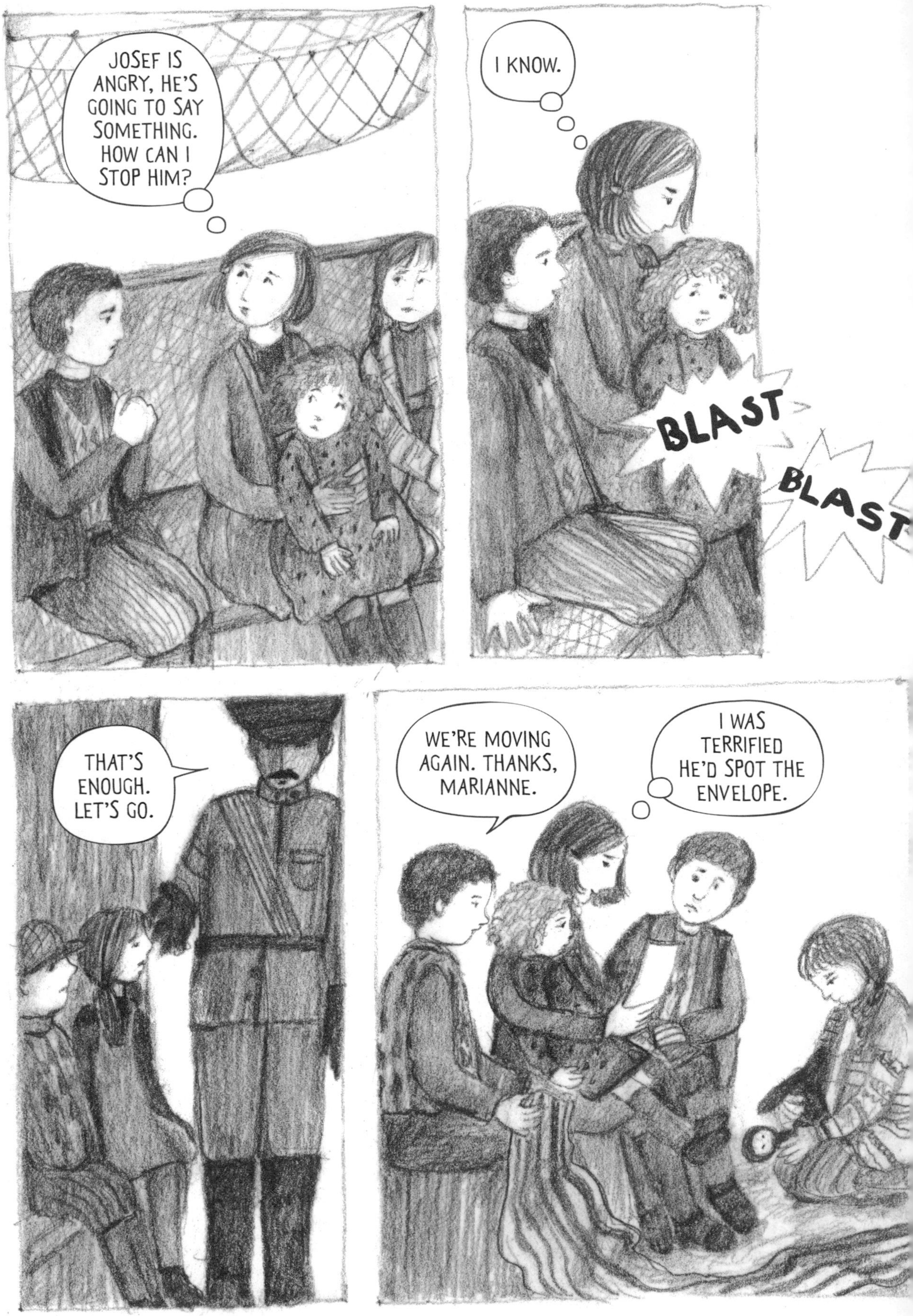
JOSEF IS ANGRY, HE'S GOING TO SAY SOMETHING. HOW CAN I STOP HIM?
I KNOW.
BLAST
BLAST
THAT'S ENOUGH. LET'S GO.
WE'RE MOVING AGAIN. THANKS, MARIANNE.
I WAS TERRIFIED HE'D SPOT THE ENVELOPE.

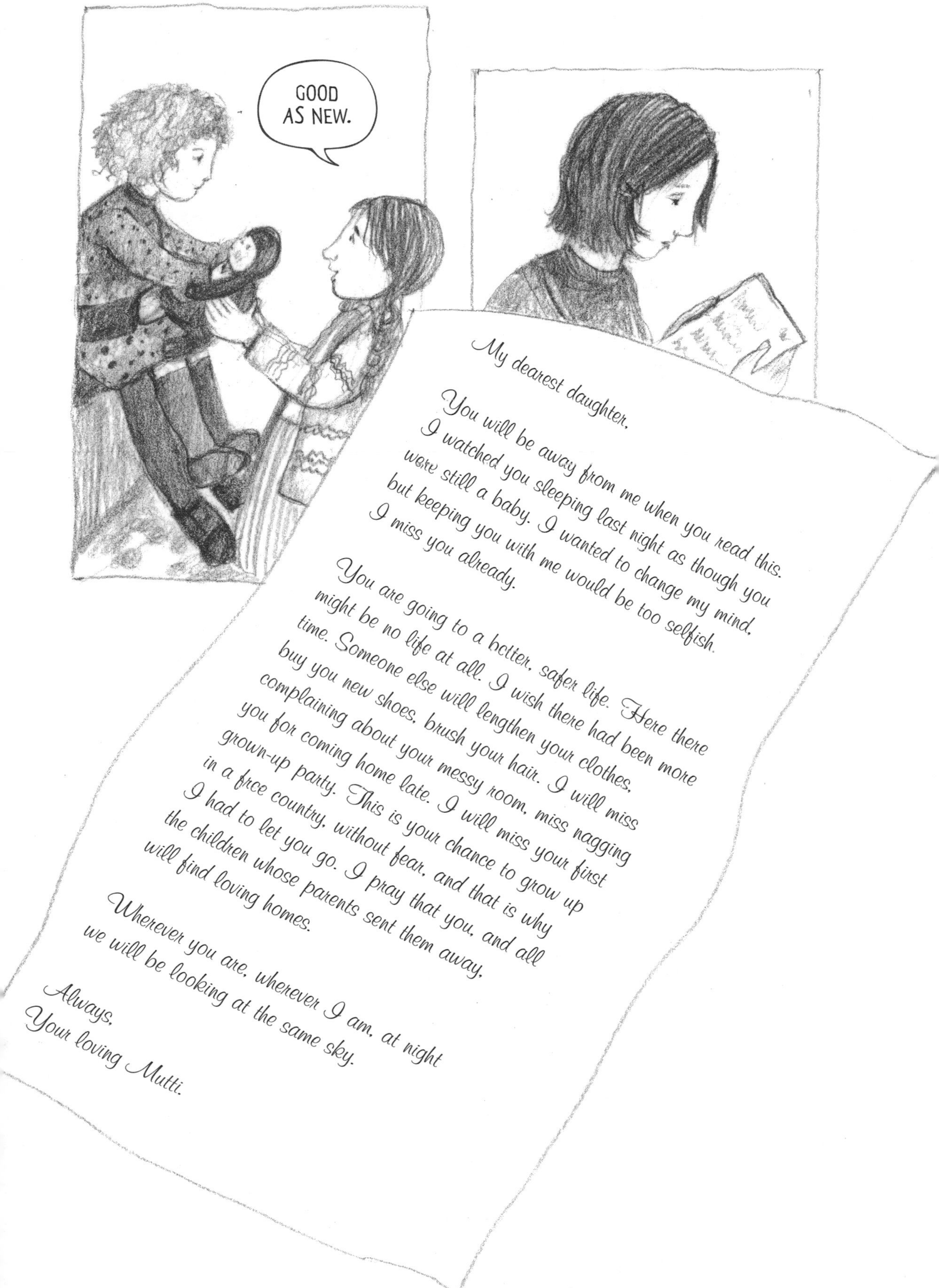
GOOD AS NEW.

My dearest daughter,

You will be away from me when you read this. I watched you sleeping last night as though you were still a baby. I wanted to change my mind, but keeping you with me would be too selfish. I miss you already.

You are going to a better, safer life. Here there might be no life at all. I wish there had been more time. Someone else will lengthen your clothes, buy you new shoes, brush your hair. I will miss complaining about your messy room, miss nagging you for coming home late. I will miss your first grown-up party. This is your chance to grow up in a free country, without fear, and that is why I had to let you go. I pray that you, and all the children whose parents sent them away, will find loving homes.

Wherever you are, wherever I am, at night we will be looking at the same sky.

Always,
Your loving Mutti.

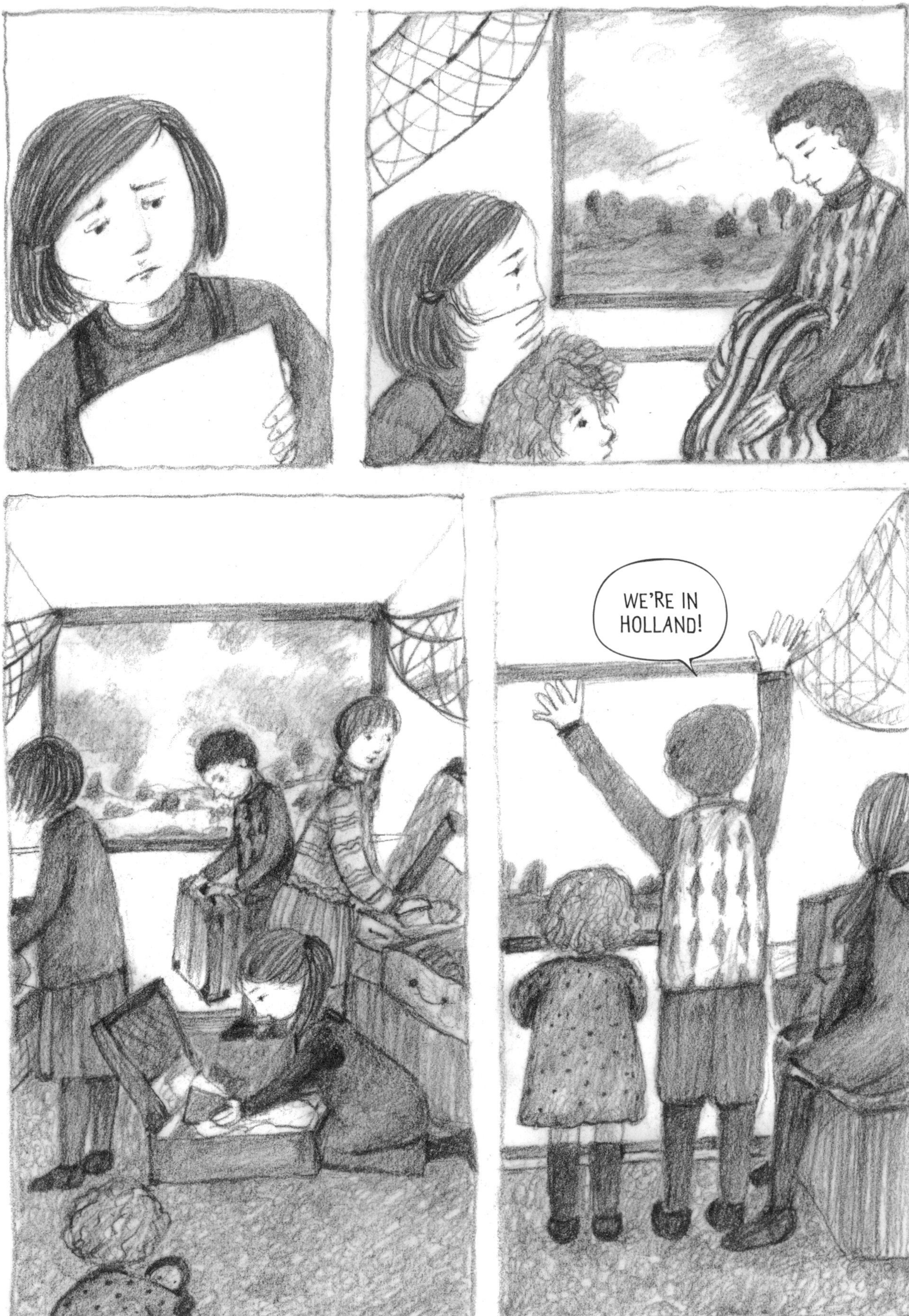
WE'RE IN HOLLAND!

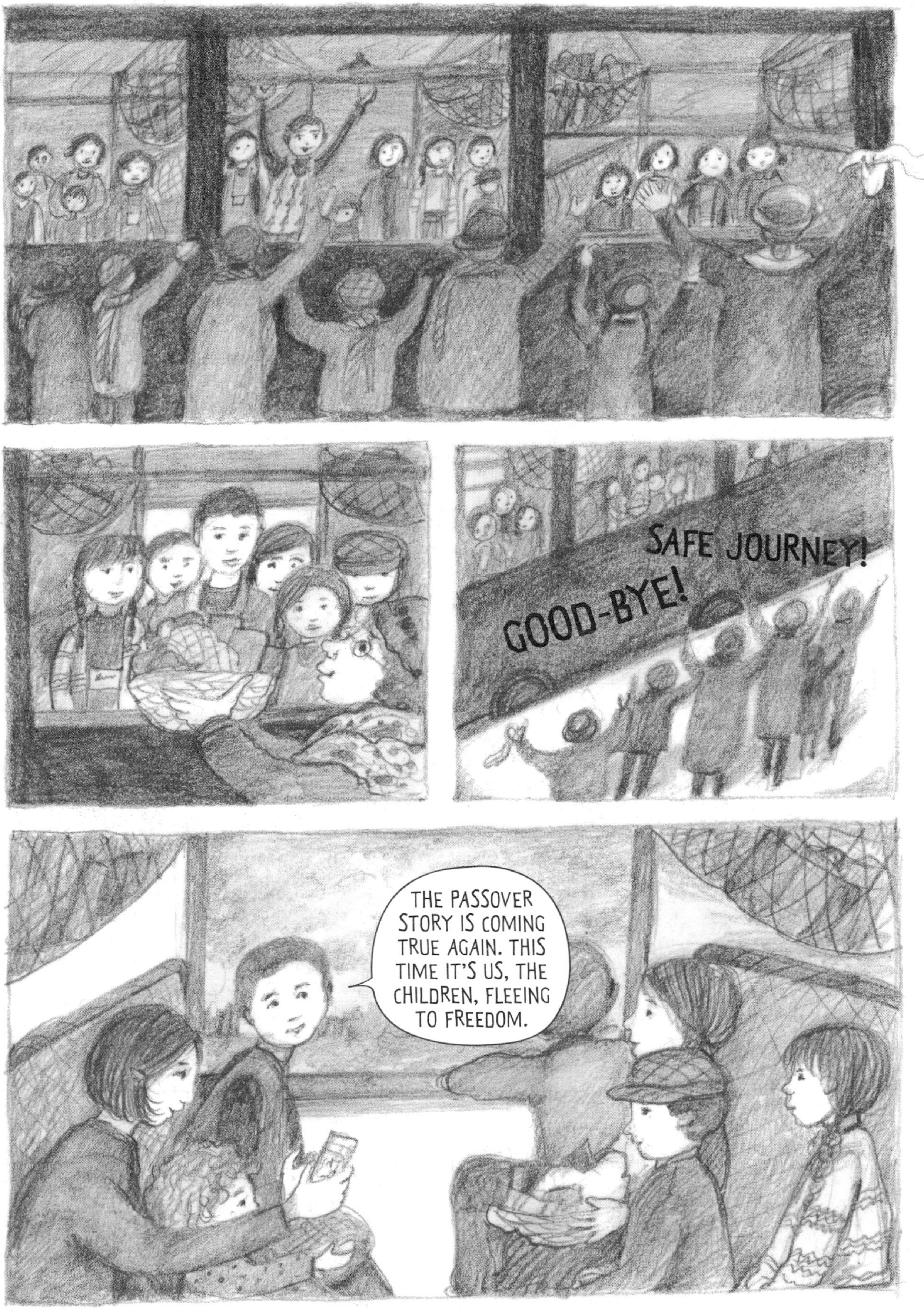
SAFE JOURNEY!
GOOD-BYE!
THE PASSOVER STORY IS COMING TRUE AGAIN. THIS TIME IT'S US, THE CHILDREN, FLEEING TO FREEDOM.

CHAPTER TEN

THE SHIP INTO THE FUTURE

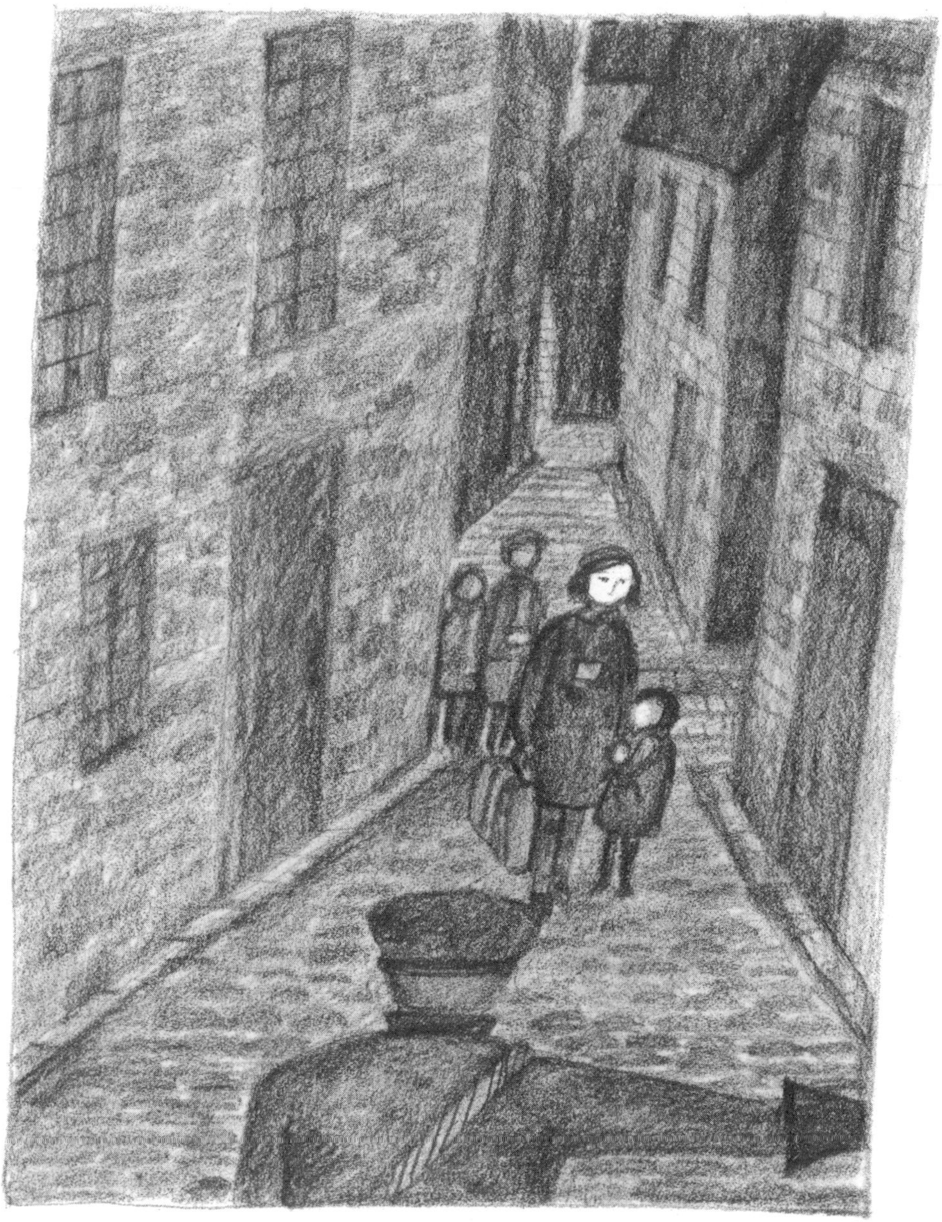

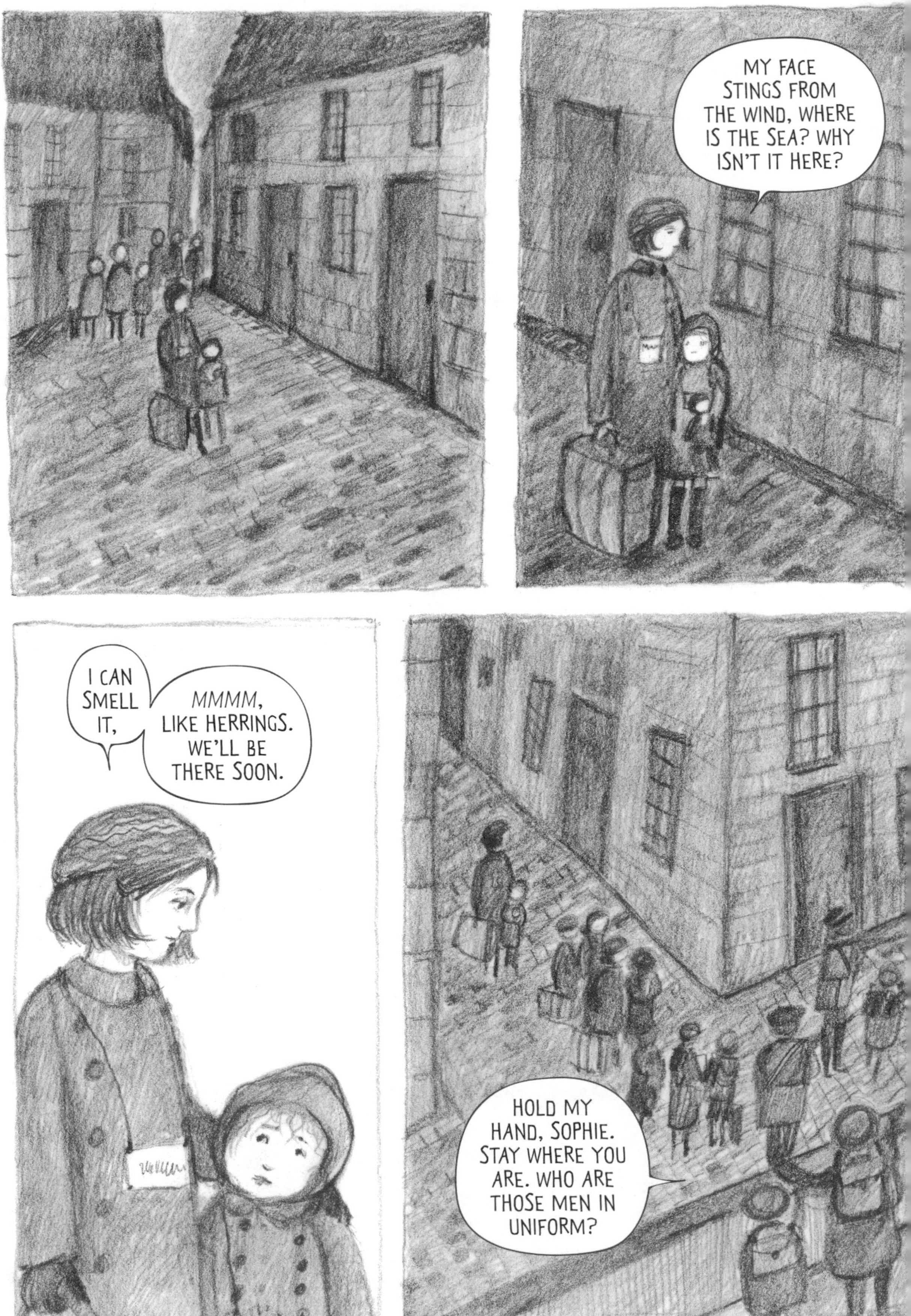
MY FACE STINGS FROM THE WIND, WHERE IS THE SEA? WHY ISN'T IT HERE?
I CAN SMELL IT,
MMMM, LIKE HERRINGS. WE'LL BE THERE SOON.
HOLD MY HAND, SOPHIE. STAY WHERE YOU ARE. WHO ARE THOSE MEN IN UNIFORM?

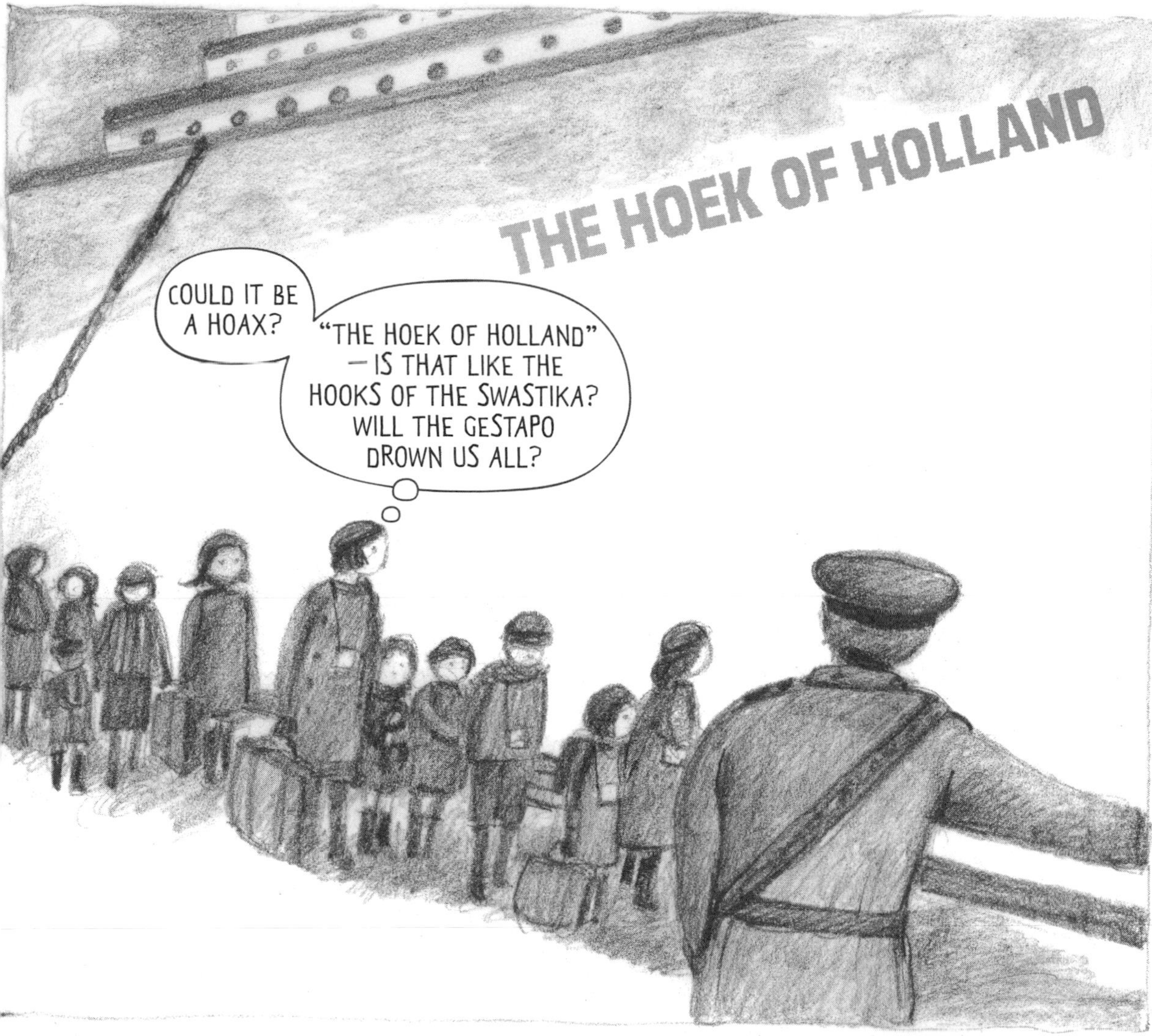
THE HOEK OF HOLLAND
COULD IT BE A HOAX?
"THE HOEK OF HOLLAND" —IS THAT LIKE THE HOOKS OF THE SWASTIKA? WILL THE GESTAPO DROWN US ALL?

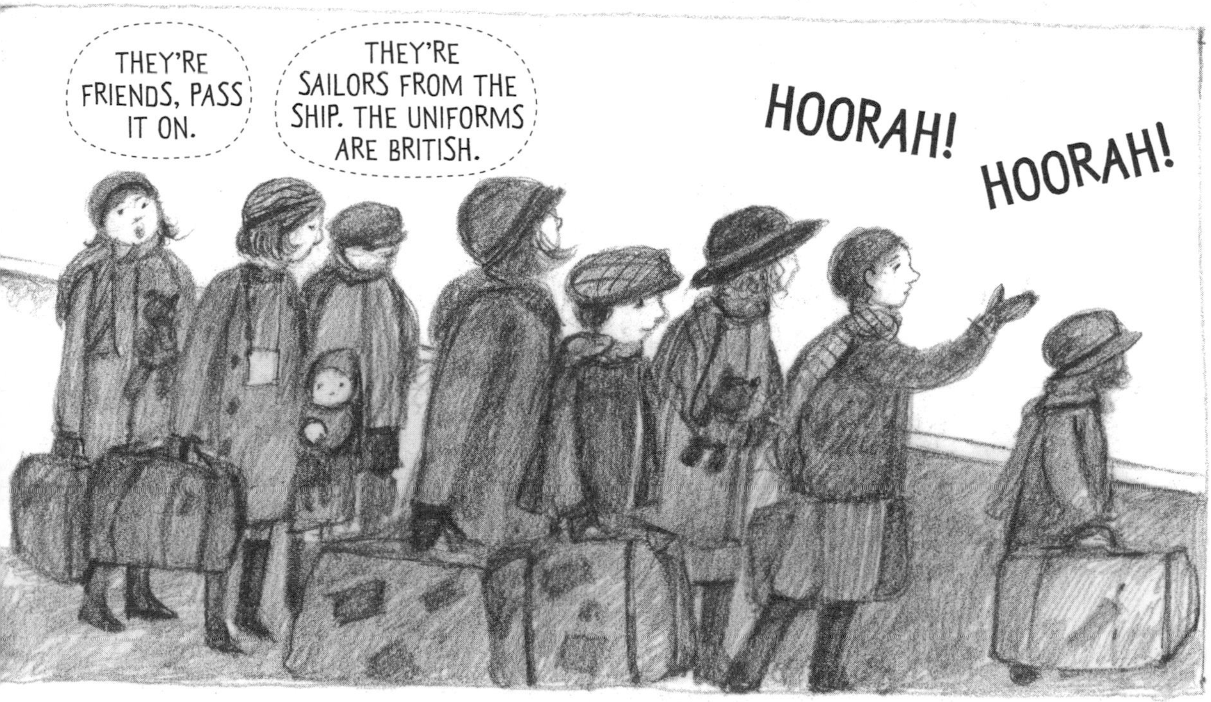
THEY'RE FRIENDS, PASS IT ON.
THEY'RE SAILORS FROM THE SHIP. THE UNIFORMS ARE BRITISH.
HOORAH!
HOORAH!

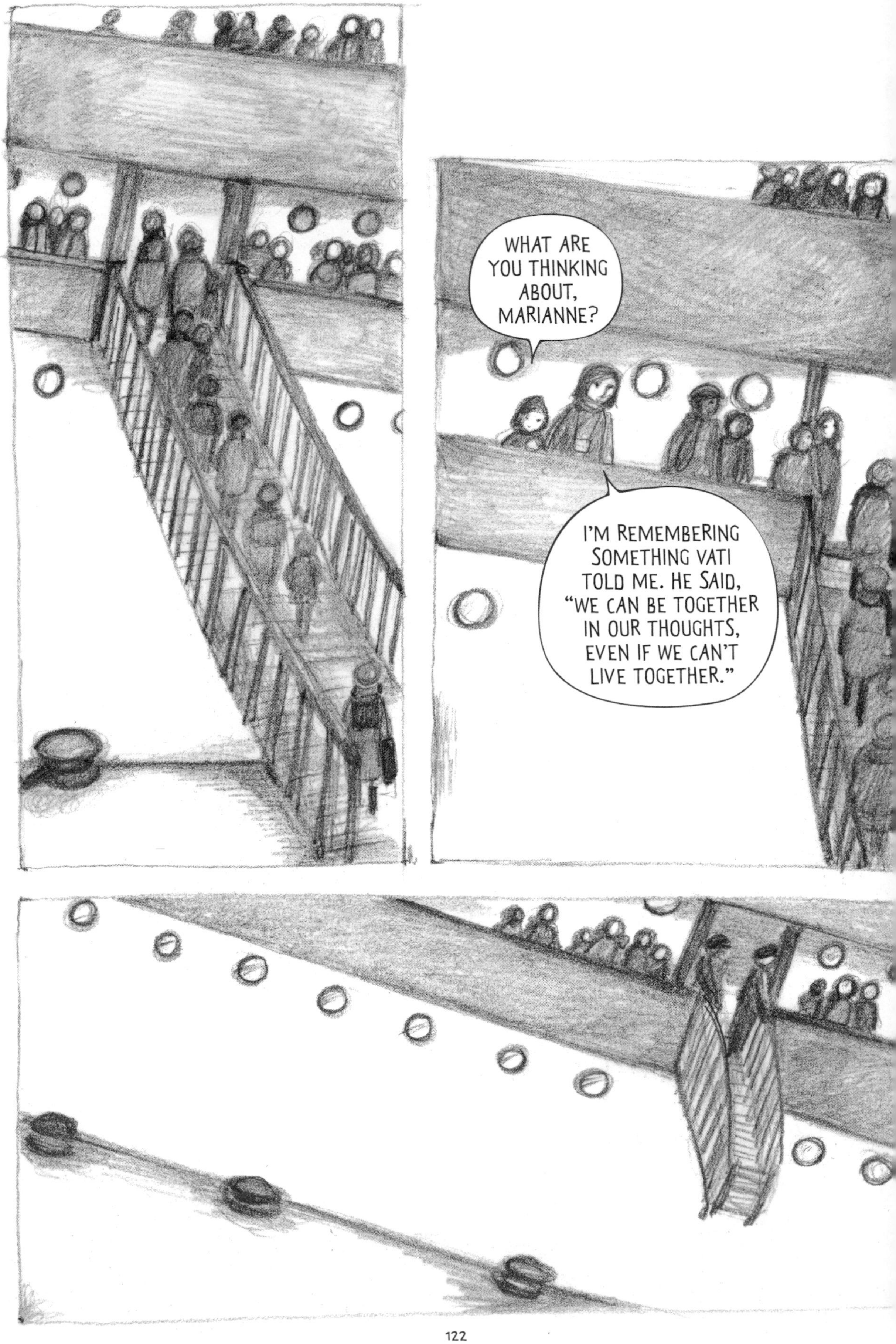
WHAT ARE YOU THINKING ABOUT, MARIANNE?
I'M REMEMBERING SOMETHING VATI TOLD ME. HE SAID, "WE CAN BE TOGETHER IN OUR THOUGHTS, EVEN IF WE CAN'T LIVE TOGETHER."

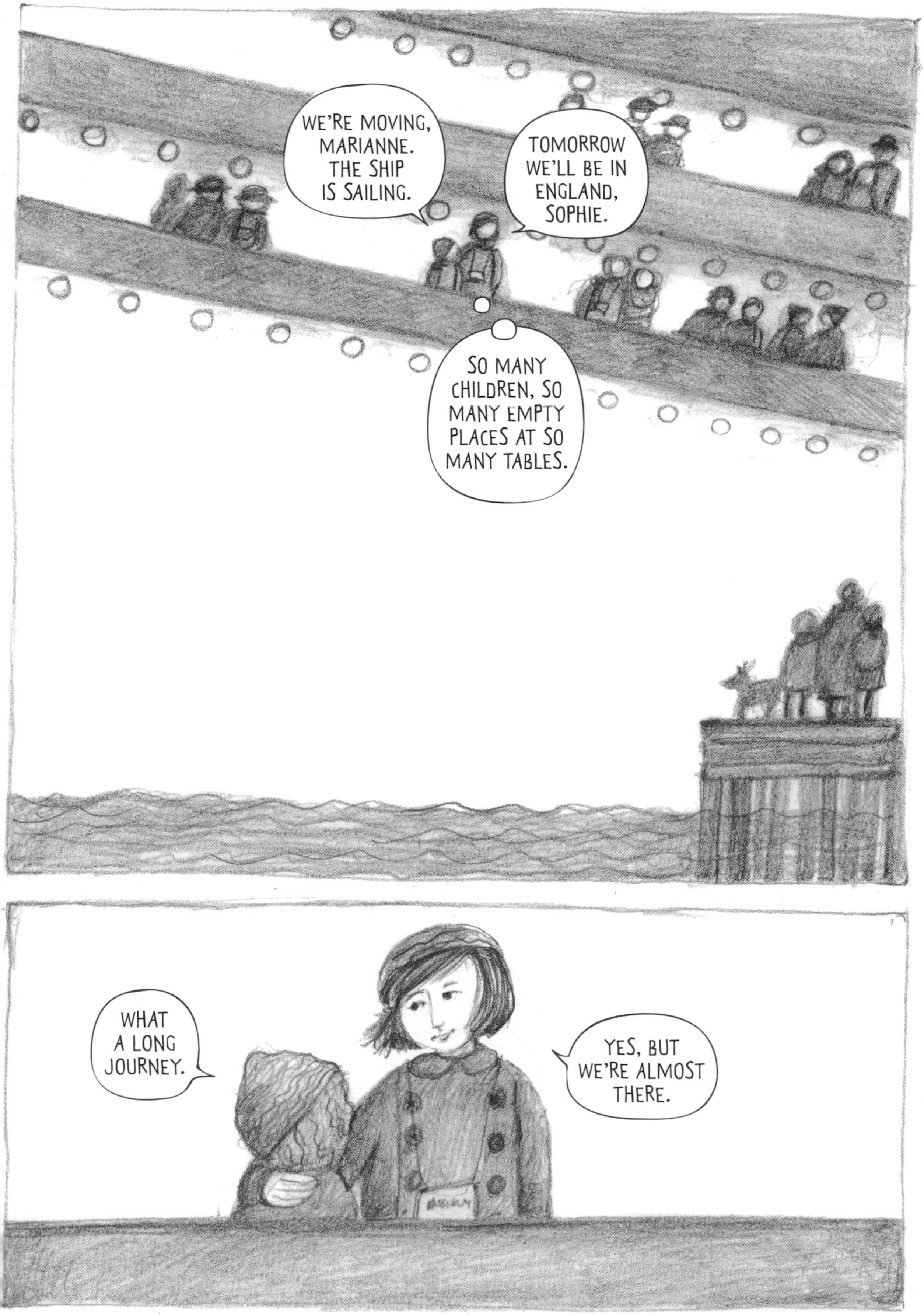
WE'RE MOVING, MARIANNE. THE SHIP IS SAILING.
TOMORROW WE'LL BE IN ENGLAND, SOPHIE.
SO MANY CHILDREN, SO MANY EMPTY PLACES AT SO MANY TABLES.
WHAT A LONG JOURNEY.
YES, BUT WE'RE ALMOST THERE.

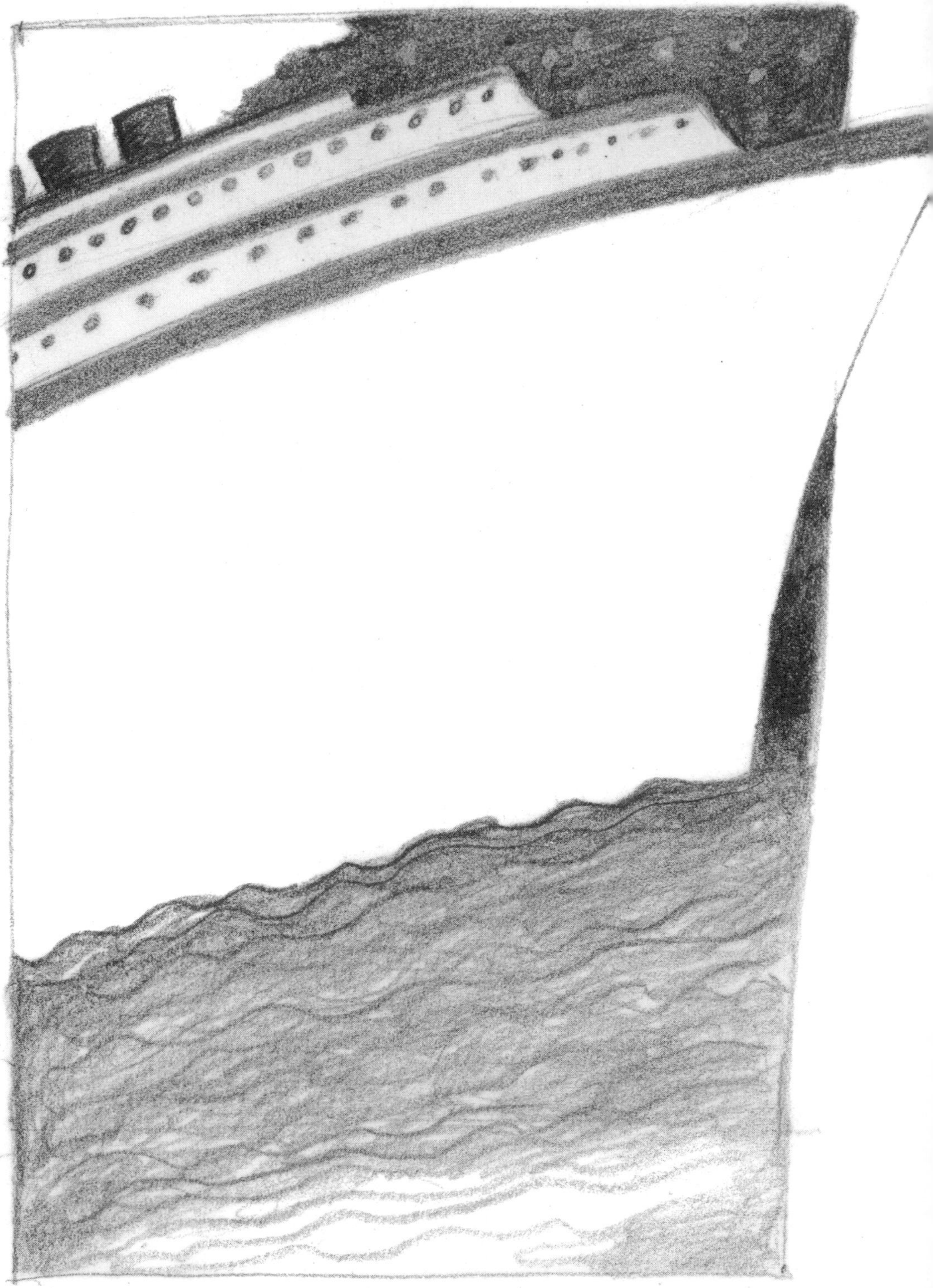

THE SHIP SAILS ON INTO THE NIGHT — INTO THE FUTURE AND INTO FREEDOM.